Praise for Nebula Award Winner
and World Fantasy Award Winner

ELIZABETH HAND
and
BLACK LIGHT

"Hand does a terrific job. . . . Once again we encounter
Hand's trademarks of hypnotically beautiful prose—she
has unarguably become one of the premier stylists
in the field—and Wagnerian atmospherics."
—*Locus*

"Hand has never been more deft."
—*New York Times Book Review*

"A fine work from a fine writer. . . . Will
delight her devoted readers."
—*Washington Post Book World*

ATTENTION: ORGANIZATIONS AND CORPORATIONS

Most HarperPrism books are available at special quantity discounts for bulk purchases for sales promotions, premiums, or fund-raising. For information, please call or write:
Special Markets Department, HarperCollins Publishers Inc., 10 East 53rd Street, New York, NY 10022-5299
Telephone: (212) 207-7528. Fax: (212) 207-7222.

BLACK Light

ELIZABETH HAND

HarperPrism

A Division of HarperCollins Publishers

📖 **HarperPrism**
A Division of HarperCollinsPublishers
10 East 53rd Street, New York, NY 10022-5299

This is a work of fiction. The characters, incidents, and dia-
logues are products of the author's imagination and are not
to be construed as real. Any resemblance to actual events or
persons, living or dead, is entirely coincidental.

ISBN 0-06-105732-0

HarperCollins®, 📖®, and HarperPrism® are trademarks of
HarperCollins Publishers Inc.

Cover design © 1999 Saska Art & Design

Cover photography © 1999 courtesy Art Resource and
Photonica/C. Rosenstein

A hardcover edition of this book was published in
1999 by HarperPrism.

First paperback edition printing: April 2000

Printed in the United States of America

Visit HarperPrism on the World Wide Web at
http://www.harpercollins.com

⌘ 10 9 8 7 6 5 4 3 2 1

And all alone on the hill I wondered what was true. I had seen something very amazing and very lovely, and I knew a story, and if I had really seen it, and not made it up out of the dark, and the black bough, and the bright shining that was mounting up to the sky from over the great round hill, but had really seen it in truth, then there were all kinds of wonderful and lovely and terrible things to think of, so I longed and trembled, and I burned and got cold. And I looked down on the town, so quiet and still, like a little white picture, and I thought over and over if it could be true.

ARTHUR MACHEN, "THE WHITE PEOPLE"

Contents

BLACK
Light

PART ONE

Decades

1 ❧
Helter
Skelter

My mother claimed to have been on the set of *Darkness Visible* when Axel Kern fired a revolver into the air, not to goad his actors but out of frustration with a scriptgirl who repeatedly handed him the wrong pages. My mother had, indeed, very briefly worked as a script-girl for Kern—this was before she settled into her eternal and prosperous run as Livia on *Perilous Lives*—so it wasn't considered good form to doubt her, or even to demonstrate normal curiosity upon hearing the anecdote repeated whenever the subject of artistic temperaments arose; which, in our family, was often.

My father was friends with Kern long before Axel became a world-famous director. When I was born in 1957, Kern was my godfather. When I was a child he was around our house a good deal, and my parents dined often at Bolerium, his vast decaying estate atop Muscanth Mountain. But as I grew older Kern stayed less often in Kamensic, and by the time I was a teenager it had been years since I'd seen him. He and my father had a long history, as drinking buddies and fellow members of a loosely allied, free-floating group of bibulous Broadway and Hollywood people. Most of them are dead now; certainly their vices have gone out of style, except as *veteris vestigia flammæ*. Only Kern made the leap gracefully from the old Hollywood to the new, which in those days wasn't Hollywood at all, but New York: Radical Chic New York, Andy Warhol's Factory New York, Black Light New York.

He was always a seeker after the main chance, my godfather. When, for a moment in the late '60s it looked as though the movie industry was turning back to the city—where, of course, it had begun when the century was new, in warehouses and a brownstone on East Fourteenth Street—well, then Axel moved back, too, inhabiting a corner of a Bowery block that could best be described not so much as crumbling as collapsed. Exposed beams and girders laced with rust, sagging tin ceilings that exposed the building's innards: particle board and oak beams riddled with dry rot and carpenter ants. The place was infested with vermin, rats and mice and bugs and stray cats; but there were also people living in the rafters, extras from the stream of low-budget experimental films Axel was filming in the city. Some had followed Axel out from the West Coast, but most of them were young people who had been living on the street, or in tenth-floor walk-ups in a part of the city that was light-years away from being gentrified. Speed freaks with *noms du cinema* like Joey Face and Electric Velvet; trust-fund junkies like Caresse "Kissy" Hardwick and her lover Angelique; a bouquet of sometime prostitutes, male and female, who named themselves after flowers: Liatris, CeCe Anemone, Hazy Clover. They were young enough, and there were enough of them, that Rex Reed christened Axel's production space the Nursery. The name stuck.

In the movies Axel shot back then—*Skag, Creep, House of the Sleeping Beauties*—you can see how a lot of those people were barely out of junior high school. Joey Face for one, and CeCe, were only a few years older than I was, with acne scars still visible beneath their Bonne Bell makeup and eyeliner inexpertly applied. None of them were beauties, except for Kissy Hardwick, who possessed the fragile greyhound bone structure and bedrock eccentricity of very old New England money. Axel seemed drawn to them solely by virtue of their youth and appetites: for food (the gloriously obese Wanda LaFlame); for amphetamines and heroin (Kissy, Joey, Page Franchini); for sex (everybody). In Hollywood, Axel had been legendary for always bringing his projects in under budget; quite a feat when you consider movies like *Saragossa* or *You Come, Too*, with their lavish costumes and soundstages that recreated Málaga during the Inquisition or fifteenth century Venice. Now, in New York, he was famous for letting a Super 8 camera run for six hours at a stretch in a blighted tenement loft, and having the results look as garishly archaic as *Fellini Satyricon*.

I visited the Nursery only once, for a Christmas party when I was twelve. Traditionally my parents held a party at our house in Kamensic, rich plum pudding-y parties where the children ran around in velvet dresses and miniature suit jackets and the grownups drank homemade eggnog so heavily spiked with brandy that a single glass was enough to set them off, playing riotously at blindman's buff and charades, singing show tunes and "The Wessex

Mummer's Carol." Axel Kern was usually a guest at these holiday gatherings, but by 1969 he had set up shop at the Nursery and wanted to throw his own party there. In keeping with the pagan tenor of the times, it was a solstice celebration and not a Christmas party; but really it wasn't even that. It was a rout.

This was before my father achieved his commercial success as TV's Uncle Cosmo. He was signed to do summer rep at the Avalon Shakespeare Theater in Connecticut, and my mother was on one of her infrequent sabbaticals from *Perilous Lives*, Livia having shaved her raven tresses and joined an Ursuline convent in the French countryside. The birth of a new decade, 1969 swandiving into 1970, seemed almost as propitious as the birth of a new century. Radio DJs rifled through the hits of the last ten years and analyzed them as though they were tarot cards. In health class we watched grainy films that showed teenagers who took LSD, staring transfixed at candle flames (*"look at the pretty blue flower!"*) before they went mad and were trundled off to the loony bin in an ambulance. To my parents, the prospect of Axel Kern's party must have seemed as much anthropological exercise as social obligation. So they put their own annual gathering on hold and we traipsed down to Axel's place on Chrystie Street, with high hopes of an urban adventure.

In fact, the Nursery was disgusting. Even my father, who had holed up with Axel in a ruined East End London warehouse while he shot *The Age of Ignorance*, was hard put to conceal his revulsion at the broken furniture and overflowing trash cans, the rats skittering in the stairwells and longhaired boys nodding out in corners. Still, neither he nor my mother would leave. At the time I thought that this was some form of grownup loyalty, on a par with playing bridge with people you hated or taking roles in plays that were doomed to flop.

But I was frightened, and only slightly reassured when numerous adult friends from Kamensic showed up as the afternoon progressed. None of them brought their children, though. None of my own friends were there, and that was odd. People in Kamensic were not usually inclined to shield their young from the kind of bohemian horrors that the rest of the country was reading about in cautionary *Life* magazine articles.

The Nursery was on the top two floors of a building that had once been a herring processing factory. Inside it smelled of rotting fish and urine. An ancient cage elevator bore us up, cables shrieking, and finally opened onto a big seemingly empty room, its bare plank floor coated with a layer of cigarette ash so thick it looked as though it were upholstered in gray velvet. In fact, there were a few people already there—it would be a stretch to call them *guests*, since they seemed to be in the process of crawling away from a terrible accident which had occurred somewhere just out of sight. Two women wearing silver Lady Godiva wigs and little else sprawled in a corner, one of them frowning as she dabbed at a series of small bloody puncture wounds in her friend's arm.

"You think a doctah, maybe?" she asked, but her friend was silent. "You think a doctah?"

In the middle of the room a boy lay groaning, his blue jeans black with grime and hiked so low on his hips that I could see his pubic hair. My parents could see it, too, but they only raised their eyes to the ceiling (not much of an improvement) and hurried me to the next room.

Here there was more of an effort at the holiday spirit. The walls were painted black and hung with multicolored lights. A scrawny Christmas tree bowed threateningly close to the floor. Beside one wall there was a table where a woman in a sequined halter dress played bartender. The stereo blared "Come Stay with Me" while a few dozen or so people flopped around on a sectional sofa.

"Well," my father said, arching one bristly eyebrow. "Will they let *us* join in any of their reindeer games?"

"Leonard! Audrina!" A man in a Nehru jacket and harem pants crossed the room to greet my parents. "So glad, *so* glad—"

While they exchanged hugs and my mother's Tupperware bowl of homemade whitefish dip, I wandered over to inspect the Christmas tree. It was devoid of lights or Christmas balls, instead was covered with marijuana cigarettes, hanging from wire tree hooks. I eyed these dubiously: Were they even real? If they were, wasn't anyone afraid of the police? In addition to the joints there was a half-hearted attempt at a decorative chain, orange thread strung with pills—Miltowns, black amphetamine capsules, a few Saint Joseph's Baby Aspirin thrown in for color.

"Looking to see what Santa left for you?" a babyish voice piped behind me. "You *look* like you've been good."

I looked around, embarrassed. A girl stood there, as old as some of the New Canaan girls who baby-sat for me. But this girl's patrician features—dark brown eyes, retroussé nose, sharp chin—were all but lost beneath a patina of nicotine and mascara. She was terribly thin, with boy-cropped black hair, her face so thickly smeared with kohl it looked as though she'd just woken up and knuckled the sleep from her eyes. She wore a very short electric blue dress, sleeveless, and long dangling earrings shaped like fish. Her hands were small and dirty and yellow-stained, with nails so badly chewed they were like ragged bits of cellophane stuck at the ends of her fingers. A patchwork bag was slung over her shoulder. As she leaned toward me I caught a whiff of something sharply chemical, like gasoline or paint fumes.

"Hey, you know what, this isn't a very good place for a kid." She smiled, showing small white teeth. "I don't want to bum you out. But maybe I could call your mother or father to come pick you up?"

I pointed across the room. "That's them there."

"Yeah? Well, that's cool, that's cool, that's cool." She fingered one of her earrings, and seemed to forget about me. After a minute I shrugged and turned to walk away.

"Bye," I said.

"Oh!" She looked up, stricken; gave me a meltingly apologetic smile. "*Nice* talking to you! Bye-bye."

She waved, a teensy little-girl wave. I thought she would leave, but she remained where she was, in the shadow of that pathetic tree, and scowled ferociously at her dirty bare feet.

"Charlotte! Oh, Charlotte, *there* you are—"

I looked up guiltily as my mother draped an arm across my shoulder. She was offhandedly elegant in black charmeuse, plastic champagne glass in one hand, cigarette in the other. "Lit, honey, will you be okay for a little while? Because there's something your father and I have to do . . ."

It turned out that my parents had been corralled into

going upstairs with a few others of the chosen, to watch Axel's most recent opus. This was an underground film of a play inspired by Aubrey Beardsley's *The Story of Venus and Tannhäuser*. It had played briefly in a MacDougal Street storefront before being loudly condemned by Cardinal Spellman, among others, and finally closed by the New York City Department of Health.

And now, despite her laissez-faire attitude toward other aspects of my education, my mother had no intention of letting me see it.

"Sweetie, I know this is awful and you're bored. We should have thought to ask Hillary to come with us. I don't know why we never think of these things. I'm sorry—"

She sighed, smoothing back my hair, and smiled briskly as a producer we knew wandered past. "But we *do* have to see this, Axel thinks it could be a *real* movie and apparently there's a part in it for your father though god only knows what *that* could be, I think the whole thing's done in the nude. Here now, have some of the whitefish, we brought it so we know it's safe, and maybe you can just curl up in a corner and read for an hour, all right, sweetie?"

She took my head in her hands and kissed me on the brow. "There! Bye now, darling—"

So I was left to wander the Nursery by myself. After a few minutes my unease dissipated. I just grew bored, and sat dispiritedly on a cinder block beneath a very large painting of a woman's shoe. I'd been to enough grownup parties in Kamensic to know that adults behaved strangely on their own, but I was also young enough to have no real perspective on what I was seeing.

And what I was seeing appeared to be some grimy street scene, complete with bums and teenage runaways, that had been miraculously picked up and then plonked down some ten stories above the Bowery. Neighbors from Kamensic floated past, like well-dressed puppets moving across a dirty stage. For fifteen or twenty minutes a band played, deafeningly loud guitars and a cello held by a bearded man in a pink dress. Later I saw the bearded man fondling a woman while someone else filmed them. I sat on my cinder block, watching the door through which my parents had disappeared the way a cat will watch a mousehole. Around me, the crowd swelled until it seemed impossible that anyone could move. Then, abruptly, the place emptied. I was alone, and frightened. Had the other guests somehow been forced to leave? If so, were my parents being held hostage somewhere in this bizarre maze of rooms and bad behavior?

The thought terrified me. From somewhere far away I heard laughter, the shivering echo of breaking glass. With a cry I jumped up and headed for the door where I had last seen my mother.

It led into a narrow corridor: bare concrete floors, walls and ceiling painted black. There were other passages leading off this one, all crooked doorjambs and rotted sills, some of them strung with Christmas lights and one with barbed wire. I started down the first hall, almost immediately found myself entering a room where the floor was covered with writhing bodies. In one corner a thin young man in a black-and-white striped sailor shirt stood behind a Super 8 camera and trained a blinding spotlight on the proceedings. As I hesitated in the doorway he looked up at me.

"Hey," he said, and frowned. "You're early . . ."

I turned and fled.

Further down the passage there was more of the same: darkened rooms illuminated by 100-watt bulbs, handheld cameras grinding away as people danced or coupled or just sat vacant-eyed in the middle of rooms that were uniformly devoid of furniture. I had no idea where I was, and my anxiety was now full-blown panic.

Where were my parents?

My hands were sweaty; I had wiped them on my velvet dress so much it began to feel like damp suede. My short hair, neatly cut and combed for the holidays, was now stiff with dust, and stank of cigarettes and pot. Every room I passed seemed crammed with strangers. But except for a peremptory nod from one of the figures behind a camera, no one acknowledged me at all. I could feel the tears starting and I bit my lip, desperate not to cry, when in front of me the nightmarish corridor abruptly ended.

"Oh, *please*," I muttered.

There was a door there, tall and painted with the same glossy black enamel as the rest of the Nursery. I stood a few inches away from it, held my breath, and listened: silence. Behind me slurred voices called out, names tossed from room to room—*"Bobbie? Has anyone seen Bobbie? Where's Bobbie?"*—and then suddenly music roared on.

Here . . . comes . . . the . . . Sun . . . King . . .

I reached for the metal doorknob.

"Ouch—!"

It was burning hot. I snatched my hand back, very ten-tatively ran my palm along the door, worrying that there might be a fire on the other side. But the door itself was cool. I knocked, softly; heard nothing but a dull metal boom. I covered my hand with a protective fold of my dress, carefully turned the knob, and peered inside.

It was empty. I glanced back at the dark hallway, then stepped in, shutting the door behind me.

I was in a long, high-ceilinged room. Not much differ-ent than the corridor I'd just left, except that there were no doors save the one I'd entered by. On the floor flick-ered a votive candle stuck onto a small white saucer. Its flame looked disproportionately large; so did my shadow, rising and falling as I stepped toward the candle. I knelt in front of it to warm my hands, then looked around.

"It's green," I whispered. "A green room . . ."

And it was. Not the lurid, concrete-stairwell green you might have expected to find in that place, but a soft, ferny green, dappled where the candlelight struck it, and so welcome after the Nursery's endless black that I almost laughed out loud. I stood, went to one of the walls and touched it, half-expecting to feel the moist warmth of foliage. But no, it was just paint, cool and slick beneath my fingertips. I crossed the room lengthwise, walking slowly and running my hand along the wall. The candle gave everything an odd velvety glow, and the way my shadow leaped beside me only added to the strangeness. I felt as though I were inside one of those fairy rings that grew behind our house in Kamensic, ferns reaching high enough to form a curved green roof above my head.

And there was a sound, too, so faint it was several min-utes before I really became aware of it—a soft, steady *whoosh*. At first I thought someone had left a tap running in a neighboring bathroom. But when I reached the end of the room, the noise grew even louder, and I realized it was not water but the sound of wind in the leaves. Not a gentle rustling, but the restless, unrelenting toss of trees in the night.

I cocked my head, puzzled. There were no windows, no doors save the one I'd entered by; no skylight. And it was dead winter in lower Manhattan—there were no leaves, either. Yet the sound was so persistent, and so near, that I almost imagined I could feel a cool breath upon my neck.

It's a movie, I thought. *They're just running a movie somewhere . . .*

I stood for a minute, listening, then turned. The votive candle had burned down to a nub. I was halfway across the room when I noticed something hanging on the far wall. Another painting, I thought, like that blandly weird canvas of a shoe. It was very big, so it was odd I hadn't seen it when I came in, but unlike the other paintings I'd seen scattered around the Nursery, this one wasn't immediately identifiable. It wasn't a famous face, or a shoe, or a box of Cracker Jack. The edges were irregular and uneven, the colors dark swirls of brown and black and a deep, rusty red. I walked until I stood in front of it, and frowned.

It wasn't a painting. Or rather, it wasn't *just* a painting, but an immense slab of rock, perhaps ten feet high and twice as wide. It didn't seem to be fixed to the wall so much as protruding through it. I could see no nails or wires, nothing on the floor that might support such an enormous weight. Its surface was smooth but uneven, with patterns in it like waves, and moist. I drew my hand carefully upward, the curved rock beneath my palm like something huge and alive, the flank of a sleek horse or bull. When I reached the middle of the stone I stopped.

There was something painted there, in colors so similar to the rock's natural tones that I almost missed it. A figure as tall as I was, its body drawn out of proportion and its limbs all mismatched, and posed in grotesque angles. It stood upright, shoulders hunched and arms drawn up before it awkwardly. Dwarfishly foreshortened arms, painted in blurry dark lines to indicate fur. But the hands were human hands, and its legs, though furred, ended in human feet. One leg was oddly foreshortened— either badly drawn or meant to indicate that the creature had been injured.

The rest was merely monstrous. A striped, swayed back like a horse's; long tail ending in a fox's white point; a slender, curved shape hanging between its legs, that I knew must represent a penis. I grimaced and looked away, trying to find the creature's face.

That was even worse. A face like a hideous mask, sitting square on its shoulders and staring straight out from the stone. The outline of the head was like that of a deer, and two asymmetrical antlers corkscrewed from its brow. Instead of a muzzle there was only a long black gash to indicate a nose or mouth, shading into lines sketched beneath to indicate a ruff.

But most dreadful of all were the creature's eyes. Huge, round, staring eyes, the irises daubed dead-white, the pupils black pinpricks: two blank orbs unsoftened by lashes or lids or anything that might have lent them the faintest breath of humanity. They could have been a serpent's eyes, or an owl's; they could have been the glaring sockets of a skull. I started to shake, and stumbled backward for the door.

That was when I saw her.

"Hi," she said. Her voice was low and breathy, as though she were talking to herself. But her eyes—wide and staring as those of the creature in the painting, but etched with green like leaves on dark water—her eyes were fixed on me.

"You know, I was going to tell you something," she went on, absently scratching her head. "But I forgot, and then you were, you know—" She made a flurrying gesture. "—*gone*. And then I got worried . . ."

She was at the far end of the room, leaning against the wall. Not anywhere near the door—but then how else could she have gotten in? There was no other entrance, and I was certain I would have heard her, or seen the door open. The sound of the wind in the leaves rose and died away as I looked around in a panic. The girl continued to stare at me. After a moment she slid down to the floor, her patchwork bag beside her.

"Hey . . ." She beckoned me. "Come here—"

I hesitated. Then I went. After all, I was only twelve; she was older, but not old enough to seem dangerous. As I crossed the room I felt the gaze of that dreadful figure in the stone follow me. But I refused to look back, squeezing my eyes shut and taking tiny careful steps until I reached the other side. I opened my eyes then. The girl smiled up at me, and my terror faded. It was like one of own friends smiling at me, welcoming and without guile, and somehow complicitous.

"I know who you are," she said. She scooched over, patting the floor as though she were plumping a sofa cushion. I settled beside her, trying to arrange my velvet dress so it wouldn't get dirty, and still being careful not to let my gaze fall on the rock painting opposite.

"Pretty," she said, stroking my dress. Once more she gave me that ravishing smile. "You're the godchild. Charlotte. Right?"

I shrugged and said, "Yes."

She looked pleased, and started playing with the hem of her dress. There were runs in it, spots where the metallic blue fabric was so frayed you could see right through.

"You know how I know that?" Her lips were dry and cracked. She licked them, over and over and over, until a seam of blood appeared. "Because I am, too. Did you know that?"

"No," I said shyly.

She nodded. "So we're sort of related. Right? So that's why I wanted to talk to you. Because of what happens to us. Just so you'll know."

She leaned toward me, and once again I caught that rank chemical smell. "No one understands about Axel. People think they do, they see the movies and read all that stuff but no one really *knows*. Except me."

She took my hand and opened it, traced the lines on my palm the way my friend Ali did when we were playing fortune-teller. The girl glanced up, her gaze flicking from me to the far wall. Despite myself I looked, too; then quickly lowered my eyes.

She pointed at the rock painting and said, "You see that." It was not a question. "Hardly anybody does. Do you know what it is?"

"No," I whispered.

"A self portrait." When I looked at her doubtfully she shook her head. "Not *mine*. His."

This reassured me somewhat. Plus, I felt flattered by her attention, the fact that she was talking to me as though I were one of her friends and not a little girl. I thought of the strange artwork some of my parents' friends collected, and the ugly paintings I had seen elsewhere in the Nursery, and ventured another glance at the rock painting. "Really?"

"Sure." She lowered her voice. "You should see some of the other stuff. I mean, I probably shouldn't talk about it 'cause you're so young—but, well, some of it is *very* sexy. Definitely X-rated."

She giggled. "That's one of the amazing things about Axel. All this stuff, you know? It's all sort of hidden in plain sight. Like the movies, and the paintings, and the books and things he collects—everyone thinks it's just, like, *junk*—but really it's all for a reason. He's been very careful about what he brings into this place, and his other houses . . .

"Like, at Swarthmore I read this book about witchcraft, and I mean, his stuff is *in* there. I mean the things he owns, the manuscripts and that collection of— well, some of those sexy things—it's all *real*. And you know what else, Charlotte?"

She placed a hand on each of my knees and drew her face to within inches of mine. "*We're real, too*. All of us," she whispered. Her expression was rapturous, her dark eyes huge. "Me, Precious; Joey and CeCe and Page . . . we're all really what he says we are. Just like you, Charlotte. Just like you . . ."

She rocked back, tilting her head and looking utterly blissful. "Isn't that amazing? All this energy, these vibrations all over the world—they're all focused right *here*, on us! All these things are happening, like this new age is coming on and there's all this amazing energy and these, like, *radical* changes, and *we're* doing it! It's happening right now, Charlotte, and you and me are *in* it. Doesn't that just blow your mind?"

She crossed her hands upon her breast, the soiled blue fabric bunching between her fingers, and I tried to look as though I understood what she was talking about. It made a certain kind of sense to me—I had seen things on TV, and in *Life* magazine. I heard the songs on the radio, and read pilfered copies of *Rolling Stone* and *Creem* and *Circus* magazine, *Viva* and *Rosemary's Baby*. I knew people thought that *something* was going to happen.

And when I saw pictures of people like this girl, or passed them in the street, with their gorgeous motley and occult jewelry, peacock-feather eyes burning like candle stubs and mouths slightly ajar, as though they had just glimpsed something marvelous, something unspeakable, something with a name that I would never know—well, then *I* thought something was going to happen, too.

"But you have to do it *right*." I was daydreaming: when the girl jabbed me with her finger I almost jumped out of my skin. "*That's* what's gone wrong all those other times. No one did it right. But that's not going to happen now . . ."

She made a funny, giddy face, shook her head so that her long earrings spun and sparkled. "Because I am strong. I am *so* strong, *I* am going to be the one who does it right! And then, Charlotte, *you'll* be able to come and visit me on Sundays!"

She laughed and clapped her hands—just once, as though she'd performed a marvelous trick. I looked at her warily, not sure if she were making fun of me. But her delight seemed genuine.

"On Sundays?" I asked.

"That's just a joke. Listen, don't you know what happens here? People come, and they stay for a while; and Axel gets stronger. And stronger. And stronger. And I mean, this has all been going on for like *a thousand years*. Not here, not in this building, but—you know how everyone thinks this is the age of Aquarius? Well, that's only part of it. That is *the tip of the iceberg*—"

Abruptly she turned and began rooting in her bag, loosening the drawstring ties and poking inside. "Where is it? God, I can never find *anything*—I *hate* this!" she cried, and upended the whole thing.

An astonishing array of objects poured onto the floor. Matchbooks, Lucite bracelets, gold hoop earrings, crushed and uncrushed cigarette packs, a spiral notebook, a pink rosary, innumerable pill bottles, a silver flask, drinking straws, loose change and rolled-up bills, an address book held together with rubber bands, wads and wads of newspaper clippings. I stared, amazed, but the girl just made an impatient noise and swept most of it to one side. Very delicately she picked through a tiny heap of dust and loose pills, choosing a black capsule and popping it into her mouth. Then she took the newspaper clippings and began smoothing them out on the floor.

NURSERY HATCHES STRANGE MONSTERS, OBSCENITY SUIT

FUROR OVER "SCAG" OPENING: "THIS IS THE FUTURE OF FILM," DIRECTOR KERN ATTESTS

GIRL & BOY TOGETHER: PRECIOUS BANE COWS 'EM AT CANNES

I craned my neck at the flashlit image of Axel Kern escorting a coy, heavily made-up blonde past a police barricade, but the girl shoved these pages back into her bag.

"Here," she said, stabbing at the single curling column that remained. "Read this."

TRIUMPH OF THE DIONYSIAN SPIRIT

Hollywood monarch turned "underground" filmmaker Axel Kern makes Art out of Life—or is that vice versa?

The recent screening of his controversial "The Savage God Awakes" brought to mind the furor a few years back when Kenneth Anger's "Lucifer Rising" was all the rage. But Anger never claimed that his hocus pocus actually *works*.

Axel Kern does.

Press releases touting the verisimilitude of a sequence wherein two teenage "chicks" ritually dismember a live goat brought down the wrath of the American Humane Society and ASPCA. But nobody seemed overly worried about the chicks, whose monokinis (designed by Kern's pal Rudi Gernreich) might pass muster at bohemian Malibu Beach but definitely shocked 'em onscreen—and off. NY society deb Caresse Hardwick ("Kissy" in the film credits) raised a few eyebrows at the La Tartine party afterward with her comment that "if the Beatles were bigger than Jesus, well then Axel is way bigger than God." The party's menu, catered by Les Trois Freres, went largely untouched as . . .

I stared at the accompanying photo, shot a surreptitious glance at the girl beside me. It was the same person, though in the picture her hair was silver and not black, her face immaculately made up, and her slim form clad in a white dress that glowed like a fluorescent tube. I read the caption.

FILM DIRECTOR BIGGER THAN GOD, OPINES DEB SUPER-STAR

"That's the joke, get it?" Kissy Hardwick nudged me. She licked her lips again. "He's not bigger than God. He *is* God."

I didn't say anything. I was only twelve years old, but at this point even I knew that this girl was nuts. Worse than nuts, she was on drugs—I'd seen her swallow that little black pill, and god only knew what else had already made its way from her magic bag of tricks into her mouth. I looked at the floor, trying to think of how I could leave, wondering if I could just bolt, when she grabbed my wrist.

"Tonight." Beneath the thin fabric of her dress her breasts moved, and one pink nipple poked out through a hole. She was breathing too fast, her head nodding crazily. "Tonight tonight tonight. December 21. The winter solstice. Get it, do you get it? And I'm ready, I'm all ready for it to happen . . ."

I tried to pull away, but her grasp only tightened.

"Ow—"

"*Right here,*" she said, ignoring me. With her free hand she slapped at the junk on the floor. Matchbooks and earrings went flying, pills skidded away as her fingers closed around something. "'Cause I'm ready, I told them I was ready—"

She looked up, still holding my wrist; grinned that horribly incongruous doll's smile and showed me what was in her other hand.

"See, Charlotte?"

It was a knife. Maybe six or seven inches long, blade and handle both carved from the same slender piece of bone. The handle end was narrow and russet-brown; the curved blade creamy ivory. As she turned it back and forth I could see tiny incisions in the handle, a series of lines intersected by smaller Xs. But the blade was bro-ken—the end had been sheared off, leaving a jagged edge. When she ran her finger along it I could see that it was dull, no sharper than a piece of plastic cutlery.

"Huh. I'll have to sharpen it I guess. But I'll *do* it, that's the key thing! I'm not afraid and—"

She stumbled to her feet, dragging me as well. Although she seemed to have almost forgotten me; I might have been another piece of awkward jewelry tied to her wrist. With a soft moan she began flailing back and forth. I thought she was having a seizure, but then she started to laugh, spinning in a clumsy pirouette with me staggering alongside, and I realized she was dancing.

"I'll—do—it—!" she sang breathlessly. Something crunched beneath her bare feet. I looked down and saw that the floor was littered with seedpods, brown and as big as my thumb. "I'll—"

At that moment the candle went out. I yelped, Kissy laughed; and the door at the end of the room flew open.

"Lit? Charlotte Moylan, are you—"

"*Daddy!*"

For a fraction of a second I could feel Kissy's hand tighten about mine. Then there was a warmth at my ear, and a voice whispering, "Don't forget!" With a giggle she let go, falling back against the wall.

"Lit! What the hell are you doing in here? Where's the light? What's that *smell*?"

My father stomped inside. "Jesus Q. Murphy, we've

been ready to leave for an *hour*, where the hell have you—"

Light flooded the room from an unshaded bulb overhead. There was a soft *crack*, and the saucer that had held the votive candle shattered beneath my father's foot. "Charlotte!" he said, hugging me to him. "Damn it, where have you *been*?"

He let his breath out in an explosive gasp and ran his hand through my hair. I leaned against his chest, smelling wine and the warm tobacco scent of his tweed jacket. "What, did you come in here and fall asleep?" he went on, rocking back and forth. "Your mother's ready to call the cops—"

"No—no, I just got lost, I was looking for *you*, and then I came in here and we were talking—"

I gestured at the wall behind me, looked up to see my father frowning.

"'We'? Who's 'we'?" He sighed, exasperated, and pulled me with him as he started for the door. "Come on, then, let's go, we're going to be ticketed as it is and it's starting to snow—"

I slipped from his arm and whirled around. "Wait—"

Kissy Hardwick was gone. So was the rock painting. Only the walls were as I had first seen them, shimmering green, and the shattered husks of seedpods sown across the floor.

And, faint as a breath against my cheek, I could hear the rustle of wind in the leaves.

"Lit."

I nodded obediently, without a word returned to my father. He draped his arm around me and we went down the hall, past other rooms that were all empty now; past the derelict Christmas tree and the shabby foyer where a boy was throwing up out the window, and where my mother awaited us by the elevator.

Neither of my parents ever said anything to me about the party; never even mentioned how strange it was that it had been Christmas, and Axel Kern was my godfather and I had not seen him, or even gotten a present. On New Year's Eve we stayed at home and celebrated quietly by ourselves, watching TV, Guy Lombardo and Fred Astaire in *Top Hat*. The next morning, January 1st, 1970, I read in the *Daily News* about the death by drug overdose of nineteen-year-old celebutante Caresse Hardwick. Her body was found on the bathroom floor of her Chelsea Hotel apartment. Medical examiners estimated that she had been dead for at least a week, perhaps two. Her involvement with Axel Kern and his films was duly noted, as were the shocked reactions of family and friends. Nowhere was there any mention of a bone knife.

The truth was that, despite their friendship with Axel Kern, the world of the Nursery wasn't my parents' world at all. My mother was far too professional for such self-indulgence.

"Amateur night," she'd always sniff when told of opening night parties where principal actors got smashed on champagne or gin. Still, in those days my father was a prodigious drinker. It showed on his face, and helped chart the odd peregrination his life would soon take as Uncle Cosmo on *Tales from the Bar Sinister*. His stories about my godfather were dark, though very funny as my father told them in his professionally Irish brogue.

Actually, *all* the stories I ever heard about Axel Kern were dark—the disturbing tales of his involvements with underage girls, the bizarre circumstances surrounding the death of his first wife and the madness of his mistresses; rumors that he slept with a loaded gun in his mouth, and especially those grotesque charges of drug use and cannibalism lodged against him by several bit players from *Saragossa*. These last of course were dismissed, but not before several weeks' worth of scandalous publicity. The actors were disgruntled over their scenes ending up on the cutting-room floor, and in those days Kern's extravagant reputation made him an easy target for lawsuits.

This was in the year following the holiday party at the Nursery. Only a month after Caresse Hardwick's death, a woman actually *had* tried to murder Axel, though with a gun rather than a Paleolithic knife. She was arrested and subsequently imprisoned; still, public sympathies seemed to lie with her and not Axel Kern. The Manson Family killings were recent history. In their wake, ritual cannibalism practiced by a leading film director didn't seem quite so far-fetched. The Nursery and Kern's Laurel Canyon home were searched. Small quantities of peyote and psilocybin mushrooms were confiscated from the latter, along with esoterically obscene sculptures from the Mediterranean and Near East. Kern himself was hauled off to jail. My father helped him make bail (while he never went over budget on any of his films, Kern was famously insolvent), and stood by him while further accounts of Kern's escapades—strange ceremonies involving Newport socialites and some livestock, a bas-relief missing from the Museo delle Therme in Rome—filled the papers and evening news.

Eventually most of the charges were dropped, save only those for drug possession. But an Icelandic shaman and two Lakota medicine men testified that the peyote and mushrooms were for religious use, and by the time the whole ridiculous episode had been supplanted in the headlines by the Pentagon Papers, Kern had paid several hundred dollars in fines and tens of thousands in legal fees. My best friend Hillary and I used to fight over the morning's *Daily News*, giggling at the front-page photos of the gaunt hawk-faced man, his long dark hair pulled into a ponytail and his eerily intent eyes unshuttered by sunglasses. A year later he recreated it all on film for Granada Television, in the prize-winning documentary *Suddenly, Last Summer*. Throughout, his lawyer hinted darkly at a mass conspiracy that, if revealed, would shake not just Hollywood but Broadway, Capitol Hill and the Vatican.

To my great chagrin, that conspiracy remained a secret, at least for another few years. But the whole affair only deepened Kern's friendship with my father. After his drug imbroglio, it was Kern who recommended my father for the part of Uncle Cosmo on *Tales from the Bar Sinister*. There wasn't exactly a lot of competition for the role—a few unknowns, a former kiddie-show host on the skids and an ailing Vincent Price clone. But my father threw himself into the audition with his usual brio and walked out of the casting director's office with a new job. He was sober by then, eager for work, and his devotion to Kern—always intense—became positively slavish. My mother used to laugh and say that the only thing my father wouldn't do for Axel Kern was promise him his only child. Of course, she was wrong about that.

2 ❧
Some of These Things First

> . . . on the first day Bumpy took me
> on a rapid tour of the nearest village
> of any size . . .
>
> FREDERICK EXLEY, *A FAN'S NOTES*

The most important thing you have to understand is that we lived in a haunted place. A town that over the centuries had survived death by fire, water, wind; a town that endured—and not only the town itself, you see, but everyone who lived in it. The village was founded in 1627 as a far-flung remnant of the old Dutch colony of New Netherland. The oldest houses—stern fieldstone dwellings with steeply pitched roofs and gables—dated from twenty years later, but there were ruins of older houses still, wooden buildings burned to the ground by the Tankiteke Indians in retaliation for the slaughter of an entire Indian village. In the late 1700s the town was burned again, by the British General Eustis "Bloodjack" Warrenton, a convert to Jansenism who met an unhappy fate—murdered by Polly Twomey, a former tragedienne (her Ariadne in *The Rival Sisters* was rumored to be superior to Mrs. Siddons's) and singer of bawdy songs, well known to be a witch. Warrenton's mutilated body was found by his aide-de-camp in the woods outside of town. Cat-a-mountain, the villagers blandly insisted, what do you think? But those with Tory sympathies knew it was the witch.

A century later the White Hurricane of 1873 left the woods along the Muscanth River as desolate as though they had been struck by a meteor. The forest scarcely had a chance to regenerate when in 1907 it was drowned, the Muscanth dammed to form a reservoir that would provide water for the great city to the south. Most people moved their houses, by horse and oxen—you can see the photographs in the Constance Charterbury Library and the Kamensic Village Courthouse (now a museum, Open Weekends)—but some refused. Their homes lie there still beneath the green murky waters of Lake Muscanth, alongside rusted-out refrigerators and doomed autos and a few unclaimed corpses.

Through the centuries, high above it all stood the strange grand mansion known as Bolerium, its mottled granite walls so covered with moss and lichen they were nearly indistinguishable from the surrounding stones, its turrets and gables and cupolas thrusting from its walls as though carven from the mountainside itself. Bolerium seemed not so much separate from Kamensic as some marvel given birth by the town, phantasm or prodigy or portent. Its whorled-glass windows gazed down upon the lake's deceptively placid dark surface as though dreaming of itself.

Bolerium was the oldest building in Kamensic. Legend had it that when the Dutch settlers arrived, the mansion was already there, torchlight guttering behind its thick panes and shadowy figures moving slowly through its corridors. This was absurd, of course. It would have taken years, decades, even, to build such a mammoth structure.

What *was* known about the house was that its granite blocks were not native to New York State, or even to the New World. During the Victorian era Owen Schelling, founder of Schelling's Market and an amateur geologist, determined that the building material came from the Penwith peninsula, on the westernmost tip of Cornwall. And because of an unusual variation in the stones, he could assign them an exact provenance: the pastel-tinted cliffs of Lamorna Cove, where ancient quarries produced greenstone and the coarse-grained granite that gave birth to that country's tors and neolithic forts and standing stones.

After Schelling's discovery, Bolerium's mysterious stones would periodically draw geologists from universities and museums across the country. They would carefully tap at the mansion's walls and take their slender samples off to the city, where the results were always the same—an unusual mixture of Penwith greenstone and St. Buryan granite. The shaved and splintered rock was examined and dated and filed away, but the mystery remained: there were no records of Bolerium's construction, no ship's manifest detailing how or when or why a million tons of Cornish granite came to New York Harbor, and thence seventy miles inland to a remote hamlet where only hardscrabble farmers lived, and red men, and witches.

Town records showed the official date of Bolerium's construction as 1743, and were attributed to the mansion's first registered owner, an Irishman named Crom MacCrutch. According to village legend, MacCrutch brought with him the last remaining herd of *Megaloceros*, the so-called Giant Irish Elk, with the intention of establishing a sanctuary for them in the New World. This fact was duly typed on a yellowing index card, where I read it during one of the elementary school's annual trips to the Courthouse Museum.

"That's impossible," Hillary announced disdainfully when I told him about it after school that day. We were kicked back in his basement watching *The Munsters*, Uncle Cosmo's only television rival. "Those things were deer, not elk. Besides which they became extinct about twenty thousand years ago."

"Well, that's what it said in the museum," I insisted, then went on stubbornly, "and Mrs. Langford said it was true. Plus how would *you* know?"

Hillary said nothing, only tightened his lips and stared fixedly at the television. But at the commercial he stalked upstairs, returning a few minutes later with two oversized volumes. He set them side by side on the coffee table and then opened the first, a heavy old book with a stained blue cover and the title *Ancient Man in Briton* stamped in gold letters.

"How would I know?" he demanded, and opened the book. Flecks of paper and dust flew up. There was a faint smell of mold as he flipped through the pages, and finally stopped. "From *this*—"

He stabbed at an illustrative plate, its sepia tones tinged with gray and feathered with the remains of silverfish.

"'Irish Elk,'" I read out loud. "'Peat burial in Hound's Pool, Devonshire, alongside of human remains.' So?"

"So that was ten thousand years ago," Hillary sniffed. "And wait, look here—"

He shoved aside the first book and opened the second. A glossy guide to prehistoric mammals, it had been a Christmas present several years earlier, when Hillary's passion for saber-toothed tigers had driven me nuts. "Look at this," he commanded, and pointed at a two-page spread.

> *Megaloceros:* Giant Eurasian Deer of the Pleis-
> tocene Era.

Above the legend were realistic illustrations of what looked like pretty ordinary deer, the same kind of deer that leaped across the road in front of the school bus or nibbled apples from the trees in our front yard. Save only this: the deer in the pictures were crowned by absolutely massive mooselike antlers, spreading upward and out like the canopy of an oak, and so huge it seemed impossible that the creatures could have held their heads erect.

"Holy cow." I whistled and read the rest of the caption.

> In a fully mature male, the palmate antlers could span twenty feet and weigh forty pounds. Even after the stag reached its full growth, each year it would continue to produce successively larger and more unwieldy crowns, which may ultimately have contributed to their extinction. With the minor ice age of 10,000 B.C., their numbers were severely depleted, although there is evidence of some having existed within the Black Sea basin as recently as 500 B.C.

I shook my head. "They weren't extinct twenty thousand years ago—it says here they found some in Europe in 500 B.C. So—"

Hillary rolled his eyes. "So that's still over *two thousand* years ago, Lit! Listen—there's no way anyone ever had an Irish Elk in Kamensic, okay?"

"I'm just telling you what the sign said in the Courthouse Museum."

"The sign in the Courthouse is *wrong*. And what the hell would Mrs. Langford know about it, anyway? She believes in Bigfoot." Hillary collected his books and swept back upstairs, yelling his parting shot. "Your dad just called. You're supposed to go home."

Hillary was my best friend and next-door neighbor. His parents were the Fabulous Wellers, Natalie and Edmund: English actors who had made their debuts alongside Laurence Olivier in a 1940s production of *Tis Pity She's a Whore*, and gone on to mainstream success in the 1950s and early '60s with a series of Ealing comedies in which they played Flo and Moe Fleck, divorced private investigators who continued to work together despite past (and continuing) infidelities. In real life, both were homosexual. Natty's youthful passions were notorious and flamboyant. She had run off with the wife of a Chicago financier and later had a long-term, dish-throwing relationship with a predatory blonde starlet named Ada Morn, before marrying Edmund, whose own lovers tended to be men of his own age and temperament: stable, soft-spoken, quietly humorous.

Now both were in their early fifties. Like my father, Natalie and Edmund were part of the repertory company at the Avalon Shakespeare Theater in Avon, Connecticut, and otherwise spent their time raising bees and restoring old-stock apple trees with names like Fox-whelp and Ten Commandments. Hillary was their only child. He was named for Sir Edmund Hillary, a family friend.

"It was actually quite a sacrifice for them to make," he remarked once when we were hanging out at Deer Park. "I mean, probably they *really* wanted to name me Bob, or Stan—"

"Or Butch."

"Or Butch." He nodded sagely and took another swig of his beer. "But they stuck to their guns and named me Hillary, damn it. They're good people, my parents. Good damn people."

I don't remember the first time I met Hillary. He was just always there, like the Wellers' old apple trees and weathered colonial farmhouse that formed the backdrop to my own house. We were the same age and in the same grade at the Kamensic Village School, and, except for a dicey few months in early adolescence when we hated each other, completely inseparable. We roamed freely between our two homes, eating and playing and later sleeping together, companionable as puppies. When my parents were away, rehearsing or performing, I stayed with Hillary. When Natty and Edmund went to England for three months to tape a Flo and Moe reunion, Hillary lived with us. Some people thought we were brother and sister, and there was a superficial resemblance. We were both tall, with shoulder-length hair, though Hillary's was jet-black and mine a rather dingy dark blonde. And we both had large, oblique eyes. Mine were such a pale gray as to seem luminous; Hillary's a deep hazel, the color of new moss on old bark. When we were fourteen we began what was to be a long-time pattern of falling in and out of love with each other, alternating between passionate declarations and equally heartfelt platonic discussions of why it was a far far better thing to remain best friends. This didn't stop us from sleeping together, usually after a night of drinking at Deer Park. Sex with Hillary was fun, the way sex with my other friends was fun: occasionally confusing but never punitive. Our parents were remarkably grown-up about steering us toward various methods of birth control, and so none of us got pregnant. My own couplings were frequent and sunlit, more like swimming than sex; the only mystery about sex was that there was supposed to *be* a mystery. That troubled me. I would have thought it was all just artistic license, troubadours and rock stars wailing about love when they might just as well have been singing about Constantine Fox's red convertible.

But then I would get disturbing hints that it was otherwise; like the fading signal half-heard on a radio late at night, the chopped echo of a song that sounds more beautiful than anything you've ever heard before, a song you never hear again. Sometimes it was a real song that made me feel that way, like the first time I heard Joel Green do "Cities of Night," with its offhand, sloping chorus and melancholy saxophone. Sometimes it was just something I heard about—a movie I'd never seen, like *Midnight Cowboy*; a book I'd never read, like *Venus in Furs*. And sometimes it was just the sound of the wind in the leaves at night, lying in bed after having left Hillary in his room, the two of us more feverish after lovemaking than when we'd started.

There were never any recriminations between Hillary and myself. In that we really were like siblings. Our sex was never perfunctory, but neither was it especially passionate—we saved that for our talk, which was endless and endlessly poignant, fueled by the shared conceit that we were soul mates, doomed in this life to never quite connect romantically but otherwise inextricably entwined. Whatever psychic wounds we exacted upon each other, they were clean ones, and healed quickly.

Which was just as well, since we were always cast opposite each other in school plays. Hillary was not an exceptional actor, but by the time we were sixteen he *was* handsome, with wry comic timing and a pleasant if unremarkable baritone. You could never capture his good looks on film—he was too animated, hands gesturing wildly as he told some ridiculous story about his parents, long hair flying wildly around his lean face. But in high school productions he was Sebastian, and Benedick, and King Arthur in *Camelot*. People fell in love with Hillary when they saw him onstage. Me, they remembered as the Aunt Abby who fell into the front row during *Arsenic and Old Lace*.

Oh, I was crazy about it all. Rehearsals, backstage intrigue, the whole tatty-golden hierarchy with its smells of sweat and spirit gum and melting gels, dust burning off the followspots and the reek of marijuana seeping down from the light booth. I would invariably beat out the competition for Rosalind or Viola or '40s ingenues—not because I was talented, but because I was boyish. I had none of my mother's aristocratic glamour. Instead, I was a throwback to my father's ancestors in County Meath—broad freckled cheekbones, wide mouth, ski nose; narrow-hipped and long-legged. I looked good in trousers or vintage suits. I could fence and do cartwheels, knew the steps to a dozen reels and hornpipes, was strong enough to handle a broadsword. In full stage makeup I could even pass for a slightly eccentric romantic lead, bedraggled Helena to my mother's Titania.

But I was absolutely bone-lazy: loathed learning my lines, hated acting exercises, refused to breathe from the diaphragm. And I had such a bad sense of direction that blocking was a nightmare. I could never remember where upstage was. The lights blinded me. I stepped on people's feet and forgot my lines, and had such horrible stage fright that I threw up before every performance. More than once Hillary had to literally push me onstage from the wings. Anywhere else on earth, I would have been banned from school productions, or sent for extensive counseling to determine why I insisted on acting in the first place.

Finally, to save face, I announced to my family and friends that I was going to be a playwright; and to this end began carrying around a notebook and a copy of *The Bald Soprano*. At night, alone in my room, I'd sit in front of an old Underwood typewriter, a filched bottle of vodka under my desk, and write. Actually, what I really did was drink, and listen to the radio through my headphones. But the line about being a playwright worked. People stopped pestering me to try out for plays. For a little while, at least, I felt as though I fit in.

Because this was Kamensic, and Kamensic *was* theater. What the village had, and has, is actors. *Real* actors, Broadway actors as well as Hollywood royalty, from Tallulah Bankhead and the Lunts, D. W. Griffith and DeVayne Smith, to lesser-known survivors like Theda Austin and the Wellers. Later there would be aging rock stars and hosts of twilight television (Cap'n Jack and

Officer Hap and Gore DeVal), as well as retired icons from *King of the Hillbillies* and *Tales from the Bar Sinister*.

This last was where my father made his living, as the eponymous watering hole's cadaverous yet elegant bartender, Uncle Cosmo, affectionately known as Unk. *Tales from the Bar Sinister* was fabulously popular on network TV in the early 1970s and had a long and happy half-life in syndication. My father couldn't go out for groceries without being recognized, and everyone from waiters at the Muscanth Restaurant to kids on 125th Street called him Unk. Years later, when the show was picked up by Nickelodeon, Unk became a genuine pop icon. Recalled fondly by his original fans, embraced by a new generation who loved his moldy tuxedo, his garish Cryptkeeper makeup, and Peter Lorre voice. *Our* magazine even ran a cover: (H)UNK! it read, beneath his kindly crepuscular face.

Back then, and like everyone else in Kamensic, I took it all for granted. My father with his horror-show garb, mother with her daytime Emmys and *TV Guide* Reader's Choice Awards. In Kamensic, Unk was spoken of as respectfully as Hume Cronyn or Jason Robards. At the annual village Christmas party my mother's reading of "A Christmas Memory" reduced everyone to tears.

"Your mother." Hillary shook his head, staring at my mother's slender figure perched on a stool at the front of the Town Hall, surrounded by banks of sweet-smelling pine boughs and clumps of ghostly white mistletoe. "In the old days they would've burned her at the stake."

"Along with *your* mother."

"Yeah." Hillary slumped down into his seat. "Actually, they probably would've burned the whole fucking *town*."

If Kamensic was a strange place to grow up, I never

knew it. My mother worked outside the home before most women did, but then so did everyone else's mom, acting or dancing or singing or designing costumes. I was lucky enough to be raised by my father rather than a housekeeper or nanny. Except for the three years when *Bar Sinister* was being shot in California, it was Unk who got up with me every morning, Unk who made my brown bag lunches and waited for me at the bus stop, Unk who met me each afternoon. My mother of course was in the city, taping *Perilous Lives*. My earliest memories are of waking at four A.M., lying in bed, and hearing her pad softly about our rambling house as she gathered her makeup bags and fashion magazines, and the more purposeful sound of my father in the kitchen, making her breakfast. Smells of coffee and scrambled eggs floating up through the chilly dark house; then the huffing of our Volkswagen squareback as my father drove my mother to the station, so that she could catch the first train to the city and make a six-thirty call.

My mother's married name was Audrina Moylan. As a girl in London she had played all the Shakespearean ingenues, Ophelia, Cordelia, Rosalind; but it was as Audrey Gold that she created the role she inhabited for forty-some years, that of Livia Prentiss on *Perilous Lives*. Livia was raven-haired and raven-hearted; a suburban Medea in Bob Mackie gowns who seduced, poisoned, throttled, baited, stalked, and reproached her television clan for sixty minutes a day five days a week. Livia's children were numerous and quarrelsome as those dragon's-teeth sown by Cadmus, and Livia herself was something of a hydra, impossible to kill, prone to ridiculously unbelievable recoveries: from cancer, coma, drowning, childbirth. The character of Livia was equally immortal, but my mother had shed her Shakespearean aspirations with as little thought as a snake sheds its skin. She reveled in Livia, collected her Emmys and displayed them proudly in the living room beside infant photographs of her only daughter and a silver-framed picture of my father and Axel Kern at the Oscar ceremonies, the year Kern won for directing *Die by Night*. My mother loved her daily treks to the city, thrived on them; and while she claimed to love Kamensic, she is the one person who always seemed immune to its disquieting charm.

I grew up in Kamensic; everyone I knew grew up in Kamensic. Our parents worked in the city, as actors or directors or designers or dancers; but I had seldom been to the city alone, without my parents. Our houses were very old—those fieldstone fortresses left by the Dutch patroons, a few colonial farms left unburned by Warrenton's raid—or else they were aggressively new, futurist machines designed by Vuko Taskovich or Michael Graves, the approximate shape and color of battleships. My family lived in one of the colonials, set within a broad swathe of lawn in that part of town known as The Hamlet. This was where the Constance Charterbury Library was, and Schelling's Market. On Sundays we had brunch with our parents' agents at the Village Inn. When my father was rehearsing for the Avalon Shakespeare season, groceries were delivered via bicycle from Schelling's. Every year at my birthday party, my father would make a surprise entrance as Unk, which would send my guests into gleeful fits and me into an absolute rigor of embarrassment.

Still, while having Uncle Cosmo as a parent was mortifying, a lot of my friends had it worse. Duncan Forrester's father had remarried a famous feminist sculptor who filled their rose garden with enormous bronze castings of her vulva. Linette Davis's mother, Aurora Dawn, had been a model and actress in the Warhol Factory who was famous now for drunk driving. Sport and Jacey Finn had six sons with golden hair and emerald eyes, all addicted to heroin. In a lot of ways Kamensic seemed like a throwback to medieval times, a walled fortress with a high child-mortality rate. There were not many children in Kamensic, certainly not as many as in the neighboring towns of Goldens Bridge and Mahopac and Pawkotan. Children were at once cherished and expendable; families were large, so that even if one or two of the older kids were lost to drugs or madness or the Ivy League, the younger ones could always be found hanging out in front of the library, or fidgeting in the back of the Congo Church during benefit performances of new works by Beckett or John Guare. The Vietnam War swept by us like an Angel of Death distracted by other things: there were enough Kamensic boys of age to fight, but somehow no one was ever drafted. Our parents were unilaterally against the war, the town was against the war; and that seemed to be enough to protect us.

We were all wild things there. Indulged or ignored by famous parents who traded psychiatrists, agents, drug dealers, spouses; shielded by the miles of wood and mountain that stood between us and the city to the south, the desultory suburbs all around. Kamensic itself stood guard against the darkness I sensed sometimes on a June day, the sun glaring off the surface of Lake Muscanth as though off a blue-lacquered plate, crimson dragonflies lighting upon my bare knees as Hillary and I lay naked in the summer warmth.

But still we knew something was there, waiting.

Sometimes I imagined I could hear it—a sound that was just barely audible, an engine thrumming somewhere deep below the water like that faerie mill that grinds salt into the sea. Ali heard it, too, and she said she knew what it was—

"The dead bell."

"The dead bell?" This was when we were thirteen or so, and Ali was reigning queen of slumber parties because of her repertoire of ghost stories and morbid lore. Ali was Alison Fox, my other best friend. She lived in a vast gray argosy of a house on the far side of Muscanth Mountain. Her parents were recently separated. At least I had both parents, even if there were times I longed to live somewhere else, Somers or Mahopac or Shrub Oak, with a father who worked for IBM and a mother who stayed home and played bridge on Thursday nights. It was a snow day and we were at my house, waiting for Hillary to join us so we could play Monopoly. "What the hell is *that?*"

"You know. Up *there*"— She cocked a thumb at the window. —"at Kern's place. That bell in the gate. It rings when someone's going to die."

"So how come it didn't ring last week when Mr. Lapp died?"

Ali cracked the window open and lit a cigarette, kneeling on the floor so the smoke would drift outside. "'Cause it's not when just *anyone* dies. It's like a banshee or something. It only rings for certain people."

"Like who?" I was dubious. Ali was weirdly superstitious—she believed "I Am the Walrus" actually *meant* something, and had a bizarre theory linking Brian Jones's death and the film version of *Rosemary's Baby*—but she was also more plugged into local gossip than I was.

"Like Acherley Darnell. And all those people who killed themselves."

"Acherley Darnell died two hundred years ago. That bell's just for decoration or something."

"Uh-uh. And you know what else—they killed someone every time they made one."

"When who made *what*?"

"The people who made that bell, in England or wherever it came from. It was a custom. They would pour the melted bronze into a mold, and then they would take a person and *zzzzt*"— Ali mimed drawing a blade across her throat. —"they'd cut their neck and put the blood in with the metal. Because otherwise the bell would crack, and you'd never get the tone right."

All this was actually starting to give me the creeps, but I didn't want Ali to know that. I gave her a disgusted look. "What a bunch of crap."

"It's true. I mean, my father said Kern told him it was true," she insisted. "Why would he make it up?"

"He makes all those movies. He makes *everything* up. That bell probably came from some Dumpster in Larchmont."

"Hey." Icy wind gusted into the room and there was Hillary, shaking snow from his hair as he tossed his ski jacket onto the floor. "How come the board's not set up?"

"Cause Ali's running her mouth again, that's why."

I pushed past Hillary, heading into the next room to get the Monopoly set. The truth was, I felt annoyed by Ali's story. Not because it was another one of her crazy anecdotes, but because I'd never heard it before. Axel Kern was *my* godfather, after all: *I* was the one who'd spent childhood evenings at Bolerium listening to his tales and watching movies in his screening room with my father, while the wind roared through the broken windows Axel never bothered to fix, and voles nested in the velvet seat cushions.

In Kamensic you could never trade much on fame, your own or your family's—everyone was either famous, or sort of famous, or had *been* famous. The exception was Axel Kern. Because Kern wasn't just famous. He was notorious, perhaps even dangerous. Like Acherley Darnell, who had been found guilty of the murders of his own daughter and her lover and hanged in front of the village courthouse, his body left on the gallows overnight. The next morning it was found swinging from one of Bolerium's parapets, throat cut and body bled as though he had been a hare.

Nothing like that had happened to Axel Kern—yet. My own childhood memories of him were complex and rather strange, shaded as much by my physical impressions as anything else. These were startlingly acute. I have a strange gift for recalling sensations, and my father sometimes joked that I was psychic, though my mother would not allow a Ouija board in the house, and when I received an Amazing Kreskin's ESP game for my birthday one year, she made me give it away. So while I recognized Kern's famous profile—the tilted, deep-set eyes and high cheekbones, the iron-streaked dark hair and tawny skin that added to his exotic, unsettling persona— what I recalled most about him was the acrid scent of his trademark black Sobranies and the taint of red wine on his breath, at once sweet and foul. Or the way his hands felt when he occasionally and absently stroked my cheeks. Kern was not overly affectionate, at least with children, though he was always kind to me. His hands were large and heavily lined, as his face would one day be; it always felt as though he were wearing leather gloves, supple and rather tough. Yet his clothes were extremely dandyish, even for that foppish age. Custom-made Carnaby Street suits of silk velvet the color of ormolu. Belgian lace shirts so fine I could see through them to his coppery skin and the thick curling hair of his chest. Embroidered Berber robes from Morocco; cowboy boots of ostrich and elephant and python and what Axel solemnly assured me was mastodon, from a corpse recently uncovered in Siberia. I recall all of these, and his voice, lilting for such a big man—Kern was well over six feet—though I remember little of what he actually said. Probably this was because he seldom spoke to me. As I said, he had scant use for children.

Still, I had always felt a proprietary claim on him. And Ali's story about the bell, ridiculous as it was, pissed me off. Now I stomped around for several minutes, hearing her laughter from the next room and the wind battering the storm windows.

"Lit?"

I looked up to see Hillary standing in the doorway. "I'm getting it," I said curtly, and yanked the Monopoly set from a bookshelf.

"You and Ali having a fight or something?"

"No. I'm just sick of her stupid stories, that's all. Look out—"

Hillary moved aside to let me pass. "Lay off her, will you?" he said softly.

"I'm not—"

He grabbed my arm before I could step back out into the living room. "Her mother has a boyfriend," he whispered. "My father told me. They're getting a divorce . . ."

I hesitated, looking out to where Ali still sat on the floor, watching cigarette smoke seep out the window cracked above her head. Beside me stood Hillary. I could hear his breathing, and when I glanced up I noticed for the first time that he had gotten taller, that all of a sudden he was bigger than I was. His hand was still on my arm. I could smell his hair, damp from the shower, and the warm scent of his skin beneath layers of flannel and wool. "Lit," he said again; but I pulled away.

"All right then." I flounced into the room, glaring at Ali. "Will you put that out, Ali? My father'll kill you if he finds out. Come on, let's play."

After that I never asked her about the dead bell. If she started telling stories about Axel Kern, or the Village, or any of its odd history, I listened but said nothing. Somehow Hillary had made me feel that we had to protect Ali, and so I did. Much of the time I did so reluctantly, because Ali could be a bully; but I knew Hillary was right. We had to protect her, as the town protected us. It would be a few more years before Axel Kern returned to Kamensic and our world shivered apart, like a crystal vase vibrating to that dimly heard note. By then it was too late to protect anyone.

Ghosts

In another house nearly a thousand miles from
Kamensic, atop a mountain far more isolated than Mount
Muscanth (though no less strange), a man sat looking
down upon the dying sun as it dipped beneath the trees.
He was a very slight man, small-boned but strong-
featured, his black hair curling almost to his shoulders
and tinged with gray. The ruddy light spun a fine web
across his sun-taut skin, but otherwise it was impossible
to guess his age—his full cheeks were rosy as a child's, his
eyes a penetrating sea-blue beneath bristling black eyebrows. His first year undergraduate students always
thought him quite ancient, forty at least; but those who
went on to more advanced and esoteric studies at the
University of the Archangels and Saint John the Divine
were nonplused to find that as years and even decades
passed, their Professor changed very little; and only the
very wisest of his protégés gradually realized that, in fact,
Balthazar Warnick never aged at all.

He sat now within an enormous bay window overlooking the Agastronga River far below. A hawk drifted

lazily past, its wings tilting as it caught the air currents and finally plummeted out of sight. In the distance stretched the Blue Ridge mountains, their peaks a sunset archipelago thrusting upward from the October mist, light like molten copper trickling down their slopes. Balthazar Warnick leaned forward, tracing the hawk's path. On the window ledge a note was perched, expensive stationery covered with the fine spidery handwriting of the Orphic Lodge's formidable housekeeper—

Professor Warnick,

I am to remind you that we have passed three weeks since October 1, and you have not yet performed the *pharmakos* . . .

Balthazar sighed. Three weeks was far too long, of course, even for such a monotonous (and unpleasant) task as the pharmakos. But still he lingered at the window, putting off his duty for one more minute as he stared into the autumn haze.

His knee bumped against something, and he looked down to see the Benandanti's orrery leaning sideways on the faded velvet window seat. A jeweled model of the solar system, sun and planets and little moons all formed of semiprecious stones. But one of the gold wires had become twisted, the lapis lazuli Venus perilously close to being thrown from its delicate orbit. Balthazar had set it here months ago, meaning to set about the careful task of repairing it with more gold filament.

But then the busy weeks of the University's spring term had begun, with their round of oral and written dissertations, the painstaking process of winnowing

Molyneux scholars and the painful one of dismissing those who had failed to live up to their promise, or otherwise crossed the Benandanti. And so the months had passed, until finally today Balthazar had returned to the Orphic Lodge, to find the Benandanti's mountain stronghold isolate and calm as ever, and the little orrery yet unhealed.

With a sigh he picked it up and set it idly upon one knee, toying with the lapis representation of Venus—marble-sized, its surface etched with faint golden striations that felt like fine hairs beneath his fingertips. He rolled the glowing bead back and forth, back and forth, until heat began to rise from it, and tiny gray fronds like steam. He drew his hand back, smiling a little as the blue orb danced upon its filament; then whistled softly as his thumb caught upon the jagged bit of protruding gold filament. The orrery bounced upon the velvet cushion and came to rest against the window. Balthazar swore beneath his breath and drew his hand to his mouth, sucking another crimson bead from his thumb. On its abbreviated transit, gold-veined Venus spun and strained at its wire lead like a june beetle on a thread, and made a noise like a woman humming.

"*In coelo quies*,'" he murmured. *There is rest in Heaven*.

Somewhere within the vast reaches of the Orphic Lodge a clock struck the hour, six sweet clear chimes that rang out like water cascading into a well. The notes hung in the air a moment and Balthazar listened, waiting for the echoes to fade.

But instead of dying away the sound grew almost imperceptibly louder, as though someone ran a moist finger around the lip of a crystal glass. Balthazar frowned.

He looked toward the door, but of course there was no one there.

He shivered. Still the sound went on, maddeningly faint, and as it did so the hairs on his arms prickled.

Because there seemed to be another sound behind that eerie note. A noise like scratching, or static, that as the moments passed resolved into a chittering whisper he could just barely hear: as though a radio droned in some far-off part of the house. Balthazar shook his head. With stony calm he turned, straining to hear.

And now the sound grew—not louder, but more distinct. He held his breath, listening. There was a crackle of static. Myriad voices chattered and whistled, with now and then an unsettling whoop like an angry gibbon. Balthazar listened, every hair on end; then grew rigid as the room fell silent.

A moment when he could hear only his own breathing. Then suddenly a voice began to speak in mid-sentence, a voice so thin and faint it was like the clicking of ants within the walls.

A voice he had last heard almost four hundred years ago.

"*Giulietta*," he whispered. "*Giulietta* . . ."

. . . *do not understand why I have been summoned here* . . .

A young woman's voice, speaking in the dialect of the Italian village of Moruzzo, her tone calm but Balthazar knew, ah! he remembered: she had not been calm at all.

—*Do you know of anyone in this village who is a witch, or a Malandante?*

A second voice now, a man's, with the airy accent of Vincenza. His tone neither threatening nor pleading but almost playful, rehearsing a well-known part with an actor who had perhaps forgotten her lines.

Of witches I do not know any, nor even of Benandanti.
The girl laughed throatily; but a moment later went on,
her voice rising. *Father, no. I really do not know. I am not
a Benandante, that is not my calling. And certainly I am
not Malandante. I do not know whether any child in our
village has been bewitched.*

At the word *Malandante* Balthazar shuddered as
though a sentence had been pronounced. The voice of
the inquisitor rang out, more sternly this time.

—*Yet you saw the son of Pietro Ruota.*

I went to see the sick child . . . The girl hesitated, then
went on. *The father asked for my help, but I could do
nothing. I told him I did not know anything about it. I—I
have not invited anyone to the games to which the
Benandanti go.* She laughed again, a sound like rope
fraying.

—*Why did you laugh?* the man demanded; and
Balthazar's throat burned as he felt the same words
welling inside him: O *Giulietta, why did you laugh?* He
saw her again, a tall girl with bold eyes, uncanny ice-blue
eyes that had already stained her with the epithet *strega*;
that and the fact that she rinsed her hair with Egyptian
herbs to give it color and strength, and lay with men but
had never borne a child.

—*Why did you laugh?* repeated the inquisitor.

Balthazar heard her feet shuffling against the bare
wooden planks as she swore beneath her breath and
finally said,

*Because these are not things to inquire about, because
they are against the will of God.*

—*And how would you know what is the will of God?*
the inquisitor cried.

Silence. Then, in a clear sure voice the girl answered, *It is said that when they assemble, the Benandanti must fight for the faith of God, and their enemies fight for the Devil's.*

—*But for the faith of what God do they fight?*

Silence. Balthazar's heart pounded and he moaned aloud. All around him was the darkened stall swept clean of hay and dung. A single small clay lamp had been thrust into an alcove to send shadows skittering up the splintered cedar walls and greasy smoke spiraling toward the mud-daubed ceiling. Beneath the stench of burning oil he could smell her, a faint musk of salt and fennel stalks, her auburn hair scrubbed with sand that still reeked of the river-bottom. Even from across the room, even from across the centuries, he could feel that she did not flinch, as the inquisitor thundered once more.

—*For the faith of whose God do they fight?*

In his corner the scrivener's quill snagged upon the parchment in front of him. Still the girl said nothing. After a moment the inquisitor took a deep breath, and asked, —*Then tell me the names of their enemies, of the witches. The Malandanti.*

The girl lifted her face. Tangled auburn curls fell back from a high forehead, and her eyes burned white in the darkness as she calmly replied, *Sir, I cannot do it.*

—*Yet you say that they fight for God. I want you to tell me the names of these witches.*

Balthazar shuddered. As though she sensed him there the girl trembled, too. She rubbed her hands along her bare arms and glanced around the room, not nervously but with great care, as though tracking a mouse by the sound of its footsteps. And then she found him; recognized him, even though his face was hidden by the sooty folds of the domino. Her linen shift made a sound like the wind in the cornstalks, counterpoint to the scratching of the *procurator ab actis* where he sat in a corner transcribing her words, his face lost within the domino's hood. He would not look up to meet her eyes. The girl's gaze remained upon his hunched figure, and Balthazar could see hopelessness settle on her thin shoulders like a rook.

I cannot name nor accuse anyone, she said at last, tearing her gaze from the scrivener. She shook herself, then gave him a thin smile. *Whether he be friend or foe.*

—*Tell me the names of these Malandanti.*

Boldly the red-haired girl met the inquisitor's eyes. *I cannot say them.*

The inquisitor pounded his hand against the wall, the folds of his domino flapping like black sails.

—*For what reason can't you tell me this?* he cried. In a neighboring recess a horse whinnied. —*For what reason?*

The girl's voice rose angrily. *Because we have a lifelong edict not to reveal secrets about one side or the other!*

—*You assert that you are not one of them—why are you obliged to obey them?* The inquisitor stepped away from the wall. Dust curled around his booted feet like smoke, and reddened the hem of his robes. He lifted his cloaked head and inclined it very slightly to where the scrivener was bent over his lap-desk, his breath clouding the autumn air; and across all those intervening years Balthazar could feel the malice of that hidden gaze, a cudgel crashing onto his back.

Because, of course, the inquisitor cared nothing about the girl. His only concern was that villagers claimed that she was a *strega*, and so might have corrupted her lovers;

and one of those lovers was under his care. She was seventeen, too young to have been taken by the Benandanti as one of their own. Besides which she was a girl, and women rarely gained entry to the Benandanti's libraries and refectories, and then only as servants. The inquisitor himself knew this, because he was a Benandante, as was the girl's lover. He sought only to learn if her young *cicisbeo* had betrayed the Benandanti's secrets to her; but now the girl had betrayed herself. He raised one white hand to his cloaked face, the fingers long and slender and seemingly bloodless as bone, and slowly shook his head.

—*Giulietta Masparutto*, he said. The words came out quickly now, his tone grew distracted, even bored. *Your words condemn you as Malandante. Our land is full of witches and evil people performing a thousand evils and a thousand injuries against their neighbors. There is an abundance of such misbegotten people, and I have been chosen to act as inquisitor general and judge over cases such as yours. With the counsel of those who are expert in the laws of God and Good Men, you, Giulietta Masparutto, are arraigned in my presence and will now hear the penance to be imposed, as follows:*

First, I condemn you to a term of twelve months in a prison which we shall assign to you . . .

What have I done? the girl shouted. Her cheeks flushed as she tossed her head furiously. *I have done nothing, you know that I have done nothing—*

—*We reserve to ourselves the authority to reduce these penalties or absolve you, in whole or in part, as we may deem best . . .*

With a cry she whirled, to turn accusatory eyes upon the hooded figure whose quill moved unrelentingly across his parchment. But the scrivener did not look up, and the girl quickly turned back to her questioner.

Please, she cried, *I am needed here, my cousin Ilario is ill—*

But already there was the scraping sound of the barn door being pulled open behind them. Sunlight slashed through the narrow stall, blinding her; a few yards away the horse whinnied again in excitement. Two barefoot young men in the soiled brown robes of cenobites stepped uncertainly through the doorway, frowning when they saw the girl.

—*This one, Father?*

The inquisitor nodded. He gestured dismissively as he strode past them, his robes sending up more dust as he tugged his domino from a gaunt face slick and reddened from the heat.

—*Yes*, he said brusquely, and fanned his cheeks. In the doorway he paused, waiting until the two men had dragged the struggling girl past him and out into the courtyard. Sunlight made a ragged halo about his black-clad figure, dust-motes a rain of golden coins about his shoulders as the inquisitor gazed at the scrivener in the room behind him, slowly gathering his things. After a minute the inquisitor spoke.

—*She did not betray you.*

The scrivener bent to retrieve a leather satchel. He shrugged without lifting his head. The inquisitor continued to stare at him. Finally he asked,

—*Is she Malandante?*

The scrivener stooped, silent, beside his bag and little wooden traveling-desk. He shook back the domino from his face, blinking at the sun.

I do not know, he lied. *But the villagers say she has the sight.*

The inquisitor gazed down at him, his expression cool. —*If that is true, you might have brought her to us.* His mouth twitched into a bitter smile. *We could have found a place for her, Balthazar. Better that she serve us than another master. A word from you could have saved her.*

He turned and walked out into the courtyard, light swirling around him like flame. Balthazar watched him go, his eyes burning; then suddenly drew his hand to his face.

Giulietta.

He closed his eyes, opened them to see about him the familiar lines of his study.

"Giulietta," he repeated, and buried his face in his hands.

4

No Fun

There was something else strange about Kamensic, and that was its suicides. Some of these had taken place so much before my time that they had the solemn, dingy aura of ancient myth. But by the year I started high school there had been ten or twelve of them: deaths by hanging, by jumping off Darnell Bridge into the reservoir, by drug overdose, by gunshot, by carbon monoxide and straight-edge razor. Almost all of them were teenagers, although the mother of my friends Giorgio and Nastassia Klendall killed herself when we were in high school, climbing to the roof of their four-story village Victorian and jumping off. The note she left in the kitchen, weighed down by an empty wine bottle, read only

Th-th-that's all, folks!

The deaths were seldom spoken of, but they were not hushed up. They were treated as normal deaths, as normal at least as dying in your bed at the age of ninety-seven with a hooded peregrine falcon on your breast, as Gloria Nevelson did, or expiring of lung cancer after smoking three packs of Kents a day for thirty-four years, like Clement Stoddard. And there was certainly no *religious* distress or stigma attached to the suicides. Despite the presence of its century-old Congregational Church, Kamensic was not what you could call a religious place. There was no minister affiliated with the Congo Church, which in any case was used almost constantly as an informal rehearsal space. Occasionally out-of-towners would arrange to be married there—it looked so charming, tucked in amidst the maple trees with the Muscanth River meandering in the background and all those eccentric, theatrical villagers mowing their lawns!—but they brought their own clergy or made arrangements with the justice of the peace.

The only time I ever saw the church used for something like its intended purpose was at funerals. And I never realized how bizarre, even disturbing, these must seem to outsiders, until I was much older and attended a funeral down at Sacred Heart in Yonkers, with Irish Catholic relatives of my father who wept while incense burned and an Irish tenor sang the "Ave Maria" in a voice so pure that I wept myself, though I scarcely knew the deceased.

It was not like that at home. In Kamensic there was solemnity but no real grief; no service save for readings from Shakespeare or Aeschylus; no music until the very end. The church's rough-hewn wooden pews would be draped with ivy and evergreen boughs, even in midsummer, and the lovely, stellated wild tulips that grew in rocky crevices on Muscanth Mountain. All of the casement windows would be opened, no matter the weather, and the doors as well; but no coffin or casket ever entered the building. Only as the brief ceremony of readings ended would someone commence playing on a flute in the back of the church, and those gathered would leave, to reconvene at the cemetery a few hundred yards away. The music was always the same, a haunting, repetitive melody, not filled with sadness so much as longing and a strange, almost exhilarating intimation that *something was about to happen.*

But what that was, I never found out. Nor did I ever learn who played the flute: I never saw anyone, either in the back of the church or in that tiny choir-loft where choirs never sang. At the cemetery a plain wooden coffin would lie on the ground, its top strewn with poppies and anemones; in winter, there would be the poppies' dried seed-heads, ivy, and holly. Beside the coffin was the grave, freshly dug, the soil protected from rain or snow by spruce boughs, and beside the grave the women would stand in a line. Usually someone would say a few words, but it would always end with my mother standing at the head of the grave and reciting in her fine clear girlish voice—

> *"Down with the bodie and its woe,*
> *Down with the Mistletoe;*
> *Instead of Earth, now up-raise*
> *The green Ivy for show.*
>
> *The Earth hitherto did sway;*
> *Let Green now domineer*
> *Until the dancing Sonbuck's Day*
> *When black light do appeare."*

Then the unadorned box would be lowered into the grave. This was always done by women; never men. Sometimes it would take only four of them, sometimes six or even ten, as when Chubby Snarks, an old vaudevillain who weighed three hundred pounds and was buried with his notices, choked to death on a cornichon. The women would strain and groan, but at last it was done. Robins and thrushes would alight upon the mounded earth, to hunt for insects there, and butterflies drawn by the flowers.

As a child I thought the cemetery was the most beautiful, even idyllic, spot in Kamensic, with its flowering dogwoods and shads and forsythia, and so many apple trees it might have been an orchard. Daffodils bloomed underfoot, and more of the *tulipa saxatilis*; there were bluebells and periwinkles and, everywhere, ivy. And of course there were the gravestones themselves, carved figures of winged foxes and men with the heads of birds, of lionesses and deer and serpents, commemorating the dead from wars and influenza, fire and cancer and noose. The strains of the flute would die into the sound of wind in the leaves, and the children would run off to play quietly among the grave markers. When the coffin was lowered the villagers shared the task of heaping soil back upon it; and when this was completed the last part of the ceremony was performed. Mrs. Langford would produce several bottles of red wine. My father or one of the other men would open them, and the bottles were passed around. Everyone drank from them, even children—I can remember spitting out my mouthful, and my mother smiling gently as she wiped off my mouth with her handkerchief. Sometimes only one or two bottles were quaffed this way; sometimes a dozen or more. Then everyone would leave—not very quietly, either, and generally to my house or the Wellers'. People would speak fondly of the deceased, but there was no sense of genuine grief or bereavement, even with the suicides of the village children. It was as though you one day discovered a dead chipmunk in the woods, half-buried in the leaves; but every day thereafter it was harder and harder to find, until at last it was gone, completely swallowed by the earth.

So it was with Kamensic: swiftly and remorselessly as an ermine, it devoured its own young.

Somehow it never appeared strange to us. After all, what else did we know? It was the early 1970s, we were thirteen, fourteen, fifteen years old. We absorbed Kent State and the Manson Family, evacuated our classrooms for bomb threats and stayed home from school when Albert Shanker called our teachers to strike. Death just seemed to be an occupational hazard if you were young. What shocks me now is how we were all expected to simply take it for granted, how often we met on the playground or school parking lot and spoke in whispers, glancing over our shoulders as a brother or sister of the deceased would arrive and take their place among us. Famous or notorious as Kamensic's residents were, there were no talk shows, no tabloid headlines, and certainly no school psychologists waiting to comfort the bereaved. Even when Phillip Lawton's son died—the *New York Times* reported it as a bad reaction to a bee sting, but we heard otherwise—and the television crews appeared, the people of Kamensic drove them away.

"Have you no decency?" cried DeVayne Smith at the train station where the reporters had gathered, his basso voice quavering with rage. "Go from here, now—*go*—"

They went. Confronted with the angry mob that had rushed to Lawton's side—not just DeVayne Smith but Gracie Burrows, Constantine Fox, my own parents, and Axel Kern—the reporters shot a few seconds of taped footage, got into their vans and fled. Fifteen minutes later, heading south on Route 684, a deer ran in front of the van and it crashed. The footage never aired. Lawton's son was buried in the Kamensic Village cemetery, alongside a weathered statue of an angel with folded wings and a wolf's muzzle.

5

Children of the Revolution

Hillary and Ali and I were inseparable as the petals of a rose. Ali had been my best friend since the first day of kindergarten. We had stood in the playground weeping as our parents left us, and then fallen into each other's arms, wailing—a story which we heard repeated, say, a thousand times over the years. Ali was slight and fey, as I was big-boned and (much against my will) commonsensical. As a girl she wore white fishnet stockings and plastic go-go boots to parties, her long black hair so thick that when you ran your fingers through it they stuck, as though it were taffy. My own hair was a mess, thin and lank. My mother finally gave up on it and brought me to her hairdresser in the city.

"Chop it off," she ordered, snatching up her copy of *Women's Wear Daily* and sinking into a pink lounge chair. And chop it off he did, leaving me with a horrible pixie cut. I was tall for my age, skinny as a rail. With my cropped head I looked like a very young ex-con and was constantly mistaken for a boy. It wasn't until I was thirteen that I rebelled and insisted on growing my hair out. It took two years, but by the time I reached high school I was a reasonable facsimile of a girl, with shoulder-length hair and narrow hips, though still too quick-tempered and clumsy as a young St. Bernard.

Hillary, on the other hand, remained blithe as ever. He was one of those kids whose popularity transcends the rigid class barriers of high school. The jocks liked him, the freaks who smoked pot between classes, the kids in the Honor Society, teachers: everyone. Once a guy from Mahopac called Hillary's father a fag, and even though Ali pointed out that, technically, this was true, Hillary sat down and patiently explained the word's etymological origins until the guy finally shrugged.

"Well, shit, if you don't care that your old man's a fag, neither do I," he announced, and bought Hillary a beer.

In 1974, nobody cared; at least not in Kamensic. David Bowie had appeared on *Don Kirschner's Rock Concert* wearing eye makeup. Duncan had seen the New York Dolls perform in drag at Club 82, and even Hillary sometimes wore electric blue mascara to parties. I made my own bid for bisexual chic by dressing à la Joel Grey in *Cabaret*, in a moth-eaten tuxedo and battered top hat. I still have a Polaroid photo that Ali took of me then: strange lunar eyes so pale they seemed to have no irises, upturned nose and dark eyebrows, a slight overbite that had failed to yield after three years of braces.

"God, *look* at me," I wailed, when the offending image dropped from Ali's camera onto my living room floor. We were going to a cast party, Ali resplendent in a red leotard and Danskin skirt, me in my tatty Marc Bolan finery. "I look like—I don't know *what* I look like."

"You look fine," said Ali, shoving the camera in her

leather satchel. "'Divine decadence.' Right, Unk?"

My father nodded, giving me one of his mock-solemn looks. "Charlotte is *jolie-laide*. Interesting-looking. Like her mother."

At this my mother frowned over her script, her face larded with Christian Dior unguents. "Charlotte is *far* more *jolie* than *laide*. And I am *not* interesting-looking."

"You're *beautiful*, Audrey," Ali said soothingly and with the assurance of someone who truly was. Even at seventeen she was petite, just five feet tall, with a round smooth body, small round breasts and milk-white skin, freckled all over. She still had that wild mane of black hair framing a wide, expressive face—freckled cheeks, sweetly pursed mouth, honey-colored eyes, a small gap between her two front teeth. Hillary teased her and called her Colette, which for a little while made Ali hope that perhaps he was in love with her. They slept together a few times, but then Hillary started going with a Swedish exchange student with even more fabulous hair, and that was the end of that.

Ali's parents did indeed get divorced. Ali lived with her father in Kamensic, and spent alternate weekends in the city with her mother, a one-time principal dancer with the New York City Ballet and former Balanchine muse. Ali's father, Constantine, was a set designer. Ali had inherited his gifts—she would have made a wonderful illustrator, with her eye for the grotesque combined with her skills as a draftsman—but Ali wanted to be a dancer. She had studied since childhood at Madame Laslansky's famed Manhattan studio, but despite the years of training she moved with an oddly stilted grace. Not like a dancer at all; more like a fox stalking, stopping to listen, and then flowing forward, always on the balls of her feet so she looked slightly tippy-toed, as though she were about to pounce. In our freshman year she auditioned for both the Joffrey and the School of American Ballet, but was turned down for both.

She was different after that. Wilder—she'd always been wild, but now there was a hysterical edge to everything she did, from dancing at parties to streaking during away football games at Carmel and Goldens Bridge. When I think of Ali I think of her naked: she shed her clothes like a toddler, unthinkingly, stripping to slide into the lake or to join some boy in the mossy woods behind school. Or else she wore leotards, black Danskins and black Capezios on her tiny feet; a ragged flannel shirt tied around her waist so the sleeves flopped against her thighs, her glossy black hair slick against her skull.

That was how she was dressed the day we met Jamie Casson. It was a damp afternoon in our senior year, the week before Halloween. The end of high school seemed like a formality to be dispensed with as quickly as possible. We'd both recently applied to the college of our choice—Hampshire College for Ali, NYU for me. Half the time we'd hardly bother showing up for class at all, save to find our friends in the parking lot and check out whose parents were out of town scoping locations for a new film or rehearsing. That was how we knew where the parties were, and that's how we spent most of our time.

It was a strange autumn; not just that one October night, but all the weeks leading up to it. Though I never spoke of it, I felt a real foreboding at the idea of leaving. Not leaving school, but leaving Kamensic—and leaving Hillary, who had aced us all and already been accepted by the Yale School of Drama. Yet in some weird way the thought of going away from the village disturbed me more than anything else. I wondered if Ali felt it, too. Sometimes she would grow silent and oddly alert, as though focused on a faint sound, thunder or the rustle of footsteps in dead leaves. But she never told me what she was thinking.

That rainy Thursday afternoon I felt fiercely restless. By the end of the day I thought I'd start screaming if I couldn't escape: from school, from the rain, from my own too-tight skin. I met Ali in the parking lot by Hillary's old Dodge Dart. Behind us the dismissal bell shrieked. The rain had slacked off, though a cold breeze shook the trees and sent water arcing onto our heads. Ali lit the butt-end of a joint; as usual, the pot made me feel worse, paranoid and fuzzy-headed. But Ali grew loopy, laughing and walking backward through the woods.

"Something's gonna happen now. Don't you feel it, Lit?" Her golden eyes narrowed as she took out a cigarette. "Don't you *feel* it?"

We cut through the trees, heading out along the railroad tracks. I shrugged and kicked at the gravel underfoot. "I guess."

The truth was I felt a vague foreboding, a sense of malevolent purpose in the way the tree-limbs moved and the pattern of raindrops beaded on the railway ties. But Ali walked alongside me happily, smoking and singing.

> *"I don't want no diamond ring*
> *Don't want no Cadillac car*
> *Just want to drink my Ripple wine*
> *Down at the Deer Park bar . . ."*

She tossed her head back. "Isn't it fucking great to be alive?"

"I dunno." I shivered. I had on one of Hillary's old corduroy jackets, too big for me but worn and comforting. "I do feel sort of weird. Maybe something *is* going to happen . . ."

Ali laughed. "I *always* feel like something's gonna happen. And nothing ever does."

She dropped her spent cigarette, veering from the tracks onto the overgrown path that would bring us to Mount Muscanth.

It wasn't a real mountain, of course, just one of those outriders of the Catskills that straggle down from the northwestern part of New York State. But on its north face there was a bare stone outcropping where you could sit and look down upon the village, and it was as though you were in another world. The air smelled of dying leaves and earth, and as we walked there were birds everywhere, and tiny things moving underfoot.

"I'm beat," Ali exclaimed. "Hang on a minute—"

We stopped before a stand of forsythia that had run wild. I was stooping to settle beneath it when the earth at its roots seemed suddenly to shiver.

"Fuckin' A—" Ali gasped. "Look out!"

At her feet the ground was fuming with a gray cloud of shrews no bigger than my thumb, dozens of them scurrying about, utterly heedless of us. At first I thought something must have disturbed them. But as we watched I saw that no, they were all *hunting*—feverishly, lunging at black beetles and ants pouring up from beneath the rotting leaves, teeth slicing through shiny carapaces and the dull gray coils of millipedes, their white claws delicate as fronds of club moss. They tore at the leaf-mold in a fury, scrabbling over puffballs that sent up clouds of spores like minute bomb-bursts. I held my breath and lowered myself to within a foot of this seething world, watching as two shrews had a tug-of-war with an earthworm. After a minute they separated and ferociously attacked each other. I was so close I could see tiny droplets of blood spatter onto the forsythia and smell their faint foul musk.

And still the shrews raced on, fighting and hunting and eating. To them, I had no more being than a tree or stone. I was entranced, and would have remained there for the entire afternoon, maybe, if Ali hadn't pulled me away.

"Enough with the fucking *Wild Kingdom*, Lit; it's gonna rain. Come on, let's go to Deer Park."

About halfway down we emerged onto a narrow ridge of stone, slick with moss. A scant yard in front of us the ridge sheared away, so that we gazed down upon the tops of red oaks and huge lichen-stained boulders. If you knew where to look, this was where you could catch your first glimpse of the ruinous beauty that was Bolerium. I edged back until I could wrap my arm around a tree—I was wearing knee-high lace-up Frye boots, well broken in but a bad choice for climbing. Ali walked fearlessly to the lip of rock and looked out.

"I can't see it," she said, frowning.

I squinted, trying to distinguish between the mansion's granite walls and the gray trees that stood between us. "It's too rainy," I said at last, feeling a vague disappointment.

Ali shook her head. "Uh-uh. It's *hiding*."

We turned and scrambled on down the path. When we finally burst out of the woods onto Kinnicutt Road, it was into a world gone gold and white, yellow leaves covering the tarmac and birches ghostly in the mist. Ali shivered in her leotard and pulled her flannel shirt over her head like a hood. I pulled Hillary's jacket tight around me, wincing as a black BMW raced past and sent water splashing over us.

"Asshole," I shouted.

If there was a wrong side to Kamensic, that's where we were now: Kinnicutt Road, a chopped-up remnant of the Old Post Road that a hundred years earlier had linked Boston to the fractured villages strung across New England. Ten miles or so along, Kinnicutt fed into Route 684, the new interstate that connected the city with the north. But here it was a scumble of cracked asphalt, broken glass winking from a shoulder overgrown with nightshade and fox grapes and jewelweed. There were no houses along this stretch of Kinnicutt, no other roads; only a defiant tributary of the Muscanth River threading alongside the tarmac.

Now it felt almost inutterably desolate. The air smelled faintly of diesel fuel. Ahead of us the road narrowed, unyielding to the woods that crowded to either side, and finally faded from sight. My dread intensified until I considered making up some excuse to head home—stomachache, homework, fever.

But then the trees fell back, revealing a drab patch of sky. In another minute I could make out the parking lot and dull mass of cinder block that was the Deer Park Inn.

"Hillary's here," remarked Ali. And yes, there was his Dodge Dart by the front door. That made me feel better, and the sight of Deer Park's venerable sign: a huge Sweetheart of the Rodeo, suspended between two worm-riddled telephone poles. Years ago during a storm the sign had been cloven right down the middle. Now only half of the cowgirl remained, one eye, one arm holding a lariat, one foot in one frilled cowboy boot; and beneath her what remained of the bar's legend:

RK INN
NTRY
TERN
NCING
LBILLY
USIC

We crossed a parking lot awash with cigarette butts and beer bottles. Once behind the squat building you found more ominous detritus: spent sets of works like crushed centipedes, crumpled cellophane envelopes, scorched spoons, empty matchbooks. Two bikers sat on the steps drinking Budweisers. They watched us pass, eyes glazed, but said nothing. Entering I felt the customary frisson of excitement and blind terror; and was relieved to spot Hillary standing by the jukebox, resplendent in an old military jacket and embroidered turquoise shirt.

"Jeez, it's packed," shouted Ali.

Deer Park was so small it never took much to make a crowd. High school kids mostly; a few more bikers playing pool in the corner; some older kids who'd moved on to college a few years earlier, and either graduated or drifted back to town. Beer lights flickered through the cigarette smoke—Budweiser, Rhinegold, Pabst Blue Ribbon—and the jukebox was roaring "Jailhouse Rock." There were Halloween decorations on the walls, leering witches and black cats. Over the bar hung a mounted stag's head with a pumpkin nestled between its antlers. As we crossed the room people yelled out to us, and somebody began chanting—

"Alison Fox, she must be
The prettiest witch in the north coun-tree . . ."

"I got to piss," Ali announced, and made a beeline for the bathroom. I turned to wave at Hillary. He was talking to a boy perched on top of the jukebox, a wiry figure with unfashionably short hair, dressed completely in black.

Hillary raised his beer. "Lit! C'mere—"

"Hang on!" I shouted, and headed for the bar. "Hey, Jim. What's the deal? It's so crowded—"

"Tell me about it." Jim Charterbury worked at the Lifesaver factory down in Portchester and moonlighted at Deer Park at night. He pointed at one of the cardboard witches and shook his head. "Fuckin' Halloween, man. Got the bikers howling at the moon. What's going on with you?"

"Not much. Who's that with Hillary?"

"Dunno, some kid just moved here. You want the usual?" I nodded and stuck a few crumpled bills on the bar. Jim poured two drafts, filled a shot glass with rail whiskey and dropped it into one of the mugs. I downed this, grimacing, and shivered.

"You look like my dog when you do that." Jim slid me the other mug, put a stack of quarters alongside it. "Go crank up something beside Elvis Goddam Presley, will you? These bikers are driving me nuts."

I took the quarters and my drink and elbowed my way through the room. By the time I reached the jukebox I wanted another beer.

"Hillary."

"Hey, Lit." Hillary handed his bottle to me. I took a swig—lukewarm, he'd been here for awhile—and glanced at the boy on the jukebox. "Jailhouse Rock" segued into "Born to Be Wild." Behind the bar Jim gestured at me frantically, and I jingled the quarters in my fist.

"Hang on, I got to do something about this music"— I looked pointedly at the boy sitting on the old Seeburg. —"but first your friend has to move his ass."

"Right." Hillary made a low bow. "Jamie? This is Lit—"

I stared at him and nodded. I felt the weird clarity that came over me sometimes when I drank, when suddenly I could see how my friends would look when they were old: where the lines would fall alongside Hillary's mouth, where his hair would thin at the temples. Other times it was an awful certainty that was like a rank taste in the back of my throat, the fear when I stared at Duncan dancing in Deer Park that something terrible was going to happen to him; the less numbing recognition that Ali was never going to make it as an dancer, no matter how much she still wanted to. These were things I didn't talk about anymore. Ali laughed at me, and when I tried telling Hillary it made him nervous.

Standing there now I felt that same strange sense of recognition, and a profound, almost nightmarish, unease. I glanced at Hillary, but he just grinned. I swallowed, my tongue thick with whiskey and cheap beer, and looked at the boy on the jukebox. He wore black jeans low-slung on narrow hips, dirty black Converse high-tops, a moth-eaten black sweater.

"What are you, Johnny Cash?" I asked.

He met my eyes disdainfully. He was rangy, a few inches taller than me, with dark blonde hair cut so short you could see the shape of his skull, sleek as a ferret's. That more than anything else made him seem otherworldly. *Everyone* I knew had long hair. The boys I hung out with, the boys I slept with, all resembled Hillary. Beautiful straight teeth courtesy of Doctor Tolmach, skin kept clear by weekly visits to dermatologists, shoulder-length hair thick and glossy as a golden retriever's.

Not Jamie Casson. His skin was faintly sallow, and so fair I could see the tracery of capillaries across his cheeks, like a leaf's fine-veined web. His eyes were huge, heavy-lidded; the flesh beneath them looked bruised. Great wounded eyes, of a startling turquoise, deep-set above a pug nose and thin, girlish mouth. The only person I'd ever seen who looked remotely like him was Lou Reed on the cover of *Transformer*, or maybe Louise Brooks in an old photograph I'd seen in the Courthouse Museum. I could imagine my parents approving of Jamie Casson's hair, if nothing else.

But I thought he looked decadent and faintly sinister, perched there on the old Seeburg. The music rattled on; he continued to stare at me. When the song ended, he raised himself up slightly on his hands, then abruptly sat down, hard, on top of the jukebox. There was the scrape of a needle on vinyl, and "Born to Be Wild" started again.

"LIT?" From across the bar Jim Charterbury yelled. "What the fuck are you *doing?"*

I mouthed *Sorry!* Hillary and I looked at each other and burst out laughing. The boy on the jukebox tipped his head to one side and regarded me through slanted eyes.

"I'm Jamie Casson." It sounded like a challenge. "What the hell kind of name is Lit?"

"Her name's Charlotte, that's what everyone calls her," Hillary explained, then added conspiratorially,

> *"She is the madhouse nurse who tends on me,*
> *It is a piteous office."*

"Don't mess with her, man," warned Hillary. "She's got a temper, she'll clock you if you mess with her—"

"Right," I said, pretending to swing as Hillary pulled me close in a bear hug.

"—*and* she's crazy," he yelled.

"Crazy like a fox." Someone poked me from behind and I turned to see Ali. She raised her eyebrows quizzically to Jamie Casson. "Umm . . . ?"

"This is Jamie," I started to say; but then I saw the two of them *looking* at each other. Like that Aubrey Beardsley black light poster Ali had up above her bed, "How Sir Tristam Drank of the Love Drink." Two beautiful children etched in violet and dead-white, so intent upon each other that the air between them all but glowed; heavy stage curtain drawn at their backs but you already suspected what lay behind it.

"Well, hey, Jamie," Ali repeated. "How's it goin'?"

I shifted and knocked up against a table. Bottles rattled; Hillary rolled his eyes.

"Sasquatch," he said, looking at my boots. I blushed, but no one else had noticed. Beside me Ali had drawn back into the shadows. Her amber eyes were half-closed, but already I could see the faint glister of desire there like a burgeoning tear. I looked away, embarrassed.

"Jamie Casson," Hillary went on, leaning over to drape an arm around Ali. "He just moved up from the city. His father's doing something up at Kern's place."

"Oh yeah?" said Ali throatily. "So you want a beer, or—something?"

I glanced at Hillary, to see if he was taking this in. Because this was nothing like witnessing love at first sight; more like watching a pair of cars approaching each other way too fast on a lonely stretch of old Route 22, and being too paralyzed with fear to yell for help.

"Great," I muttered. I edged toward Hillary, wanting his opinion on this. There was a *thunk* as I bumped against a chair, and with a clatter it toppled onto Hillary's feet.

"Ow—god *damn* it, Lit!"

Ali laughed. "Man, you are such a klutz!"

Only Jamie said nothing; just looked up and for a long moment held my gaze. Light blazed from the jukebox, making him seem washed-out and insubstantial, the shadow of another figure I couldn't quite see. There was something odd about the way he looked at me. His pale eyes were questioning, almost pleading, as though he was waiting for me to speak. But I felt awkward and ugly in my heavy boots and Hillary's old jacket. So I just stared back, challenging him to recognize me as something besides Hillary's clumsy best friend.

Finally, "I got to get back," Jamie said. He swung off the jukebox, ambled to a table and hooked a worn suede windbreaker onto his thumb. "I'm broke, anyway . . ."

I felt a pang, until Hillary nodded. "I'll give you a lift. Lit? You want to come? Ali?"

I nodded, hurrying to the jukebox and sliding in the quarters Jim had given me. "Yeah—I'll meet you at the car—" I punched in a half-dozen songs, downed a beer that had been abandoned on the old Seeburg, and went to join them in the parking lot.

The rain had stopped. The sun was going down in a smear of orange and black, and a small crowd had gathered on the steps, passing joints and bantering. Duncan Forrester and his girlfriend Leenie, Christie Smith, Alysa Redmond: the usual suspects lowlighting with bikers and trying to score. If the cops ever decided to bust up Deer Park, the papers would have a field day; there were enough Famous Children at that dive to fill an inch of column.

"Charlotte!" Duncan shrieked, throwing his arms around me. "Don't say you're *leaving*—"

"*Ouch!*" I cried, wriggling free. Duncan was skinny and lank-haired, with a hatchet face that was so enormously improved by stage makeup he'd taken to wearing it on weekends, whether or not he was in a show. Even more incongruous was Duncan's voice, a rich baritone that (in my father's words) could charm the teeth from a snarling Doberman. When he'd played Billy Bigelow in *Carousel* last year, entire busloads of cheerleaders had wept during his death scene. "Dammit, Dunc, that *hurts*. I got to catch a ride with Hillary."

Duncan looked stricken. "*C'est terrible*," he cried. "How will we have *any fun* without you?" Last summer, someone had told Duncan he looked like Marc Bolan. Since then, he'd affected a ridiculous accent along with Yardley midnight blue eyeliner. "*C'est impossible*—"

"Oh, try." I licked my finger and wiped a blue smudge from his cheek. "God, you're a mess, Dunc. See you—"

I hurried to where Hillary's decrepit car was parked beneath a tree. Ali and Jamie stood sharing a cigarette, while Hillary swiped yellow leaves from the windshield.

"You always lived here?" Jamie dropped the cigarette. We all nodded. "Man, I don't know how you can stand it."

"It's not so bad." Hillary slid into the front seat and began sorting through a pile of eight-tracks, adding, "You just need the right *attitude*."

"And a ton of money," said Ali as she swung in beside Hillary. "And good teeth."

"Fuck that. This place creeps me out."

Ali looked bemused. "Deer Park?"

"No. This *town*—" Jamie got into the back, rolled down his window and stared to where Muscanth Mountain rose above us, mist lifting slowly from its slopes. "It's weird. I don't like it."

I clambered in beside Jamie, pushing empty beer cans onto the floor. The eight-track roared on with considerably more power than the car, blasting Slade as we bellied slowly out of the lot.

"You're up at Kern's place, right?" yelled Hillary.

Jamie hunched down in the seat. "Yeah."

We drove back into town, turning off Kinnicutt and onto the labyrinthine road that wove through the village and then up Muscanth Mountain. The dying sun cast a milky haze over the rough contours of the surrounding hills and forest. A kind of light I have only ever seen in Kamensic in autumn, light like powder shaken onto the landscape, mingled gold and green and a very pale opalescent blue. The air smelled sweet and slightly rotten. The old houses and ramshackle mansions took on a detached glamour, their stones and clapboards softened by a golden haze of oak leaves, the neglected lawns smoothed by distance. Pumpkins sat at the end of driveways alongside sheaves of corn, and on the front doors appeared those idiosyncratic emblems of Halloween in Kamensic—ugly little terra-cotta masks with gaping eyes and mouthes, hung by bits of coarse twine. Crude versions of the traditional masks of comedy and tragedy, they appeared every year at the end of September in the Scotts Corners Market, along with jugs of cider and ornamental gourds and coils of hempen rope. Cub Scouts and the League of Women Voters sold the masks and donated the money to the volunteer fire department. I never knew where the masks came from. They were heavy lumpen things, with dried clay coils for hair and clumsy, almost primitive features—a tiny depression to indicate the nose, hollow eyes, gashed mouths. I hated them. They embarrassed me, and in some strange way they frightened me, too. Once at the Courthouse Museum I asked Mrs. Langford what they were for—

"Well, they're for Halloween," she said, frowning. She reached for her thermos of black currant tea spiked with sloe gin, poured herself a cupful, and sipped. "Just a local custom, that's all. To show our allegiance to the gods, you know."

And she fingered the brooch she wore on her breast, a pair of beautifully figured masks of gold. One mouth curved into a delicate smile; the other was less a frown than a grimace. No one would ever tell me more than that, nor why the masks were never saved from one year to the next but instead were broken.

"That is an *idiotic* superstition," Hillary yelled once at his mother. This was a year or two earlier, when we were fifteen and Hillary facetiously wore a NIXON'S THE ONE! button to school every day. Natty stood in their backyard wielding a hammer and a mask wrapped in a tea towel, surrounded by neatly raked piles of leaves and burlap sacks.

"Oh, hush, Hillary," she said impatiently. "Oooh, I *hate* this—" She winced and brought the hammer down. There was a muted *crunch*. The towel opened like a blossom, spilling shards of broken terra-cotta.

"Then why do you *do* it?" Hillary demanded.

"It's good for the soil. Good drainage." She began gathering the pieces into the towel, humming. "Hand me that basket, will you, dear?"

"Not until you tell me why," Hillary insisted. "You don't go to church, you don't even *vote*—why do you mess around with those stupid masks?"

Natty ran a hand across her face, leaving a trail of dirt. "Oh, Hillary." She turned and set the broken mask on the stone wall. "Look at Lit, *she's* not complaining—"

"Yes I am." I nodded emphatically, walked over to inspect the bits of terra-cotta. "They give me the creeps. I hate those things."

"Really?" Natty looked genuinely surprised. She wiped her palms on the front of her baggy jeans, set her hammer on the wall, and started for the house. "Why ever would you hate them?"

We followed her into the kitchen. Natty heated some cider and we drank it, warming ourselves as she washed up at the sink. "You shouldn't be afraid of the masks, Charlotte. You of all people."

"Why? Because my father is scary Uncle Cosmo?"

"Noooo . . ." Natty dried her hands, looking very English with her sturdy pink face and pink Shetland sweater, her pants smudged with dirt. "Because you're an actor, darling!" she said in her plummy voice. "Because you were born to it—"

"*I* wasn't born to it," I snapped. Only a week before I'd made a fool of myself in *Arsenic and Old Lace*. "I *hate* it, and I hate those things—"

"Oh, don't say that, Lit." Natty's gaze widened. "It's what we all *live* for—"

"It's a job, Mom. It's just a stupid job." Hillary hunched over his cider and stared at her balefully. "I mean, *you're* not doing Shakespeare—"

"Oh, that doesn't matter," said Natty. "Besides which, Lit's parents, and your father and I, *have* done Shakespeare—"

"Oh, come on! Unk is starring in an *Addams Family* ripoff and you guys are—"

"*It doesn't matter.*" Natty's cheeks glowed bright red. "'No profit grows where is no pleasure ta'en, In brief, sir, study what you most affect.'"

Hillary sneered, "I'm not going to waste my life on goddam sitcoms—"

"Don't you swear at me!"

"—and all this superstitious bullshit."

Natty stood with her back to the counter, head thrown back. She looked as though she was about to burst into tears. I put my hand placatingly on Hillary's and said, "Those masks just seem so tacky, that's all, Mrs. Weller."

"*Tacky!*" She sounded like Lady Bracknell contemplating a handbag. "Tacky? You children grew *up* on them."

"Give me a break, Mom!" Hillary said, exasperated; but his fury was gone. "We grew up on takeout from Red Lotus—"

But Natty was already striding out of the kitchen. I slid off my chair and trailed behind her, and after a moment Hillary followed. We found her in a small, narrow, very cold room that had been the old farmhouse's pantry, but which now housed Natty and Edmund's books and theatrical memorabilia—tattered broadsheets, yellowed newspaper clippings in dusty frames, dogeaten scripts.

And plays, of course: the entire Oxford Shakespeare and all of Noel Coward and Oscar Wilde, as well as numerous lesser lights that had quickly burned out—*A Sun for the Sunless*, *From Arcadia to New Rochelle*, *Madame Levinskey's Hat*. Except for the absence of certain titles, and the obviously British slant, the collection could have belonged to my own parents.

"Oh god, Mom," Hillary moaned. "Look, you don't have to—"

"Hush," commanded Natty. She began squinting at titles. "Where *is* it . . . ?"

I wandered to one corner and picked up an ancient publicity photo of Hillary's father, playing the lead in a Manchester production of *Charlie's Aunt*. I was always torn between embarrassment and sentiment by this old stuff, as though it had been our parents' baby shoes. I stared at the photo, trying to find some resemblance to Hillary in the white-faced, pie-eyed performer wearing full matronly drag.

"You know," I began thoughtfully, "you really do sort of look like—"

"Lit! Cut it out—"

"Here it is!" Natty crowed, and held up a book. "*The Mask of Apollo*. Your father gave me this for our anniversary, oh, almost ten years ago . . ."

She thumbed through it, raised an admonitory finger and began to read.

"'It is hard to make actors' children take masks seriously, even the most dreadful; they see them too soon, too near. My mother used to say that at two weeks old, to keep me from the draught, she tucked me inside an old gorgon, and found me sucking the snakes.'"

She finished triumphantly. Hillary and I looked at each other, then burst out laughing.

"Oh, *right*, Mom! So where're the snakes?"

Natty frowned, with a sniff replaced the book on its shelf. "Obviously you two are not old enough yet to appreciate the subtleties of our profession," she said, and headed for the door. "Tell your father I'm going up to the market for some more milk."

Now, as Hillary drove past our house I could see this year's mask, a bland face with two small eyes poked above puffy cheeks and a surprised O of a mouth. My mother had draped ivy around it, carefully clipped from the back wall.

"Doesn't it make you feel weird?" asked Jamie Casson.

"Huh?" I started. "What?"

"All this bizarre stuff . . ." In the front seat Hillary and Ali ignored us, continuing a longtime debate about David Bowie. "I mean, what the hell are *those*?"

Jamie pointed as we passed the cemetery. Strange stone animals stood guard over the oldest graves, their features worn away so that one could only guess their species: insect? bird? wolf? Clay masks leaned upon some of the mounds; others were extravagantly draped with wreaths of ivy. "It's like *The Exorcist* around here . . ."

"I know what you mean." I glanced at Ali, willfully oblivious to us, then leaned toward Jamie. "About Kamensic—"

I wondered if I could tell him what I was thinking. That the town frightened me, too, even though I'd grown up there; that sometimes when I drank I could see things in the faces of my friends, and hear the echo of something like distant music, the dying notes of a bell.

"It—it feels dark," I said. "Even in the morning, it feels dark—"

Jamie stared at me, his pale eyes luminous, and slowly nodded. "*Right*. And the roads . . ."

He gestured at a dirt track snaking off behind the

cemetery. It was marked as were all the streets in Kamensic, by a wooden fencepost topped with a long, arm-shaped signboard that ended in a pointing finger. "We came into town *that* way, right?"

"Yeah."

"And from Kern's place, you can *see* that road coming down the mountain."

"Right . . ."

"But you don't see *this* road—the one we're on now. And this is a much bigger road."

I shrugged. "Maybe the trees block it or something?"

Jamie shook his head. "No way. It's *weird*. Like at Grand Central, you go to check out the stops up on the boards, and Kamensic isn't even *there*. It's not listed anywhere. Same thing with the train schedule—*nada*."

In the front seat, Hillary glanced over his shoulder at us. "So?"

"So how the hell do people *get* here? I mean the train stops in town, right? There's a train station, the conductor calls out the name—but if it isn't even on the schedule, how do people know to come here?"

Ali rolled her eyes. "Oh, *please*. Anyone who needs to get here, gets here. It's not like it's fucking Brigadoon."

"No! I'm right, I *know* I'm right!" Jamie jabbed at the window with one nicotine-stained finger. "Every time we come down that mountain it's like a different road. Like when Hillary drove up before, we passed this cliff looking down on the lake. How come we're not going that way now?"

"Because we're going to murder you and dump your body in the reservoir," said Ali. "Christ, where'd you move from, the South Bronx? Relax, will you? Enjoy the ride—"

Jamie sighed and leaned against the door. For a moment he looked very young: I could see where his chin had broken out, and how his fingernails were bitten down to the quick. "This is just a weird fucking place. You hear all kinds of stuff at night—"

Hillary laughed. "Those are called animals, Jamie." He turned the car up the narrow switchback that ran along Muscanth's southern face. "Like deer and things like that. Foxes."

"Nothing dangerous," said Ali. "No grizzly bears. No wolves."

"Someone was killed here by a mountain lion," I said.

"That was two hundred years ago, Lit." Hillary made a face, then yelled, "Oops, there's one now!" He swerved to avoid a chipmunk in the road.

"It's still creepy," said Jamie obstinately. "Plus it's like *Hollywood Squares*, all these old actors. That weirdo lives here, the guy who's Uncle Cosmo on *Bar Sinister*—"

Ali whooped. "Oooh, scary Unk!"

"That's my father," I said.

"Damn straight," Hillary agreed heartily. "Her damn Dad. Never say a word agin' him, Jamie—"

Jamie slumped down, defeated. "Oh, forget it. Anybody got a joint?"

"Nope," said Ali. "Sorry."

"Plus we're almost at your place. There's Bolerium—" Hillary tipped his head, indicating where the mansion's gray walls gleamed faintly through the trees. "But I don't remember where your driveway is, so tell me when we're coming up to it—"

Jamie pointed behind us, at a road nearly hidden by the ruins of a stone wall. "That was it."

"Whoa!" Hillary yanked at the wheel, frantically

steering the car away from a pile of rocks. Jamie laughed.

"Hey, man, sorry. Watch that ditch there—"

The driveway was so narrow only one car could pass at a time. In places the dirt and gravel had been completely washed away, so that we drove on sheer bedrock. Hillary swore as the Dodge Dart scraped against stone and fallen branches.

"God damn, the muffler's going to go—"

I squinted out the window. Twilight was falling quickly now, the autumn haze fading into a fine clear evening. To either side of the road a hedge reared, easily eight or ten feet high, a brambly mass of quince and dog roses and the tangled creepers of fox grapes. Birds darted in and out through gaps in the hedge. Winter birds: chickadees, blue jays, a raven carrying a dead vole.

"Wow," I said. "Look—" But already it was gone.

"How much farther?" asked Hillary. "'Cause this car ain't gonna make it . . ."

"Just up here." Jamie frowned. "I *think*. Soon, anyway."

He stuck his hand out the window and tugged at a grapevine "Hey, check this out—"

A small explosion of leaves as the vine snapped. Jamie held up something like a plant from a Dr. Seuss book, all spiraling corkscrews and bright purple clusters.

"Cool!" said Ali. "Grapes!"

"Sour grapes, I bet." Jamie pinched a violet bead, popped it into his mouth and grimaced. *"Yech—"*

"Let *me* try one—" Ali snatched the vine from him. An instant later she turned and spat out the window. "Ugh, that's disgusting—"

The vine fell onto the floor, where I rescued it from

between empty cans of Budweiser. The grapes were small but perfectly formed, and sticky with juice. I sniffed tentatively, inhaling their heavy, almost animal, musk; then bit into one.

"This one's sweet." Though the skin was slightly acrid—numbing, almost, like rubbing your lips with cocaine. I sucked it thoughtfully before swallowing it, tiny seeds and all.

"Here we are," announced Hillary as the Dodge Dart humped over a fallen log. "Jesus, that road sucks. Can't Kern pave it or something?"

"He'll never pave it," said Jamie disdainfully. "Mister Famous Director. He's so cheap he squeaks."

Ahead of us the corrugated drive gave way to meadow, a wide sloping expanse of knee-high grass. Patches of goldenrod nodded in the evening breeze, so bright a yellow it was as though the sun still shone in spots. Crickets buzzed softly. There was the intermittent drone of a power saw. We stepped out, blinking in the half-light, and Jamie peered into the distance.

"My father's around somewhere," he said as the power saw roared on again.

Ali yawned. "He mind if I smoke?"

"Hell no. My dad's a really groovy kind of guy. A really groovy kind of asshole."

Ali nodded. She pulled off her damp flannel shirt and tied it around her shoulders, smoothed the front of her leotard and looked around appraisingly. "Well, it's a nice place."

She grinned, a flash of white teeth with that odd little gap between them, and wandered away from the car. The boys started after her. Jamie said something to Hillary and Hillary laughed.

"Fuckin' A, man . . ."

I hung back, shivering, and buttoned up Hillary's old jacket. Underneath I wore a floppy white peasant blouse, intricately embroidered with long green tassels that dangled from the too-long cuffs. The blouse had seemed like a wonderful piece of exotica when I bought it at a head shop during the summer. Now it was nowhere near warm enough, and the thin cotton felt clammy against my breasts. I poked the tassels up into the sleeves, and hesitated before following the others.

Before me stretched the meadow. The scent of fallen leaves mingled with the fragrance of woodsmoke drifting overhead, and crickets chirped mournfully in the dusk. I glanced down, saw my boots coated with moisture pale and insubstantial as mildew. When I looked up again it was as though I were gazing at the world through a fogged window. The outlines of everything were blurred. Ferns faded into a fallen rock wall, its stones indistinguishable from the trunks of trees. The trees themselves receded into a greater darkness. The wind rattled their bare branches and I stared, my heart thumping.

Because suddenly I wasn't looking across a twilight field, but into a pool, black and depthless beneath a haze of mist. I no longer saw my friends moving in the distance, but only their reflections on the water's surface, flattened images stirred by a cold wind that made the hair on my arms rise. Within the dark reaches other creatures moved, recognizable by their shadows: the flash of a tail beneath the surface, the flicker of something like a wing. The hum of insects faded into the ripple of water on stone. I took a deep breath and tried to focus on something familiar: Hillary's jacket chafing at my neck, the way my boots pinched . . .

It was no good. Dizziness swept over me. The meadow's autumn incense gave way to another smell, the dank odor of standing water, rotting wood. My mouth grew dry, my tongue hard and swollen. Something horrible seemed caught in the back of my throat, a viscous strand of water hyacinth or old-man's beard. I coughed; the putrefying smell grew stronger, moist tendrils thrusting against my tongue as I struggled to cry for help. In front of me the air billowed, liquiscent.

I screamed then, but it was like screaming underwater. In the distance three bright shapes shivered and disappeared. I blinked. In front of me shone an unwavering sweep of pure blue, so beautiful that my eyes filled.

Because I recognized that color: it was the blue that shades the sky sometimes in your dreams, the blue you see when a kingfisher dives and for an instant everything before you coheres into one thing, bird lake sky self: and then is gone. That is the color I saw then, and somehow I knew that this was *the* sky, a truer sky than I had ever seen, and that I was gazing up into it from the bottom of the deep and troubled mere that was our world.

But before I could fully grasp this, or wake to find myself drowning, something moved above the surface of the water.

I thought it was a falling tree, its branches clawing at the sky. But it moved too slowly for a falling tree, and when it seemed almost to touch the water it halted. No leaves grew upon its tangled limbs, and I realized that they were not branches at all. They were monstrous antlers. What I had at first perceived as the tree's grotesquely gnarled bole was a head—not a stag's head, but a man's. His staring eyes were huge, the irises strangely variegated. Tawny yellows, moss-greens, the murky brown of leaves at the bottom of a lake; the colors radiating from a pupil that was ovoid, like a cat's. His mouth was parted so that I could see the moist red gleam of his inner lip and the tip of his tongue. As he gazed into the water I trembled, afraid that he would see me there.

But after a minute passed a deeper dread filled me—because he did not see me at all, and surely he should? Surely it was impossible that something so huge would not notice another creature scant feet in front of it?

Yet it did not, and as this realization grew in me, so did my terror. That I could be so insignificant, that it was possible for me to move through the world and have my presence as unremarked as that of a spider spinning its web in the tall grass. And like the spider I could be casually destroyed, my passing neither mourned nor noticed by this monstrous being. An arm's-length away from me the hornéd man dipped his head closer toward the water's surface, as though he would drink there. He did not, but hesitated an inch or so above it. The surface remained smooth, the glassy air untroubled. Only those daedal eyes moved very slightly within its great head, as though it gazed questioningly upon its own image.

I shuddered. Because there was something horrible in that gaze, a sort of mindless potency that made me think of water lilies choking a pond, infant voles squirming in their nest of cast-off hair. The odor of fetid water melted away. A sweetly aromatic smell filled my nostrils, oak mast and burning cedar, grapes warming in the sun. The immense figure swept its head from side to side, and I could hear its antlers slicing through the air. I was terrified it would catch my scent, but instead the creature

turned. I saw it clearly against that elysian sky, its speck-
led eyes ravenous as an owl's. Then it stepped away,
moving in an odd, stilted manner. I caught a glimpse of
its torso, arms smoothly solid, legs and chest and but-
tocks well-shaped as any man's. Save only between its
thighs, where its phallus mounted, grotesquely large and
rigid as though hewn from wood. Once, Ali and I had
found an image like this in one of Hillary's books—an
ithyphallic carving from ancient Greece, its face worn
away to nothing save the faint indentations of eyes and
lipless mouth; armless, legless, only its ludicrous member intact.

"Ooh, Daddy, buy me one of *those*!" Ali had squealed.
But seeing this creature now I felt only horror, and panic
lest it turn and catch sight of me.

It did not. Its long legs swung stiffly through the
underbrush, its antlered head swung back and forth as
slowly it receded from view. For one last instant I
glimpsed its silhouette fading into the trees, and could
almost have believed I imagined it: a strange manlike
pattern formed by leaves and shadows and darting birds.
But then I recalled its eyes, at once empty and devouring. I took a deep breath, as though struggling to wake
from a dream, and stepped forward.

Around me the evening air shivered. I could feel it
sliding like cool water across my face, and once more
smelled fallen leaves, damp earth. In the distance an owl
hooted. Something struck my upper leg and I looked
down to see a cricket tumbling into the shadows at my
feet.

"Lit! Move your ass!"

All was as it had been. In the tall grass Ali hopped up
and down and waved impatiently. Beside her Hillary

made faces, moving his arms semaphore-wise, and Jamie Casson stood atop a pile of stones with his shoulders hunched against the chill. I stared at them, frowning. My eyes ached the way they did after I'd fallen asleep in the sun, and I wondered if I *had* somehow fallen asleep, or experienced some kind of acid flashback.

But whether I had or not, I knew I was stuck with it. Whatever I had glimpsed—a man with leaves in his eyes and the terrible slow gait of an avalanche destroying a hillside—was etched upon my mind's eye as clearly as my father's face, or my own.

"Lit!"

"Hold on, I'm coming—" I began to wade toward them, getting soaked by wet goldenrod and Queen Anne's lace. "Did you—did you—"

I paused, feeling sick to my stomach. *Did you see the world turn to water? Did you see a man with horns?*

"You looked like you were trancing out there, Lit." Hillary grabbed my shoulder. "You okay?"

"I—I think so. I guess I just sort of spaced or something."

"Like, wow. Played Black Sabbath at 78 and saw God, right?" Ali leaned against Jamie, and he dropped his arm companionably around her. "Let's go before you totally wig out . . ."

"I'm *fine.*"

Hillary continued to stare at me, finally shrugged. "If you say so."

We walked across the field. Overhead the sky deepened from gray to violet. A few stars appeared. I forced myself to stare at them, and to count the seconds between a cricket's song: anything to make the night seem mundane. I still felt shaky, and clung more closely to Hillary than usual. It felt weird to be here with his arm around me and the night wind biting into my neck; weirder still to look over and see Ali and Jamie the same way, as though they'd known each other for years instead of just an hour.

And it was strange to find myself this close to Bolerium again. I knew kids who used to come to the abandoned guest house, to get high or fuck in the empty bedrooms, but I hadn't been here since I was seven or eight. Back then it was all neatly mown grass and stone walls, with hollyhocks and delphinium shading the cottage.

Now the guest house wasn't abandoned anymore. At the edge of the overgrown field rose the stands of oak and hemlock and beech that comprised the old-growth forest covering Muscanth Mountain, one of the only virgin tracts left in the Northeast. Within their shadow stood the house, looking even smaller than I had remembered. Another one of Kamensic's fey architectural artifacts, like the Mies van der Rohe mansion that had a tennis court on its roof, or the sixteenth century Austrian longhouse that had been reconstructed on Peter Nearing's estate.

This was nowhere near as grand as either of those. It was someone's idea of a French country cottage, built in the 1920s when the first wave of silent film stars settled in Kamensic. I remembered my parents talking about it during a visit to Bolerium. One of Axel Kern's mistresses had lived here, before she had a nervous breakdown. It was an awful story—my parents absolutely refused to tell me what happened, but over the years I'd combed together most of the details. Drugs, and a murdered infant, or perhaps it was stillborn; the mistress found in the woods, a struggling fawn in her lap and her breasts bloody where the frenzied animal had bitten her. Her family hauled her off to Silvermire for electroshock and primal scream therapy. It was later rumored that she became a Jesus freak, before starting her own business selling real estate in Chappaqua.

The cottage had been unoccupied since then, and still looked it. Two gnarled lilac trees clawed at its walls, their branches shedding leaves like withered hearts. Layers of paint had been badly stripped from the front door, which was half-open so that you could hear opera blaring from inside. Beside the lilacs leaned a pair of rusted bicycles, and a huge and incredibly fake-looking sort of effigy.

"What the hell is *that?*"

I walked over and poked it—a gigantic green head, twice my height and made of molded plastic. Somehow it made the memory of the hornéd man less dreadful, more like the residue of a bad dream or bad drugs. It had round staring eyes and a grinning mouth filled with peg-like plastic teeth. Wormy green rubber spirals drooped from its head. A long red plastic tongue protruded from between its gaping mouth, flapping in the breeze like flypaper. On top there was an empty beer can and a wooden sign, with letters picked out in bottlecaps.

VILLA OF THE MYSTERIES

"That's the gorgon," Jamie replied, as though addressing an idiot. "Didn't you see *Hercules in the Underworld?*"

"Uh, no." I scrunched down to peer into its mouth. Water had pooled behind its grimace and become a trap for yellow jackets and daddy longlegs. "How disgusting. What's it doing in front of your *house?*"

"My father designed it. He also did the monster bees in *Empire of the Anguished*. Also Sirena the Ageless in *Blood Surf* and the talking rocks in *Satan's Hammer*. Ever see those?"

"No. Sorry."

"No one did." Jamie looked tragic. "That's how come we're living in this dump."

He edged past me, shoving the half-opened screen door so that we could follow him inside. "Watch your step," he said and stooped to pick up an electric drill. Ali and Hillary wandered past him, kicking aside a newspaper. "This place is a fucking bear-trap—"

"You're not kidding," said Hillary.

Inside smelled of mildew and marijuana smoke, the hot reek of carpenter's glue and solder. The low ceiling was traversed by heavy beams hung with bundles of rope, a hacksaw, wire mesh. There was hardly any furniture—an old horsehair sofa and two unsprung armchairs. Sheets of plywood leaned against one wall; two-by-fours were stacked alongside another, and there were mason jars everywhere, filled with nails, screws, nuts and bolts, metal hinges. India-print bedspreads were pinned over some of the windows; in others you could clearly see the great webs made by golden orb weavers, and the spiders themselves poised in the center, like flaws in the glass. A big old wooden hi-fi console stood beside a crumbling fireplace, opera blasting from its torn speaker.

"Welcome to Hodge Podge Lodge," said Jamie.

"I thought it was the Villa of The Mysteries," said Ali.

"Uh-uh. *That* was from *Medusa Enslaved*." Jamie crossed to the stereo, scowling. He turned off the opera and began flipping through a stack of records, finally found something and put it on. There was the crackle of dust on the needle, and then music, the same few notes picked out on a piano. "You guys hungry?"

We drifted into the kitchen, a dim room with rough-hewn cabinets and a few battered chairs. Hillary flopped down at a trestle table strewn with the remains of breakfast—a jar of imported marmalade, half-eaten toast, tin mugs of cold tea.

"Yeah, as long as I won't catch something," said Ali.

I plonked down beside Hillary, moaning. The beer and whiskey had burned off, and I could feel the beginnings of an early hangover. "I would *kill* for some coffee."

"How about some ants?" He held up a piece of toast filigreed with tiny insects. "Mmm mmm good. Can you imagine Flo and Moe here?"

"No. I can hardly imagine *me* here."

At the sink Ali clattered and smoked. Jamie filled a teakettle and put it on to boil, and I rested my head on the table. From the living room music echoed, and Hillary sang along in his reedy baritone—

> *"If you had just a minute to live, and they granted*
> *   you one final wish,*
> *Would you ask for something like another chance?"*

And then I must have dozed off, because the next thing I knew I was jolted awake by the teakettle's piercing whistle, and a man's voice booming.

"Why aren't you kids in school?"

I sat bolt upright. Ali dropped her cigarette in the sink and looked around furtively, but Jamie only took the kettle and began to pour boiling water into a brown ceramic pot.

"Hello, Dad," he said. "How's it goin'?"

It was like a fast-forward glimpse of how Jamie would look in twenty years. Into the kitchen strode a wiry man in faded coveralls and carpenter's belt heavy with tools, his shoulder-length blonde hair going to gray and receding from a high sunburned forehead, so that you could see the taut lines of face and skull. The same haunted eyes, mocking as Jamie's; the same wry mouth. He walked over to his son and jabbed him with the blunt end of a screwdriver. As he passed me I caught the distinct smell of marijuana smoke.

"You young scalawag, you," he said, peeking into the teapot. "Wait'll the truant officer gets here."

"It's night, Dad." Jamie gestured at the window. "See? Dark: night. No school."

The man turned to survey the rest of us. "Well, well. Our nation's youth in revolt. I'm Jamie's Dad. Ralph Casson." He nodded and shook my hand, then Ali's, then Hillary's, repeating his name solemnly each time. "Ralph Casson. Ralph Casson. Ralph Casson."

I glanced at Hillary, but he just grinned. "Hi, Ralph. We met this morning."

"Of course we did." Ralph Casson slid the screwdriver back into his toolbelt and grabbed one of the enameled mugs. He sipped, made a face, and handed it to me. "So. Which ones are you? Debutante daughters of Miss Broadway 1957? Antonioni extras in town for the fall foliage tours?"

Ali found a windowsill wide enough to perch on and settled there. "I'm Alison. This is Lit—"

"'Lit'? What the hell kind of name is that?"

"It's for Charlotte," I said, and felt myself reddening. "But nobody calls me that."

I stared at my clunky boots. My hair cascaded into my face but I let it stay there, until I felt a hand brush it away.

"Charlotte. You're right, I don't think you're a Charlotte." I looked up into Ralph Casson's frank, slightly manic gaze. He pulled his fingers gently through my tangled curls, let the hair fall back into my eyes as he drew away. "How about Thalia?"

"How about Bigfoot?" suggested Ali. Hillary and Jamie laughed, but Ralph shook his head.

"'A lovely being,'" he said, "'scarce formed or moulded, a rose with all its sweetest leaves yet unfolded.'"

"Oh, bra-*vo*, Dad." Jamie's sarcastic voice drowned out Ali's hoot. Ralph Casson winked at me, then crossed to the sink and began washing his hands.

"Watch your step, Jame," he remarked over his shoulder. "You don't want to get into bad company in *this* place."

"*Who's* bad company?" said Ali. Ralph turned and shook his hands, sending water over all of us.

"You." He tilted his head at Ali, then me. "Her."

Hillary pretended to be affronted. "What about me?"

"You?" Ralph regarded him disdainfully, then said in an arch, Glinda-the-Good-Witch voice, "You have no power here!"

"And they do?"

"Oh, Christ, *please* don't get him started—" begged Jamie.

"Don't you know the *Mahamudratilaka*?" Ralph raised one hand as though delivering a benediction. "'*Go not with young women over twenty, because they have no occult power.*'" He sighed. "Kids these days. What *do* they teach you?"

"You sound like my old man," said Ali.

"Does *he* know the *Mahamudratilaka*?"

"Probably," said Hillary. He sniffed at a glass of milk left over from breakfast, then poured it into his tea. "So what are you doing here? Fixing up this place for Kern or something?"

"Or something." Ralph began rummaging among canisters and mason jars on the counter, finally settled on a large Earl Grey tin. He pried off the top and fished out a plastic baggie full of marijuana, opened it to remove a packet of ZigZag papers, and began rolling a joint. I quickly turned my attention to a jar of marmalade, trying not to look shocked. I knew adults in Kamensic who smoked (there were certainly enough who *drank*), and probably did other things as well, but I had never actually witnessed somebody's father crumble a bud into a rolling paper. Ralph finished rolling the joint, lit it, and inhaled deeply.

"Hillary?" Smoke leaked from his nostrils as he leaned over to pass the joint to Hillary. Hillary waved it on. So did Jamie—he seemed wary around his father, not afraid exactly but tense.

But Ali took the joint and sucked it eagerly. I did the same. I actually hated getting high. It made me cough, and I worried so much about saying something stupid that I would just sit in paranoid silence until it was time to go home. But I was too self-conscious to refuse, certainly in front of Jamie's father.

"Thanks," said Ali.

"No prob." Ralph leaned against the counter and ran a hand through his thinning hair. "So. Axel's coming back this weekend. I gather you guys know him?"

Hillary cocked a thumb at me. "He's her godfather."

"Oh yeah? That's cool. So you heard about the party, right?"

"No." I took a spoonful of marmalade and sucked it. "What party?"

"There's a big bash this weekend. Halloween party. I gather there's gonna be a lot of the usual suspects around. Rock musicians. Pulitzer Prize winners. Norman Mailer, local riffraff. You see Axel much?"

I shrugged. "Not for a long time. He's hardly ever here. I think my folks saw him, I dunno—maybe two years ago? He doesn't stay in Kamensic much."

"Why would he want to?" Jamie turned to Ali. "How come he's not *your* godfather?"

"I wasn't born with a caul."

"What's a caul?"

"It's a joke," I explained. "He and my father've been friends for a while, that's all. I didn't even know he was back in town."

"He's not, yet," said Ralph Casson. "He's getting the money together for *Ariadne*."

Ali frowned. "Ari Who?"

"*Ariadne auf Naxos*. The sublime music that was playing when you arrived, before Jamie put on whatever the hell *this* crap is. It's an opera. You guys know what an opera is?"

I laughed, but Hillary cleared his throat and warbled in his best falsetto—

> *"There was a thing of beauty called Theseus—*
> *Ariadne,*
> *that walked in light and rejoiced in life."*

Ralph gave him a thumbs-up. "Hope for the future!

Yeah, that's Axel's new baby. He's got some big backer in Italy, one of the DeLaurentises or somebody, wants to sink a bundle in it. That's why we're here—I'm doing the sets."

Hillary and I glanced at each other. Anything connected with Axel Kern would be a plum assignment, and Ali's father could have used the work. I stole a look at her. She seemed surprised by this revelation, but said nothing.

"Well, anyway, some kind of Big Do this weekend. Maybe catch some of you there." Ralph stretched and began patting absently at the tools dangling from his waist. "Okay. Back to work. Jame, you seen my T square around here?"

"Nope."

"What about my X-Acto knife?"

"Uh-uh."

"Yeah, well, keep an eye out for 'em, okay?" He ambled across the room. "See you later, Hillary. Ali." In the doorway he paused to flash me a grin. "Thalia."

When he was gone Jamie sank into a chair. "God, I'm sorry."

"He's all right," I said.

"Hey, he's cool." Ali gave Jamie a stoned smile. "Can he read auras? Harmony Shakti did that for me when I was over there last week."

"Who's Harmony Shakti?"

"Rachel Meyerson's mother." Hillary tilted his chair back and wedged his knees beneath the table. "A total fruitcake. Your father doesn't seem like a *total* fruitcake."

"Yeah, well, everything's relative." Jamie tapped the butter dish with the wrong end of a fork, his turquoise eyes a little too bright. "You oughta meet my mother."

"Where's she?" asked Ali.

"Getting her aura read somewhere down in Tennessee." With a loud *tink* Jamie dropped the fork into an empty mug. "She's part of an experiment in expanding the radical sexual and spiritual consciousness of our nation."

Ali frowned.

"She dumped me and my father and joined a commune."

"Cool," breathed Ali. Hillary gave her a disgusted look.

"That's a drag," I said, but Jamie only sighed.

"I'm beat. I think I'll crash for the night." He eased from his seat, hands slung into his pockets. "Hillary, man. Thanks for the lift. Lynn—"

"Lit," I said.

"—Lit. I'll see you later." He got halfway across the kitchen and stopped to look back at Ali.

"Hey," she said, suddenly bouncing up, "where's your bathroom? I gotta take a leak—"

"C'mere, I'll show you."

Hillary and I watched them go. We waited for Ali to return, but after a few minutes Hillary said, "I think they've gone to look at his etchings."

"His aura." I brushed the hair from Hillary's eyes, and pointed at the front door. "Come on. I'm pretty beat, too."

We went outside. Above us stars blazed, and the wind was no longer chilly but downright cold, sending acorns rattling down from the trees. The sound made me think of the hornéd man and I shivered, buttoning my jacket and wrapping my arms around Hillary.

"Well, gee, Charlotte." He gave me a rueful smile and drew me close. "Isn't it nice to make a new friend?"

"*And* his groovy asshole father."

We got into the car and I looked back at the cottage. All the windows were dark; the front door was shut. But as we pulled away Ralph Casson emerged. In one hand he held a hammer, swinging it lazily back and forth. The other cradled a long two-by-four like a shotgun. When he saw us he waved, raising the hammer in a triumphant pose.

"All power to the People's Party, Comrades!"

"Right on," hollered Hillary. The Dodge Dart groaned as it crept away, and crickets flew up around us like water spraying from a ditch. When we reached the bottom of the driveway Hillary grabbed my arm and squeezed it hard, the two of us giving the mountain a quick backward glance as the car slammed onto the paved road.

"This will end in tears," said Hillary. He smiled but his eyes were grim. "Big fat fucking tears." He gunned the motor and drove much too fast the rest of the way home.

6 ❧
Things Behind the Sun

In his study, Balthazar Warnick stood in front of the window, gazing into the twilight of the Blue Ridge but seeing only the anguished face of Giulietta as she was led away by the agents of the Benandanti. When someone touched his shoulder he gasped, and held up his hand as though warding off a blow.

"Professor Warnick?"

He blinked. Beside him stood Kirsten Isaksen, the Orphic Lodge's forbidding housekeeper. Her thin mouth was pursed, her customary scowl tempered with concern. "You have forgotten your supper, Professor. I've brought it up on a tray for you."

Balthazar drew his hand across his eyes. "I'm sorry, Kirsten, I—"

"It is here." Kirsten turned and busied herself with setting a heavy silver tray upon Bathazar's desk, moving aside heaps of paper and a long, coiled parchment scroll. "*Grillet laks med dill*, also *kurkkusalaatti*. And please see that *you* eat it all, Professor, the cat is ill when you give her salmon. The dill is *very* fresh"— She picked up a yellow-green sprig and waved it admonishingly at Balthazar. —"and there is Tosca cake for dessert. And I am to remind you yet again that you have not performed the *pharmakos.*"

Balthazar nodded, composing himself. "Yes, yes of course. Thank you, Kirsten, thank you very much—" He pulled an immaculate green paisley handkerchief from his pocket and dabbed his thumb with it, wincing as blood welled from the cut left by the orrery. "Dinner looks very nice, and yes, I promise, I won't feed it to the cat ever again—thank you, that's very nice, you can bring my coffee up in a few minutes . . ."

He escorted her into the hall, Kirsten towering above him. When they reached the head of the stairs, she turned. "The coffee is already made, you may get it for yourself. I am going to Front Royal to see a movie. Good night, Professor."

Balthazar watched her go downstairs, waiting until her brisk footsteps echoed into silence. Then he allowed himself the luxury of a long and heartfelt sigh, and returned to his study.

The salmon was, indeed, very good—Kirsten was a famous if imperious cook—the new dill fragrant as clover, the Tosca cake perfumed with almonds and heavy cream. He tried to force Giulietta's memory from his thoughts and focus upon the long and irredeemably tedious recitation that was the first rite of the *pharmakos*—a task he hated, and which it was always a good idea to be well fortified against. When he had finished eating, Balthazar diligently brought his tray down to the kitchen, murmuring apologies as the Lodge's cat ran to meet him at the head of the stairs.

"I'm sorry, but you are very ill when I give you salmon. Please forgive me." The cat regarded him through contemptuous yellow eyes before stalking out of sight.

Slowly, Balthazar made his way through the Orphic Lodge's labyrinthine halls. Past rooms where stacks of books tottered beneath windows draped in velvet the color of claret and very old port, but smelling of myrrh and lemons; past rooms filled with blown-glass globes strung like drying gourds across the ceiling, globes which, if one peered into them, revealed tiny seashores aglitter with azure surf and crimson sails cast like confetti upon impossibly distant swells; through doors that opened without a touch as Balthazar's shadow grazed their panels, and by other doors that in all his years he had yet to see inside; and last of all, through a corridor filled with monastically simple rooms all made ready for the annual autumn retreat.

Finally he reached the end of the east wing. He walked down the servants' stairway to the kitchen. There he found a reassuringly utilitarian demesne, and hot coffee in the old electric percolator. His cup and saucer were set reproachfully beside it, along with a plate of Kirsten's ginger cookies and another note—

> *Tolle moras!*
>
> *semper nocuit differe paratus!*
>
> —K

Don't delay! Even when prepared it is dangerous to postpone what must be done! He laughed. "Very well, Kirsten. I won't delay . . ."

He poured his coffee, feeling the profound melancholy that always assailed him at the thought of the *pharmakos*, and looked up. High above one of the gleaming institutional stoves a plaque was suspended. Its legend swirled in gothic lettering, blue and gold and emerald green:

OMNIA BONA BONIS

All things are Good with Good Men. The motto of the Benandanti, "the Good Walkers," "Those Who Do Well."

Though sometimes—this was one of them—Balthazar felt more like an unwilling gaoler than a good man. For several minutes he stood, sipping his coffee and watching the twilight deepen. At last he crossed to the kitchen door and stared outside. A short distance away there was a small declivity in the lawn, four or five feet across, and just beyond the shadow of the encroaching woods. In the middle of the hollow stood a pillar, man-high, thrusting up from the tangle of grass and weeds like an overgrown grave marker.

But it was no grave marker. It was a herm, a granite stone that was thousands of years old, filigreed with lichen and bird droppings. Its base was just wide enough that Balthazar could have wrapped his arms around it, and it narrowed very slightly toward the top. Words were carved up and down the column, some in ancient Greek characters, others in Latin, and the most recent—going back only a few centuries—in English.

WITHIN A GREATER GNOMON ALL THE NIGHT

The herm was crowned with a carven man's face. Time had softened it, so that the features were blurred, the cheeks pocked and bearded with moss. One side of the nose had been chipped away. But you could still make out the deep-set, almond-shaped eyes and thin curve of its mouth, and see quite clearly the outlines of ivy twining through its hair and around the broken stubs of two small horns poking from its head. Once upon a time, and very far away, the herm had been venerated. More recently, like others of its kind, it had been thrown down by an angry mob of Puritans. The Benandanti had salvaged it and brought it here, where students on retreat thought it one of the Lodge's myriad oddities, like the winged homunculi in Brother Vaughan's study, or the housekeeper's narwal tusk. Those impertinent enough to question Kirsten about the herm were told brusquely that it was a sundial.

But it was not a sundial. It was an oubliette, a prison; and Balthazar Warnick was its keeper. Now he stared out at the somber pillar and once again sighed, recalling Giulietta's face and putting off his duty for one more minute.

"Ah, me . . ."

It had been warm enough that Kirsten had left open the door leading out onto the veranda. Moths fluttered against the screen, and he could smell damp earth where she had watered the rows of fuchsias in their hanging baskets. On its shelf an arm's-length away, the kitchen Timex glowed faintly.

Crack.

Without warning the sound ripped through the kitchen. Echoes trailed after it throughout the Lodge like gunshots. Balthazar jumped, then raced onto the veranda, the screen door banging behind him.

Above the western mountains the clouds had darkened to black and violet. But directly overhead the sky was a strange flat silvery-gray that gleamed like falling rain. As Balthazar stared down onto the lawn he winced and shaded his eyes—the silvery light *hurt*, as though he gazed into an unshaded incandescent bulb. At the same time there was a weird murkiness to the light: it cast no shadows, so that when he tried to focus on individual objects below—a clump of hostas, the stone birdbath that Kirsten religiously filled each morning—he found them shadowed as by heavy fog.

But a fog that coruscated and gave off threads of metallic brilliance, and made a shrill sound as it did so; a fog that *hummed*. Sweat stung Balthazar's eyes as he fought to see something in the deathly haze. The humming grew louder, but no matter how he struggled to find its source he could not. It seemed to come from everywhere, a horrible resonate note that made the air shiver, so that he imagined he could see individual atoms dancing like beads of water upon a red-hot stone.

And then he could no longer hear the note, but only feel it, a vibration that made his very bones tremble. The pressure in his ears became a spike driven through his temples. Around him the silvery air wheeled and sang, as though it were a pool that had been stirred by some great ship's passing. There was a stifling smell; when he breathed he tasted burning leaves.

"What is it?" Balthazar screamed into the shining vortex; but could not hear his own voice. *"What is it?"*

And then an answer came to him. The roaring did not diminish, but it began to focus, so that he could track its source: a point some twenty yards down the sloping lawn. The whorl of silver light thinned like mist before the sun. The humming faded into silence. Balthazar took a deep breath and gazed out upon the lawn.

The last streamers of uncanny light were lifting. Overhead the night sky was a calm sweep of indigo strung with stars. Yet at the same time a faint glimmer still hung about the grass, so that he could see the shadows of tiny cloverheads, the serrated edge of a fern. The charred odor faded. A sweetly vegetative fragrance filled the air, a scent that made Balthazar think of fruit ripening and then rotting in the heat. When he swallowed, pollen rasped the back of his throat, and he coughed.

In answer, low laughter sounded from somewhere below. Balthazar looked but could see nothing but the tops of ferns moving as though stirred by the wind. Suddenly he cried out.

"No!"

He ran from the porch. Fingerlings of light flashed around him, and again he heard that soft mocking laughter.

"No," Balthazar repeated, and stopped.

The herm had been destroyed. It lay upon the grass in two pieces, severed through the middle as though someone had taken an ax to it. A black streak ran across the granite's coarse veining. Balthazar stooped to touch it. When he withdrew his finger, it was greasy as with soot. He sniffed, grimacing at the reek of sulphur, then stood and walked slowly around the fallen pillar.

The head had been driven a good six inches into the ground. Upturned earth surrounded it like black foam. In the lingering twilight it seemed to glow, so that Balthazar could see every detail of the carven visage: its oblique slanted eyes, the mouth upturned into a faint smile, hair curled tightly as bunches of grapes atop its head. Beneath its face the legend could still be clearly read:

WITHIN A GREATER GNOMON ALL THE NIGHT

Somewhere above him laughter rang out once more. Balthazar's hands tightened into fists. He took a step closer to the pillar, rage roiling in his chest; but even as he drew his foot back to kick it, the herm's features began to fade. Carven curls and etched mouth, ivy tendrils and stubs of horn all melted into the granite, as though they had been traced there in ice; as though they had never been at all.

Except for the eyes. Instead of fading, these grew more distinct, iris and pupil and long black lashes darkening, *thickening*, until Balthazar was staring into a gaze as keenly alert as his own.

"No!"

With a cry he recoiled. The eyes blinked, once; then tracked back and forth as though searching for something—until, finally, they focused on him.

Balthazar could not move. He felt blind horror, as though he stared into the lidless orbs of a great shark: the same raw hunger, without the faintest shading of human thought. The laughter came again, louder now; and suddenly the ravening eyes squeezed shut. A dark tear appeared at the corner of each one, twin arabesques that swelled until they were as large as Balthazar's clenched fists. The air shivered as with rain. Like mouth and nose and face before them, the eyes melted into the granite and were gone.

Yet for just an instant longer the tears remained, shining upon the dark granite. Then, soundlessly, they burst and streamed down the sides of the fallen pillar. One last time the laughter rang out and died away, and Balthazar thought he heard the echo of his own name.

About him the night was still. From the woods a whippoorwill hooted. Inside the Orphic Lodge a clock softly chimed. Very slowly, as though settling into sleep, Balthazar crouched beside the broken herm.

Wind rustled the trees and sent the first autumn leaves

flying. A cricket leaped onto the fallen stone. At the edge of the lawn something moved in the high grass; something that made a guttural sound. There was a smell of the sea, and roasting flesh. Balthazar extended his hand to where dark liquid pooled in the hollow of an ivy leaf that had blown against the pillar. Tentatively he dipped his finger into it, then brought it to his tongue.

And tasted wine, a fire that seared his mouth and made his eyes water even as he thirsted for more: wine and earth and the coppery taint of blood.

7 ❧
Dancing Days Are Here Again

Hillary's parents were still out of town, taping an episode of *The Love Boat*, so after we left Jamie Casson's house he came over for dinner. I was relieved. I felt exhausted and a little sick from drinking, and was glad to let Hillary chatter with my mother about industry gossip—whose agent was screwing whom, which characters were going to be killed off next season when the cast of *Perilous Lives* boarded an airplane that would crash into the Bermuda Triangle.

My father seemed to have caught my mood. He sat brooding at the head of the table, picking at his spaghetti carbonara. He watched me so closely that my stoned paranoia went into overdrive. I decided to feign illness and flee to my room.

"Umm, you know, I sort of don't feel so hot—" I cleared my throat, fidgeting in my seat, when Hillary turned to my father.

"So, Unk—did you hear Kern's back in town?"

My father hesitated. "Yes. I'd heard," he finally said.

"Is he? That's nice." My mother tore off a tiny piece of Italian bread and nibbled it, gazing at tomorrow's script beside her plate. "Who's he married to now?"

"I didn't ask—"

"You should have. I was so embarrassed that time with Marlena Harlin, you really should think to—"

"He's mounting an opera," my father went on. "I think he said *Die Fledermaus*—"

Hillary shook his head. "*Ariadne auf Naxos*."

Unk glowered, the same look he gave recalcitrant customers—usually zombies—at the Bar Sinister. "Would somebody let me finish? Whatever the hell it is, he's gotten backers for it and he wants to rehearse it here—"

"Where, dear?" My mother poured herself more Chianti. "I mean, here in Kamensic, but where?"

My father sighed, defeated, and reached for his coffee. "The Miniver Amphitheater."

"Oh, I have been *longing* for someone to restore that place! At the last town meeting I—"

"So there's a party there tomorrow, or something?" Hillary asked, all innocence. My mother stiffened. After a moment she shot my father a look.

"Oh, surely not. I mean, he hasn't been back in *years*, Bolerium must be an absolute shambles—"

"It's time," said my father. "You knew he was coming . . ."

My mother's lips tightened. She shook her head emphatically and stared back down at her script. My father turned to Hillary, his voice as archly guileless as Hillary's had been a minute before. "So. Where'd *you* hear about the party?"

"Uh—this new guy at school. Jamie Casson. His father told us. I gave him a lift home—"

My father's voice rose sharply. "Ralph Casson?"

"No—his son, Jamie. He's in my—"

"Ralph Casson? He's here? You met him?"

Hillary fell silent and glanced at me for help. *Thanks a lot*, I thought; then said, "Yeah. They're staying in the caretaker's cottage. Ralph Casson's designing the sets for the opera."

"No, he's not." My father's voice was fierce, almost angry; but for some reason that only made me want to argue with him.

"Yes he is. He told us he was doing the sets."

"He may be *building* them. He's *not* designing them. He's a goddam handyman—"

"He's a master carpenter," my mother broke in gently. "And he's very good—he studied ancient architecture at university, before going into the theater." She turned to Hillary and explained, "This is just another example of masculine rivalry that goes back long before you children were even born . . ."

"Oooh la la," said Hillary.

"*Not* that kind. And it doesn't even involve *us*, really—" She gave my father a warning glare. "It's between Axel and Ralph and—some friends. And it goes back a *very* long time. Unk sided with Axel—"

"And Ralph went independent," finished Hillary. He looked very pleased with himself, but when I watched my parents I saw something complicated, almost disturbing, pass between them. My stomach lurched: all I could think of was that snowy morning when Hillary had whispered that Ali's parents were getting divorced.

"Right," my father said after a moment. "Ralph remained—independent."

I knew by his tone that he was talking over our heads. Hillary didn't even notice. He speared some spaghetti, wolfed it down and asked, "So this party's tomorrow? What time?"

My mother's delicate eyebrows rose. "Are the children invited?"

"Everyone's invited." My father sighed. For an instant I thought he was going to leave the table. He pushed his chair back and stared out the darkened window behind us. In the distance the ragged bulk of Muscanth Mountain blotted out the stars; but at its very tip I could see a faint glimmer of gold, as though bonfires burned there. My father stared at it for a long time. At last he said, "It's not an invitation you can turn down."

"Cool." Hillary grinned. "Too bad my folks're out of town."

My mother shook her head, striking her best Livia Defending Her Young pose. "Darling, are you *sure*? After that trouble in—"

"*Absolutely.*" My father turned with such force that everything on the table bounced. "Axel hasn't seen Lit for years. He's her goddam *godfather*, Audrey—"

My mother set her mouth and glanced down at another page of script. "Do you have something nice to wear, Lit?" she asked calmly. "We'll have to go to Lord and Taylor if you don't."

"I can always borrow something from Ali."

"Fine." She nodded without looking at me, and I almost pointed out that any dress that fit Ali would only come up to my crotch. But my mother had deliberately lost herself once more in Livia's world, slitting her eyes as the wickedest woman in daytime television plotted her family's downfall.

When we finished eating I walked Hillary next door, the two of us scuffling through piles of leaves and hunching our shoulders against the chill. "What the hell you think was going on at dinner?" he asked.

"I don't know. I—Do you think they're getting divorced?"

Hillary laughed. "You nuts? Your mom and Unk are, like, the only people in this whole town who would *never* get divorced! No *way*." He grabbed me and rapped my head with his knuckles. "You idiot. Is that what you're worrying about?"

"I guess. I don't know. They were just acting so weird."

"What, somebody in Kamensic is acting weird? Wow, alert the media." He shook his head, clambering atop the tumbledown stone wall that was the dividing line between our property and his. "*Everyone* here is *always* acting weird. No, this is something about Ralph Casson. He's bizarre, man. Jamie hates him. I mean, he *really* hates him."

"How come? He seems okay to me."

"I don't know." I followed him to his front door. Hillary stood there for a minute, staring at the terra-cotta mask hung on the knocker. The porch light spilled too brightly onto its blank face, two small holes for eyes, its mouth a black slit. "It *is* weird," he said, almost to himself. "We never think about it, but Jamie said you never see stuff like this in the city. Or anywhere else, probably."

Suddenly he gave the mask a tug, yanking the hempen cord from the door. "What the hell does it mean, Lit?" he asked in a low voice, and held up the ugly grinning face. "What does it *mean*?"

I shrugged. "I don't think it means anything," I said, but that wasn't true. As I stared at the tiny mask between Hillary's fingers I felt revulsion and something very close to fear. Again I saw that terrible figure moving slowly through the trees, and heard the rustle of its antlers as they tugged at the leaves. "Hillary . . ."

Hillary's eyes remained fixed on the mask. His expression grew dark. Before I could say anything more, he tossed the mask into the drift of leaves beside the porch.

"I just want to get out of here," he said softly. "I just want to get to New Haven and never see this town again."

He opened the door and slipped inside. For a moment he hesitated and I saw him framed in shadow, the porch light igniting his face so that he resembled the mask, his mouth a livid gash and his eyes blackly staring. He dipped his head in farewell.

"'Night, Lit. See you."

"Yeah . . ."

He shut the door. I waited, half-expecting him to come back, to ask me in, to act like Hillary again. But he didn't. After a minute or so I turned and started back to my own house, glancing at the pile of leaves where the mask had landed. There was no sign of it, and even when I kicked through the heap, sending a spray of gold and brown and scarlet up into the night, the mask remained hidden.

When I got home my parents were already in bed. I called Ali; her phone was busy, and after three tries I stopped. I went into the darkened living room and sat in the wing chair by the window, staring out at the silhouette of Muscanth Mountain. Lights still burned from the promontory where Bolerium stood, but whether these were indeed bonfires, or just light glowing from the mansion's windows, I couldn't tell. After a while I stood, yawning, and crossed to the fireplace mantle, where my mother's awards and the photo of my father and Axel Kern leaned against the brick.

But the photo was gone. I frowned, glancing around to see if my mother had moved it to one of the end tables cluttered with old scripts and issues of Italian *Vogue*. It wasn't there, either, and when I checked to see if it had somehow fallen on the mantle I found nothing. Finally I gave up. I went to my own room, a small haven under the eaves with a map of Middle Earth on the wall and George Booth cartoons torn from *The New Yorker*, the ceiling covered by a collage I had made of magazine and newspaper pictures.

"That's your whole problem right there," Hillary had said once, pointing to a photo of Lou Reed thumbtacked onto a publicity still of the Moody Blues. "You can't make up your mind whether you want to be a freak or just totally uncool."

He was right. I was tainted by the same impulse that made my parents adhere to their Oriental rugs rather than shag carpeting, oak harvest tables rather than glass-and-chrome bookshelves. I stared up at the ceiling, then hopped onto the bed and peeled away the Moody Blues, in their place stuck a page torn from *Creem*, showing a silver-haired Iggy Pop in a recording studio. Then I collapsed back onto the unmade bed, kicking its flimsy India-print spread onto the floor, and turned on the radio.

> *It was the nature of the thing:*
> *No moon outlines its leaving night,*
> *No sun its day . . .*

Alison Steele's dusky voice filled the room. She read a poem and an excerpt from *The Prophet*, segueing into trancey music. Tonto's Expanding Head Band, Lothar and the Hand People, a band I'd never heard before singing about the Autobahn.

"Fahn, fahn, fahn . . ."

I reached for a broken-spined paperback on the floor: *Greek Plays for the Drama.* I was weeks behind in my reading. With a sigh I thumbed through it until I reached the selection from Euripides I was supposed to have memorized for class on Monday.

> *'When is this worship done? By night or day?'*
> *'T'is most oft performed by night:'*
> *'A majestic thing, The Darkness!'*
> *'Ha! With women worshipping?*
> *Tis craft and rottenness . . .'*

Behind me the radio pumped out its strange music, muted voices chanting over a synthesized drone. It made my head ache, that and the last vestiges of Ralph Casson's pot. After a few minutes I turned off the light. I felt edgy and frightened, the way I felt anticipating a test I hadn't studied for. But I fought the urge to sneak over to Hillary's house for comfort—he'd just lecture me again on my drinking. So I pushed Euripides onto the floor, switched off the radio, and crawled under the covers with my clothes on. My window was cracked open; chill air threaded into the room, bringing with it the acrid smell of damp birch bark and fallen leaves, the creak of insects. At last I fell asleep.

In the middle of the night I woke. The crickets had fallen silent, and the night was given over to the wind. Just a front blowing in, but hard enough that the windows rattled and I could hear tree limbs rapping at the walls.

Hhhhhhhuuuhhh . . .

I pulled the paisley spread tight around my shoulders and held my breath, listening.

Hhhuuuu . . .

Dread seized me then—dread but also a sort of exultation, an unbearable longing. The realization that something was going to happen, was happening *now*.

This is a weird place . . . you hear all kinds of stuff at night . . .

I remembered how Jamie had looked, sitting on the jukebox with light welling up around him like a wave; and the shiver of recognition when I realized I had never seen anything so beautiful, so *solid*, in my life.

Outside the wind rose louder still. With it there came another sound, the wail of a train making its way southward past the far shore of Lake Muscanth. I lay on my back and focused on the beating of my heart, the rhythm of my breathing: anything so as not to hear the wind.

The next thing I knew I was wide awake. Something had disturbed me, a sound like the nervous tapping of a foot. It came from within my room, and even in those first hesitant moments of wakefulness I knew absolutely what it was *not*—not the sound of water dripping, not a mouse moving within the walls, not one of my parents padding to the bathroom. This sound was at once more subdued and more insistent. There was a manic quality to it, like a restless child rapping for attention, but a child who has forgotten why she wanted your attention in the first place. I sat and listened, sleep falling from me, and waited for the sound to fade away.

It did not. Neither did it grow louder, but as the moments passed the rhythm of the tapping quickened. I could see nothing, not even the pale outline of my window. My breath came harder; I began to suck air through my mouth as loudly as I could, trying to drown out that sound. But I could not.

Nor could I look away. And very slowly I began to see something take shape within the corner of the room. The relentless tapping continued, but now I could see that the noise was connected to blots of darkness jumping within the gray, and tiny silvery sparks. The flickering interplay formed a pattern, and I had the terrible feeling that I should *recognize* it, that it should somehow make sense.

And then, in one awful flash, it did. The thing in the corner was a man. Not a man, but *half* a man, bisected down the middle so that I saw one side of its head, one arm hanging loosely beside its truncated torso and worst of all, one long pale leg hopping like a pogo stick. The jots of black I had discerned were its eye, its rib cage, the broken crescent of its mouth. There was no hint of carnage. No bloody shreds of flesh, no shattered bones.

And somehow that was worst of all. That this cloven thing should be within a few feet of me, jigging mindlessly as a scarecrow in the wind, for no reason whatsoever.

But it was not mindless. Because now the asymmetrical features of that face began to come into focus. A swollen scar of an eye like a bullet wound; the white triangle of its bifurcated chin; a lopsided mouth curving into a leer: all cohered into the dark reflection of a face I knew. The eye blinked; the mouth grinned. The rhythm of its movement grew suddenly, obscenely clear as I recoiled on the bed.

"No—"

It was Axel Kern. His grin widened, a poisonous quarter-moon. I thrashed across the bed until my back jammed against the wall. The black shape bobbed up and down, up and down. With each moment it drew closer to me, until I could smell it, animal musk and the odor of charred leaves. It was close enough now that it could touch me: its single arm lifted, fingers knotted and dark as it reached through the darkness.

"*Lit . . .*"

I screamed and kicked out. A hand tightened around my ankle, nail and bone biting into bare flesh. With a shriek I tried to fling myself from the bed. Then there was light everywhere, and someone shaking my shoulder.

"Lit! Lit, wake up!"

"No—god, let *go*—!"

"Lit!"

I looked up to see my father in his pajamas, hair awry, eyes wide but bleary with sleep. "Lit—are you all right?"

"No! No, there's—"

But of course the room was empty. My India print spread lay where I had dropped it. Beside it *Greek Plays for the Drama* crowned a heap of dirty clothes and record sleeves. My father stared down at me, his face torn between concern and annoyance. "Charlotte. I think you had a nightmare."

"Yeah . . ." I took a deep breath. "Yeah, I guess I did."

He glanced pointedly at the clock. It read three-twenty. "Well, your mother has a six o'clock call. I'm going back to bed."

"Right. Sorry, Dad, sorry . . ."

He stumped back to his room, switching off the light as he left. I watched him go, then sat up in bed watching the numbers flip over on my digital clock while the window went from black to violet to gray. When I woke, the room was filled with light, and my father was pounding on the door, shouting that I was going to be late for school again.

"Oh, fuck," I groaned. I started from my bed, and stopped.

Something was strewn across the bedroom floor. At first I thought they were leaves, but no—they were the pages of a book, torn and scattered everywhere. Between them were heaps of seed-pods, round and dull brown, almost black, with a tiny raised ridge around the flattened top. I scuffed across the floor, pods rolling beneath the bed. At the window I stopped.

There were more pages here than elsewhere, more dry husks. I crouched, sifting through the mess until I found the book's cardboard jacket. Its spine was split, the cover scorched so that the twin faces of Comedy and Tragedy were almost unrecognizable.

Greek Plays for the Theater

"Damn it," I whispered.

I stood and kicked angrily at the pages, snatched one as it came fluttering back down. It was blackened from top to bottom. As I held it, the paper shivered between my fingers, then crumbled into ash. Only a fragment remained, like the damp impression of a leaf, the letters jagged and black as though stamped upon my hand—

Join us.

PART TWO

Twenty-Four Hours

How Do You Think It Feels

At breakfast that morning I couldn't eat; only sipped at some orange juice while my father read the *Times*.

"You'll miss the bus," he said, reaching for his coffee.

I nodded and stared into my glass. I'd made a quick job of cleaning my room, shoving the torn pages into the wastebasket and sweeping most of the seedpods under the bed. Now I felt exhausted and depressed. I'd never been very good at shaking off bad dreams, and last night's clung to me like a fever. I considered pleading sick and going back to bed, but the thought of being alone in my room was worse than almost anything else I could imagine—except, perhaps, seeing Axel Kern that night at his party.

"Lit?" My father frowned over the top of the Arts and Leisure section.

"Okay, I'm off," I sighed. "Don't worry, Hillary'll drive me—" I kissed him, grabbed the canvas bag that held my schoolbooks and started for the door.

"Your mother won't be home this afternoon." My

father put down the paper and looked after me, his mournful face unusually pensive. "I have to go down to the city to see a casting agent. Then we're going to meet your mother for dinner with the Kingsleys in New Canaan, and *then* we'll all go over to Axel's for this party. What are your plans, Lit?"

"I dunno." I hesitated. I would never admit it, but the thought of going to Axel's party without my parents now frightened me. "Actually, I'm not feeling so hot. I was thinking that maybe—"

My father gave me Unk's best bone-freezing stare. "I want you there tonight, Lit."

"But—"

"No 'buts.' Be there."

"Right." I nodded, defeated. "I'll just go to Ali's after school, I guess. Or Hillary's—"

"Not with his parents gone; not if we're not here. Call us from Ali's house if you need a ride up to Bolerium. We expect to see you there this evening, Lit."

"Yeah."

I shouldered my bag and headed outside. It was a chill morning. The sky was dark and forbidding; to the east a thin line of blue was eroded by swiftly moving clouds. Alongside the road the trees were bare, save for a few oaks clinging to tatterdemalion crowns. I went next door, slowing to walk through the leaves in front of Hillary's house. My unease was now fullblown dread: worse than when I listened to one of Ali's ghost stories, worse than when I took the SATs, worse than anything I could remember. I knew this was ridiculous, but I couldn't shake it. I stopped and stared down at the leaves, nudging them around to see if I could find the mask Hillary had tossed there the night before. There was no sign of it, and finally I gave up. I let myself in the front door and found Hillary in the kitchen beside the stove.

He raised a spatula in greeting. "Hey, Lit. French toast?"

"Yeah." I poured some coffee and peeked through the window at my house.

"What's going on?" Hillary dropped a chunk of butter into a skillet. "Is he, like, watching?"

"I don't know. Wait—"

I pointed at my father striding out the side door of our house. He wore a long black greatcoat that flapped behind him in the wind, and even from this distance I could see his saturnine face scowling furiously as he swiped leaves and fallen twigs from the car windshield. Against the backdrop of stark trees and lowering sky he looked faintly threatening, like a wicked parson.

"He's going now," I whispered, as though my father could hear me. He clambered into the old VW square-back and backed it out into the road. I held my breath, fearful that he'd see Hillary's car still in the drive and realize I hadn't left. But he didn't; only turned and headed off for the village train station. "He's—*gone.*"

"Ali called." Hillary handed me a plate swimming with maple syrup. "She wants to go to the Elephant's Trunk. She can't cut Interdisciplinary again, so I told her we'd pick her up afterward."

I slid behind the table and ate while Hillary cleaned up. He seemed pensive, even brooding, and with his usual offhand grace had dressed the part—an old tuxedo shirt of Edmund's tucked into his patched and embroidered jeans, a dark blue naval officer's jacket. I watched him stalk across the kitchen, loading the dishwasher and gathering his books for school. I said nothing, recalling his anger last night. But I felt uncomfortable—it wasn't like Hillary to stay mad about anything. When I finished eating we went out to the car, still without speaking, and drove to pick up Ali.

"I need earrings if we're going to this thing tonight," she announced as she clambered into the front seat beside me. She shivered dramatically. "God, it's cold."

Hillary eyed her outfit—short-sleeved black leotard, black ballet slippers, bell-bottom jeans so frayed her skin showed through. The same thing she'd been wearing yesterday, as a matter of fact. "Maybe you should put some clothes on."

"Screw you."

Ali leaned her head against my shoulder. I wrinkled my nose. She smelled of smoke and patchouli oil and something I didn't recognize, a sweetish, faintly chemical odor. "Didn't you go home last night, Ali?"

"Uh-uh. I crashed at Jamie's." She yawned, and I felt a stab of hopeless envy, seeing her in bed with Jamie Casson. She had dark circles under her eyes; her lips looked swollen and bitten, and there was a tiny greenish bruise on one arm. "You guys didn't bring me any coffee, did you?"

Hillary snorted. "Yeah, sure, Ali! And pancakes, too! *No*, I didn't bring you coffee. Wasn't there any at his place?"

"No. Ralph won't buy coffee. He says it's, like, a capitalist plot to steal money from the Aztecs."

"The *Aztecs?*"

"Or *something*," said Ali defensively. "Gimme a break, I feel like shit."

"That's good. Cause you *look* like shit," I said, and ducked as she elbowed me.

Hillary drove us to the Elephant's Trunk, a head shop in Mount Kisco, where Ali bought a little brown vial of amyl nitrite (HEART-ON EXOTIC FRAGRANCE, the label read) and I tried on an orange-and-green paisley Indian print dress. It was low-cut and calf-length; long shirred sleeves, flowing skirt, no tassels.

"What do you think?"

Great, Ali mouthed. She sat on the floor, eyes huge as teacups, the open vial cupped in one unsteady hand. "Grrr—unh . . ."

She slumped against the wall. Ignoring her, Hillary stepped over to examine me. He frowned. "It's sort of a funny color. It's sort of *two* funny colors."

"It's orange," I said.

"Well, yeah, that's what I mean. It's sort of a weird shade on you. I mean, isn't it sort of a weird color on anyone, orange and green? I thought you were going with your mother—"

I gave him an icy look. "What, to Lord and Taylor? I *like* it—" I ran my hands over the bodice. "It's cool."

"Don't listen to him, it's great." Ali got up and stumbled toward me. "And it looks really cool with those boots. But you need a necklace or something. C'mon."

I picked out a pukka-shell necklace and a handful of silver bracelets so thin and supple it was like wearing a Slinky on my wrist. For herself Ali chose a pair of very large earrings, Mexican silver inlaid with mother-of-pearl, and shaped like peacock feathers. Hillary flipped through a bin of used albums, every now and then holding one up for me to see.

"Wow. *In the Wake of Poseiden*. Do I have that, Lit?"

"Dunno."

"What about this: *Supersnazz*."

Ali cozied herself back onto the floor and put on her new earrings. "Cool, huh? Hey, you want some of this?"

She unscrewed the vial of amyl nitrite and inhaled loudly. Behind the register the store manager looked up, glaring.

"Oh, *great*," Hillary groaned. He shoved the album into the bin, turned to the manager, and smiled apologetically. "Boy, she sure loves that exotic fragrance, huh? I was just going to—"

"I said *not in here*. Get her out," the owner commanded, pointing at the door. "*Now*."

We went. "I don't believe that stuff is legal," Hillary fumed as he herded Ali into the car. "It *can't* be good for you."

"It's not," I said. "The next sound you'll hear is her cerebral cortex hitting the floor."

Ali laughed. Her pupils had shrunk to black specks and her wide tawny eyes looked gormless as a kitten's. "Yeah. And the sound after *that* will be Lit picking it up again."

Hillary shoved in an eight-track and started the car. "You're a fucking mess, Ali."

"Sure, man. But I'm *cute*."

It took us most of an hour to get back, winding along old Route 22 through the maze of backroads and villages threaded into the foothills of the Siwanoy Mountains. Ali and Hillary fought over the eight-track.

"Black Sabbath."

"T. Rex."

"Black Sabbath."

"T. Rex."

"Duck season."

"Wabbit season."

"*Duck season*—"

"You are both total idiots." I stuck my head out the

window, trying to escape from flying tapes and Ali's cigarette smoke. "Next time I'm walking."

"Forget it, we'll fucking *compromise*—"

Hillary punched off the tape player and fiddled with the radio dial. Finally he homed onto a faint signal.

I have to be careful not to preach
I can't pretend that I can teach . . .

Ali joined in with her hoarse sweet alto, and after a moment Hillary did the same—

"And on the dance floor broken glass,
The bloody faces slowly pass . . ."

Then the signal faded, and the car filled with the soft hiss of dead air. I stared out at the late-autumn vista— golden hills, lowering sky—and recalled Hillary's stricken voice the night before.

What the hell does it mean, Lit? What does it mean?

I rubbed my arms. Ali lay passed out on the seat between us, her head on my lap and her fist jammed up against her mouth. Now and then her leg kicked reflexively against his, and Hillary would gently push her away. I fixed on that tiny star-shaped bruise at the crook of her elbow, and tried not to think of Jamie Casson kissing her there.

"What is it, Lit?" Hillary said at last.

I shook my head. I had felt uneasy for so long it was like a dull pain in my breast, or a throbbing headache; not something that could possibly come from outside me. I gazed out the window a long time before answering.

"I—I don't know. Just this—"

I gestured at the trees gone glimmering gold and crimson beneath tungsten clouds, the leaf-strewn river winding alongside the highway. I had always loved this stretch of the road, the secret knowledge that Kamensic Village was crouched behind that last dark curve of the river. Now I could hardly bear to look at it.

"All this . . ." I said numbly.

Hillary stared straight ahead, after a moment nodded. "Yeah. I know what you mean."

No you don't, I thought. *None of you even have a fucking clue.*

I glanced down at Ali snoring in my lap. Then with all my strength I slammed my hand against the door.

"Lit!" cried Hillary. "What the hell are you doing?"

A long red welt immediately bloomed across my knuckles. Ali opened her eyes to gaze at me blearily, then dropped back to sleep. Hillary glared. "*Lit—* "

"This fucking life—this *place*, you're just bored here but I feel like it's *killing* me—"

Hillary reached across Ali's snoring form and tried to take my hand, but I pulled away. "You know it's true, Hillary. It's not so bad for you—everyone loves you, everyone loves *her*—"

I poked at Ali, still oblivious, and Hillary sighed.

"I know," he said. "But it's not that long now. Probably you'll miss it when you're gone—"

"*Never.* I will *never* miss it. If Kamensic fell into the goddam river I wouldn't shed a single tear—"

"Oh, come on. You'd miss *me*. And you'd miss Livia, and Unk—"

"I'm *sick* of Unk. What Jamie Casson said last night was true—all these has-been actors—"

"DeVayne Smith just won the Oscar, Lit. And Mariel Gillian's doing that new Beckett one-act—"

"But it doesn't *matter*. What difference does it make, even if they were all Shakespeare? Which they're *not*—my mother's in a goddam soap opera and my father is *Uncle Cosmo*—"

"Give him a break, Lit! Unk played Toby Belch last year at Avalon—"

"It's all bullshit." I set my mouth and stared straight ahead. "*Bullshit*. Eighteen million versions of *Oedipus Rex*, but it's always the same goddam play, it's been the same goddam play for two thousand years—"

For the first time Hillary looked pissed off. "So stop talking about it and write a goddam *new* play, Lit."

"How can I *possibly* write anything here?"

"Maybe if you were sober once in a while . . ."

"Fuck you, Hillary. Just *fuck* you."

"'The lady doth protest too much, methinks—'"

I turned away. Outside railroad tracks appeared alongside the Muscanth River, so that I had a momentary vision of three parallel trajectories, road river rail, all arrowing into the heart of the village. A few minutes later, Kamensic itself came into view.

"That toddlin' town," Hillary sang to the tune of "Chicago." In my lap Ali chimed in sleepily.

"*Kamensic, Kamensic my home town—*"

I stared resolutely out the window. And, despite myself, shivered at the sight of it—snowy church spires and courthouse bell tower, bare chestnut trees and white-gabled library all rising from the autumn haze like the memory of the drowned village that lay beneath the reservoir. Even after all these years, it still took my breath away.

Not because it was beautiful. Though it was, deceptively wholesome as a Currier and Ives print. Shops neatly tended, dogs sleeping peacefully on the sidewalk, a young boy leading a black horse alongside the railroad tracks. Healy's Delicatessen, where lemons bobbed like turtles in a huge vat of iced tea; the library with its incongruous sphinxes standing guard beside the steps; and, hidden behind a bend in the road, the black depths of Lake Muscanth.

And everywhere the trees—four- and five-hundred-year-old oaks and ancient beeches, huge dark hemlocks and the pair of massive holly trees that fronted Mrs. Langford's tiny cottage beside the courthouse. Like Bolerium they seemed to protect Kamensic, that phantom village, so lovely that even now I ached to see it.

Yet what haunted me was not its beauty, but the way it shut me out. For all that I had lived there my entire life, for all that every face that passed me on the sidewalk would greet me by name, remember my birthday—and not just my birth date, but the weather on the day I was born—still somewhere within the town there was a mystery.

And it was a secret kept from *me*. I was convinced of that, the way some children believe themselves to be adopted. What I had seen at Jamie Casson's house proved it. A man with living trees in his eyes and horns sprouting from his skull; and for all I knew everyone in Kamensic had seen that creature, and had never bothered to tell *me* about it. So like any cast-out lover, I longed more than anything else on earth to hold Kamensic within my embrace. But the village only looked deep into the lake that mirrored it; and, dreaming, saw Bolerium's decaying horns and turrets, and the shadows of the mountain.

A rattle as Hillary's car bumped over the wooden bridge spanning the river, willow leaves like calligraphy upon its surface. Ali sprawled across the seat, her head bumping my knee.

"See?" she crowed. "My brain's falling out, but Lit's catching it!"

"Lucky for you," said Hillary with a touch of bitterness. "I'm hungry. You guys want to eat?"

Ali was up like a shot. "Deer Park."

"Okay with me. Lit?"

"No . . ." I shifted, trying to get comfortable. "Damn it, Ali, move *over*."

"But aren't you hungry?"

"*No*." I couldn't bear the thought of being in that car another minute; couldn't bear the thought of sitting with Ali or Hillary or anyone else.

"Hey, suit yourself—"

The car scraped against gravel as we passed the courthouse museum. And suddenly I knew where I wanted to be.

"Listen—drop me off here, okay?"

Ali grimaced. "I'm *not* going to Healy's—"

"Me neither. I'm going to see Mrs. Langford."

"Mrs. Langford? *Now*?" Ali looked at me as though I had just opted for a life of chastity, but Hillary silently angled the car in front of the courthouse.

"I just feel like dropping by. Plus I ate about five hundred pieces of French toast, so I'm *not* hungry. Here, keep this until I come over later—"

I shoved the shopping bag with my new dress into her lap. Ali made a face. "How're you gonna get there?"

"I'll hitch or something. See you—"

She waved as I bounced from the car, but Hillary said nothing; only pulled slowly back into the street. I waited to see if he'd look back. He didn't, and I turned away.

The courthouse was older than anything in the village save Bolerium. When Bloodjack Warrenton burned the town, his men had inexplicably left it standing—Acherley Darnell in his *Northern Sketches and Fireside Tales* quoted a Leftenant Adams as saying it was "occupied by evil sprites." Later, after Warrenton's mysterious death, Polly Twomey was tried (and acquitted) there, and Darnell himself met his death in front of the small clapboard building. On the gallows he recited the First Pilgrim's speech from *The Duchess of Malfi*, bringing tears to the eyes of those who convicted him as he cried, "Fortune makes this conclusion general, All things do help the unhappy man to fall," and fell.

By the early 1900s, all cases were tried in county court fifty miles to the south. The Kamensic courthouse fell into disrepair, its cupola home to hundreds of little brown bats and its doleful bronze bell silent.

All that changed when Mrs. Langford arrived. Stage name Theda Austin, neé Hopiah Lee Magillicuddy, known as Hoppy to her friends—Mrs. Langford had been a celebrated stage actress, and the original Stella Dallas back in radio days. She and her husband, the actor Lawrence Langford, retired to Kamensic in 1931. Lawrence continued to work intermittently until his death in 1972 at the age of 101, but Hoppy took her retirement seriously. She devoted herself to reviving the courthouse, first getting its name on the Register of Historic Places, then raising the money to have it restored and turned into a museum. As such, it attracted perhaps a dozen visitors a year, who would push open the decaying screen door and be immediately absorbed by a zenlike torpor. I walked in now, the door wheezing shut behind me, and shaded my eyes against the steely light that spilled down from the clerestory windows.

The scrubbed pine floors and rows of wooden benches gave the place an air of prim sanctity, as did the portraits of gimlet-eyed magistrates on the whitewashed walls. This was offset somewhat by the very elderly woman in black velvet tam-o'-shanter and lime-green houndstooth tweeds who sat in the judge's dock, peering through heavily bandaged spectacles at a newspaper. Beside her perched a voluminous carpetbag that in happier days had carried Mrs. Langford's beloved toy poodle, Tinker. At her elbow a transistor radio leaned against a thermos. I could just make out the carnival strains of "C'mona My House" segueing into the Bossanova.

"Hello, Mrs. Langford? It's Lit—"

"Is that Charlotte?" Mrs. Langford lifted her head, blinking. "Hello, hello . . ." She waved vaguely in my direction, then swatted at the radio, which gave a faint shriek and fell over. "I *hate* this music, it doesn't make any sense whatsoever . . ."

I picked up the radio—like her glasses, thickly swathed with masking tape—and switched it off. "How are you today, Mrs. Langford? Any customers?"

"Oh, fine, I'm just fine. I don't think we'll see anyone today. Didn't you hear? Axel Kern is coming back tonight—" Her vibrato rose thrillingly and she gave me a look of utmost rapture; then slumped back into her seat, shaking her head. "I just don't know what will come of it, after all this time."

"What do you mean?"

She gave me an inscrutable look, lifted a hand clattering with costume jewelry and draped it suggestively upon a cashbox with a neatly-lettered index card taped to its lid.

ADULTS $1.00

CHILDREN OVER TWELVE $.50

CHILDREN UNDER TWELVE FREE

CHILDREN UNDER SIX **NOT PERMITTED**

"I think you're over twelve now?" she said hopefully.

I laughed. "I'll be eighteen in March—" and put a dollar into her palm. Her hands shook slightly, and I had to stop myself from helping her as she fumbled with the cashbox.

"Eighteen." Mrs. Langford was eighty-six. "When I was eighteen I was playing Maria in *Twelfth Night*. It was a small part but I stood out. That's how Larry noticed me, you know—I stood *out*." She lifted her trembling hand in the gesture I recognized from her old publicity stills. These invariably showed the Amazonian Theda Austin cowering unconvincingly before the menacing villains played by her slight husband. Now her face was creased as crumpled paper and blotched from sun and drink. Her kohled eyes rolled skyward as she cried, "*Never* be afraid to stand out, Charlotte."

With a sigh she shut the cashbox, and tapped her thermos with a gnarled finger.

"Darling, would you mind opening that for me? My hands are bad today, the arthritis you know, I *think* I need to take a little something hot—"

"Sure." I unscrewed the thermos. A wisp of steam emerged, fragrant with the scent of black-currant tea and sloe gin. I watched as she poured a hefty shot into the plastic lid.

"Thank you, darling—"

She sipped, eyes closed so that I could see where the kohl bled into the violet labyrinth of broken capillaries. Then they opened once more: brilliant green eyes, the whites unclouded, lashes still thick and black as a girl's.

"Now. What brings you here? How is your mother?"

"She's fine. I guess she'll be there tonight. I—I just wanted to check something, that's all."

Mrs. Langford nodded and took another sip from her thermos. "Good, good. You go ahead and walk around, take your time, it's not going to get very busy . . ."

She clicked the radio back on. I went upstairs, trying to keep from breaking into a run. I wasn't sure what I was looking for, and there didn't seem much chance I'd find it even if I did. The second floor was even colder and darker than downstairs. I felt a surge of genuine fear, stepping between unlit curiosity cases and assiduously avoiding corners, and hoped Mrs. Langford was right about there not being any other visitors.

The museum's collection was an ill-sorted mass of Tankiteke Indian amulets, woven oyster baskets, old shoes, and arrowheads, as well as hundreds of tattered books and scripts used by actors renowned in their times and now utterly forgotten. *The Devil to Pay*, *The Iron Chest*, a version of *Romeo and Juliet* where the lovers were miraculously revived at the final curtain. Beneath me the floorboards creaked. The slanting light darkened from steel-gray to lead. From downstairs I could hear Mrs. Langford's radio announcing the three o'clock news. My head ached from trying to see anything in the early darkness; I wished I'd asked Hillary to come with me, or even Mrs. Langford. I was ready to give up when I bumped into a small case in the corner.

"*Right*," I whispered nervously, and stooped beside it. A wooden square raised on four spindly legs, its glass top filthy with dust and dead flies. I blew on it, sending up a gray plume, then did my best to clean the glass with my sleeve. Set into one side was a small brass tag that read DONATED BY THE HONORABLE EDWARD P. FOOTE, 1964. IN MEMORY OF A FELLOW PLAYER. Inside, upon a bed of ragged velvet, was a frayed, leather-bound copy of Acherley Darnell's collection of supernatural tales, *Northern Sketches and Fireside Tales*.

I had seen the book before, of course, here and in countless reprints, and like everyone else I had watched the Disney cartoon version of Darnell's most famous story, "The Dancer at the Burial Ground." But I had never actually read anything else by Darnell. I sat back on my heels and eyed the case warily, as though it might know what I had in mind. I took a deep breath and began to prise it open. There was no lock, but the hinges were so rusty that for a moment I was afraid I'd have to give up. I could hear a few mothballs rolling around inside it, and I tugged harder. There was a puff of mold and the smell of camphor. The wood strained and creaked, until with a final groan it gave way.

"Okay." I bit my lip, tasted blood and dust. "Let's get a look at you—"

I picked up the book, nearly dropping it in my urgency. It was heavy, bound in leather and brown cloth and with the title picked out in gilt letters. When I opened it a pressed leaf wafted from between the pages, tissue-thin, brittle as lichen. I tried to catch it, but as it fell the leaf disintegrated, melting into the air as though it had been made of snow. I sank to the floor and opened to the title page.

NORTHERN SKETCHES

AND

FIRESIDE TALES

The frontispiece showed the author himself, with the legend DARNELL AS PROSPERO. A lean, dark man in a black cape, not at all the avuncular white-haired patroon I had imagined. Old theatrical engravings usually made me laugh, those pursey-lipped images of plump men in wigs as Hamlet, or fat-cheeked matrons playing unlikely Rosalinds.

But there was an unpleasant intensity to Darnell, with his thin, upcurved mouth and piercing eyes, long black hair falling disheveled about his gaunt face. He looked less like Prospero than Caliban. I tried to turn to the first tale, but the pages stuck together, and the book fell open at random to a page illustrated with a drawing of a shrieking man pursued by black shapes with huge glowing eyes.

THE MOON-HOUNDS, BEING AN ACCOUNT OF THE STRANGE AND TRAGIC DEATH OF A HUNTSMAN IN THE SIWANOY HILLS.

I do not think that Menheer Vanderbiin ever believed that he would meet his end with his throat torn out within sight of his own doorstep, nor that his wife e'er thought that their children would come to their majority fatherless. I do know that Vanderbiin scoffed at local superstitions, and most especially at those rumors which circulate within the foothills of the Siwanoy Range; namely that the Devil's own hounds hunt upon those desolate slopes . . .

I glanced uneasily over my shoulder. Mrs. Langford seldom navigated the steps, but I had a sudden irrational fear that someone else might. Around me the room had fallen almost completely into shadow. A single shaft of pale light streaked a windowpane curtained with cobwebs and insect husks. I thought of what I had seen in my room last night, and decided I didn't want my back to any more windows, no matter how empty they seemed. I crept behind the glass case, leaned against the chill bare wall and flipped through the book.

"Waitstill Finch, or A Tragic Romance." "The Tolling of The Muscounth Bell." "A Tragic Tale of Olden Times."

Page after page of thick brown-edged paper, interspersed with more gory drawings and the occasional engraving. "Heathen Customes in Modern Dress." "A Savage Lover." "The Infernal Hind."

But then I turned to a plate that made the breath rasp in my throat.

"That's *it* . . ."

A crude black-and-white print showed a maniacally smiling figure, a man with the lurid grimace and goatish expression of a Restoration devil. He was naked, save for a swag of furs and bones around his waist, and capered wildly in front of a bonfire where several dithery-looking captives ineffectually waved their hands as they burned. The demon's feet were clad in high laced boots, and from his head sprang two branched horns.

"The Wae-Be-No, A Savage Relict," I read on the facing page.

> There is amongst those austere men who have made their dwellings here long centuries before the advent of the European race, a tale that is repeated—nay, not a tale, but a most severe

admonition; for such is their belief that they will plead most piteously with any White Man who seeks to ignore their warning, and have been known to slay innocent trespassers, not for malevolent purpose but to spare these unknowing interlopers a fate which the Tankiteke abhor unto death. It is thus that they speak of a devil they call the Wae-Be-No, which takes the form of a hornéd man dancing in flame. Human flesh is what the devil consumes, preferring it above all other sustenance . . .

"Charlotte?"

I gasped and looked up to see Mrs. Langford peering at me from the shadows.

"Oh! Jeez, you scared me!" I stumbled to my feet, trying to hide the book under my arm.

"I didn't know where you were." She glanced around, frowning at the cobwebs hanging from the ceiling, the pallid light that fell through dingy windows. "Good lord, this place is filthy. Hasn't that girl come to clean?"

She took off her tam and swiped at the thick veneer of dust on a caseful of arrowheads. Then, as though she'd just remembered me, she turned and said, "We're closing, dear—a little early, but there's the party . . ." She stared pointedly at the volume under my arm.

"Right. I—I was just looking at this. I'm sorry. I'll put it back—"

"Which one is that?"

She flapped the dust from her tam o'shanter and put it back on her head; then crossed to me, her cane thumping loudly. "Oh, yes, the *Fireside Tales*. That's a *very* valuable book—"

I handed it to her, shamefaced. "I know—I was just, there was something—"

Mrs. Langford held the volume in one unsteady hand, straightening her glasses as she peered at the illustration of the hornéd man. "Well!" she murmured. She studied the picture as though she'd never seen it before. At last she gave it back to me and said, "Better put that back where you found it. Thank you, dear. Now, if you don't mind waiting for me to close up, you can walk me home . . ."

I replaced the book, making a great show of closing the case. Then I escorted Mrs. Langford downstairs.

"There!" she exclaimed breathlessly when we reached the bottom. "Thank you, dear—"

I followed her to the judge's dock. It was almost five, already so dim that the shapes of benches and chairs could only be guessed at. I turned on the electric lamp, and sank onto a bench to wait for Mrs. Langford to gather her things.

"I'm just going to finish my tea, dear." She poured what remained and sipped it noisily.

I watched her, then finally blurted, "What was that a picture of?"

"What picture, dear?"

"In that book. The thing in the Indian legend." I thought of sneaking in to watch *The Exorcist* a year before with Hillary. "Is it—is it like the Devil or something?"

Mrs. Langford put down her tea and stared at me, her green eyes wide. "The *Devil?*" She laughed, costume jewelry rattling. "I don't think the Indians thought it was the Devil. Have you read the story?"

"No."

"Well, Acherley Darnell says it was a god."

"An Indian god?"

"Oh, no. Or, well, not *just* their god. The god of *this place*." Her fingers fluttered and she stared thoughtfully at the ceiling as she went on, "He says it came over with the stones—but you should read the story."

"Well, could I borrow it?"

"Lord, no!" Mrs. Langford looked affronted, then hiccuped loudly. "Pardonnez-*moi*. No, no, Charlotte—that book is worth a fortune, it *never* leaves here. You can find a copy in the library, I imagine . . ."

With a sigh she screwed the cap back onto her thermos, dropped it into her carpetbag and gave me an odd, almost avid, look. "Why are you asking about the book, Charlotte?"

I hesitated. If anyone in Kamensic might know about what I had seen, it would be Mrs. Langford. But the hungry expression on her mottled face and the way she continued to stare at me changed my mind. "No reason. I was just curious, that's all."

"Were you, Charlotte." Her green eyes glittered: it was not a question. "Well, well."

She tilted her head, the light from the single lamp igniting her features so that it was as though I gazed upon one of those terra-cotta masks, all empty eyes and gaping mouth. Then she lifted her hand and in a tremulous voice recited,

> "Blessed is she among women who is given these rites
>   to know,
> But the uninitiate, she whose mind is not touched,
> Goes blindly into that darkness which awaits the
>   dead."

As she spoke the memory of the gruesome apparition came to me, its horrible humping motion and lunatic tapping at the floor of my room. Then it was gone. But for an instant there lingered in the darkness before me the ghostly afterimage of a face, swollen and pale as the egg sac of a spider. This faded into the wide fervid eyes of Mrs. Langford. I stared back at her, repulsed. My mouth tasted sour; there was a heavy pressure at my temples, as though someone sought to drive their fingers into my skull.

And still Mrs. Langford gazed at me. I shook my head, wanting to yell, to gouge at those glittering eyes; but then she was laughing, her dime-store bangles clanking as she stood and struggled into her moth-eaten wool coat.

"But I have to hurry if I'm going to get dressed!" she exclaimed. "Lila Moncrieff is supposed to pick me up at seven—"

I remained on the bench, my heart thudding. When I touched my cheeks they felt like scorched paper.

"Charlotte?"

I looked up. There was Mrs. Langford gazing at me with grandmotherly concern. Gone was the frightening intensity of a few minutes before. Her coat hung askew from her bent shoulders and her tam was plopped crookedly on draggled white hair, like a crow on a woebegone nest. I nodded and automatically started to my feet, crossed to the judge's dock, and let her take my arm.

"Thank you, darling. Here, make sure that light's turned off—"

We made our way slowly to the front door and then out onto the sidewalk, where I waited as she locked up. Above us bare-limbed trees scratched at a sky marbled black and purple. To the west heavy clouds massed like the shadow of Muscanth Mountain, their edges tinged scarlet. The wind had risen and sent leaves pinwheeling across the lawn. I walked Mrs. Langford to her little clapboard cottage nestled behind its paired holly trees. As she searched for her keys I stared at the mask that hung from her door, Bacchus leering from within a starburst of orange bittersweet.

"Thank you, dear." Mrs. Langford withdrew a key hanging from a length of bright yarn and poked it ineffectually at the lock. When at last it gave way the door swung open, onto a cold dark hallway rank with the scents of mildew and old newspapers. "I'll see you this evening, I imagine . . ."

A light clicked on. I had a glimpse of walls covered with ancient framed images of forlorn stars and playwrights. She stood for a moment, catching her breath, then turned to close the door.

"Good night, Charlotte . . ."

I waited until I heard the latch click. Then I walked out to the overgrown sidewalk and started down the street. I looked back to see if anything was revealed by the dingy windows fringed with tattered ivy, but hardly a glimmer of light shone through. There were no shadows, no flicker of movement; nothing at all.

9

Houses
of the Holy

I ended up walking to Ali's house. As I crossed the village green the courthouse bell tolled five-thirty. Too late for me to run into anyone I knew driving home from school, too early for the commuters leaving Kamensic station. I stuck my thumb out once or twice when cars appeared, finally gave up and shouldered my bag, buttoning Hillary's old jacket tight against the chill. I walked quickly, scuffing through piles of leaves and gazing wistfully into the village shops with their warm haloed windows, the smell of roast turkey erupting from Healy's as the door flew open and Mr. Healy emptied his pipe onto the steps. I hurried by with head bent, and felt my melancholy fade as the village disappeared behind me.

It was two miles to Ali's house. Not far, but the road wound precariously up Muscanth Mountain, and dusk fell early there. I knew the way by heart. My boots found smooth purchase between the stones and fallen branches covering the road, and the chill faded as I began to pant with the effort of climbing. Now and then I stopped, perching on one of the stone walls that bordered the road until I caught my breath. By the time I reached Ali's driveway I could hear the Courthouse bell chiming faintly: six o'clock. I was at Foxhall.

The gravel drive spilled out onto the road. Behind it you could glimpse trees—birches mostly, Ali's father had cut down everything else—their branches laced with light flowing down from the house. The stone walls were inset with two concrete pillars, one etched with FOX-HALL, the other showing a stylized vulpine face, all pointed ears and sharp nose. I headed up the drive. A few minutes later I stood in front of the house, a dun-colored monstrosity that looked as though it had been constructed out of toilet paper tubes.

"Ali—it's me—"

I went inside, shouting. From upstairs music pounded, Ali warbling along with "Gimme Shelter." I stuck my head into the living room, a cavernous glass-walled space with built-in white furniture that made it look like a cross between a space capsule and a sepulchre. No sign of Ali's father, save for an empty pitcher beading a glass coffee table with condensation.

"Lit!" Ali bellowed. "Get your ass *up* here—"

I went upstairs. Ali grabbed my arm and yanked me into her room, dancing over to turn down the stereo. There were Pre-Raphaelite posters on the walls alongside the Beardsley image of Tristan and Isolde; Polaroids of Ali and Hillary and Duncan and myself; a picture of Noddy Holder torn from *Circus* magazine. A cone of jasmine incense smoked on Ali's desk, but I could still smell pot and tobacco smoke. "Where the hell you been? 'Cause I had this great idea—"

"Is it about food? Because *I'm*—"

"No—your hair, I'm going to henna your hair—" I scowled, but Ali ignored me. "I *know* I've got some henna left—"

"But I'm starving, *please*, Ali—"

She pushed by me and made for the bureau. "This'll be great, you'll look so fucking *great*—"

It took her a while, fumbling through drawers jammed with mascara wands and Biba lipgloss, *L'air du Temps* perfume and plastic envelopes of birth control pills, worn-out ballet shoes and innumerable black leotards.

"Hah! Here it is—" She held up an enameled metal tin decorated with hieroglyphs. "I was afraid I'd thrown it out."

Resigned, I sank onto her bed. "Will it still be any good?"

"Definitely. This stuff lasts forever. Cleopatra probably used this same box—"

She pried it open and stuff like greenish smoke filled the air. Ali pinched some henna between her fingers, redolent of dried grass and incense.

"It looks like dirt," I said.

"Oh, shut up and sit down. And put this over your shoulders. Just wait, Lit, you'll be *beautiful*—"

She mixed henna and water in a cracked Wedgwood bowl, then carefully smoothed the greenish clay onto my hair. "Oh, man. At the party tonight they'll be *crazy* for you. It'll make you gorgeous."

What it did was turn my hair flaming orange, the precise shade of a fox's pelt in full winter growth. I shrieked when I looked into the mirror. Ali grinned.

"*Wow*. It looks great, Lit." She dried my hair, leaving muddy streaks on the towel. "God, it looks *so great*. See, your hair should *always* have been this color. You just want to pet it—"

She touched it gingerly, that glowing mass that didn't really belong to me. "Ooh, yeah. *Excellent.*"

I stood in front of the full-length mirror and glared. "God damn it, Ali. I oughta kill you—"

"One of these days your face is gonna stay like that," Ali said, and tapped my nose. "*Smile.*"

"I look like that thing at Jamie's house."

"What? The sitar?"

"No, you idiot. The gorgon. The Medusa."

She went to the window, hoisted herself onto the sill and lit a cigarette. "I think it looks totally cool. Before your hair was so—well, it was just *beige.* This is much better. Here, hold this—"

She shoved the cigarette at me and hopped off the sill. "—*I'm* getting dressed."

She slid out of her Danskin and pulled on a velveteen Norma Kamali minidress with heart-shaped cutouts in the bodice, fluffed her hair, and proceeded to spend forty-five minutes putting on mascara. I kicked off my boots and jeans and got into my dress.

"Don't you *dare* put your hair up," Ali yelled when I started tugging my damp curls into a braid. "Just *leave* it. Look"— She stood behind me, close enough that I could catch the smoky smell of her skin, sweat and tobacco and jasmine. —"see how pretty it is now?" She thrust her fingers into it. "Medusa. Is that the one who started the Trojan War?"

"No, Ali. Medusa is the one who turned everybody to stone."

She laughed. "So *you* can be the one who *gets* everybody *stoned.* Ha!"

I put my boots back on and we went downstairs. Despite the chill, Constantine, Ali's father, was sitting out on the back deck overlooking the woods, a pitcher of screwdrivers on the table beside him. He was a slight man, with dark hair and Ali's golden eyes, his sharp features starting to go slack from too much drink.

"Charlotte!" he said. "What happened to your face?"

"My face?" I clapped my hands to my cheeks in dismay.

He pointed at my dress. "It's the only part of you that's not orange."

"C'mon, Dad, leave her alone." Ali peered at a sheaf of blueprints stretched across the table. "What's that?"

"Just some sketches I'm putting together for Axel's opera."

"I thought Ralph Casson was doing design for that," Ali said innocently. She plucked an ice cube from the pitcher and ran it across her cheeks. "I mean, that's what I heard."

Constantine looked annoyed. He refilled his glass, took a long swallow, and said, "Well, he's not. Ralph Casson is *building* the sets. *I'm* designing them. And I don't want you trashing the plans, okay?" He replaced his drink and reached for one of the designs, but Ali grabbed his hand.

"Oh, *please*, Daddy—can we see?" Ali leaned over the table. "Hey, this is pretty cool. Check it out, Lit."

She poked her finger at the blueprint, tracing something that looked vaguely like a chambered nautilus. "Dad? What is this? A pyramid?"

He shook his head. "It's supposed to be a labyrinth—see, it's kind of a cutaway view, so from the audience you're looking inside it. These are all just preliminary sketches"— He picked up his drink. —"it's actually a bitch to get the sightlines right. I have no idea how it's going to work."

I stood beside Ali and looked at each design as she flipped through them. All showed the Miniver Amphitheater, a small open-air theater on the Bolerium estate that dated back to Acherley Darnell's time. Actually, calling it a "theater" was stretching a point. Despite the Kamensic Village Preservation Society's continuing (and unsuccessful) efforts to have it declared a National Historic Site, the amphitheater was little more than a natural declivity on the mountainside, with stone and wooden benches set into the surrounding slope. Over the decades, the granite slabs had gradually sunk into the earth; their mossy tops now thrust at odd angles from the grass, like the remains of an ancient barrow. In Acherley Darnell's time, the writer and his cronies often staged plays there, for their own amusement and the entertainment of the villagers.

Since then the amphitheater had fallen into decay. I dimly recalled attending a child's birthday there when I was six or seven, and every few years the Preservation Society hosted a garden tea with Mrs. Langford officiating. But the staging area was small. More than sixty or seventy people would crowd the hillside.

"Isn't it kind of dinky?" I asked. "I mean, for an opera?"

"Yup. But *Ariadne* isn't *Aida*—it's just one act and a prologue, small cast, no elaborate sets. In fact, Axel is actually dropping the prologue"— Constantine tapped a finger alongside his nose. —"and *this* is where it gets kind of neat. He's gotten his hands on a fragment of a lost play by Euripides called *Theseus at Knossos*, and he's going to stage it as the prelude to *Ariadne auf Naxos*."

"Wow." Ali yawned. "Don't want to miss *that*."

Her father ignored her. "The amphitheater would actually be a very nice place to mount it, pretty alfresco setting, all that. I think he's going for some sort of modern staging—you know, kind of Beckett, kind of *Godspell* . . ."

He crunched an ice cube, then sighed. "Actually, I'm not sure exactly *what* the hell he's up to. I think he's doing this for the backers, trying to get the money to mount a full-scale version next fall. Or this could be just another one of his vanity productions. Who the hell knows. It's a goddam job, that's all I care about."

Ali nodded absently, and I scrutinized the plans strewn across the table: sketches of crude, boxy mazes and prisonlike edifices of stone, elaborate topiary labyrinths and pop art meanders and designs like the rose windows of a cathedral.

"They're great," I said. I glanced over to see Constantine giving me a bleary smile. "Really beautiful. Is that what he's going to do? Build a maze in the amphitheater?"

Constantine shrugged. "Who knows? He's got some wacko conception about archetypal images or some such shit, the labyrinth of the mind. That kind of thing. There sure as hell isn't a maze in the opera, though I guess the part about Theseus has a Minotaur in the labyrinth."

He downed the rest of his drink, gently moved me aside, and started gathering his prints. "I better get these back together. You girls about ready? Okay—give me a couple minutes to change. I'll meet you at the car."

Constantine's car was a vintage red Triumph convertible, the only vehicle in Kamensic that was even less reliable than Hillary's Dodge Dart. Ali and I scrunched into the minuscule backseat, our legs tangled, as the car inched up the mountain toward Bolerium. It was nearly full dark now, and cold. I huddled against Ali's small form, warming my hands beneath her velvet cape.

"You want us to push?" she shouted, as the Triumph crept almost to a halt.

"*NO!*" bellowed Constantine. He'd changed into a blue blazer and white shirt, boat shoes, no socks, with a red-white-and-blue Hermès ascot tucked under his chin. He looked (and drove) like a demented Cary Grant.

"Dad! It's not going to—"

"NO *PUSHING.*"

"But—"

I closed my eyes while they argued. My hair was still damp; I knotted my fingers about it, breathing in the henna's sweet scent of grass drying in the sun, and hoped I didn't look too ridiculous. The bizarre things I'd seen, or thought I'd seen, now seemed very far away. It was difficult to believe in antlered men or ghosts with Constantine Fox singing Judy Henske songs off-key in the front of a red convertible. I'd had a hit off a joint with Ali back in her room, and felt a pleasant anticipatory buzz about the party. My parents would be there, which wasn't so great. Neither was the prospect of watching everyone in town suck up to Axel Kern. But I shivered at the thought of seeing Jamie Casson again, his languid mouth and bruised eyes and insolent voice . . .

"Hey, Lit—" Ali nudged me, hard.

"Ow! What?"

"Get out. We're pushing."

I groaned, clambering out as Ali squirmed by me. Constantine got out as well, and the three of us pushed until the car gave a low rumble.

"Get in!" yelled Constantine. Ali leaped in beside him, laughing hysterically, and I flung myself onto her lap, the door hanging open as we barreled up the hill.

"Very important to make a good entrance!" shouted Constantine.

"Yeah, like the circus," Ali hollered back.

We puttered up the last few hundred yards, the road weaving among the great old-growth forest: hemlock, poplar, beech, white oak, all slashed with crimson and yellow and glowing in the headlights. Up here the cold wind ripped across the mountaintop and the trees creaked like a ship under full sail. Other than that there was no other sound. No music, no party voices. No other cars making their way up the mountain; nothing to suggest that anything lay behind those sentinel trees but wilderness.

But then the Triumph bounced over a rut. The chassis scraped against stone. Ali shrieked; Constantine swore. I sat up too fast, blinking and feeling slightly vertiginous, as though I'd just stepped onshore after days at sea.

"Hey! Dad, watch out!"

"Hold your horses, for chrissakes let me park . . ."

A few feet ahead of us a sawhorse had been set up as a roadblock. In front of it a spare figure in white shirt and black vest and trousers was directing traffic. Constantine snorted in annoyance and pulled the Triumph into a long row of cars parked at the side of the road. "I guess we walk from here."

Ali hopped out before he could cut the engine. I followed, turned to see Constantine perched on the edge of the driver's seat. The rolled-up blueprints lay across his knees. His hands curled around them protectively as he stared up the road to where guests milled around, laugh-

ing as they made their way toward the main entrance to
Bolerium. Constantine's bronze cheeks glistened faintly
in the twilight, and even from where I stood I could see
his dark eyes, at once tired and expectant.

"Thanks, Mr. Fox," I said.

"Hmm? Oh, Lit—sure, sure." He smiled and got out of
the car, pausing to pat my shoulder. "You girls behave,
now."

I watched him walk unsteadily toward the others, who
greeted him with more laughter and raucous cheers. In
the darkness I could just make out Ali's white face as she
rushed to hug Duncan Forrester. I was heading toward
her when a voice rang out.

"You left the door open. Hey! You left your *door*—"

Someone grabbed my arm—the formally dressed guy
who'd been directing traffic. I stared at him blankly, then
said, "Jamie."

He nodded wearily. "Your car—"

"It's not my car."

"Whoever—that drunk left his front door open." He
turned to motion at a Mercedes barreling toward us.
"Fucking assholes," he muttered, then shouted, "Over
here! Sir—over here, please—"

I walked to the Triumph, closed the door, and
returned to Jamie. "You're working here?"

He gritted his teeth in a fake smile and beckoned
another car. "You got it. Part of the deal my old man
made with Asshole Kern. What a goddam cheapskate,
like he couldn't *hire* someone to do this? Yes, ma'am,
right there! Thank you, sir! Hey, Lit—look out, will you?
You're gonna get killed"— He grabbed my arm, pulling
me to the side of the road. —"and then I'd lose this nice
job."

I frowned, trying desperately to think of something to say. But Jamie just went on, "God, this bites. It's only till nine, though." He lit a cigarette and eyed the line of cars with revulsion. "But I don't know who the hell's gonna get all these drunks home."

For a few minutes no new cars appeared. Jamie smoked silently and stared down the road, and I stared at Jamie. Finally he glanced at me sideways, eyes narrowing.

"Hey, you got a joint? No? What about Ali? She around?"

I gestured at the enormous stone gates flanking the estate's entrance. "Yeah. I came with her. She was just here, I don't know where she—"

"Shit—" Jamie tossed his cigarette and strode away from me as more cars hove into sight. "Back to work. Hey—*hey*! You can't go in there—"

He shouted at a Karmann Ghia, then spun on his heel to wave at me. "See ya, huh?"

"Sure. Later."

The knot of waiting guests had disappeared, and except for the occasional roar of a car mounting the hill, the night was quiet. I hugged myself against the chill and headed toward the gate. Seeing Jamie had given me a sharp burst of elation, but now that was fading into anxiety. Where the hell had Ali gone? I thought of Jamie sitting on the jukebox, fixing me with his prescient gaze; I thought of the antlered man moving with slow and dreadful purpose through the trees.

Blessed is she among women who is given these rites to know . . .

The wind came rushing up the mountainside, cold and smelling of woodsmoke. For one last moment I stopped to look at Jamie in the distance, his sullen swaying dance as he beckoned a car closer and then sidestepped out of its way, dust staining his trouser cuffs and his bow tie coming loose to flop around his neck. Then I hurried on.

I kept to the left of the dirt road, past parked cars, smoldering cigarette butts, an empty bottle of imported beer. Ahead of me Bolerium's gates arched like a smaller study of the mountain itself, black and threatening. It made me feel faint and muzzy-headed, already drunk. I looked up guiltily when I heard voices.

". . . don't know *what* he's thinking, it'll be frost by the time they open . . ."

In the shadow of the gates people stood talking. Friends of my parents, men and women in late middle age, faces sun-creased, their voices brittle with drink. The women wore designer minidresses or ankle-length Halstons in harsh colors—bronze and silver, gunmetal blue—beneath furs still smelling of storage. The men were dressed like Ali's father, in navy blue or tweed; a few wore tuxedos. I tried to will myself invisible to them, but it was no good.

"Charlotte *Moylan*! I didn't *recognize* you—" The casting agent Amanda Joy, a plump woman resplendent in velvet cossack pants and gold brocade, raised her wine-glass to me and grinned archly. "So *this* is what it takes to get you into a dress."

"Hi, Mrs. Joy." I gave her a limp wave as the others turned. "Hi, hi, hi . . ."

"Where's your mother, Charlotte?"

"Unk going to make an appearance tonight?"

"Your dad here?"

I shook my head. A lock of hair fell across my face, vivid as a pheasant's wing, and I felt myself blushing.

"Uh, not yet." I forced myself to nod pleasantly as I passed. Behind me their voices faded into laughter and affectionate mockery, the familiar rhythms of people who measured their acquaintance by the titles of shows forgotten by anyone but themselves—

". . . when he was doing *Volpone*, that dreadful musical—"

"*Not* him, darling, that was Michael *Rothman* and you're thinking of *Antigone*—"

A minute later I was safe beneath the gate—a monumental stone arch, elaborately carved, its threshold consisting of the same coarse-grained granite that formed Bolerium itself. I leaned against the wall and stared at it hopelessly. "God damn you, Ali," I whispered.

I loathed going into parties by myself. And how could I skulk into Bolerium unnoticed, with my orange dress and flaming hair? I decided to wait beneath the arch until someone I knew arrived. Even entering with my parents would be preferable to entering alone. I tried to remember when I'd last visited Bolerium—five years ago? seven? We had always driven up to the main house, and so I'd only glimpsed the strange figures carved into the stone, like graffiti on a tunnel wall.

Now I saw that there were hundreds of fantastical creatures, so many that they seemed to be giving birth to each other. Birds with the heads of men; cats whose forked tongues unfurled into flowering vines; leaping stags with multifaceted eyes like those of dragonflies or bees.

But then my gaze was drawn to a single figure, carved amidst a thicket of coils and chevrons that seemed now to be eyes, now breasts, now huge-eyed owls with triangular wings. The figure sat cross-legged, its back very straight, its eyes wide and expressionless. From its brow rose two horns, stiffly divaricated as a child's drawing of antlers. One hand was raised, palm out; the other rested in its lap. When I looked more closely I saw that it clasped a penis, thick as a cudgel and circled by what appeared to be a grinning snake. I grimaced, then very tentatively touched the carving. For an instant I felt a sort of motion there, a faint vibration, as though the ground beneath me sent a warning tremor through the arch.

"Hey—!" I reared back against the far wall. "What the . . . ?"

The grotesque figure was gone. I squinted, trying to find it among the crude representations of birds and eyes. I ran my fingers over the carvings, stood on tiptoe as I searched: all in vain. Where it had been there was only an ornate mob of attacking owls and arabesques.

My fear returned in a slow, steady pulse. I had seen no one else since I walked beneath the arch. The trees blended into a darkness impenetrable as stone. I took a deep breath, fighting panic, and stepped back into the road.

It was empty. My parents' friends had disappeared. So had Jamie, though the parked cars remained and I could see footprints in the dust. But not only was I alone. I could *hear* nothing. No cars, no echo from the village; no faraway wail of trains. There were no crickets, no night-birds, no music.

Nothing.

The silence was a horror. Before I could lose my nerve I turned and walked quickly back beneath the arch, into the domain of Bolerium.

By some trick of the light—perhaps the moon was ris-ing?—I could see better here. The dirt road widened into

a driveway, its tarmac in such disrepair that Indian grass
and sumac had sprung up between the cracks. To either
side reared a line of white oaks, and beyond the trees I
could glimpse the estate's rolling lawn. And *surely* I
should be able to spot someone I knew there . . .

But there was no one, and I could only imagine the
cold had driven the party inside. I walked on, amazed at
how terrible everything looked. The grounds at Bolerium
had always been disreputable. Right now they seemed a
wilderness, overgrown with dead stalks of meadowsweet
and joe-pye weed taller than I was. I couldn't even see
the house, hidden behind its gnarled hedge of rhododen-
drons at the hill's summit. There were no lights to hint
that anything was there, no sound beyond the thrum of
blood at my temples. A twig snapped beneath my boot;
there was a faint popping in my ears.

And suddenly I could hear again. Tall grasses whispering; the susurrus of dried milkweed pods. But nowhere
the sound of music or laughter. Nowhere the sound of
anything human. A few more minutes and I reached the
top of the slope. I stopped and looked back.

Behind me stretched the driveway. Little more than a
track it seemed from here, beaten earth winding between
oaks and beech and hemlock. I shoved my hands into my
armpits to keep warm and looked in vain for Axel Kern's
house.

It was gone. Instead I saw only a wasteland of grass rippling as the wind rushed past, acrid with the scent of
dying leaves. There was an unmistakable salt tang to the
air, though I knew the ocean was miles and miles away. I
shivered, my hair whipping into my face and my dress
blown taut against my legs. Above me stars blinked into
view, faint at first but growing more and more brilliant,

until the sky glittered and the grass shone silver with frost. I stared at the sky, feeling stoned and dreamy and bitterly cold; unsure if I was still awake, or sober, or even myself.

But gradually I became aware that there was something else upon the desolate summit. At the edge of the high moor reared some kind of pillar or column. It reminded me of the stones in the Kamensic graveyard, those carven animals with neither name nor epitaph upon them, standing watch over the graves of patroons and dead movie stars.

I was too far away to see if it was, indeed, a monument. But inexplicably I found myself walking toward it, as though it had been my destination all along. The wind grew colder. My ears ached and my fingers grew numb. There was an overpowering reek of the sea, of ebb tide and decay; of the wasteland for which the standing stone served as sentinel and threshold. In a few minutes I stood within its shadow.

It was a granite pillar twice my height. Upon its rough surface letters or symbols had been carved. The capital bore the crude outlines of a face, and I could make out the pitted remnants of eyes, nose, gaping mouth. Beneath this the stone had worn away so that only a few written characters remained, sinuous letters that ran from its weed-choked base to the decayed visage at its top. There was something repellent about those undulating characters, as though they held hidden representations of awful things: the spoiled swollen coils of entrails, the burst vesicle of an oak gall that reveals teeming spiders in its husk. I shut my eyes but that was even worse. The grotesque characters writhed across my eyelids, entwined with the spectral tendrils of capillaries, nerve endings, muscle tissue, as though burrowing into my skull. After a minute I opened my eyes.

In the darkness voices echoed. A sustained despairing wail was joined by a chorus of howls and yelps, and the unmistakable sound of footsteps.

"... *oooyyyehhh* ... "

And now I could hear panting, a tormented sound louder than any human voice; the clatter of hoofbeats and those unrelenting cries of pursuit all coming toward me.

"... *ooyehh* ..."

Desperately I looked around for a place to hide, but the hillside was barren of anything except the ruined column. I shrank back, crouching, scrabbled in the dry grass for a weapon but found only cold earth and bits of shattered rock. I yanked at the folds of my dress, steeling myself to run if I had to, and waited.

An instant when the landscape was still. Then beneath me the ground shook. Pebbles bounced against my bare knees. A black shape blotted out the horizon then broke away from the greater darkness. Its head swept back and forth, droplets of blood flying from its mouth. It halted, swaying slightly, then stumbled toward the column.

It was a deer. No: not a deer: a stag, a huge heraldic creature that towered above me black and silent as the pillar. The span of its antlers was greater than that of my outstretched arms. Behind them I could see its humped back, like glimpsing a hilltop through leafless trees. It moved with painful slowness, stones flying where its hooves struck them. When it was only a few yards from where I hid it halted and dipped its head. I covered my mouth to keep from crying out.

It had been flayed, the flesh stripped from jaw and muzzle and brow-ridge so that the entire skull was laid bare. I could see the smooth concavities where its eyes should be, its curved mandible and great peglike teeth fixed in a skeletal grin. Bloody furrows led to where its exposed vertebrae burrowed into the hair of its back. As it panted its breath spurted in white gouts from its nostrils.

"God, no—"

I staggered to my feet, but before I could flee the stag turned. Cries rang out all around us. The stag stood with one foreleg raised, and I gasped.

The skeletal visage was gone. In its stead was the image I had seen in Hillary's book so long ago: the *megaloceros*, the Irish elk. It lifted its massive head and stared back at me. Its eyes were each the size of my fist, golden brown, with striations of green and amber radiating through the iris. Behind us the cries grew louder, but the stag seemed to take no notice. I could hear its breathing, like the rhythmic pumping of a bellows, and see its breath silvering the air. When a howl rang out from the darkness the stag tilted its head to gaze at the sky, and its antlers blotted out the stars. Then the hunt was upon us.

It was as though a wave broke upon the hilltop. A dozen figures crested the rise. They ran like dogs, bodies bent close to the ground and long hair flying behind them, and so swiftly I could not tell if they were men or women, or even if they were clothed. A few carried spears or cudgels. Most were unarmed. I could smell them, rank sweat and dried grass and carrion. I don't think they saw me at all.

They raced toward the stag, and I slipped behind the column so that I could watch without being seen. The stag stood silently. Only the vapor staining the air about its head indicated that it was alive, and not some grotesque monument. One of the hunters broke away from the rest and darted beneath the great beast, jabbing at its leg with a spear; then thrust it upward into the stag's breast.

"No," I whispered.

It was like watching a tree fall. The immense crown of antlers trembled as it twisted its head, vainly seeking its assailant. Then slowly, as though its legs were roots being torn from the earth, the stag tumbled to the ground.

With a shriek, first one and then another of the waiting hunters raced toward it. One plunged a spear into its belly; another clambered onto its side and began hewing its neck. Still another darted toward its face, thrusting a lance into its eye.

I could watch no more. I turned and ran down the mountain, catching myself when I stumbled, not stopping until I once again felt the familiar ruts and furrows of a path underfoot.

I slowed, panting, and looked behind me for signs of pursuit. There were none. I shivered: my dress hung limply, damp with sweat; my arms and legs were scratched and smeared with dirt. Voices drifted down from the hilltop, their somber undercurrent heightened by a single sharp cry of grief, like a blade drawn against a stone. On the summit I could see the thrusting finger of the column; the elk's curved antlers, like the rib cage of some extinct reptile; the stooped figures of the hunters intent on disemboweling their prey. I was far enough away that I felt safe, but now that I *was* safe I perversely wanted a better look. So I made a half-circuit of the hillside, keeping low until I found a natural hollow that hid me, even as it gave a better vantage point.

Above me the hunters worked without talking. The only sounds were the wind and the measured hack and crunch of bone against bone, bone against rock, stone against skin. In the grass, the slain *megaloceros* loomed like the remains of an ancient fortress. The wind shifted and brought with it the stench of slaughter. Blood and fat, excrement and trampled grass, turned-up earth. I gagged, wiping tears from my eyes and moving uphill slightly to escape the shifting breeze. When I looked up again, the scene had altered.

The great stag was gone. Or rather, it had *diminished*. What I saw now was not the massive creature felled by the hunter's spear, but something smaller, its curves more graceful—and familiar. Even in the half-light I could make out its color, pale brown darkening to gold, and its antlers, a dozen tines still furred with autumn velvet. A twelve-point buck. Magnificent in its way, but no dream-elk; no enchanted stag.

The figures crouched around it had changed as well. There were still a dozen of them, with one slight man standing apart from the rest. He alone spoke, chanting in a high, almost boyish voice; words that were meaningless to me. The others worked deftly and in silence, slicing chunks of raw meat, tugging strands of sinew and glistening fat from the hide. But the knives glinting in the dimness had metal blades now, not flint or obsidian. Their clothes, too, were less primitive, dun-colored robes or loose trousers of cloth, rather than ill-cured hides and pelts. I thought I could smell smoke and my eyes stung; but when I blinked the scene changed again—

—yet O so slowly this time, so that I could actually *see* it change, centuries passing, millennia perhaps: the figures blurring as though I glimpsed them through a rainy

window. Now they stood solemnly in a line, their eyes
dark holes and their mouths open, though they made no
sound. Only the slight sharp-featured man continued to
chant, his arms raised above a figure on the ground
before them. At first I could not see it clearly, but then it
seemed that this, too, changed, so that I was no longer
half-crouched upon the hillside but standing in their
midst.

"*I so ylikitatos, I so oreos,*" sang the man beside me. The
eerie light made him look as though he had been cast in
lead. All save for his hair, black and singed with silver like
ash, and his eyes. These were deep-set, sea-blue and sor-
rowing; the most melancholy eyes I had ever seen.

"*Dionysos, Zagreus, eho pi i aftos . . .*" He tilted his
head, staring at the slaughtered deer at his feet, then
glanced at me and made a graceful, almost welcoming
gesture. I looked down and began to shake uncontrol-
lably.

The deer was gone. In its stead was a human corpse.
He lay on his side, naked, arms pulled in front of him and
bound at the wrists; his legs taut and angling away from
his body, ankles tied. His skin was so pale that it seemed
to glow, and his dark hair fell in ropy tendrils across his
face. Here and there small dark crescents gleamed—
beneath his rib cage, above his groin, on his neck and
both thighs. At first I thought they had been scored by
knives.

They had not. Each little half-moon held even smaller
wounds like tiny beads: the imprints of human teeth.
Beside one nipple a pistil of torn flesh gleamed, and
blood seeped from it like nectar. Ivy twined about his
wrists and throat, its tendrils braided into his hair. His
eyes had been gouged out, and blossoms forced into the

empty sockets, poppies whose white petals littered the ground. Poppies filled his mouth as well, cleaving to his tongue and lips. Beside his head two antlers had been set, their upcurved tines like skeletal fingers.

". . . *to maheri*," sang the slight man. He opened his hands to let more petals fall upon the corpse's face. "*To maheri is tas hiras o kozmos. Apopse ekaika zontanos, apethanon: i me ta stafilia! i me to meli, i me to krasi—*"

"*I se to krasi,*" the others replied. The wind rose and the petals spun into eddies of light and dark. "*I se to krasi—*"

"*I me to krasi.*" Another voice, so faint it was like the wind in my ears. "*I me to krasi apethanon . . .*"

It was the bound man; the man I thought was dead. With nightmarish slowness his head moved, until it faced me. His mouth opened, lips curving into a smile as ruined petals spilled upon his breast. His teeth were stained black with blood; when his tongue thrust between them shining larvae spun from it like thread.

"*Blessed is she among women who is given these rites to know,*" he whispered; "*Blessed are you who comes willingly unto the god . . .*"

And then, jarringly, the scene changed one last time. Instead of the malign archaic figures upon the hillside, I now looked upon a young man perhaps ten years older than myself. He wore khaki pants and a white shirt rolled up to the elbows, unfashionable black eyeglasses and unfashionably short hair. Behind him the outlines of the hillside blurred. I could just make out the ruins of a building, russet and sepia-toned like an old photograph. The young man was crouched in front of a tumbled arch, its pedestals still bearing great honey-colored blocks of stone. Beside him a wooden box held hammers and a pickax. His hands moved back and forth, back and forth, with dreamlike patience; as though he had been doing this for centuries.

It was a few seconds before I figured out that he was holding some kind of screen, sifting earth and smiling absently as he did so. Now and then he ran a hand across his brow, leaving a smear of dust in its wake, and looked up, grinning at the sky, the shattered arch behind him.

Unlike all that had gone before, there was a palpable sense of *warmth* to this scene. Despite the wind gnawing at my back, despite the rustle of grasses around me, I knew that if I could only touch that fallen arch it would be hot beneath my fingertips, and the young man's cheek would be slick with sweat. I took a step forward, but before I could do more a second figure appeared behind the first. A slight man in a dark suit, head down so that I could only see a crown of dark hair smooth against his skull.

He stepped from beneath the arch, though I had not seen him there a moment before. As he did so, the first man turned and greeted him, smiling. I could not hear their words, but the young man looked delighted. The other man's expression was infinitely sad. Slowly, almost reluctantly, he lifted his head, and I covered my mouth to keep from crying out.

It was the same man who had presided over the slaying of the great elk and the human sacrifice I had witnessed minutes earlier. Now he wore modern dress, but his gestures had the same mannered grace as before. He walked until he stood beside the young man, who was motioning at the sieve in front of him. The older man nodded and lifted his hand. Behind him, upon the arch's twin columns, a stone began to move. The young man continued to speak. The second man stepped backward, his hands held in front of him as though in supplication. Above them, the stone inched forward, until it perched at the very edge of the arch. The young man's mouth moved, his brow furrowed. He turned, glanced up and saw the stone. For one terrible instant they all were there before me, stone boy man. Then in utter silence the stone plunged from the column, toppling until it landed upon the young man and crushed him.

Overhead the sky was blue-white. Eddies of dust rippled like miniature dunes swept by the wind. A huge block of stone lay near enough for me to touch. As I stared something moved from beneath it, the glistening head and eyes of a crimson serpent that turned into a skein of blood unraveling at my feet, and the white tip of a finger that twitched and then was still.

I did not see what happened next. I was already gone, running blindly down the hillside with the wind roaring around me and my own voice burning in my throat. I ran and ran and ran, finally collapsing at the edge of the drive. There were trees here strung with Chinese lanterns, and tiki lights on poles. In the near distance shadowy figures passed in and out of the golden portal that was Bolerium's massive, open front door. I was on my hands and knees, my bare legs scraped and raw, my hair tangled with dead grass and falling into my eyes. At the sound of footsteps I tensed and closed my hand around a rock.

"Lit?"

Someone touched me on the shoulder.

"Get the fuck away from me!" I shrieked and threw the rock so that it careered wildly into the darkness, stumbled to my feet and began to run. I only got a few steps before strong hands grabbed me.

"Lit! Lit, for chrissakes—calm *down*—"

I shook my head. "No—get *away*!" I gasped. "Get the—"

"Lit—come on, come on, sweetie—*look* at me!"

I looked.

"Ralph Casson—remember? We met yesterday, my son Jamie—"

"Ralph!" I began to cry with relief. "Oh, my god, you have to get the police, you have to get *somebody*—"

"Hey—sit down over here for a sec. Okay?" He put his arm around me, hugging me to him, and for just an instant let his palm rest against my forehead. "Oh, dear—you're burning up. Come on, this way—"

He led me away from the drive and onto the over-grown lawn. I wiped my cheeks and looked up at him gratefully. "I—I was—"

"Shhh." He squeezed my arm. "Let's go over here where it's quiet, and you can mellow out for a few minutes . . ."

I nodded. He stared down at me, unsmiling, his pale eyes wide with concern. Instead of faded coveralls and carpenter's belt he wore a shiny ultramarine jacket, and his gray-blonde hair hung loosely to his shoulders.

". . . mellow out," he went on. "Right? And tell me what happened . . ."

My terror faded. I felt disoriented, slightly dizzy; as though I'd been yanked from deep sleep into daylight. And seeing Ralph Casson there unsettled me, even more so than when I'd watched him rolling a joint in his kitchen. I fidgeted, but Ralph only held me tighter, so that I could feel his heartbeat, and smell the too-sweet scent of jasmine oil.

"Let's go," he said.

We headed toward the back of the mansion. Above us, Bolerium's chimneys and crumbling turrets rose like the skyline of some fantastic city. The north tower's famous stained-glass windows had an infernal glow; figures could be seen moving behind them, small and serenely intent as spirit puppets in a shadow play. On the lower stories, the casements of all the arched gothic windows had been flung wide, voices and music drowning out the wind. Laughter, a man's falsetto shriek; the mingled strains of Telemann and "Rebel Rebel" and an old song by the Nursery's house band. I was so conscious of Ralph Casson's arm around me that I thought I might pass out. I swallowed, my mouth dry, and pointed at the base of the house, where a broad flagstoned patio extended out onto the lawn.

"What's—what's that?"

Along the border of the patio, all the French doors were open. A strange velvety light poured out onto the flagstones, so rich and deep a blue it was like spilled paint. I blinked: the light made the edges of things appear soft, as though grass and trees and wrought-iron furniture had all grown cobalt fur.

Ralph shrugged. "Black light. Axel's doing the whole light-show trip, hired some company from Far Rockaway—"

As he spoke, a woman in a gypsyish dress with absurdly long sleeves stepped outside and began dancing by herself, eyes closed, hands drawing imaginary pentagrams in the air.

"Oh, goody," said Ralph. "I was so afraid Isadora wouldn't be able to make it." He gestured at a stone bench overlooking the patio. "Your chaise awaits, *ma princesse tenebreux*. Sit."

I slipped away from him, sat down too hard on the bench. It was cold, the surface crinkly with lichen. "Ouch," I said, moving as far from Ralph as I could. He just fixed me with that brazen stare.

"So. Speak."

"Do I have to play dead, too?"

He laughed and settled himself beside me. I looked away, at the baroquely weird scene in front of us. The Stooges had edged out Telemann and David Bowie in the Background Music Sweepstakes. In some of the downstairs windows banks of candles had appeared, silvery sparks flickering against a lurid blue cyclorama. The wind shifted; instead of woodsmoke, it carried the headier fragrance of marijuana and roasting meat.

And the woman on the patio had stopped dancing. She stood with her head slumped, arms hanging limply in front of her. After a minute or so she began to lift them. She swayed back and forth, eyes still shut tight and mouth slack. Her long skirt was hitched up so that I could see she was wearing only one desert boot; her other, bare, foot was black with grime. Watching her I felt the return of that horror and strangeness I had felt on the mountaintop; a growing fear that it might break through here. When Ralph touched my knee I jumped.

"I actually would like to hear what spooked you up there," he said. "You looked pretty freaked out."

I bit my lip. "I *can't*," I said at last, hopelessly. Because how could I ever explain anything about Kamensic to someone who hadn't lived there all his life? Especially a grownup; especially Jamie Casson's father. "It's—it's just so . . ."

"Listen. *Lit*." Ralph lowered his voice and let his hand

rest upon my knee. "Is this some kind of—*drug thing*? Because if it is, I won't tell your parents—I can *help* you, but you'll have to tell me what it was you—"

"*No*! I mean, I wish it *was*—but it wasn't, *I* wasn't— I'm not on anything."

"So . . . ?" He turned and took my chin in his hand. His fingers were rough and calloused and smelled of jasmine. "Hey, come on—you know you'll feel better if you talk about it."

So I talked about it. Somehow the angry music and marijuana smoke and velvety light made it seem not so strange to be telling an adult I barely knew about something I wasn't sure I had seen.

". . . was like I went the wrong way up to the house, but there's only one road, and anyway the road was *gone* . . ."

As I spoke Ralph Casson nodded and his eyes widened, not with disbelief but as though I were confirming something he already knew. When I faltered, trying to think of a way to describe the stone column I had seen, or the terrible sound the stag had made when it was wounded, Ralph didn't interrupt, or question me. He said nothing at all; only let his gaze lift from my face to rest upon the black hillside behind us. All the while he continued to hold my chin in his hand, and gradually he let his fingers creep upward until they splayed across my cheek, stroking it.

I didn't pull away. His touch was hypnotic, it made me feel as though he were gently pulling the story from me, as one carefully plays out the string of a kite against a steady wind. He didn't say a word, until I mentioned the slight sharp-featured man who had chanted over the slaughtered deer and a living corpse bound with ivy.

"Describe him," Ralph broke in. The scent of jasmine flooded me as he trailed a finger across my upper lip. "Tell me."

I shook my head, puzzled.

"Describe him." Ralph's voice rose slightly. He moved his hand so that his fingers knotted in my hair, then pulled my head back. Not forcefully but irresistibly, so that my neck was exposed to him. He ran a finger down the ridge of my windpipe and probed at the hollow of my throat; then traced the skin above my breasts. "Lit. You have to tell me. What did he look like?"

"He—he was small." I wasn't sure if I should be frightened; if so, what precisely I should be frightened *of.* "About as tall as me, and he had sort of gray hair. Black hair, but turning gray. And blue eyes. I think."

"Balthazar." Abruptly Ralph let go of me. He smiled, those intense eyes glowing with reflected light. With deliberate slowness he slid his hand beneath the front of my dress, until it caressed my breast. I felt my nipple harden as he circled it with one finger. But he drew no closer, made no move to kiss me; only tipped his head to regard me measuringly.

"Well," he murmured. "Aren't you the lucky girl." His palm covered my breast and for a long moment he held it there, so that its warmth seeped into my skin. A sharper scent cut through the smell of jasmine. Unexpectedly he slipped his hand free, and raised it to brush a strand of hair from my face.

"'Meet the new boss,'" said Ralph Casson lightly. He stood and stretched, his back to me, and stared at Bolerium's glowing violet windows, the patio empty now save for a cigarette smoldering on the flagstones. "'Same as the old boss.'"

I shook my head, trying to hide confusion and arousal, and anger that he'd drawn away from me so suddenly. "Who—who was it? Do you know him?"

"Know him? Sure." He didn't bother to glance at me. "Balthazar Warnick. I studied under him at the Divine. Cultural anthropology. Comparative religion. We had a falling out, over—well, call it structuralism."

I looked at him blankly. "What's that?"

"The way the world is arranged. I thought he was wrong, but I've come to see the error of my ways. Now I can find him and tell him he was right all along," he added.

"But I don't get it—what was he doing up *there*?" I jabbed a finger toward where the standing stone had been. "Nothing's there now! It was—is it *witches*?"

"Witches?" Ralph Casson began to laugh. "Oh, you poor benighted child! No, it's not *witches*. Don't you know what this place is? This little bedroom community Shangri-la you have here? This incredibly groovy little place conveniently located just seventy-two minutes north of Manhattan?"

I glared at him. *"No."*

"Why, it's the sacred fucking grove!" he exclaimed bitterly. He pointed to a neighboring hillside that blotted out the sky to the east, then to the service road winding down from the far side of Bolerium to the village. "I mean, right there you've got Sugar Mountain, and Muscanth here's your fairy mound, and down there's the river where boys drown trying to fuck Undine, and here at Bolerium—"

"Charlotte! Where have you *been*?"

I turned to see Duncan Forrester weaving across the patio. He was wearing his sister's fuchsia tank top over ragged blue jeans, blue eye makeup and Ali's black cherry Biba lipgloss. The blouse was too small for him: the seams had split across the front, so that you could see glitter sparkling in his chest hair. He stopped and stared at me, grinning with totally blitzed good humor; then leaned forward to frown at the top of my head.

"Tell me, Charlotte—is it my eyes, or has your hair turned quite gold with grief?"

"It's henna. Ali did it," I said dully. Because Duncan's appearance had the opposite effect of reassuring me. As clearly as though it had been spelled out on a banner overhead, I knew that everything had changed. Whatever happened next, neither Duncan nor any of my other friends were going to be able to stop it.

"Ah: another mystery solved!" Duncan raised his eyebrows, shedding tiny flakes of silver. "Miss Fox in the bedroom with the curling iron. *Trés rouge*, Charlotte, *trés trés rouge*." He turned to Ralph. "Hi. I'm Duncan Forrester."

Ralph stared at him in distaste. "Ralph Casson," he finally said.

"Charmed, charmed . . ." Duncan wandered off a few steps and gazed at the sky. "Is there a full moon tonight? Is there a moon at all?"

"I think I'll leave you to your little friend," said Ralph, and walked away. As he passed Duncan he made an elaborate show of giving him a thumbs-up. "Groovy threads, man."

"Who the hell is that?" asked Duncan, throwing an arm over my shoulder. He held up a fifth of Tanqueray, already half-empty, eyed it wistfully before taking a swig.

"He told you. Ralph Casson." I watched until he disappeared around a corner, turned back to Duncan. "He's doing sets or something for Axel. His son is that new guy Jamie—"

"Oooh, yes." Duncan lowered the bottle. He flicked a drop from one corner of his mouth, then smoothed out his lipgloss. "I met him. Jamie Casson. The new guy. He has a sort of—*spiritual* quality, don't you think?"

"Meaning?"

"Meaning I think he's a *junkie*." Duncan pursed his lips. He looked less like Marc Bolan than Don Knotts in drag. "Hillary is inside having a fit looking for you. *Trés formidable*. And you know who's here? Precious Bane! *And* Hillary said there's supposed to be a band later, or a movie, or something . . . Tell me, Charlotte, do you like what I'm wearing?"

He spread his arms to model the tank top. I heard another seam rip. "Damn." Duncan sighed. "Do you know, I spent an hour picking something out, this beautiful old peach organdy Balenciaga gown of my mother's—and then I got here and walked inside and there was some guy and you know what? *He was wearing the same dress.*"

He made a tragic face. More mascara and glitter rained onto his cheeks. He took another mouthful of gin and started for the patio.

"You're not going to get sick, are you?" I asked.

"Never mix, never worry." He handed me the bottle. I sniffed it and took a sip. "Don't look like that, Charlotte, Tanqueray is mother's milk to me. *My* mother puts it on her muesli. Come on, you're missing everything. It's like the Tomb of the Unknown Hairdresser in there. Give me that—"

I handed him the bottle. "Wait till you see inside," he announced when we reached the patio. The music had momentarily died away, though the rumble of conversation was loud enough that Duncan had to yell for me to hear him. Beside the doors, windblown asters and chrysanthemums erupted from terra-cotta vases shaped like amphorae. In the ultraviolet light the swollen flower heads looked dark as blood, but everything else had an edgy dark-night-of-the-soul glare. A jackknifed cigarette stained with lipstick lay on the ground, still smoldering. Without pausing Duncan swooped down to nab it. He toked it as though it were a joint, tossed it into the bushes, and propelled me through a doorway.

"Don't bother thinking. Just *go*—!" he shouted.

It was like diving underwater; like being pushed into one of those huge, extravagantly lit aquariums you see at louche nightclubs or fabulous Malaysian restaurants, where nightmarishly beautiful fish dart in and out of coral ziggurats, skeletons and organs visible through their skin; then devour each other before your eyes. From outside, it seemed that the UV lights were trained on the entire main hall, but they were not. They were fixed in upright columns all along the outer perimeter of the room, so that I walked through a glowing cobalt corridor; then almost immediately was in darkness so profound I thought the power must have blown.

"Dunc?" I called nervously. *"Dunc!"*

But he had already disappeared. I stood and tried to get my bearings, after a minute figured that the lights actually had *not* gone out. I was in the broad inner hallway that ran along the back of the mansion like an extension of the patio. But once past the rows of black lights, there were only candelabrums for illumination. These hung by long chains from the vaulted ceiling: great clusters of horns and antlers like knotted fingers with candles thrust between. The soles of my boots grew slick with wax; directly under some of the larger candelabrums fragrant stalagmites thrust up from the slate floor.

The noise was deafening. There were people everywhere, half-seen through candlelight and a veil of periwinkle smoke. They looked like those ghostly afterimages you get when you stare into the sun and then look away; figures so swaddled within their flamboyant clothing that I couldn't tell if they were really human, let alone male or female, old or young. A grotesquely tall, emaciated woman with a white afro and skin lacquered gold and crimson; twin matrons in chaste Chanel suits and pearls, their heads shaved; a boy wearing lederhosen and an ammo belt. Bare, glitter-encrusted breasts like the ripple of light on a trout's belly; eyes like holes gouged in a green melon. For one split second I had a vision of Duncan Forrester, laughing beneath a tapestry; but as I took a step toward him he disappeared. In his stead there was only a suit of armor hung with plastic Hawaiian leis, a yellow happy face beaming from its visor.

—TV eye on you—

With a roar the music suddenly came back on. The whole place erupted into laughter and cheers.

—My TV eye on you—

I covered my ears and started threading my way through the dark, to where I knew a doorway opened onto the music room. Drinks spilled on me, a girl shouted my name. I almost tripped over a prone body but was held up by the crowd.

"Hey, Red! Here—"

Someone thrust a joint into my hand. I sucked on it, my fingers damp with someone else's spit; then held it up over my head to be snatched back. Before anything else could come my way—magic needles, wreaths of poppies, an arrest warrant—I lurched forward, and at last found the way out.

There was no door; just a high arched entry, so wide you could have driven a VW bus through it. For all I knew that was how all those guests arrived. A small cluster of relatively sedate-looking people stood in the passageway. Men in tuxedos; Amanda Joy and her rival, the agent Margot Steiner. Opposite them lounged my high school classmates Christie Smith and Alysa Redmond, in matching white silk jumpsuits, whispering to each other with fingers interlaced. As I walked by they glanced sideways and smiled.

"Hi, Lit."

"Hi, Lit. *Great* party . . ."

As though I had something to do with it. I gave them both a wobbly smile. "Hi, Alysa. Christie. Have you seen Hillary any—"

I stiffened. One of the tuxedoed men was laughing at something a companion had said. He turned casually in my direction—a short slight man with dark silver-touched hair, a keen blade of a nose and disarmingly alert blue eyes. When he saw me his laughter did not stop, but there was a nearly imperceptible change in its timbre, as though he'd drawn a breath of cold air. His gaze caught mine and held it. Not challengingly, not fearfully, but with disbelief—

But a sort of disbelief that seemed almost like ecstasy, a raw surge of emotion that I had never observed before, and certainly never directed at *me*. His brow furrowed and his blue eyes narrowed, as though he was not quite sure of what he was seeing. Then he turned away again, so that I saw only the back of his bespoke tuxedo jacket.

It was not quickly enough. I had recognized him. The man I had seen atop Muscanth Mountain; the man Ralph had named Balthazar Warnick.

Yet what terrified me, what sent me pushing past that little crowd and into the reassuring silence of the music room, was not the memory of slashing wind or the soft dreadful cries of the dying stag. What was most horrible was that, somehow, in that flash instant, Balthazar Warnick had recognized *me*. The unguarded look he had given me was not mere disbelief. It was the joy I had seen on Peter Burke's face when he learned his son Evan was not dead in a place crash, but had missed his flight. It was the look my mother had one dawn when I hadn't bothered to call first and returned home from an unexpected party; the look of a man seeing a loved one he thought dead. And the revenant was me.

10 ❧
The Punk Meets
the Godfather

I stumbled into the music room. After the shrill, over-
heated melee of the outer hall, it seemed positively
monastic. Tiffany lamps and austere Prairie School
lanterns cast a cozy glow over worn leather furniture—
hassocks, oxblood couches, armchairs large enough for
two people to sleep in side by side. Which at least one
blissed-out couple was doing, the woman's miniskirt still
hiked up to her waist while her partner snored.

Otherwise the place was empty. Oriental rugs were
scattered across the floor, not the elegant Chinese silk
pastels favored by my parents but thick rough-textured
rugs from Turkey and Afghanistan, wool so heavy it left
your fingers sticky with lanolin, with intricate mazelike
patterns dyed in the autumnal hues of the wines Axel
Kern loved: claret, burgundy, the golden bronze of
Armagnac, pale sunlit sémillon. The floorboards were
worn and creaked underfoot; the plaster ceiling cracked
and blotched with water-stains. There were music
stands holding black-and-white photographs of a naked

Marilyn Monroe, a harp hung with a Soviet flag, a Steinway covered by a fringed paisley shawl. A shabby polar bear rug lay in front of a huge stone fireplace where a fire crackled. The room was so big, and so inadequately heated, that I hurried there to warm myself. I avoided the polar bear—its fur matted, the color of city slush—instead stood on tiptoe on the tile border in front of the hearth.

The fire must have been blazing for hours. There were logs as large as I was angled across the brass firedogs, and a mountain of ash beneath. After a minute or two I blinked, my cheeks burning, and stepped backward until I leaned against the Steinway. I could still hear laughter and thumping music, and fainter strains from other parts of the mansion. I was debating whether to brave the hall again or head off in search of Hillary, when someone grabbed my ankle; someone beneath the piano.

"Lit Moylan," a voice intoned drunkenly. I tried to pull away but the hand moved up to my calf and gripped me. "Where the hell have you been?"

"Hillary?"

I had to lift the fringed shawl before I could see him, lying on his stomach, his flannel shirt open and his long hair sticking out like Struwwelpeter's, a heap of apple cores beside him. "Gee, Hillary, I thought you were prostrate with grief looking for me."

"I am. I'm completely housebroken. Get down here—"

I slid beside him. He kissed me sloppily, his mouth tasting of red wine and apples, then drew back, puzzled. "Your hair smells funny—Christ, your hair *looks* funny! What happened?"

I pulled away. "Nothing."

"*Nothing?* You look like—well, I don't know *what* you

look like." Hillary reached behind him and grabbed a
wine bottle. He took a long pull, then regarded me
thoughtfully. "Actually, you know what you look like?
That picture in Ali's room."

"Really? 'The Lady of Shallott'?"

"No. The creepy one, that girl with the red hair and
the ripped white dress who looks like she's pulling her
hair out—what's his name? Stuck? Gluck?"

"You *idiot*." I turned angrily and crawled back out. "I
hate that picture—"

"Munch," Hillary said, snapping his fingers. "That one!
Hey, where you going?"

"Leave me alone! And it's *orange*, not white."

Hillary stared at my dress. "Yeah, no lie."

"Fuck you."

I stormed from the room, not even noticing which
doorway I left by. I was such a roil of pure emotion—
embarrassment, fear, excitement, arousal, rage—that I
felt sick to my stomach. I was halfway down a darkened
hallway before I stopped to catch my breath. Overhead
the ceiling was so ornately carved it seemed hung with
dark crumpled linen. I glanced back for the telltale glow
of firelight from the music room.

It was gone.

"Damn," I whispered.

I was in one of those labyrinthine oak-paneled passages that wound through Bolerium like the trails bored
by deathwatch beetles, opening upon anterooms and
stairways, pocket libraries and maprooms, and even upon
a tiny private chapel where it was said Acherley Darnell
had been shriven the night before his execution. As a
child I had sometimes wandered in these halls, when the
adult conversation bored me and I'd tried unsuccessfully

to find my way to the kitchen in search of normal food, rather than the robust and inedible spreads that Axel and my parents loved: morels, imported truffles and dark bread, venison studded with juniper berries; fiddleheads and shad roe.

But I could never make any sense of the corridors. Sometimes I found the kitchen, and Axel's housekeeper would give me turkey sandwiches and a glass of milk before sending me back. But just as often I would wander for what seemed like hours, futilely jiggling doorknobs, climbing narrow stairways where the ceiling grazed my head, staring out lead-paned windows onto the slope of Muscanth Mountain and the distant play of light upon the lake. Eventually, of course, I always found my way back; but ever after was haunted by dreams of dim passages, muted voices speaking behind walls; doors I could never quite open and words I could not understand.

Now I felt that same dread returning. And I was starving. So I went on, trying to ignore the pulse of music from behind the walls, the flicker of movement behind half-closed doors. In front of one there was a stack of unopened mail that came up to my waist; by another someone had dumped an ashtray. The walls held some of the artifacts scattered throughout Bolerium like the detritus of a fabulous library. Old, sepia-tinted photographs of places in western England: Land's End, The Lizard, a group of standing stones called The Merry Maidens. A huge gilt frame that held an oil painting in the style of Landseer, its colors so dark I had to squint to determine its subject: ravening hounds and an embattled stag, the deer poised upon the edge of a cliff with its head thrown back. An engraved brass plaque gave its title, "AT BAY."

And after this, an entire hallway filled with a series of maps, the earliest dating back to the 1600s. All depicted the changing contours of Kamensic's boundaries—a farm, the Indian burial ground overlooking Lake Muscanth, the Old Post Road. I stopped to peruse these, looking for my own house. I never found it, which was puzzling—it was on the Register of Historic Places, and often mentioned in local histories.

What was even stranger was that the one local landmark which should *not* have changed over the centuries—Muscanth Mountain—*did* change, at least on these ordnance maps. The oldest chart, dated 1601, showed a vast Himalaya of a peak, snow-covered, with black stones thrusting from its side like a reptile's dorsal spines. Only three years later, Muscanth was a mere hillock, the silhouette of Bolerium already blotched onto it in tea-colored ink.

But the next map showed yet a different view, and then another: as though the mountain were a lake or marsh whose environs swelled or shrank according to the seasons. Its placement never varied. Neither did the shadowy outline of Bolerium. Only the exact size and shape of the mountain itself seemed to be in question.

This was odd, though of course old maps are notoriously unreliable. Yet even the more recent charts, dating from the 1930s, shared this anomaly. I stared at one, frowning, and recalled Jamie Casson's complaint—

Every time we come down that mountain it's like a different road . . .

But what if that wasn't it, I thought, and shivered. *What if every time we come down that road, it's like a different mountain?*

As if in answer a tide of laughing voices rose and ebbed

somewhere just out of sight. I lingered another moment in front of the maps, then went on.

The air grew cooler, as though I had wandered far from where the other partygoers held court. The cracks beneath closed doors hinted at what was inside: candles, a halogen glare that meant 16mm cameras; the ubiquitous fuzzy glow of ultraviolet. Occasionally I caught a whiff of something other than lemon polish—marijuana smoke, candle wax; a woman's perfume, heavy with the sweet notes of vanilla and jasmine. My stomach growled, and I had the beginning of a headache stabbing at my eyes.

"Come on, come on," I muttered, squinting as I tried to figure out where the hell I was: absolutely nowhere. In front of me the passage wound on. Behind me there were only all those doors, like the sets of some demented game show. *"Shit."*

I stopped and ran a hand through my knotted hair, steeling myself to kick in the next door I saw, when light flooded the hall in front of me, brilliant red. I stiffened, saw yet another door that opened inward. There was someone inside—two people. Their shadows rippled at my feet, and I stepped quickly to one side.

". . . *knew* you'd find her! Why else would you be here?"

"Don't be a fool. I had no—"

Abruptly they grew silent. I pressed myself against the wall and held my breath. I knew the first voice. It was Ralph Casson, his tone nearly strangled with rage; and the second voice, too, I almost recognized, a voice so oddly familiar that at first I thought I must know it from a movie or song.

But then the shadows moved closer. The pool of crimson light at my feet diminished and disappeared. In the doorway stood two figures, staring at me. Not in complete shock, but not quite as though I were expected. More like they had expected me sooner, or later, or in other clothes.

"Lit," Ralph Casson pronounced. "Here you are."

"*Giulietta,*" breathed the second man: Balthazar Warnick. He ran a hand across his brow, glanced quickly at Ralph, then at me. "You—he said you were here, Giulietta, but . . ."

He stepped toward me and I shrank from him. "I don't know you," I said, sounding unaccountably childish. I looked at Ralph, who cocked his head and beckoned me to him.

"Lit," he said, correcting Balthazar. "This is Lit Moylan." He put his arm around me, leaning his head so it rested atop mine. "She and my son Jamie are in school together."

Balthazar Warnick continued to stare at me. Behind him I could just glimpse a room, not much bigger than a closet, really, bare of any furniture and lit by a single red bulb in the ceiling. After a moment he stepped out into the hall, seeming disconcerted, almost fearful. But then he nodded, smoothing the lapels of his tuxedo jacket and gracing me with an ironic bow.

"Lit," he said. "I am delighted to meet you."

He extended his hand. I glanced at Ralph. He gave me a reassuring nod, and so tentatively I took Balthazar's hand in my own. I thought he would shake it. Instead he drew it to his lips and kissed my knuckles. Mortified, I looked down at my boots.

"*Please,*" I said. Balthazar smiled coolly and withdrew his hand.

Ralph laughed. "They teach you that at Greenwich Country Day School, Lit?" I flushed, and started to snap back at him when another figure appeared in the red-lit room behind us.

"Boys, boys, boys," a voice scolded. "You must learn to *share*."

I looked up. Someone stood there, head and shoulders above Balthazar and Ralph, glowing as though just pulled from a kiln. An aureole of cerise hair; milk-white face save for two slashes of rouge like arrows drawn across her cheeks; a voluptuous mouth green as poison apples. A gold sequin winked above her upper lip, and her eyes were so thickly mascaraed they looked like spiders. She stared at me and smiled, then with a flourish raised her hands. She placed one upon Balthazar's shoulder, the other upon Ralph's, pushed them aside and walked between them.

"I learned that from Charlton Heston in *The Ten Commandments*," she explained. Her voice was deep but breathy, very hoarse, as though it was a continuing effort to speak. She put a long, blunt-tipped fingernail under my chin and tilted my head back, until I was gazing directly into those liquid brown eyes.

"Charlotte Moylan?"

I nodded.

"I'm Precious Bane."

"I—I know."

How could I *not* know? Precious Bane, née Wally Ciminski, the Jersey City steno pool speed freak turned transvestite hustler and Nursery film idol, imperiled star of *Necromancer* and *House of the Sleeping Beauties*. Heroine of Russ Greer's anthemic 1972 hit "Cities of Night," with its teasing refrain and daring references to sexual acts even I, liberated child that I was, could only imagine; Axel Kern's confidante and, it was rumored, lover, though my parents refused to believe *that*.

Looking at her now, I had difficulty believing it, too. Precious Bane was just too huge. She towered on silver platform shoes, her linebacker's shoulders expansive as a condor's wings, enhanced by a Barbara Stanwyck jacket wide enough that Barbara Stanwyck herself could be hiding in it. The halo of cerise hair shimmered when she moved, and a very short black polyester skirt skimmed the tops of her thighs. The effect wasn't exactly what you would call a paragon of feminine beauty, but neither was it laughable. She was like a statue damaged by time and weather, her beauty increased by exposure: she was too much *herself*, her gift stemming from her own unshakable belief that she was fabulous. And so you thought so, too.

"Your godfather sent me to find you, sweetie." She smiled, showing a lot of big, yellow teeth. "Ready?"

I swallowed and looked around uncertainly. "Uh, sure. I guess."

Precious Bane plucked at my hair, frowning. "Maybe we better stop by the little girl's room first? You're a bit *untidy*. Here, this way—"

She steered me into the red room. Ralph Casson started after us, but Precious Bane turned and held up her hand like a crossing guard.

"Uh-uh-uh. No boys allowed. Sorry."

"But—"

"I'm sure we'll all find time to have a nice visit later."

I peeked around her, trying to catch a last glimpse of Balthazar Warnick. But the door slammed shut before I saw anything except Ralph Casson staring after me with a greedy, almost gloating, look.

"There." Precious Bane shook her head. "People come and go so *quickly* here," she said, and clomped across the room. There was a single door set into the far wall, its glass knob sparkling beneath the crimson bulb. "I don't know why Axel comes here—I *loathe* it. Those trees, this house—I always expect to find Mrs. Danvers rummaging through my underwear."

She yanked the door open and announced, "Ta da."

Before us was a small room shaking with the roar of a stereo and crowded with people I knew. DeVayne Smith and Amanda Joy; Mrs. Langford, resplendent in frayed taffeta; Constantine Fox and a woman I recognized as the opera singer Yvette deMessieres, wearing a velvet pantsuit and an extremely pained expression; my parents and several of their closer friends. At the front of the room hung a motion picture screen, where black and white figures moved jerkily as subtitles flashed.

UN FILM DE AXEL KERN

It took me a minute to figure out exactly what room we were in—Acherley Darnell's private chapel—and to discern the sparely elegant figure standing off by himself to one side, eyes closed, a rapturous expression on his face as he listened to the music blasting from speakers perched atop a fireplace mantel: Axel Kern.

"Ooh!" Precious Bane clapped her palms over her ears. *"Too loud."* She hesitated, then shrugged, put a hand on my shoulder, and gestured at the chapel.

"His Satanic Majesty awaits," she shouted, and we went inside.

Once upon a time the chapel had actually resembled a mid eighteenth century New England place of worship. Whitewashed walls, stern wooden pews, an altar of unpolished hemlock and wrought-iron lanterns suspended by chains from the ceiling. This at least was the image on display in engravings from various Darnell biographies.

But every picture *I* had ever seen, in the courthouse museum or Bolerium itself, showed a distinctly more sybaritic temple, hung with the heads of animals hunted by Darnell and his ancestors, the windows draped in ivy that had crept through cracks to spread like mildew across the walls. I had never actually been in the chapel before; right now I would rather have been just about anywhere else. All eyes turned as I entered. Constantine Fox gave me a watery grin. My father beamed. At his side, my mother looked pale, her eyes red, but when she saw me she smiled thinly and I could see her mouthing my name, though of course I heard nothing, except for that music and its ominous bassline.

With the shriek of a phonograph needle the music ended. In the near-silence I could hear only the whir of a projector. I shrank closer to Precious Bane, catching the powdery-sweet scent of her pancake makeup, the acrid odor of sweat-stained fabric. She looked down at me, brows furrowed in a Kabuki representation of concern.

"Are you all right, sweetie? Aw, shit—we never got you cleaned up. Oh well, *he* won't care—"

She led me to one side of the room, walking past the little mob of revelers. Slowly people began speaking again, voices scarcely raised above a whisper. I hoped they were just embarrassed by the sudden stillness, but I couldn't help thinking that they were talking about me. I craned my neck to see my parents, but they had turned away to greet another friend from summer stock.

"Don't slouch," commanded Precious Bane. She glanced at the bodice of my peasant dress and frowned. "And you ought to wear a bra. You don't want to end up looking like those ladies in *National Geographic*, do you?"

I laughed, but she only shook her head. "Youth is wasted on the young."

We were alongside the first pew, a few feet from where Axel stood gazing at the ceiling. His hair was longer than when I had last seen him, iron-gray but streaked with black. Yet he looked no older; he had the same chiseled, hawkish features, the same deep-set eyes set above a face heavily lined yet oddly youthful. There was a rawness to Axel, an understated feral quality as disturbing as it was compelling. You could always smell him; not some expensive cologne, nor yet the smoky afterthought of his Sobranies, but Axel himself: his sweat, the earthy scent of his hair, an unnamable attar that I knew must be grown-up sex. Some people mistook this rawness for mere vulgarity, and shunned him; women mistook it for shyness or vulnerability, and suffered. There are photos of Nureyev that remind me of him, Nureyev and perhaps the young Klaus Kinski, with their Slavic grace and that tinge of cruelty about their mouths, like the spot of blood on a house cat's paw.

But it was on a class trip to the Met, when I saw a golden burial mask from a Scythian grave at Pazyryk, that I truly recognized Axel Kern. The same gypsy eyes, the same glint of festal savagery. He knew the power of his appearance and played up to it, favoring clothes that would not have seemed out of place in a cossack's regiment or opium den. Flowing trousers of canary-yellow, blood-red, sky-blue; cracked leather boots; knee-length tunics embossed with gold medallions and violet starbursts; plain black turtlenecks and black leather pants. The effect was not so much psychedelic hangover as it was a deliberate affront. No matter how you dressed when meeting Axel Kern, you never had on quite the right clothes.

Tonight he wore a long, emerald-green kimono patterned with ferns, his hands swallowed by sleeves long enough to trip over. He stared at the ceiling, his expression so intent that I looked up, too, saw nothing but coppery-green leaves and tendrils. When I brought my gaze back down, Axel Kern was staring at me, his eyes the same verdant, mottled shade as the ivy overhead, his pupils the size of poppy seeds.

"The girl with the mousy hair," he said, his voice thick. "Charlotte Moylan—but look how you've changed! Little Lit, little Lit . . ."

He smiled, extending one silk-emblazoned arm to beckon me closer. I went reluctantly, looking over my shoulder for my parents or even Precious Bane.

They were gone. Everyone was gone. I had a glimpse of Constantine Fox, hesitating in a small side doorway and looking confused, as though trying to remember where he was. His eyes locked with mine and I caught a flicker of something, warning or admonition or perhaps just drunkenness. Then he, too, disappeared. I was alone with Axel Kern.

"I'm so glad you finally got here," he said. On the screen behind him the film rolled on, a woman's face going in and out of focus, a man throwing feathers in the air. "I've been waiting all this time . . ."

He looked as crazily blissed-out as any of his guests as he pulled me to him, the folds of his kimono falling around my face as he whispered, "Ah, Lit . . .

"Welcome home."

11 ❧
Beyond the
Green Door

Balthazar Warnick stood in the hall at Bolerium and stared at the closed door in front of him. It was of wood stained a rich deep green, the color of moss in the darkest part of the forest; through seams and chinks in the paneling he could feel a fine cold breeze. His hand clasped its polished brass knob as he leaned against the portal. An observer might have thought he was striving to hear something on the other side of the door. Frightened whispers, urgent cries, the soft thunder of a heaving bed.

But Balthazar was not listening. Or rather, what he was listening for was not beyond the door but in the hall behind him. His heart was beating so hard that he thought, absurdly, that someone might hear it and take him by surprise.

And that is very nearly what happened.

"Professor Warnick."

Balthazar whirled. When he saw Ralph Casson he stared at him in silence for a long time, at last drew a long breath.

"You found her. How did you find her?" he asked.

Ralph Casson smiled. "You're really surprised, eh, Professor? You really never thought I was very good, did you?" His tone was light, bantering even, but his blue eyes clouded as he leaned against the wall, angling himself so that he could look down upon Balthazar and have a clear view of the corridor beyond him. "Man, you really blew me off last time I saw you—you know that? When we were at that cocktail party with all your tight-assed friends—"

Balthazar shook his head, his expression pained. "Not my *friends*, Ralph. The Conclave. You knew when we started—"

"I knew fuck-all!" Ralph cried. "I joined you in good faith, Balthazar—good faith! I spent six years at the Divine—I worked for you, I went to Herculaneum when you told me to, I never even *questioned* what you did to Corey Lesser there, I typed your *fucking index cards*!"

His finger stabbed at the air between them as Balthazar watched, unblinking. "And how did you repay me? Exile, man—fucking *exile*, like I was some neophyte!"

"You betrayed us, Ralph," Balthazar murmured. He moved ever so slightly, so that his hand remained on the doorknob but was hidden by a drape of black tuxedo jacket. "The day you joined Kern in Malta, it was over." He shook his head regretfully. For the first time his eyes met the other man's. "I warned you. I went to the airport—"

"Fuck that," Ralph spat. "When the hell did you *ever* use an airport—did you fly *here*, Balthazar? Did you?"

"The choice was yours, Ralph. It was always yours. You went with the Malandanti. You're here now—"

"So are you!" Ralph crowed, banging his palm against the wall. "You're here, too, Balthazar—so what does that make you? Why are *you* here? Where's *your* invitation?"

Balthazar forced himself to keep his tone even. "I came because of Giulietta, Ralph. You know that. You called me—"

"That's *right*!" Ralph said with vicious triumph. "*I* called, and *you* came—just like that! What did the Conclave have to say about that, Balthazar? Do they even know? Did you tell them—"

"They know." Balthazar broke in quickly: it was not precisely true. "Verrill knew even before I did. There was a disturbance at the temple of Dionysos Limnaios. Trees moving; a voice crying out that Pan is free—"

He hesitated before going on. "If I had not been remiss in my responsibilities at the Orphic Lodge—"

"You could have done nothing. You understand? *Nothing*," Ralph said. "They're moving, Balthazar—all your old enemies are waking. Here; in Penwith and Akrotiri and Rajputana—everywhere!"

He took a step closer to the other man, his hand sliding down the wall until it was only inches from where Balthazar clasped the doorknob. "How does that feel, Professor Warnick? Knowing that all your vigilance is for nothing? Knowing that your whole world is going under"— Ralph snapped his fingers and drew back, laughing. —"just like *that*."

"Oh, I think the world has a few revolutions left in it, before it all spins out of control. And the—events—at West Penwith were not unexpected," Balthazar said lightly. He smiled, was rewarded by Ralph showing an instant of discomfiture before the older man continued, "But you and I both know that's not why you went to all the trouble to get me here. Where is she, Ralph? Where is Giulietta?"

"*Lit.*" Ralph drew the word out. "Got that, Balthazar? At least for this particular turn of the karmic wheel, her name is Lit. Kind of a funny name, considering all that bad stuff that came down back in Moruzzo—"

"Stop it." Balthazar's voice broke. His face grew pale. "Stop it."

"—and I mean, it's kind of ironic, don't you think it's sort of *funny*, here you've spent, like, what? Five thousand years? Ten thousand years? Anyway, a really, *really* long time, battling these Malandanti—and there you were back in Moruzzo, in love with a girl who was actually *one* of them. Your own *masters* were the ones who burned her at the stake and where the hell were *you*, Balthazar? What were you thinking, why didn't you—"

"*Stop.*"

Between them the air crackled, flickers of electric blue and gold like iron filings swirling around a magnet. One of the sparks flew dangerously close to Ralph's face; he cried out, slapping a hand over his eye.

"You bastard! You blinded me—!"

With a groan Ralph fell back against the wall. His fingers splayed across his cheek, blood seeping between them. Balthazar stared, remorse welling up in him like panic; then turned and flung the door open.

"*No!*" shouted Ralph.

Framed within the door's opening was the landscape of a dream: a corrugated expanse of hills bare of any trees, their summits crowned by stone ruins and overgrown with yellow-blooming gorse and tiny, thorn-spun roses. Overhead the sky was dark gray, swept with clouds that scudded toward the western horizon, showing gashes of soft blue between them. Then the clouds dispersed and all melted into an endless vista of indigo ocean, its surface scarred by white cresting waves. Birds wheeled overhead, and there were bees in the flowering gorse; but the scene was utterly silent, a vivid film with the sound turned off. From where he stood in the doorway, Balthazar gazed upon it as though poised on a neighboring hilltop.

"*In nubibis*," he whispered, and stepped through the portal.

A sickening instant in which he seemed to plunge, his head roaring and the wind raking his face. Dimly he was aware of a voice shouting, the dulled sensation of something tugging at his hand as at an anaesthetized limb. Then there was a smell of salt and wet granite, the pounding of waves against the cliffs and the unbearably sweet, high-pitched cry of a linnet. Balthazar stumbled upon the rocky ground, caught himself, and straightened.

He stood upon one of the tor-capped hills crowding the westernmost point of Cornwall. Maps showed the place as West Penwith, the peninsula that toed into the Atlantic at Land's End. But the Benandanti had another name for it: *Affon*, the land between. Affon stretched here but also at myriad other spots across the globe. Places that existed both within and without of time, places that the Good Walkers had created and stood guard over for countless millennia; places where they watched, and waited, and prepared for the great conflict that had been building over the entire history of their world, and others.

Penwith was one such place. The Orphic Lodge in West Virginia was another, and the University of the

Archangels and Saint John the Divine a third. The rest were scattered throughout the world that the Benandanti and their enemies had shaped: in the Aegean and Anatolia, across the subcontinent and the vast Eurasian steppes; in London and Rome, amidst the ruins of the ancient Dravidian cities of India and Pompeii. Any place where the ancient gods of the earth had walked and been worshipped, in Crete or along the Ganges, in Siberia or the Orkneys—there the Benandanti had built their own temples and places of learning, their banks and basilicas and steel-lined bunkers. All were linked by the Benandanti's portals, each bearing the Benandanti's motto—*Omnia Bona Bonis*—in carven script or hidden cantrip. If you were to look at a map of the world the Benandanti had made, it would be webbed with these portals and the occult paths between them, the way a lacquered globe can be webbed with cracks. And in the same manner that the globe will break, its veneer shatter, when the cracks overtake it, so the Benandanti had shaped their assault upon the old world and old gods that had preceded their own: by stealth and manipulation, thievery and coercion, auto-da-fé and conversion.

But yet there were places on the earth where the Benandanti did not hold sway. And it was to one of these that Balthazar Warnick had come after witnessing the destruction of the herm—

Bolerium. He went unwilling, but unable to resist the summons.

For summons it had been, just as Ralph Casson had said. No vision of Giulietta Masparutto could have gone unanswered, no thought of her brushed away; no matter that it scorched him, left him breathless and burning as though he had stuck his hand into a bonfire. Balthazar could no more ignore the memory of that voice and its whispering echo through the eons, than he could have torn his soul and mind from the battle he had entered into when the hills around him were covered with trees, and the standing stones stained red with wine and blood.

So he had entered Bolerium; uninvited, unseen. It was a sacred place, as sacred to the Malandanti as the Divine was to the Good Walkers. For two thousand years Bolerium had been one of their last refuges, and no one of the Benandanti's portals would vouchsafe entry there. Instead Balthazar had made his journey from the Orphic Lodge and entered Affon, and from thence had used one of the ancient propylons that served as stepping-stones between past and future, joining the holy places of Benandanti and Malandanti alike.

Because Heraclitus was wrong. You *could* step into the same river twice. Time itself was that river, the Benandanti and Malandanti its navigators; their respective gods the stars they steered by. But in going to Bolerium, Balthazar had made his way through treacherous shoals, and risked more than he cared to think about.

Now he could see the propylon that had served as his way station: a granite pillar twice man-high, plain and unadorned where it sat upon the very top of the hill. At its base thistles nodded in the wind, and bright yellow finches worried their seeds with plaintive voices. Balthazar gave a sigh of relief. He stepped toward the propylon, and immediately went crashing to the ground.

"No—you—*don't*—" a voice gasped behind him. Someone grappled with his legs; Balthazar kicked out awkwardly and pulled away. He sat up, panting, and saw Ralph Casson sprawled in the high grass. Around his right eye a series of fine crimson lines radiated, as though it were a medieval image of the sun. Drawn in the air behind him was the blurred outline of a door, and within that faint rectangle Balthazar could just make out the corridor he had fled, vying with the misty stretch of sky above the sea.

"Tag," Ralph said, and grinned. "You're it."

Balthazar stumbled to his feet. "You can do nothing here!"

"Nor can you," retorted Ralph. He stood and brushed grass from his suit jacket, its vivid ultramarine muted in the brilliant light. He looked around, blinking. For an instant sheer wonder washed across his face, and Balthazar could see a ripple of the boy in the ruins of the man he had become. The ardent undergraduate too easily moved to tears; the older student infuriated by the revelations of Procopius, himself a loyal Benandante, and that vengeful courtier's venomous attacks upon the imperial consort Theodora; the longhaired young man with head bent over Girardius's account of the Necromantic Bell in one of the secret libraries at the Divine, his lips moving as he first uttered the words of the incantation that would make final his betrayal, and his expulsion.

But then Ralph turned to face his former mentor. Amazement faded into mistrust and restrained fury as he gingerly touched the web of broken skin around his eye. "You should not have done that, Balthazar," he said softly. "I came to you in good faith, to bring you news of your lover—"

Balthazar broke in angrily. "You manifested a sending at the Lodge—"

"I did not. That was no vision, Balthazar—the god walks, the cycle begins. He drinks and fucks and readies himself for his rebirth, even as we speak. This is what your carelessness has cost the Benandanti, Professor. You should have been more vigilant. The times were propitious for his return, the world is ready—as ready as it gets, these days," he added with a shrug. "Time to face the music, Balthazar! Your reign is almost over. And that"— He swept his hand out, indicating the ghostly door in the air behind them. —"*that* is where it will all end: in Bolerium."

"In delirium, more likely," said Balthazar. He had calmed himself enough that his voice was steady, though he kept his hands in his pockets so Ralph would not see how they still trembled. "He's not a very *reliable* god, is he, Ralph? And Axel Kern is rather a poor choice of avatar—he's too well-known! Who would dare kill him? The cycle will never be completed," he ended, and allowed himself a smile.

"You're wrong, Professor Warnick. His followers—"

"*Lackeys,*" said Balthazar derisively. "Drug addicts, prostitutes, inverts—none of them could do it. They wouldn't dare—that would be like tearing up their meal ticket, wouldn't it? And I imagine most of them possess a minute degree of feeling, or common sense, certainly enough to keep them from *murdering* him. Not to mention the complicated legal situation that would devolve—some deranged hophead slaying a famous film director in the name of an ancient religious rite!"

Balthazar laughed. "No, I just can't see it, Ralph. Who would do it? Willingly, mindfully, in accordance with the mysteries? No one—"

"The girl would." Ralph's face had turned crimson; the outlines of the wound Balthazar had given him bled into his rage. "The girl you remember as Giulietta: Charlotte Moylan. Lit."

Balthazar froze. "You're lying," he whispered. Though he knew, had always somehow known, it was the truth.

"No, Balthazar. I'm not lying. She was chosen years ago. She's his goddaughter, she grew up within the enclave—"

"Does she know?" Balthazar's voice cracked. "Does she—"

"She knows nothing," said Ralph. Relieved, Balthazar closed his eyes for an instant, opened them to see the other man staring at him. "*Yet*. In Kamensic they all grow up under the Malandanti's protection, but the children never know, not at first . . .

"But she will learn, Balthazar. She is with him at this very moment. And you know what happens next—"

"I forbid it."

Ralph burst out laughing. "*Forbid* it? Don't be an idiot! You're not her father—you're not even her lover, now. No, there's nothing you can do, Balthazar, except maybe watch the proceedings . . ."

His laughter trailed off into the sound of waves and birds wheeling overhead. He threw his head back, staring into the sky as Balthazar watched him measuringly. For several minutes neither man spoke. Then,

"I will go to her," Balthazar said. Absently he plucked a yellow gorse blossom, rubbing its petals between his fingers. "She'll listen, she'll remember—"

"She will be afraid of you." Menace undercut Ralph's tone as he tore his gaze from the sky. "There *was* a sending, but it wasn't of the fallen herm. I showed her you, Balthazar. In various fancy dress, and doing an estimable job of presiding over various rites—"

"She'll know it was false!"

"But it *wasn't* all false, Balthazar. I showed her Corey

at Herculaneum—hard to forget such a thing if you see it at an impressionable age, isn't it? And as for the rest, why would she doubt it?" Ralph shot the other man a look composed equally of pity and disdain. "She's just a girl, Balthazar. She has no knowledge, no memory of you or your history. Her parents serve the god but they aren't adepts—they're *actors*. Mediocre actors," he added with a trace of viciousness. "Ignorant. That is what the great Dionysos is reduced to now—whores and speed freaks."

"Then why do you serve him, Ralph?" For the first time Balthazar's tone was genuinely curious.

"I serve nobody. I told you that ten years ago—"

"Then you're a fool. We all serve something. I do so with full knowledge—"

"You do so as a thief," Ralph said. "You and all your kind. The Good Walkers—nothing but poachers and thieves. And murderers." He extended his finger and drew a figure in the air. Faint gold letters appeared, almost immediately faded.

"'God is the author of all good things,'" Ralph recited, lifting his eyes as though reading the words in the sky above him. "'To continue the good customs which have been practiced by idolaters, to preserve the objects and the buildings which they have used is not to borrow from them; on the contrary, it is taking from them what is not theirs and giving it to God, its real owner.' Saint Augustine," he ended. "See, Professor? I really was paying attention in class, all those years ago."

Balthazar shook his head. "If you think you act freely, he has deceived you, Ralph. 'The god of illusion'—"

"Oh, no. *'The god of ecstasy,'*" Ralph drawled. "Tell me something, Professor: why does the Devil have all the good music? At least *I* have sense to know which way the wind blows, right? Oh, she'll go to him *very* willingly, and the rest—the rest will follow. Twenty-four hours from now the cycle will already have begun again. The Malandanti will be that much stronger. Unless . . ."

He lifted his hands and waggled them suggestively. The gorse petals dropped from the blossom that Balthazar held, and the older man tossed the spent flower into the wind.

"Unless what?" he asked wearily.

"Unless the Benandanti initiate me into the Conclave."

Balthazar snorted. "That's impossible! You betrayed us, Ralph—"

"No. I refused to murder Corey," Ralph replied. "I refused to kill my best friend, when it turned out he wasn't going to be as useful to you as you first thought. I refused to be your straw man—"

"You obstinately refused to obey my command: you invoked Erichto, you stole entry to our portals, and you paid the price. And Corey died all the same," Balthazar added regretfully. "And for what? For nothing, Ralph. We will *always* triumph. Why didn't you listen to me? How could you have imagined you would get away with it?"

"I *did* get away with it. I'm here now, right?" Abruptly Ralph turned and began striding toward the hilltop. Balthazar watched him, his mouth tight; then quickly followed. Around them tiny blue butterflies dipped in and out of the gorse. The sun burned down, strong enough that the bracken crackled dry as autumn leaves beneath their feet. On the westernmost edge of the sea a fog bank was beginning to take shape, like a wall between land's end and the world beyond.

They climbed in silence, their suit jackets flapping in the wind. When he reached the summit, Ralph halted and turned, waiting for Balthazar to catch up.

"So you won't petition the Conclave on my behalf."

"There would be no point." Balthazar stooped and picked up a stone. He drew his hand back and threw it, a black jot like a bird arcing higher and higher, until it disappeared. "None."

Ralph wiped sweat from his cheek, wincing as his hand grazed the scar around his eye. "Well. I didn't think you would, actually. But I thought I would at least show you common decency, and give you the chance. You've really fucked yourself, Professor—you know that, don't you?"

When Balthazar said nothing the other man went on. "She'll go with the god. When she kills him it will start all over: Finnegan, begin again! *You* will have the pleasure of seeing your eternal love betray everything you've lived for. And *I* will have the pleasure of watching the Conclave find out about your negligence. By then it will be too late: the first gods will return, and the Benandanti will be defeated."

Balthazar looked at him with contempt. "You always were a rebel without a clue. Wasting your life, thinking that Dionysos or Erichto or Spes will prove kinder masters than the ones you had at the Divine! Would you spend your years rooting in the dirt with them? You could have worked with the Benandanti, you could have served us—"

"As a goddam foot soldier. Forget it, Professor. It's over."

Ralph turned and walked to where the granite pillar loomed against the gathering mist. A few feet away, tucked amidst the thistles and the gorse's reddish thorns, grew a small laurel bush. Its leaves were jade-green, smooth as marble. Ralph stood eyeing it contemplatively. Then he stooped and took one of its gnarled branches in his hand, twisting it until it pulled loose.

Balthazar watched in silence as Ralph crushed one of the laurel leaves between his fingers, sniffed it and then put it into his mouth. He chewed, grimacing; then spat into his hand. He took the branch and began to rub it between his palms, faster and faster, the leaves switching back and forth in a green blur.

Daphnomancy, thought Balthazar.

"That's right," said Ralph.

"Parlor tricks," Balthazar retorted, but Ralph only stared at the branch whirling between his hands. The solar scar upon his cheek began to glow. As though catching a spark from it the laurel burst into flame. There was a harsh scent, black wisps of ash, and the crackle of burning leaves. Ralph continued to hold the branch, turning it this way and that so the wind fanned the little blaze.

"There," he said, pleased. "Have a look, Balthazar."

Within the flame were two tiny figures, a girl whose fiery hair trailed into the edges of the blaze and a robed man with saturnine features. The man was speaking, his voice thin as the wailing of the birds overhead.

"*. . . the amazing thing about Fellini, he's always doing the same thing, it's always the same thing . . .*"

The girl said nothing, only rubbed her arms as though she was cold. Watching her Balthazar felt tears score his eyes. He swallowed, his mouth dry and throat aching, and turned to Ralph.

"Free her."

Ralph shrugged. He dropped the branch into a patch of gorse. Yellow flames devoured the girl's image. With a soft hiss the fire went out. A coil of smoke rose into the air and joined the mist that had begun to cloak the hill-top.

"I'm not holding her, Balthazar." Ralph sighed and ran a hand across his face. He suddenly looked very tired. "She's a part of it, that's all. There, in Kamensic—I have no more power over her than you do . . .

"What was it you always used to say, Professor? That we all have our parts, that they never change and we only fuck ourselves if we try to change them—"

Balthazar allowed himself a small smile. "I'm certain I never said *that*."

"Well, words to that effect. We do the same things over and over and over again, down through the centuries; we worship the same gods and slaughter them and wait for them to be reborn. The pattern repeats itself endlessly. Nothing ever really changes—"

"But that's exactly why we must be resolute!" cried Balthazar. "To keep the chaos at bay, to maintain *order*—"

"One man's order is another guy's ordure. If you take my meaning."

Ralph stood, shading his eyes. The mist had thickened until it was impossible to see more than a few yards in any direction. Sunlight charged the fog with a preternatural brilliance, so that it was like staring into the milky glowing heart of an opal. Ralph blinked, trying to find the portal within the shifting clouds. For an instant the mist cleared and there it was, a dark lozenge hanging in the air like a watercolor by Magritte.

"I have to get back to the party," said Ralph. He looked at his former mentor, stoop-shouldered, graying hair blown across his melancholy face, and unexpectedly felt a spasm of regret. "I—I guess I'm sorry, Professor Warnick. That we couldn't find any common ground.

That we couldn't reach an understanding."

"Let her come to me," Balthazar pleaded one last time. He opened his hands to Ralph beseechingly. "Please." In the blanched light he looked small and wizened, a goblin in black formal wear grasping for something that would forever be out of reach.

"She's not mine to give, Balthazar," said Ralph softly. He turned and strode toward the portal, raising his arms as though to embrace it. At the last moment, before stepping through, he looked back. "She's pledged to the god of illusion. And you know what *that's* like. She'll fuck him, and then she'll kill him. Or else he'll drive her mad, and she'll kill herself. There's nothing you or I can do about it. Except watch the fireworks."

He entered the portal, one hand lifted in farewell. His figure grew dark, as though obscured by smoke, and faded. The outlines of the portal remained. Balthazar Warnick stared at it, his mouth contorted with grief; then buried his face in his hands and began to weep.

12 ❧
You Set the Scene

Acherley Darnell's former chapel was freezing. The rows of clerestory windows were open and the night wind blew through, stirring the ivy clustered around the leaded glass. After a few minutes it started to rain. Sleety drops came splattering inside, and drifts of tattered oak leaves that made the stone floor slickly treacherous and gave the entire room a dank, graveyard smell. There was a hole in the elbow of my new peasant dress. When I poked my finger through, my arm felt like something dead, icy and goose pimpled. But I was too embarrassed to tell Axel Kern I was cold, and he appeared to be too stoned to notice.

"The amazing thing about Fellini, he's always doing the same thing, it's always the same thing."

Axel stood in front of the movie screen, swaying back and forth. His voice was at once drifty and impassioned, a tone I recognized from my own friends when they were totally wasted, but which I had never heard coming from an adult. On the screen behind him, the man pulling feathers from a pillow was now part of a daisy chain of dancers against a blinding white sky.

"*That's* what's so amazing about Fellini." Axel scowled at me, as though I had argued with him. "While everyone else is, like, *consumed* by creating something new. New new new *new*. Whereas *real* art lies in finding those things that are always the same. You know what I mean?"

"No." Discomfort made me bored and defiant. "I have no fucking idea."

"Yes, you do. You're a smart girl, Lit. And I don't just mean art—I'm talking about everything. History repeats itself; so does politics, and religion. So do individual human beings. It's all like *this*—"

Teetering slightly he drew a big, loopy circle in the air with his finger. It seemed to make him dizzy. "See? It all goes like that. The eternal return. In my end is my beginning. Over under sideways down. When will it end?"

He leaned back on his bare heels, almost fell but grabbed the edge of the table doing stand-in for an altar. "Oops. That's what people don't understand about my movies. They're all about tradition. The importance of tradition in the modern world. Future shock, past perfect. You know what I'm saying?"

I looked at him dubiously. "*Necromancer* was about tradition?"

"Of course. What'd you think?"

"I thought it was about that guy's head spinning around while snakes came out of his mouth."

"Oh, *please*. We're talking *subtext* here." Axel lifted a hand and made a fey gesture at the movie screen. As if by magic the black-and-white film clip ended; leader scrolled across the screen, and then an out-of-focus color shot of Richard Burton in a library. "Protest engenders revolution. Chaos presages rebirth. *The Exorcist* begets *The Heretic*. Precious Bane gives birth to—well, to your friend Duncan. *Nothing ever happens only once.*"

He let his arm drop, sighing. "*That's* what no one understands. All this talking about a new age, all this *stuff*—it's just part of the cycle. The world can only stagger on for so long before it has to shake everything off and start all over again. Like a snake"— He wriggled suggestively, the emerald kimono sliding off to reveal his bare shoulders, the skin smooth and dusky gold. —"the world has to shed its skin. Things have to change. Radically."

I was only half-listening. On the screen Richard Burton was shouting at another priest.

"You never told me there were mysteries!"

The second priest shook his head. *"My whole life has been about a mystery."*

"Lit?" Axel Kern put his hand atop my head. "Listen to me. Things are happening. Right here, right this minute. And you're a part of it—whether or not you believe me, whether or not you want to be."

Suddenly he no longer seemed stoned or drunk; suddenly he looked very sad. "Just as I am," he whispered.

He drew me close, not as a lover might but protectively. The way my father used to hold me sometimes, when I'd had a bad day, or he had. "Tell me what you've seen, Lit. Here in Kamensic since the leaves began to fall. Tell me what you saw."

I stared at my hands, the hole in my orange paisley peasant dress. I remembered that awful four A.M. vision of Axel Kern and the leaf-struck eyes of the hornéd man; the heat of Ralph Casson's hand on my breast and the way he had stroked my arm as I told him about what I'd glimpsed on the mountaintop. Not at all the way Axel held me now; not at all as though he wanted to save me from something.

"Weird stuff," I said at last, falteringly. "This—well, like some kind of human sacrifice, up there behind Bolerium—"

I pointed at the open windows, rain slanting behind them like bars of black metal. "And the other day, at Jamie Casson's place. I saw this man. But not a man—he had horns, he was moving in the woods—"

"The god," Axel said softly, nodding. "That's who you saw."

"But *what* god?"

"The first one. The oldest one, except for *Her*," he added, glancing at the open window as though he expected to see someone peering in at us. "The dying god, the hunter who becomes the hunted. The bull from the sea. The sacrificial lamb. Giles Goat-Boy. Drain this cup, drink his blood. Eat and be eaten."

I would have thought he was making fun of me, or just going off on another crazy riff—except that I *had* seen something, in the woods and on the mountain.

And what else could possibly explain it? Unless I was insane, or drunk, or someone had slipped acid into my orange juice that morning—none of which seemed totally out of the question. I looked at Axel warily.

"That's what it was? A—some kind of god?"

Axel nodded.

"But how?" I asked. *"Why?"*

"Why not? 'All men have need of the gods.'" He raised a finger, tapped his brow. "Homer. And when the half-gods go, the gods arrive. Actually, it's been happening for a long time—haven't *you* noticed, Lit?"

His gaze was piercing, almost angry. I stared uneasily at the window.

"No."

"Don't lie to me." His hands tightened around my arms, not painfully, but so that I could not edge away. "I know you have. Because I've seen you."

He tilted his head, unsmiling, put a finger beneath my chin and tipped my head back until I was staring at him.

And there, for just an instant, I saw him: the leaf-eyed figure moving through the trees, horns tangling with the branches above him and the smell of oak mast. But before I could react the vision was gone. Instead there was something else flickering there, a face pale as my own but frowning, with great bruised eyes and hair shorn so close it was like gazing at a skull, threads of light rippling up and down his arms from the Seeburg and cigarette smoke in my nostrils.

"What?" demanded Axel. He shook me gently, pulling me so close that his unshaven chin grazed my forehead and the panels of his kimono opened about my face. "What do you see? Tell me . . ."

I blinked, dizzy; then Jamie Casson's image was gone as well. I could feel my heart racing, but before Axel Kern could notice I edged away from him—carefully, pretending interest in the ivy twining down the walls.

"It's—it's gone," I murmured. I reached to touch the underside of one heart-shaped leaf. "But it was the same as what I saw before. The hornéd man. The thing in the woods . . ."

Suddenly I was rent by such horrible yearning that tears sprang to my eyes. I gasped—and everything tumbled together inside me, the feeling I had when I'd met Jamie Casson, the memory of a song played on a flute and the haunted rush of wind in the leaves, the shadow of the doomed stag upon a hilltop and a boy silhouetted on a jukebox: all of it somehow was the same thing, and if I could only find the pattern between it all, trace the lines that ran like veins within all those shadows—then I would be free of them. Then I could escape.

But not yet. Axel towered beside me. His hand covered mine, moved it from the ivy until my palm lay upon his breast. Beneath his green kimono he was naked; my fingers tangled in the thick hair on his chest and the fabric of my dress bunched up around my thighs. He leaned forward, raising his arms until they rested against the wall, the heavy drape of his kimono forming a canopy so that I was surrounded by him. Dim light filtered through the green silk; flaws in the cloth shone like stars. He put one hand on the back of my neck and thrust my head forward against his breast, pushed me until my mouth found his nipple. My lips closed around it and he moaned as I kissed him, ran my tongue over his nipple until it stiffened, became a small swollen seed in my mouth. My cheek rubbed against the hair of his chest, damp now and hot as though sun-warmed. There was a smell of musk and balsam, the acrid tang of salt upon my tongue. When I drew my hand across his breast I could feel the steady thump of his heart, like another hand beating beneath mine. I started to move, reaching to embrace him and pulling up my dress; when he murmured, *"No,"* and drew away from me.

"What?" I asked hoarsely, half-blinded by the sudden surge of light as he pulled his kimono back around him. "What is it?"

Axel looked at me muzzily, as though uncertain where I'd come from. The rapt intensity that had candled his eyes a moment before was gone. Rain silvered his gray-streaked hair, and his cheeks looked raw and red from the cold. Suddenly he just seemed stoned, a little tired, the lines around his eyes more pronounced when he smiled.

"Later." He plucked a sprig of ivy from the wall and tucked it into my hair. Behind him dancing figures stretched across the movie screen, the screen itself rippling as the wind nudged it. "It's cold in here . . ."

He turned and began to walk a bit unsteadily, holding on to one of the pews for balance. I stared after him, my bewilderment giving way to anger.

"Tell me!" I demanded. I ran after him, grabbed his wrist and tugged it imploringly. "Axel, please—tell me, you said it was real, tell me what it is!"

He stopped and drew a hand across his eyes. Above us the hanging lanterns swung slightly back and forth. "God, I'm tired. But—yes, it was real. It *is* real. But it's probably impossible to explain, even—even to you."

He leaned forward to stroke my cheek, his hand cold and smelling of some sweet resin. "Because the hardest thing to understand is that nothing ever really changes, Lit. Nothing really dies. Not even very old things; not even gods. They flicker in and out of view, that's all"— he gestured at the screen above us, then at the simple chapel altar. —"they go underground and they seem to die but they only sleep, they gather strength until finally they're reborn. Because gods have seasons, too, time moves differently for them, it might take a hundred years or a thousand, but then their seasons come round again and they always return, they always return . . ."

He began to chant, so softly I had to strain to hear him.

> "We will try for the best.
> And the more we try, the more we will spoil,
> we will complicate matters till we find ourselves
> in utter confusion. And then we will stop.
> It will be the hour for the gods to work.

The gods always come.
Some they will save,
others they will lift forcibly, abruptly
. . . and when they bring some order they will retire.
And we will start over again."

He fell silent. There was no sound save the rain tapping against the windows and the midnight hum of the film projector, and faintest of all an echoing reverberation of music through the stone walls. Beside me Axel Kern stood deathly still, as though listening for a reply. For a long time I said nothing. Then,

"If that *was* a god," I said, "if it *was* some kind of—thing—what is it doing here? In Kamensic? Why isn't it in Greece or someplace like that?"

"Because this is where he will be born, this time. This is where his children live. It is his sanctuary. Not the only one, but a place where his worship is strong."

I looked incredulous. "Kamensic Village?"

"Why not? This is where the stories come from, Lit. Come on—haven't you ever noticed anything strange about this place?"

"Yeah." I shrugged. "I guess so. But normal people live here. My *parents* live here. They have jobs. I go to school. It's not like they're out performing human sacrifices or something."

Axel raised an eyebrow. "Just how normal do you think Kamensic is, Lit? How normal do you think I am?"

He peered down, brushing the hair from my forehead and tracing a circle there. "Walking in the woods and seeing things like you saw, walking into this house and talking to people like Precious Bane and Ralph Casson and me—

"How normal do you think *you* are, Lit Moylan?"

I pulled away. "Look, I don't care! I *hate* Kamensic, I can't wait to get the fuck out of here, I *hate* it—"

"You shouldn't. It protects you, Lit. Just like it protects all of us . . ."

He pulled the kimono tighter about him and said, "Didn't you ever wonder about things like that, Lit? Synchronicities? Like sometimes you dream about something and then it happens? Like when you're thinking about an old song, a song you haven't heard in years, and then you're in the car and suddenly it comes on the radio?"

"Well, sure. I mean, yeah, that happens all the time. To me."

Axel nodded solemnly. "Me too." He began to sing in a low voice, as though trying to remember the words.

> *"There is a place called Nysa,*
> *a high mountain,*
> *surrounded by woods . . ."*

He started to pace across the room, head cocked and hands held out from his sides. It was like some clumsily executed dance, and I felt embarrassed watching it, embarrassed to be here at all. Axel was drunk, or worse; the spliced-together bits of films were just another fractured indulgence. Faded figures moved across the screen; there were a few black frames, and then a burning pyre filled the white square. Above it a laughing woman was suspended on a rack, while another woman in modern dress looked on, her expression more bemused than horrified. I could hear the hum of film scrolling through the projector, the slap of Axel's bare feet upon the stone floor.

"And they will cut you up
into three parts,
And ever since then,
every three years,
men will offer you
perfect hecatombs."

At the front of the room Axel stopped. He lifted his head, shadows spilling upon him so that his face looked ravaged, no longer the golden death mask but the split skull beneath. His voice sounded cracked and hoarse.

"We, the poets,
begin
and end our singing
through You—
it is impossible without You,
without our memory of You
we cannot voice our sacred song,
and Your children, the poets, perish."

He fell silent. The screen behind him went white, covered with balloons of magnified dust. From the back of the chapel came the insistent flapping of loose film on the projector.

"Don't move a muscle," commanded Axel. His head snapped forward and he raised his arm dramatically, like the Ghost of Christmas Yet to Come.

"Page!" he bellowed. His eyes narrowed as he reached into a hidden pocket of his kimono, withdrew a box of Sobranies and lit one, frowning. All of a sudden he looked like the imperious director who had punched out a *Time* magazine photographer on the set of *You Come, Too*. "Get the fucking reel, Page!"

From behind the second-to-last pew a head popped up.

"Got it, got it—" the man yelled in a raspy Bronx accent. "I'm gettin' it for chrissakes, keep your panties on . . ."

He clambered over the pew, heading for the alcove where the projector was, its spool of film spinning maniacally. He wore black jeans and a ratty black-and-white striped sailor shirt. From behind he could have been one of my friends, rangy and stoop-shouldered.

But when he reached the projector light splashed across his face and I recognized him. The same man I had seen at Axel Kern's holiday party when I was twelve, filming an orgy; the same man who had looked at me then, perplexed, and said *You're early*. Thirtyish, with thinning black hair and a swarthily handsome face, broad cheekbones scarred by acne and a thin remorseless mouth: Page Franchini. Sometime NYU film student, he was Axel's chief cameraman and general Nursery flunky. He'd followed Axel to Hollywood but had never been able to find work there—he wasn't union, he wasn't reliable, he wasn't even a very good cameraman. I knew him from "Cities of Night" and also from one of his solo efforts, an "experimental" film called *Gravity Train* which was notorious for a thirty-four minute blow-job sequence involving Precious Bane and a man dressed as an Apollo astronaut.

"Well. I'll see you later, Lit—"

I turned as Axel smiled at me absently. He lifted his hand in farewell, turned and strode toward the door at the front of the chapel. I watched in disbelief as he left, not even bothering to close the door behind him.

"Hey, you." It was a minute before I realized Page Franchini was yelling at me. "Sweetheart, jailbait, whoever you are—c'mere and give me a hand, huh?"

I swore beneath my breath, stared resentfully at the man fiddling with the projector. He looked up and glared, a cigarette hanging from his mouth. "Come on! I'm not gonna tell your parents you're making out with their friends—"

"Asshole," I muttered, but I walked over. The projector was sitting on an upended stereo speaker, surrounded by silver film canisters and cigarette butts and a battered paperback copy of *Sanctuary*.

"Okay, you hold this piece of leader here, it's torn, see, just hold it so I can get the rest of this crap where it belongs—"

He shoved a ragged tail of loose film at me, yanked the reel from the projector and slid it into a can. Then he took the leader, threading it between his fingers as he held it up to the light.

"It's shot," he said regretfully. "Ruined. I duped that for him ten years ago. *Juliet of the Spirits*. He wanted a few of the frames for *Saragossa*. That scene when they burn the girl at the stake? There's, like, six frames of Giulietta Masina in there, totally subliminal, I guess it's supposed to secretly make you think Axel is Fellini." He dragged at his cigarette, exhaled and rolled his eyes. "Sure, Axel."

I picked up one of the opened cans, breathed in the sweetish scent of new film stock. When I looked up, Page was watching me, brow furrowed.

"I remember you," he said at last. "That party. You were the little girl in the black velvet dress. I was tripping my tits off, I thought you were a hallucination."

"Maybe I was."

"Ha ha. No, it's crazy, I thought you were—" He stopped. "Well, never mind what I thought. What are you, sixteen?"

"Seventeen. I'll be eighteen next March."

He dropped his cigarette on the floor and ground it out. "I was your age when I met Axel. First time a guy ever fucked me. Why don't you be a good kid and go on home, huh?" He reached over and roughly took the film can from my hands. "It just gets old after a while, you know?"

I watched as he began sorting through a box alongside the projector. I felt defensive of Axel, and humiliated that this guy had seen us together. I tried to come up with some retort, finally said, "He's my godfather."

"Always a godfather, never a god."

"He's just like a really good friend—"

"Oh, please, spare me." Page put the last of the film cans into the carton, straightened and shook his head. "Look, I don't know who you are and I really don't give a flying fuck what you do, sweetheart. But if you'd seen as many pretty little girls as I have, lying on the floor with a spike in their arm or drinking so much they walk out a sixth-floor window—"

He laughed bitterly. "Well, you'd turn right around and go on home to momma."

"Oh, yeah? Then what are *you* doing here?"

"Me? I'm part of the floor show, sweetheart. I couldn't leave if I wanted to. He'd kill me." He reached out, took my chin between two fingers and looked straight into my face. I stared defiantly back at him. "But maybe you're different."

He gazed at me, then laughed. "Maybe you're really a tough cookie, huh? *'Voutes etes vraiment une déguelasse.'*"

"What does that mean?"

"Forget it." He hefted the box of film and cocked a thumb at the back of the chapel. "That your boyfriend?"

I turned to see Hillary standing in the doorway, hands

in his pockets and looking hangdog. When he saw me his face lit up.

"Lit!"

I walked over to him. "Hey, where'd you go?"

"Me? You were the one who—"

"Later, kiddies," said Page Franchini as he edged past with the film carton on his shoulder.

"I'm sorry." Hillary sighed and put his arm around me. "Look, you want to go home? This is all kind of bringing me down. I'll drive you back—"

"No. I—I'm supposed to go home with my parents," I lied.

"Really?" As we went into the corridor Hillary shook his head. "But they already left. I mean, I think they left, it looked like your car. That's why I was so bummed, I thought you'd gone without me . . ."

"Oh." There was an awful hollow feeling in my stomach, and I stammered, "Are—are you sure it was my parents?"

"Well, no, I'm not positive. But—yeah, it looked like Unk. Why?"

"Nothing. I just—well, they didn't tell me, that's all."

"So come on, then. I'll drive you back."

I pulled away from him. "No. I don't want to go. I'm just surprised."

"Probably they couldn't find you." Hillary grinned, pushing the long hair from his face. "I know I couldn't. Well, okay, if you're staying, I will, too. Listen, Ali and that guy Jamie said they were going upstairs to find Dunc, he had some hash or something—"

He pointed and I looked down the hallway, frowning. "This isn't how I came in."

"Yeah, well, this is how we're going out. This way . . ."

He took my hand and we walked down the passage, more brightly lit than the corridor where I'd seen Ralph Casson and Balthazar Warnick. A few people floated by us, giggling blondes and middle-aged couples in formal wear, a very drunken Margot Steiner. When we passed a tall, narrow window I stopped and looked out.

Below stretched the downward slope of Muscanth Mountain, and the black reflection of the lake. Rain gave everything a creepy, urban sheen; made the bare trees look sleek and metallic and the overgrown lawn brittle, as though encased in ice. I could just make out the road snaking down to the village, the rows of parked cars like overlapping scales on a butterfly's wing.

"Is Jamie done parking?" I asked.

"I think so. He was only supposed to do it till nine or nine thirty."

"What time is it now?"

"Not that late," shrugged Hillary. "After midnight."

"Midnight! It *can't* be after midnight—"

"Time flies when you're having fun. Come on, Cinderella . . ."

We slipped into a stairwell, climbed until we came out onto a wide landing where a chandelier made of deer antlers hung from the ceiling, a hideous thing webbed with dust and dead moths. Only one of the bulbs was working; it made our shadows look shrunken, and did little to dispel my unease when something scuttled across the uneven wood floor.

"Ugh! What was that?"

Hillary laughed. "Wait'll you see what Kern gave Jamie as a tip. It's in here, with the rest of the zoo—"

I followed him across the landing. This part of Bolerium looked as though it had gone a very long time without visitors. Dead leaves covered the floor, and acorns. A single window had cracked panes taped over with cardboard, and beneath it a window seat was covered with wet, moldering newspapers. Music pounded from behind a closed door, a reassuring wail of guitars and feedback. Hillary pushed the door open and we entered.

"Greetings, my children," he announced. "It's showtime."

We were in a large room, lit only by an ultraviolet bulb screwed into an ornate fixture in the center of the ceiling, a plaster medallion shaped like a flower. There was a mattress on the floor, covered with pillows and an India-print spread, and a circle of small rocks that glowed with spectral brilliance in the black light: acid green, cyanic blue, sickly chartreuse. A stereo was shoved into one corner, a cheap Kenmore lift'n'play model with a bunch of albums queued above the turntable.

"Hey . . ." someone said thickly.

One of the pillows moved: Ali. Next to her Jamie Casson sat cross-legged, still in his uniform of tuxedo pants and vest. The sleeves of his white dress shirt were rolled, the shirt unbuttoned so I could see his pale chest, hairless, his skin tinted ghastly blue by the light. His head was tilted back and his eyes closed; his features disquieting, almost disturbing, in repose. There was something poisonous about him: if you cut him his blood would burn you. More acorns and dead leaves were strewn across the floor, drifting atop album covers and soiled clothing.

"Oh, very nice," said Hillary. He kicked his way through a heap of flannel shirts and bent to retrieve a small envelope folded from a magazine page. He smoothed it open, licked it tentatively, and scowled.

"God damn it." He looked at Jamie, then tossed the empty packet aside. The floor was covered with them, like spent matchbooks among the acorns. I stooped to examine one of the envelopes, and saw then that they weren't acorns at all. They were the seed-heads of poppies. Scores of them; hundreds. Not the little dried husks nodding in Kamensic's gardens, but pods the size of small plums, their skin smooth and slightly moist. I held one up, squinting in the weird blue light, and scored the rounded surface with my fingernail. Thick liquid oozed out.

"Fuckin' A," whispered Hillary. He looked at me and shook his head helplessly. "They're gone."

I hurried to the mattress, bent until my face was inches from Ali's. Her breath touched my cheek, cool, scented with lactose and wintergreen. The blue light gave her skin a niveous gleam, as though it had been thickly powdered. Sweat pearled in indigo beads upon her upper lip.

"Ali," I whispered, fighting panic. "Ali, can you hear me?"

Without warning her hand shot up, closed around my jaw and pulled me down. She kissed me, her mouth cold and her tongue tasting of sugar; but when her eyes opened they were bright and feverishly excited.

"Lit," she said hoarsely, and grinned. "Where'd you go?"

"Christ! You scared me! I was downstairs, remember? Where'd *you* go?"

"Here." She sat up groggily, reached to tug at Jamie's short hair. "Jame. Company."

"Leave him." Hillary sank onto the blanket. "Listen to me, Ali—"

Ali smiled. "Fuck off, Hillary. Chipping, I was just popping—"

She tapped the inside of his elbow. Hillary slapped her hand away.

"God damn it. God damn it, Ali—"

"Look who's talking." She swept one arm lazily across the floor, brought up a handful of dried petals and tossed them into his face. "Pussy."

"Ali. Please—" Hillary grabbed her hand and Ali gazed back at him, eyes glittering. His cheeks flushed; he blinked, holding back tears, and turned to the boy on the mattress beside her. "Jamie, I'll fucking kill you . . ."

"Leave her alone." Jamie's voice rose ghostly from the mattress. He pushed himself up, his eyes gone to black and his lips dry and cracked. "Hillary, man. Leave her alone, huh?" When he stood petals fluttered around him. He took a few uneasy steps to the far side of the room, shuddered and for the first time noticed me. "Lit. How's it goin'?"

"Great. Oh, I'm just great."

Ali watched me, still smiling; then reached to curl a tendril of my hair around one finger. The album ended. In the brief silence before the next record dropped I could hear the staccato chirp of crickets somewhere in the room. There was a sudden gust of sound from the party below, laughter and the thump of a bass; then the album fell and music started once more.

"Look at you, Lit." Ali reached for a cigarette, struck a match against the floor. "Do you eat men with your new red hair?" She reached forward to link her hands around my waist. Between us rose a thin plume of smoke. "Beware, beware."

Ali flopped back onto the mattress. Hillary stood watching us, and I couldn't tell if he was still enraged, or just depressed. Beneath the black light bulb Jamie swayed and stared at his hands.

"Show her Camille. That's Jamie's sun scorpion," Ali explained. "Axel gave it to him."

"I thought it was a spider," said Hillary.

"It is." Jamie stumbled to the wall, bent and picked up a glass globe the size of a soccer ball. He turned and held it out to me. "Sun spider, sun scorpion they sometimes call it. He brought it back from Oaxaca."

I peered inside. Upon a bed of sand and small stones rested a creature the length of my hand, chocolate brown and covered with short stiff hairs, with long front legs that ended in pincers. It had myriad black eyes, clustered like currants upon its head. Suddenly it leaped in my direction, bashing itself against the side of the globe.

"Jesus!"

"Calm down. It's not poisonous—" Jamie pointed at the spider, now tensed into a brown hairy fist. "She hunts things and crushes 'em with her jaws. See? No poison."

I made a face. "Next time get a pony."

"Wait! Come here—"

He moved until he stood directly beneath the overhead bulb, angling the globe so that it was bathed in ultraviolet. "Check this out."

I looked cautiously. The sun spider had hunkered down with pincers raised. Beneath it the stones were nearly invisible in the black light. But like magic, as Jamie tilted its prison the ghostly image of a purple death's head appeared on the spider's carapaced back. I whistled.

"Whoa! That's amazing—"

Jamie grinned. "Cool, huh? Axel showed it to me. It only appears under UV light. Like certain kinds of rocks and stuff."

"Like all of this." Ali rolled onto her stomach and gestured at the dingy room. "Like this whole place.

Kamensic. Everything . . . it only comes out at night. You know. It moves when you're not looking. It's like a fucking ghost town. Wanna know what *I* think?"

"No," Hillary blurted. "You're too fucked up to think anything—"

"Yes," said Jamie. "Tell me."

"I think the real town is down there under the lake," Ali said. "I think everyone is there. When they moved the houses and dammed the river and made the reservoir . . . I think all the real people went under there. I think all the real people were drowned."

Hillary rolled his eyes and I snorted. Only Jamie nodded, walking with precise stoned steps to where Ali lay. He placed the globe on the floor and knelt beside her. "Yeah?" he said. "Then who are we?"

"Ghosts. We're all ghosts. Of course."

"Don't be a jerk, Ali." Hillary looked so furious I was afraid he might hit her. The black light made him look like some weird statue, Avenging Spirit or The Spurned Lover or something even worse. "Why are you even saying that?"

But Ali and Jamie were out of it. Jamie was stroking her back, not with anything like desire but absently, the way you stroke a cat. And Ali was utterly heedless of him; her eyes were dark bruises in a face the color of twilight, her black hair bleeding into the shadows. Wasted as she was, I knew by her expression that she was on a roll: the Ali of all those slumber parties where I would be too scared to fall asleep, the Ali who knew stories about girls named Topaz and Juniper and Sweet Lavender: girls who all disappeared before dawn, stories that all ended with a scream.

"This is the story of Giulietta," she said, raising herself

so that she stared straight out at the closed door, her eyes wide and black. "She was a girl a long time ago in Italy, in a small town in the mountains. After the Black Plague, during the Insurrection—"

"The Inquisition," hissed Hillary. I put my hand on his arm to silence him.

"—during the witch trials. She was not the most beautiful girl in the village, but she had many lovers, though she did not become pregnant, or marry any of them. And because of this the villagers said she was *una strega*: a witch. And they talked about her, and made accusations, until finally the priests came from the cities, the investigators—the inquisitors—and they questioned her.

"She was not a witch, of course. There *were* no witches. There were only the people who worshipped the old gods, and the priests hated them and killed them, and they called their gods devils. If they found out you were one of them, you would be brought to trial, and if you did not renounce your gods then the priests would burn you. But Giulietta would not renounce the gods, because she was a chosen one. She had her mortal lovers, but she was also the beloved of the god of the mountain. And she was also the lover of a priest—"

"A *priest*?" interrupted Jamie.

Ali nodded. "Sure. Back then priests all had lovers. Some of them had *wives*. He was a man from the village who had gone to Rome to study, and remained there as a librarian. He was not an inquisitor but a scholar; but when the complaints reached the Holy Office and they sent their interrogators to the village, this man was asked to accompany them and to aid them in their work, since he knew the villagers and the surrounding countryside.

"He had not seen Giulietta for several months, and

while they were in the village preparing for their task he visited her and tried to warn her. He went to her at night, and begged her to recant.

"'But I have done nothing wrong,' she said.

"'I know that,' said her lover. Though he did not quite believe her: he was a priest, after all—and even though he loved her, he couldn't stop believing that she was wrong—but still he wanted to save her.

"'Recant and marry me,' he begged her.

"'Will you give up your god?' she asked.

"He said no. But he loved her—she knew that—and she loved him. So she stayed with him that night, and the next morning after he left the inquisitors came, and took her. They questioned her but she would not admit to having done wrong: she *had* done no wrong. But she would marry no one and none of her lovers would stand up for her.

"'Where is your god now?' asked the priests; but Giulietta said nothing except 'He will come. He will come.'

"And all the while her lover was there in the same room with her, writing it all down . . .

"They found her guilty. They told her she would only be imprisoned, they told her lover the same thing. But they lied. The next day they took her to a field outside the village and they burned her alive. Her lover went mad: the other priests struck him on the head with stones, to make him unconscious, and so that he wouldn't bring shame on them by killing himself."

"What about the god?" I broke in. I had crept forward until I was sitting on the floor beside the mattress. My heart was pounding, just as it always had during one of Ali's stories—but there was something worse about this one, something about it that made me feel nauseous and dizzy and revolted.

I wasn't going to tell Ali any of that, though; so I only repeated my question.

"Oh, he came." Ali was sitting up now on her knees, hands flat upon her thighs so that she looked like a sphinx. "After they left the field, after they all went home, he came . . .

"Her lover woke—they had brought him to the back room of the village church—and that evening as the sun was setting he returned to the field. There he found the ruins of the fire, and what remained of his beloved. They had not even bothered to take her remains for burial, when they learned of her execution not even her parents or her brother or any of the other men of the village had come to claim her. Only the priest was there, alone. He found her bones in the embers, bones and grease, that was all that remained of her. And he *did* go mad, then—

"And that was when the god came.

"He thought it was the Devil, because of his horns. He walked down from the mountain, through the trees at the edge of the field, and when he got to where the priest lay upon the ground the Devil spoke to him.

"He said, 'Go to the top of the mountain and remain there; otherwise you will die.'

"And the priest said, 'Without her I want to die.'

"But the Devil shook his head and said, 'No.' He bent and picked up a fragment of her rib, and in his hands it became white and not black, and when he raised it to his lips it was no longer a bone but a bone flute. 'Because of you my beloved Giulietta is dead,' he said to the priest. 'It will be your punishment to live with that always. And because you have named me your enemy and are among those who seek to destroy me, you yourself will never die; but it will be no joy to you but torment everlasting.'

"And then the Devil began to play upon his flute. And the song that he played was so full of grief that the mountain wept, and as it wept it became a torrent, and the tears of the Devil and the tears of the mountain swept down and became a flood that overtook the village. And it was drowned, and all who lived there died; all except for the priest who had been Giulietta's lover.

"When the waters receded, people from the towns and neighboring farms came. Where the village had been they found a lake of black water that seemed to glow blue-black from somewhere deep within its depths, and which reflected the face of the mountain that rose above it. And it was upon the mountaintop that they found the priest who had betrayed Giulietta and brought about the destruction of the town. He had been bound with strands of ivy to a tree there; it had kept him from escaping, it had kept him alive. When they freed him he said not a word but returned to the city and his masters there.

"The village itself remained within the lake. Over the centuries people would try to dive and bring up the treasures that were rumored to be there, but no one ever succeeded. The lake was cursed. No one who ever went beneath its surface returned. Sometimes late at night, people in the neighboring countryside say that they can hear the sound of bells ringing, a tocsin warning the villagers of the flood that would engulf them; but other people who have heard it say that it is the sound of a bone flute."

All this time the album had been playing, a steady sonic tide of feedback and guitars. Now, as though on cue, it ended. The room was silent except for the metallic scrape of crickets and the ceaseless background din of the party roaring on behind Bolerium's walls. Ali bowed her head, smiling slightly, like a child waiting to be rewarded. Beside her Jamie lay on his back, one hand across his eyes and the other on Ali's shoulder. I couldn't tell if he had nodded out or was still listening. His mouth was parted in a half-smile, his chest moving slowly up and down as he breathed.

"Nice, Ali," Hillary sneered. He still stood a little apart from the rest of us, but despite his tone he seemed to have relaxed somewhat; at least he no longer looked as though he intended to strangle Jamie. "What, you get that from *Night Gallery?*"

Ali just smiled and shook her head. I took a deep breath, trying to make myself look and sound less frightened than I was. "Ali. Where did you hear that?"

"Axel told me."

"When?"

"I don't know. I mean, I can't remember—a long time ago, maybe?"

Like someone roused from deep slumber Jamie suddenly groaned and turned, so that he was almost straddling Ali. "Nice bedtime story. I told you, this place is fucking weird. The whole town is nuts. Your buddy Kern is running around giving out shit like it's candy—not that I'm complaining, don't get me wrong—"

"Forget it," Hillary said. "God, I can't take this. I'm not going to stand here and watch this . . ."

He stooped and ran his hand across the floor, stood and opened his palm to display broken poppy calyxes, the cracked plastic casing of a hypodermic needle. He looked at me, his face rigid. "Lit. I gotta go. I—"

He turned, throwing the needle and crushed seed-heads onto the mattress. Ali squealed, Jamie swore and ducked. A moment later the door slammed.

"What's his fucking problem?" Jamie sat up, fumbling with the bedspread until he found the needle; then leaned over and picked up an ashtray filled with spent matches and a blackened spoon. "C'mon, Lit . . ."

I shook my head. Ali peeked up at me, brow furrowed. "You do opium, Lit. All that stuff. It's the same thing."

I thought of smoking opium in Ali's room, the little smoldering bit of resin impaled on a needle with a glass cupped over it to capture the smoke; then looked down at Jamie carefully opening one of the little envelopes. It was empty. He licked the paper and tossed it aside, probed under the mattress and withdrew another packet.

"No," I said. "I–I'm going to go talk to Hillary."

Ali nodded. "Tell him not to be pissed off, okay?"

"Yeah," said Jamie. "Don't go away mad. Just go away."

Outside the hall was empty. "Hillary?" I called softly, then louder. "Hillary—"

There was no sign of him. I retraced our steps, returning to peer down the narrow stairwell, its risers filthy with dead leaves and twigs. It was too dark to see anything there, and behind me only a thin glowing band of ultraviolet showed where I'd left Ali and Jamie. Rain beat relentlessly at the eaves, a moth battered at a windowpane. From downstairs echoed the faint wail of "Stairway to Heaven."

Well, Hillary *hated* that: he wouldn't have gone that way. I went back across the landing, shivering, my stomach knotted.

"Hillary?"

The hall continued, up a few rickety steps that threatened to give way when I walked on them. It smelled dank. Not the closed-up, mildewy odor of an old house, but wet and somehow alive, the scent of a marsh or rotting stump. To my left was an exterior wall, crosshatched with small windows through which lavender-tinged light seeped into the corridor. To my right was the other wall, barren of anything—no doors, no lights, no paintings. I walked very slowly, scuffing the toe of my boot on the floor to make sure I wouldn't trip on a sudden loose board or step. After a minute or two I reached to touch the outer wall, for balance; and was surprised to feel not paneling or plaster but stone. It was cold and damp, the surface rough. When I flattened my palm against it I could feel lichen, so brittle it crumbled at my touch.

"Damn it, Hillary, where'd you go?"

My voice echoed back at me, too high and shaky to fool anyone into thinking I wasn't scared. The passage took a dogleg to the right. I turned the corner, saw a window that took up most of the outer wall, and through this I could glimpse what seemed to be a dormer, thrusting outward high above the hillside. Sure enough, when I passed the window I found a door, the first I'd seen since leaving Ali and Jamie Casson. The corridor wound on. Chunks of stone littered the floor, and shards of broken glass. The air above me was crisscrossed with rafters formed of immense logs. Even in the darkness I could see pale hanks of cobwebs strung between them, patterned with the ghostly remains of insects. Rain lashed the dormer windows, finding its way through cracks to spatter me. Still I stubbornly kept on, head bowed against the rain; when behind me echoed a deafening crash.

"Oh—!"

I shrieked and backed up against the inner wall. On the

floor beneath the window lay a twisted piece of wreckage. It stirred wildly in the wind, and at first I thought it was alive, struggling amidst the glitter of rain and broken glass. But then I saw it was a branch, ten or twelve feet long, rain-blackened and so thick with lichen it resembled a piece of coral dredged up from the sea. I stared at it, then stood on tiptoe to peer through the shattered dormer.

There were no trees. Far, far below, Bolerium's ragged lawns gave way to the black swathe of old-growth forest. Oaks and hemlocks tossed angrily in the wind, and skeins of dead leaves like a net thrown up against the sky.

But between here and the first trunks rearing up from the mountainside was a good quarter-mile. There was no way any branch could be hurled such a distance, not with enough force to reach Bolerium's upper stories. I stepped back and nudged the tree-limb with my boot. A slab of bark fell to the floor, revealing a soft white pith like marrow. I stooped to examine it more closely when the dormer above me shook. There was a dull roar, a violet flash that left skeletal afterimages burning in the air around me. Something bit at my neck. I clapped my hand there, saw my fingers gloved in red. Glass and wood flew everywhere; acorns rattled down like hail. The window's lead muntins buckled as a massive branch ripped through them. With a cry I fled, stumbling blindly until I found the door just past the window—an arched wooden door made from a single board, furrowed with dry-rot and scabs of grayish moss.

But there was no knob, no handle; nothing that would serve as a means of opening it. Behind me echoed the steady crash of glass, and worse. When I glanced back, I saw tree-limbs thrusting through the ruined dormer. The corridor was impassable, a black thicket of glass and broken tree-limbs; but when I looked desperately in the other direction I saw only darkness, with not even a seam of light to show where I might escape. The wind rose to a howl, the wall of tree-limbs shook as though something moved within them—

And then it seemed that something *did* move there. Something black, its head crowned by spars of lightning, its forelimbs jagged as the dead branches. I could hear it breathing and measure its approach by the sound of glass and wood splintering beneath its tread. Frantically I pounded at the door, kicked and pushed until with a grinding sound it gave way. An explosion of rotten wood, and there was a hole big enough for me to pass through. I forced my way in, the splintered panels scraping my arms. Cold air rushed by, the floor felt rough but I saw nothing save the pall of dust swirling around me. Only when I straightened, wiping grit from my eyes and coughing, did I see where I was.

"Jesus . . ."

I stood upon a vast plain, a dead white sky burning overhead and stands of birches scattered everywhere like standing stones. Wind beat relentlessly against me, a wind that had beaten down the trees as well—they all grew leaning in the same direction, branches rippling as though trapped in a dark current. Tiny midges swarmed everywhere, evil things with rust-colored wings and red eyes. I slapped at them but it did no good. They bit at my flesh and clustered so persistently around my face that I began to run, half-crazed.

"Get away, get *away*!" I could scarcely hear my own voice for the wind. I stumbled on, my boots crushing the undergrowth; then stepped into a hole and fell, wrenching my ankle. "*Ow—*"

Underfoot was a springy mat of moss and some coarse shrubby plant, clouds of lichen and small gray stones. The midges were even worse down here, but I refused to get up. I was bleeding from scores of tiny cuts, my dress torn and blotched with dirt. I felt numb, no longer frightened but completely blank, as though I'd just come out of some beer-stoked blackout. I lay there as the midges crawled across my hands, watching as crimson beads welled up behind them and the insects lifted back into the air. The wind wailed, my fingers grew white with cold. I knew I could freeze to death but I didn't care. I buried my face in my arms and cried, wishing I were home in bed; wishing I were asleep, or dead: anything but here.

I must have fallen asleep then, and dreamed. Not a dream of home, or even of Bolerium's damned chambers, but a dream in which the wind became the sound of my own name.

"Lit . . . Lit . . . Lit . . ."

I was dimly aware of the cold and thorny underbrush, the ripple of insects across my face. But gradually the voice became as irrevocable as those other things, persistent as water falling on my face. I stirred, blinking painfully. Dried blood adhered to my eyelids; when I licked my lips they felt cracked and raw.

"Lit."

I lifted my head. Overhead the sky had gone from deathly white to a violet dark and rich as claret. The horizon was slashed with red so brilliant I had to shade my eyes. It took me a full minute to make out anything in the unearthly light.

"Lit . . ."

A figure was moving across the plain. I whimpered,

thinking of shadows taking shape within fallen trees; but as the figure drew nearer I saw that it was not some awful spectre but a man in an ultramarine suit jacket, his long hair a bright corona around his face. He had his hands in his pockets, and walked matter-of-factly to where I had fallen, as though this were the most normal thing in the world.

"Hey," he said, and stopped. For a moment he stood looking down at me, face glowing in the carnival light. His expression was tender, tinged with what might have been regret or just exhaustion. A halo of midges formed around his face. He waved his hand absently; the insects flashed bright as embers, then in a burst of white ash disappeared. "Are you all right, Lit?"

He crouched in front of me, smoothing the hair from my face, ran a finger along my eyelid and winced. "You're hurt," he said. "Come on—"

I held my breath, fighting tears; then nodded and let him help me to my feet. My fingers and toes throbbed, but Ralph seemed immune to the cold. He shrugged out of his jacket and I put it on, its warmth enveloping me as though it had been a down parka.

"B-b-b-but you'll f-f-freeze," I protested.

Ralph laughed. "Neither rain nor snow nor hellfire can touch me, kiddo." He lay one hand against my cheek, and yes, it was warm—not merely warm but *hot*.

"H-h-how—"

"Something I learned at college. Feel better? Yeah? Think you can walk? I want to show you something . . ."

We walked, me huddled in his jacket, Ralph with one arm slung over my shoulder. Reindeer moss crackled beneath our feet, and while the midges buzzed everywhere, they now stayed away from us.

"Where is this place?" I asked when several minutes had passed.

"The Land of the Dead." Ralph's voice was flat, his arm around me the only comforting thing in that vastness. "The charred forest. The taiga—"

He extended his free arm, indicating the endless steppe, bowed birch trees like the ribs of fallen giants and lichen covering the earth like mist. The wind was a wall crashing down; the sunset the world behind the wall, nightmarish yet inescapable. There were no stars, no moon. A few yards in front of us stood a single large birch tree, its bark tinged pink from the sunset, its leaves blade-shaped and yellow as buttercups. Behind it the sky glowed like a furnace, black edged with purple, the horizon riven with crimson and a single brilliant ribbon of gold that spewed from the earth like a flame. It was so beautiful it made me shiver; but it was a beauty composed mostly of terror. I could imagine no people living there, nor even animals; nothing save those bloodthirsty midges.

"Oh, but people *do* live here, Lit," Ralph said, in the same soft, vague tone he had used before, as though talking in his sleep. He let his arm drop from me, bent, and began to dig in the ground. I crouched beside him, watching. The earth was hard but when he broke through the surface it became friable, falling in small chunks from his hand. He continued to dig, pausing now and then to examine what he found; finally held up a small piece of reddish rock.

"Ochre." He rubbed the stone between his fingers and it crumbled, staining his hands. "'*Farben auch, den Leib zu malen, steckt ihm in die Hand, dass er rötlich möge strahlen in der Seelen Land.*'"

He turned. With the chunk of rock he drew upon my forehead and upon each of my cheeks; then carefully smoothed the ochre across my skin. "That's from Schiller. 'Put ye colors into his hand, that he may paint his body so he will shine redly in the Land of Souls.'"

"What—what do you mean?"

He stood, rolling the piece of rock between his fingers and staring at the horizon. Very carefully I touched my cheek, drew my hand away and smelled damp earth and another odor, cold and faintly metallic, like old pennies. I looked at Ralph; he raised his arm and with a flick of his wrist threw the stone toward the sunset. It arced high above the lone birch tree, and by some trick of the light seemed for an instant to hang there and glow, not like a spark or star but like some glittering aperture, a watchful eye in the void. Then it was gone. I did not hear where it fell.

"There they are," he murmured.

I looked where he pointed. On the horizon, a dark smudge appeared. I squinted, thinking at first it was another stand of birches suddenly made visible by the angle of the sun. But the smudge grew larger, broke into smaller jots of darkness and then regrouped. Soon it was near enough that the wind brought its sound. A jingling as of many small bells, unmelodic but constant; voices calling back and forth; an occasional explosive *huffing*. I glanced at Ralph uncertainly, but he only continued to peer into the deepening shadows.

Minutes passed. The breeze became a cold blast, and now along with the walking music of the caravan the wind carried its scent. Woodsmoke, birch leaves, the pungent and recognizable stench of unwashed bodies. But most of all a dense, warm, animal smell, far stronger than any familiar grassy barn odor—the only thing I could liken it to was the sharp, almost angry musk one encounters at a zoo. I moved closer to Ralph. He did not acknowledge me beyond nodding, his eyes fixed on what was approaching.

A moment and they were only twenty feet from us, near the birch where I had last glimpsed the bit of ochre that Ralph had tossed away. It seemed to me that full night should have fallen by now, but the eerie twilight had not corroded into darkness. If anything, the sky had grown more brilliant, the colors a tumult of lavender and violet and crimson.

Certainly it was bright enough that I could see clearly the little group that had stopped in front of us. I counted eleven of them, slight slim-bodied figures, most no taller than myself. Their clothes were archaic but gorgeously designed—long skirts of hide or fur, dyed red or sky-blue and hemmed with ropes of beadwork and bone; strange open jackets of the same material that were almost like frock coats, trimmed with white fur and small triangular brass pendants. I could see their features very clearly, high cheekbones and skin the color of bronze, onyx eyes and hair. The men wore small conical caps of short dark fur. Their facial hair was sparse but unshaven, their chins ending in wispy black beards. The women had their hair in long braids, strung with still more beads and white feathers; all save one, whose braid was laced with leather tassels dyed red. On their feet were flat-soled shoes of carven wood and hide. They spoke in soft fluting voices that were more birdlike than human, broken now and then by laughter or the cries of two small children toddling behind the grownups. As they moved across the taiga clouds of insects sprang up about them, gilded by the sunset. Watching them I felt a profound, almost childish joy—

Because, marvelous as the people were, what was most wonderful of all was that every one either rode or walked beside a reindeer. Not huge and terrifying stags like the one I had seen slain; nor were they the graceful, golden deer that leaped across the roads in Kamensic. These animals were like nothing I had ever seen before, save in the fairy-tale posters by Edmund Dulac that hung in Ali's room—small, graceful, almost dainty creatures, their fur the soft gray of a kitten's belly. Even their antlers seemed toylike, the tips sawn off and strung with gold filigree and brass bells, a child's memory of Christmas Eve and restless movement upon a rooftop. Small as they were, they seemed to bear their slender riders with ease; all save the two animals which brought up the rear of the cavalcade. The first of these carried no rider, but only a large bundle wrapped in deerskin and bound with leather thongs.

But it was the last reindeer that was truly a creature from a dream. Snow-white, its fur dazzling in the eternal twilight. It alone bore antlers that had not had their prongs sawn and blunted, and it alone carried neither saddle nor any other ornament. A solitary figure walked alongside it, head bowed and hidden beneath a fur hood. A figure slight as the others but wearing garb that seemed at once more archaic than their own, and more hieratic— a long tunic of supple hide, and over this a long open-fronted jacket, white and unadorned save for bands of white fur at cuff and hem. At the neck hung a necklace formed of myriad loops of crimson beads, heavy and pliant as a woven scarf.

The figure walked in silence, its feet moving in step

with the animal's. The white reindeer drew closer to its fellows, cropping at the coarse moss beneath their hooves, but before it could join them its keeper raised a hand bearing a long thin wand and slapped it upon the flank. The white reindeer halted. The figure struck it again, and this time I could see that the wand was in fact an antler, all its points shorn save two which formed a *V* at the tip. At the wand's touch the reindeer shook its head and snorted in protest. The figure cried out a word of command; the animal immediately fell silent and began to nose the moss at its feet.

"See how it listens to you," a voice breathed beside me. I started—I had forgotten Ralph was there—but before I could question him the figure took a step away from the animal and stood directly beneath the birch tree. The wind tore at the milky folds of the tunic and made ripples in the hood's thick fur. The figure stood for a moment, wand in one hand. Then it tugged the hood back, and turning to the white reindeer cried out again. Louder, so that the other people stopped milling about and stood docile as their little herd. The command meant nothing to me, of course; but this time I recognized the voice. I began to shake my head, mouthing the word *No* over and over again until Ralph had to cover my lips with his hand.

"Yes, Lit." With his other hand he forced my head up so I could see. "Oh, yes, yes, yes . . ."

Where the furred hood had been was a brilliant corona of red hair, unbound and streaming in the wind like a pennon. It framed a face sun-coarsened and angular as the others', but even in that remote place utterly unmistakable. The same tilted nose, the same black eyebrows belying that bright hair; the same pale, almost silvery gray eyes. I had stepped through a portal in Bolerium, to stand beneath an eternal arctic sunset and gaze upon myself.

"*No!*"

I yanked free from Ralph, shouting. As I did the red-haired girl jerked her head upright and stared at me, her expression mirroring my own.

"Stop it!" hissed Ralph. Before I could dart away he grabbed me again. "Can't you tell? *She sees you!*"

I froze. Because indeed the girl continued to gaze at me, pale eyes narrowed, mouth pursed as though about to speak. The others remained apart from her, tending their herd and the two children, who were busy gathering twigs and brush for a fire. At the red-haired girl's side the white reindeer nuzzled at the ground. After a minute she reached to lay one hand upon its flank. Her eyes never left mine.

The realization that she could see me was terrifying. I buried my face in Ralph's jacket, but it was no use. Within moments I was peering out at her once more. He began to stroke my hair, murmuring wordlessly; and that suddenly made me think of something.

"It *can't* be me. *My* hair isn't real. Ali hennaed it for me this afternoon . . ."

Ralph shrugged. "Neither is hers—"

He held up his hand, thumb and forefingers still stained from the ochre he had toyed with earlier. "It's what they do—"

"Who? *Who* does it? Who *is* she?"

"She is as you see her: a girl, your age. I do not know her name, but perhaps she does not have one; at least, not what we would recognize as a name. She is their go-between, their navigator. Their pathfinder. She travels between this world and the realm of the dead. Her people call her *samdanan*, She Who Dances. But if you were to study ethnology under Professor Warnick at the University of the Archangels and Saint John the Divine, *he* would tell you that *samdanan* is just another word for *shaman*, and that it shares its roots with the Sanskrit *sraman*, which is not dissimilar to the Mongolian *samoroj*, or the Manchurian *sam-dambi*, which means 'to dance.'

"Yet if you were to visit the village of Moruzzo several hundred years ago, the farmers would call her *strega*: a witch; just as they named Polly Twomey here in Kamensic. But there is still another word for what she is, Lit—

"*Malandante*."

As I listened the scene in front of me began to blur; not as though I were passing through another portal, but as though a pale scrim had descended from the twilit sky. But it did not hide the taiga, or the redhaired girl and her antlered familiar. Instead other, more shadowy figures began to move beside her. They were no more of that time or place than I was, and yet they were somehow *known* to me, as though I had dreamed of them long ago, or seen them in a film which until now I had forgotten. A girl in a white shift, her face streaked with soot. Another girl in a blue dress and bright earrings. A rangy longhaired figure in a veil which I at first thought was another girl, but whose face beneath coarse linen was that of a man, clumsily rouged and with blackened lips. They walked back and forth in front of the redhaired girl, insubstantial as smoke and completely oblivious of each other. When a few moments had passed, first one and then another began to execute a crude sort of dance. So awkward were they that it was several minutes before I realized they *were* dancing—hopping up and down on one foot and moving in gradually widening circles, away from the girl

Ralph had named *samdanan*, dust rising where they stepped.

And this, too, was grotesquely familiar. It filled me with horror, even as I struggled to recall where I had seen such a thing before, this clumsy, almost monstrous display of—

What? Mockery? Revulsion? Their movements were too crude to seem part of any sacred ritual, and yet they were undeniably choreographed, and undeniably alike. Even if the dancers took no notice of each other, even if they somehow were taking part in this bizarre performance over a period of thousands of years: still *it was the same dance*. In the midst of it all the redhaired girl remained motionless, her hand still upon the reindeer's flank, her eyes watching me across the centuries.

"She sees you as you see them," said Ralph. "And as you see her—as patterns in the dance. It is the one thing she can recognize down through the ages, the one thing that is not bound by the taiga or by her own time—

"—just as it is the only thing that *you* perceive, Lit," he ended softly.

"I don't know what you mean." The hopping steps of the ghostly figures was hypnotic; it was an effort for me to form the words. "I don't know anything about dancing, or—or any of this . . ."

Ralph shook his head. "I didn't say you knew anything about the dance, Lit. I said you could *see* it. Just as she does. Do she think she understands? Do you think she recognizes us, or knows any more of our world than we do of hers?"

"But—but we *do*," I said weakly. "You said so, you said she was called—a magician or something, you said Professor Warnick taught you—"

"Professor Warnick knows nothing!" Ralph's voice rang out, so keen with rage I shrank back and expected the dancers to do the same. But he might have been a moth fluttering in the night sky, for all the notice they paid him. "He and his masters give *names* to things, that's all, and think themselves wise! As though naming a thing is knowing it!

"Do you know what they call them, Lit? *Malandanti*. It means *Those Who Do Ill*—yet it means nothing, because it is only a perversion of what the Benandanti call themselves! And they have ever been blind to those things which they did not create, those things they did not name—

"But what this means is that they are blind to the entire world. Because even though they would like to believe that their god created it, and that their god watches over it as though it were a naughty child—still the world escapes them. They have no more understanding of its true nature than you or I do of *theirs*—"

He pointed at the phantom dancers. Their steps had become synchronized, so that even though they moved without seeing each other, they now formed a single chain, heads bobbing and arms extended as they hopped in a widening circle beneath the solitary birch. Of the herders, only the redhaired girl appeared to see them. The weird twilight had grown deeper. It touched her with a soft purplish glow and made her hair spark like copper wire, and flowed between the dancers so that they seemed to be stepping in and out of a moving stream. Now it was those others and their antlered mounts who seemed insubstantial, bright streaks upon a moving backdrop. I shook my head, struggling with a sensation that was not so much drowsiness as a deadening languor. I felt as though I had been dropped in amber and was slowly turning to stone. When Ralph placed his hands upon my shoulders I did not move; nor when he stroked my collarbone, pushing back the jacket I had been wearing so that it dropped to the ground. I no longer felt the cold, or the wind; though I could see where it rippled the leaves of the birch tree, and stirred the rustling mat of undergrowth. I could feel nothing but Ralph Casson's touch.

"Tulamaka."

The word came to me as though breathed in my ear, but it was not Ralph's voice. Beyond the circle of dancers the redhaired girl's eyes locked with mine. If I had any doubt before that she could see me, at this moment I had none; nor that she recognized me.

"Balthazar would say that she called you 'fire-spirit,'" whispered Ralph. "Or 'guardian of the forest,' or 'beast-wife,' or 'mistress of animals,' or 'bacchante.'

"But what she actually said is none of those things. Her name for you is unknowable, because it is no one thing. That is what the Benandanti will never understand. There are gods upon gods down the eons, and goddesses as well; and other things which the Benandanti have no name for—and thus they have no knowledge of them.

"But these are what the Malandanti serve. The unknown: the unknowable. That is why they give themselves no name, and also why their gods have many names; whereas the Benandanti believe that their master has but one."

I tried to shake my head, found I couldn't move. With great effort I spoke. "But—what are the Benandanti?"

Ralph's voice grew harsh. "It is what they call themselves—'The Good Walkers,' and also 'Those Who Do

Well.' That is how they see themselves: as the protectors of this world, keeping it safe from what they perceive to be dangerous to its order, and their own. But those who set themselves against the Benandanti are not treated gently, Lit—do not ever fool yourself into believing that. Even those who have served them loyally for time out of mind, may one day find themselves cast out, and—"

He fell silent. His hands upon my neck relaxed, and as they did I discovered that I could move again—though slowly, painfully, as though I were recovering from some injury. I turned to see the dance continuing before us, the dusk unaltered except where a few brilliant stars now blazed within the sky. There were more dancers now, some of them dressed in clothes that seemed less archaic though still strange to my eyes—robes and loose trousers, ribbons of bright yellow like saris or sarongs, the bright motley of harlequins. Many of the dancers were naked, or nearly so, their garments torn; and as I watched I saw another figure join the endless chain—one of the herders I had first glimpsed upon the taiga. Before I had thought its panoply of beads and leather ribands belonged to a woman, her long hair braided with bright red tassels.

But now as the figure took its place within the circle I saw that it was a man dressed as a woman. His face had been carefully scraped of any hair and his lips reddened, the same coppery color as the girl's unbound tresses. When he moved it was with an elaborate effeminacy, his hands drawing circles in the air as he stood on one leg, like a heron, and then began the same strange hopping dance as the others. I thought of what Ralph had just told me, that the Benandanti—whoever they were—could name these things but not comprehend them.

I believed him. The man-woman ducked in and out

between the other dancers, his arms snaking through the air. He did not look ridiculous, but frightening: his eyes wide and staring, his mouth a red gash in a face powdered white with wood-ash. As he leaped his braid tossed wildly, and its crimson tassels crowned his head like feathers, or horns.

And suddenly I knew what he reminded me of—the cave painting I had seen in the Nursery five years before. The same blankly staring eyes; the same slashed mouth. But strangest of all was the way one leg was raised, a clumsy accessory to the dance—and that, too, reflected the image of a man in animal costume, his foot injured or grotesquely foreshortened.

"But I've seen him!" I cried, pointing.

"Who?"

"That one, there—"

But already the man-woman was gone, lost within the moving circle. I pulled away from Ralph, no longer caring if it was cold, no longer caring if I was a million miles or a million light-years from Kamensic. "I saw him," I repeated angrily. "At the Nursery when I was twelve. There was a painting there—a cave painting, it was hanging in one of the rooms. Kissy Hardwick saw it, too—she sat and talked to me for a while. It was right before she died . . ."

My voice trailed off. I thought of the girl in the torn blue dress, her patchwork bag spilling open on the floor between us to scatter its glittering array, pills and peacock feathers, tarot cards and earrings and a knife carved of bone . . .

"She had a knife," I said. My eyes widened but I no longer saw Ralph, only that archaic blade, its handle burned russet and scored with minuscule lines. "She said she was his godchild, too, and that we were all real—she said that we were all real . . ."

"You are," whispered Ralph. "Watch—"

In my mind's eye a small dirty hand still grasped the bone knife, turning it so that light touched the tiny incisions, momentarily causing them to glow. Then it was as though someone tossed dust into my face. My eyes teared as I drew back and raised a hand before me.

But there was no dust clouding the air; only a small spare figure standing alone beneath a birch tree. The circle dance had retreated, so that they were small black columns ranged against the purple sky. So had the little group of reindeer herders. They were perhaps fifty feet away, no longer tending their animals but aligned side by side, watching the redhaired girl. Beside her stood the white reindeer, head upraised.

And it remained thus, absolutely still. Were it not for the way its skin shuddered beneath the skeins of midges upon its flanks, I would have thought it a statue carved of stone or snow. Beside the reindeer lay the bulky, fur-wrapped bundle that had been carried by its mate, and above it stood the girl, gazing at the birch with her hands cupped in front of her. In the eerily charged light I could see her clearly—the too-vivid stain of cinnabar and ochre upon her hair, a network of reddish lines striating her cheeks. Her eyes were wide open, the pupils lost within silvery irises, and that, too, gave me a flash of the figure in the cave painting with its maddening stare.

"Why does she look like that?" I whispered.

"Poppies," said Ralph. *"Papaver somniferum . . ."*

He bent and let his fingers play with a dried stalk, one of thousands nodding in the night wind; then straightened, stripping dead leaves and an oval seed-capsule from its tip. He held it out to me, a small brown globe with a ridged crown about its top. I shook my head.

"No," I said. "I—I don't want it—"

Ralph ignored me, taking my hand and prising it open so that he could place the seed-head in my palm. "Don't worry," he said, his smile edged with disdain. He closed his hand around mine, squeezing it shut so the seed-capsule splintered and cut into my palm. "It's outgrown its usefulness, except for the seeds. You have to pick them after they bloom, before the capsules are fully ripe. And to get any kind of high you have to eat a *lot* of them"— he inclined his head toward the girl beneath the tree. —"like she has."

As though she had heard us, the girl started, blinking; then turned away. She walked slowly, stumbling and catching herself in a stoned parody of the circle dance. When she reached the bundle on the ground she hesitated, then knelt beside it and began to fumble with its leather bonds.

It took her several minutes, unraveling thongs and layers of hide and tossing them aside. Despite my fear I found myself inching forward to see.

"*Oyum kami,*" she said, and leaned to embrace what lay before her.

It was the body of a man, naked, his dark hair falling loose from beneath a conical leather hat. His face was gaunt, the high cheekbones scarified with straight lines; his eyes had been sewn shut. But even from that distance, even across all those thousands of years, I knew him.

"Axel," I breathed.

"*Kami bö,*" whispered the girl. She took the ravaged face in her hands and kissed it, lingeringly, moving from brow to mouth to chest. Then she pressed her open palms upon his breast, threw her head back and began to wail. It was a horrible sound, made more dreadful when the others of her tribe joined in. I clapped my hands over my ears in a futile attempt to drown it out, while beside me Ralph watched raptly. The lament went on and on, the girl's voice rising to a scream and abruptly falling silent. The rest, too, fell still, though there remained an ululating echo that took a minute to die away. I looked around, and saw the distant circle of stationary dancers silhouetted against the twilight.

"She is preparing him for sky burial," said Ralph in a sleepwalker's voice. "He is her father. Her father and her lover, and their god."

"How—how can he be a god? He's dead and I—I can see who he is."

"He is dead because she killed him."

"But *why*?"

"Because it is what must be done. Because he is the god who travels between worlds. Between animals and men, between this world and the world of the dead. He is a god, and goes willingly; but we must help him on his way. That is the compact men and women made with the gods, long ago. That is what the Benandanti forget, or refuse to remember—that death is a journey, too. It's all like this—"

He made a circular motion in the air, the same words and the same gesture Axel Kern had used in the chapel at Bolerium. I shook my head, too tired to argue or question him.

Ralph did not to notice. "The Benandanti see all other ways as chaos, and that is what they fear more than anything," he said. "*Mysteries*. They seek to explain away all that they can't control. When all else fails, they destroy what they do not comprehend. They made themselves the foes of the great mystery religions and their adherents, and for millennia have stood guard against the rebirth of those forces which they believe will undo all their own great works. And *this*—"

He swept his arm out in front of him. Light streamed from it like sparks from a smoldering log. "*This* is where—and when—the Good Walkers were born."

A few yards away the redhaired girl lifted her head, staring at the sky as though she saw her own image reflected there. In the distance the waiting circle was still. Between the two, silent girl and assembled dancers, only the scattered members of the reindeer tribe seemed alive, the air before them touched with vapor where they breathed. We might have been there for a quarter-hour or a thousand years, frozen figures on a great chronometer, when suddenly something else moved upon the horizon: a black cloud that broke apart and reassembled as it drew toward us, dispersing the motionless dancers as though they were rotting fenceposts.

At the same time, the girl bent forward—slowly, with no sense of urgency—and began to gather the corpse in her arms. It seemed weightless, or else she was far stronger than I. She hefted the body and started toward the birch tree. Her expression was so far beyond grief or normal human sorrow that it was masklike, almost peaceful. It was the face of the virgin holding her son, or Demeter carrying the grain to be winnowed. I could not imagine this girl laughing or weeping or even sitting in repose; could imagine nothing but this solemn bearing away, repeated for all eternity. When she reached the foot of the birch tree she paused, head bowed.

That was when I realized what the moving figures on

the horizon were. They were horsemen, riding steeds hardly bigger than the reindeer but far more fleet. The air rang with the sound of their hooves, the jingling of harness and their voices, high and clear and jubilant, as though they had just awakened to a morning golden with sun and all of life a promise.

And perhaps it *was* morning, because now I had to shade my eyes to see them. The uncanny twilight that had bathed the steppes was breaking up. Tatters of gold shone between indigo clouds. Stars flickered in them like fish in a net, then disappeared. The sudden flood of light made even far-off objects seem distinct, crisp as though cut from paper. I could make out tufts of hair bristling along the horses' necks, the serpentine patterns embroidered upon harnesses and the same patterns repeated in tattoos upon the bared breasts of the horsemen. There were women, too, their hair in pigtails like the men, their expressions no less fierce and joyous.

But what was strangest about them, and most unsettling, was that each horse wore a kind of headdress, tasseled and heavily embroidered in bold colors—blue, red, black, green. The headgear covered their skulls so that only their eyes were visible through small holes, and rose in two leather pillars between their ears. Gorgeous branching pillars, tasseled and hung with ornaments of gold, and unmistakably meant to signify antlers.

"See how it begins?" said Ralph in a low voice. "They are like cuckoos, leaving their young to nest in the homes of others, until eventually of course all the others are driven out, driven to extinction by them."

"But who are they?"

"They are the Benandanti, although it will be centuries before they give themselves that name. Right now they are little removed in time and belief from their origins, which are as you see them—"

He nodded toward the girl. "And this, too, the Benandanti can neither accept nor forgive—that they issued from the same stock as those mysteries which they most despise; that their gods and monuments are formed of the same blood and stone as ours. That if you go back far enough and long enough, you will see only two faces staring at you from the darkness: the hunter and the mother. The Benandanti deny one and have debased the other; but they will not be denied forever. Gods do not die any more than we do. They sleep, and are awakened, and sleep again. They weave the same patterns endlessly, and all through time we are only bright bits of color picked out across their work."

And then I saw not just the taiga unfolding beneath the sunrise, but an entire world, a glowing diorama with colored globes whirling overhead and small bright forms moving on the earth, like miniature puppets or gaming pieces. There were the reindeer people, frozen beside their hornéd steeds, and there the invaders upon their caparisoned horses, a carpet of dust beneath their hooves. The reindeer tribe did not move, not until the horsemen were upon them; and then they toppled like chesspieces scattered by a child, the undergrowth beneath them and red.

As though it were a time-lapsed film, the scene changed, to men and women standing quietly between cattle with huge curved horns; and yet it was not different at all. The men raised knives and slaughtered one of the bulls; a woman wept, and another coupled with a man in the dirt. And then again there was a circle of girls and boys, holding hands and executing an intricate dance, leaping from one foot to the next while in the center a man was bound to a tree with looping strands of ivy. The dance broke up but the man remained, a girl holding a cup to his lips while he drank, red running from the corners of his mouth and staining his breast. Flames rose about him, and once again the horsemen came, though they were different this time, their mounts heavier and the riders armored. And yet again there was a young girl, redhaired, naked, embracing a woman while others stood in a protective circle about them. The woman became a man, but the redhaired girl did not change. The man stood motionless while she tore his robes from him and drew him to her until the two of them collapsed to the earth. There was a burst of crimson and gold; the man disappeared. The girl remained, consumed by fire.

And then I saw before me the same scenes that had been enacted upon Muscanth Mountain. A boy lying upon the ground, bound with ivy; a stag crashing down as hunters rushed to draw blood from its breast.

Only this time I did not run away. Like all those other figures suspended between earth and sky I was caught in the pattern. I turned to Ralph Casson, and he nodded.

"Yes," he said, as though I had finally guessed the answer to a riddle he'd posed hours ago. "It's all real, Lit. As real as anything gets, actually."

"But—but I don't *know* anything!" I cried. "How can I be a part of any of it, your Malandanti or the rest, when I just heard about them tonight?"

"Doesn't matter. When has ignorance ever excused anyone? Gods need to be born, and they need avatars to assist them. That's you."

I kicked at him angrily, succeeded only in sending up a spray of twigs and moss. "Avatar? What the fuck's an avatar? And if it's so goddam important why don't *you* do it? Why aren't *you* it?"

For an instant I thought he'd strike back. His eyes narrowed, his mouth grew tight, but almost immediately his expression softened.

"Oh, Lit . . . I wish I were. More than anything—more than I have ever wanted anything on this earth, love or money or children, I've wished to be one of them. *Any* one of them—Benandanti or Malandanti, I never cared which!—but one doesn't choose these things. One can only be born to it, or chosen. "

"Then what *can* you do?" Fear stoked my rage as easily as alcohol did. I began to feel buzzed, and stared challengingly at Ralph's disconsolate face. "Why the fuck do they even bother with you?"

A tremor ran along one side of his mouth. "Oh, but they *don't* bother with me, Lit," he said, almost in a whisper. "That's the whole problem. That's what the problem has been for, oh, about twenty-two years now, ever since I went to college and made the mistake of trying to join a club that didn't want me for a member. Have you ever had that happen to you, Lit? Has it?"

"N-no," I said. "I mean, I don't think so . . ."

"Of course not," he murmured. "Of course not, how could you? Growing up there in Brigadoon—you're *one* of them. Even if you're not with Balthazar and his fucking Conclave, you're still one of the Chosen Ones. How could you know anything about what it's like, *not* to be chosen? To have this whole magical world open up to you for a little while, and then suddenly to have it all end—to have all the doors slam shut in your face? How could you know anything about that?"

How could I know anything about what you're even talking *about?* I thought, biting my tongue.

Ralph didn't notice. His hand remained on my arm, but I might have been a tree, for all the attention he paid me.

"I was hardly older than you are now when it happened. I wanted to be an architect. I'd been accepted at Yale and the University of the Archangels and Saint John the Divine—both great places to study. I chose the Divine, but instead of architecture I was seduced by archaeology. Literally seduced, by a doctoral student named Magda Kurtz. Because of her I changed my major to classical archaeology—I was eighteen, what did I know?—and that was when I met Balthazar.

"Have you ever fallen in love with a teacher, Lit? Because that's what I did. Not physical love, of course, but this complete, all-consuming *obssession.* I couldn't sleep, because I was so *thrilled* by him. By his ideas, his vision, his methods . . . This was in the fifties, remember, when you would go someplace to study law, or medicine, or physics, or English lit; and that was pretty much what you learned. Anything else, any kind of liberal arts education—well, that was just sort of going through the motions, pretending that any of these disciplines might have any bearing on each other.

"But that's exactly what Balthazar Warnick taught. That everything *was* connected, that nothing ever happens by mistake. That there's a—a sort of master plan for the world—".

I frowned. "It sounds like religion."

"It *is* religion. Or, rather, all Western religions are *it*: part of the Benandanti and the system for control that they've developed over thousands of years. And the school itself is a religious school, administered by an ancient order—so, well, it comes with the territory, doesn't it?"

He looked down at me, smiling. The color had rushed back to his cheeks; not even the strange wavering light could cloak how happy he looked, remembering. It seemed pathetic, and it depressed me; to think of somebody's *father* feeling like that. I made a face but Ralph went on, oblivious.

"I began studying Cycladic cultures; the influence of ancient Anatolia on the Greek islands. Balthazar encouraged me. The bastard! He let me believe they would take me on, that if I worked hard enough, long enough, the Benandanti would accept me. But they never did.

"I finished my undergrad work at the Divine and went on to graduate school there. Magda helped me—she was the one who first told me about the Benandanti, and she showed me how I could recognize them. Because once you know they're there, you see them everywhere—in government, in the Church, the military, universities—you name it. I went on several digs—Pamphilia in Turkey; the library at Herculaneum. I was still *thinking* like an architect. I explored the Roman mausoleums at Pamphilia, and was struck by how much they resembled the Ecclesiasterion at Prieme. Sacred spaces, theater and tomb, both defined by thresholds, by porticos and prosceniums—

"And by something else. I discovered that there were hidden passages that served as entries to secret chambers in the tombs and theaters. Not just tunnels, but words of power carved within the entablature. Magda knew of them, because she was a Benandante. She showed me how to find them myself. Which was forbidden, of course, but that was when I began to learn about the

Benandanti's portals—the doors they use to travel in time and space. That was how you got here"— He swept his arm out grandly, as though he had personally brought the taiga into being. —"and that's how you got to see everything you've seen. *Lit*," he ended, and tousled my hair.

I pulled away. "What do you mean?"

"I mean all those things you saw—on the mountain, and by our house. The sacrifice, the hornéd god—"

"You put them there? *You?*"

"No. I didn't *put* them there. I opened the doors, that's all. The portals. They're everywhere, like the Benandanti are everywhere. You just have to know how to look for them. I spent six years, studying at the Divine—six years of learning how the Benandanti created the portals, and where, and why . . ."

He fell silent. I thought of the hornéd man moving through the trees by Jamie's house, the standing stone atop Mount Muscanth and the crumbling doorway in Bolerium that had opened onto this wasteland. Cautiously I asked, "Well . . . what happened then?"

"Nothing." Ralph's tone was so light he might have been giving the punch line of a joke. But his expression was anguished. "Not a fucking thing. I was dismissed. My dissertation panel said my work was stolen, and they threw me out."

"Stolen?"

"Plagiarized. They knew it wasn't—it was an excuse, that's all. I went home that afternoon and found my apartment had been ransacked. All my notes were gone, the copies I'd made of manuscripts and books in their libraries all over the world, the maps I'd drawn up—all gone. They took them—*he* took them. Balthazar Warnick. *But*—" Ralph tapped his forehead. "The one thing they *couldn't* take was what was in here. 'Cause I'd memorized a *lot* of it. And I'd already been through some of their portals—in Herculaneum, and at their retreat house outside D.C., and again in Italy and—well, here, for chrissakes! Oh, yeah, quite a few places, you'd be surprised! *Balthazar* would be surprised," he said maliciously. "It was too late to change that, and so they did the best they could to ruin my life. Blackballed me every time I'd try to enter another doctoral program, got me fired from jobs, turned my own goddam wife against me—

"But not this time. The buck stops here, now—'cause I've got *you*, Lit Moylan."

He grinned and all the malice was gone. He looked like the same cheerful, slightly stoned hippie dad who'd first greeted us in Jamie's kitchen. "A smart pretty girl like you—I told Jamie he'd make new friends here," he said, and laughed. "*Lots* of nice people, here in fucking Brigadoon . . ."

He took a quick step backward. At the same time he raised his hand, twisting it so that his fingers seemed to ripple, a magician performing a complicated card trick with no cards there. Then he cried out and his voice died into the crackle of flames. Around us there sprang a circle of blazing light, fire leaping until it arched above our heads like a gilded dome. But there was no heat, and while smoke thickened the air between us it had no scent. I tried to lunge past it but Ralph stopped me, shouting.

"No! It protects you—and me, while I'm with you—"

I shaded my eyes, struggling to see past the column of flame. I could just make out the slender figure of the girl, standing with arms outstretched beneath the tree, her mouth a gaping O of fear and dismay. In the branches above a dark form seemed to thrash, but then I saw that it was the corpse, its limbs beaten back and forth by flame. Fire raced along the branches, white bark crackling as the wood beneath blazed a searing blue. Behind her I could dimly see the line of horsemen, rising and falling in place like some infernal carousel, riders and mounts shifting from antlered masks to golden armor to white robes and red crosses, green and black and yellow uniforms streaked against a fiery field, and then back to those first horsemen again; and between them all like shadows on a cavern wall the images of animals, running, leaping, grazing animals. Bison and lionesses, reindeer with salmon splashing about their cloven feet, mammoths and bears and owls with the eyes of men.

Then it was gone. A flare of purplish light and the figures collapsed, disintegrating into falling ash. Only the girl remained, gazing at a tree where the skeletal remains of a human corpse could be seen, white bones tangled amidst white branches. She looked calm, unnaturally so, her eyes half-opened and her hands limp at her sides. The reindeer herdsmen had disappeared. Behind her stretched the taiga, the lichen-covered plain broken by stands of charred birch trees, and here and there a lone slab of granite thrusting up from the earth. Twilight had somehow eroded into dawn, with no real night between. The eastern edge of the world had begun to glow deep red, a shade so dark it had the blackish humor of a wound that will not heal.

"No . . ."

I could not bear to see whatever awful sun might rise there. I shut my eyes and buried my face against Ralph's arm. He moved to embrace me, but then something impelled me to look up again.

I saw the redhaired girl moving as if in mockery of my own fear, into the arms of a tall form standing behind her. I wondered if this was some psychic projection of Ralph Casson, but no. The figure stirred, long braid falling to brush against the girl's cheek, revealing a face smeared with ochre and wood-ash.

The man-woman. Gone was the creepy aura that had frightened me before; gone, too, any semblance to a real woman. He held the redhaired girl gently, big hands stroking her hair, his chin nestled against the top of her head. There was nothing remotely sensual about their posture, but at the same time it was so intensely intimate that I lowered my eyes. I was too conscious of Ralph there beside me, the way he was different from any boy I'd ever been with. Not just bigger but somehow more solid, more *real*; even though I could feel that his arms were slack where Hillary's were not, his hair thinner, his skin harder and more coarsely textured. It was like leaning against a tree and being able to feel it thrum with life. I was confused but also turned on; to hide it I pointed at the girl.

"What's her power, then?"

"I told you: *'Go not with young women over twenty, because they have no occult power.'*"

"That's bullshit." I stared at the girl, still locked in embrace with her shaman consort, or brother, or whatever the hell he was. "Even if *she* does, *I* don't."

Ralph looked amused. "And why the hell do you think you would even know if you did, Lit Moylan?"

"I—well, I *don't* know," I said. "But I'm not some goddam sacrificial virgin, I'll tell you *that*."

"Oh, I know." He took my face between my hands and held it firmly. It didn't hurt, but when I tried to move he slid his thumbs until they sank into the flesh beneath my jaw. He pressed, hard, against my windpipe. "Believe me, Lit—neither Axel Kern nor Balthazar Warnick nor anyone else would have any interest in you at all, if you were a virgin."

He shifted. One hand remained tight about my jaw; the other moved slowly down, tracing the ridge of muscle that marked my windpipe, then fanning out so that it covered my collarbone, the fingers slipping beneath the top of my dress. A flicker as I recalled sitting with him on the bench outside of Bolerium, feeling drowsy, nearly hypnotized as he pressed his palm against my breast—

But there was nothing of that now. I began to struggle, the knot in my stomach tightening as he pulled me to him. "You fucker," I choked, and tried to kick him. His hand swept from my throat to my hair, yanking my head back as he shoved his leg between mine. I cried out; he pushed my face up to his, and kissed me.

"They owe me this," he said. He stared at me, his blue eyes soft. "Oh, yeah—"

He kissed me again, teeth clicking against mine as I clenched my mouth shut. He made a low frustrated sound but before he could do more I angled my head sideways and bit him, hard, on the mouth.

"Ah—you *bitch*—!"

Blood spurted against my cheek and I spat at him, kicking viciously. His shout became an enraged growl,

"Don't you *dare*, don't you *dare* bite me—" I tried to break free but he held me, no pretense of gentleness this time. "You goddam bitch—"

"Let her go."

Ralph looked up, his head snapping back. "Who the fuck are—"

"*Let—her—go.*"

It was the man in the long robe and woman's braids; the man who had been embracing the redhaired girl. Only now he seemed taller—wild-eyed, his breath rank—and undeniably *real*, not some diorama figure from a fever-dream. Ralph stared but it was as though he didn't really *see* him—Ralph's eyes were unfocused, his mouth working as though he continued to shout at me. The other man loomed beside us; I could feel the nap of his deerskin robes, the soft tufts of colored wool that formed tassels along his sleeves as he raised his hand. I thought he would hit Ralph. Instead he let his arm fall, the leather fabric rippling down to hide me.

"This way!" the man hissed. He grabbed my arm and I stumbled after him, underbrush crackling underfoot. I looked back and saw Ralph staring at us in disbelief, and behind him the spectral silhouette of the girl who was my double, still motionless beneath the birch tree with all the taiga surrounding her, bathed in the crimson glow of sunrise.

Then the light shifted and grew more diffuse, as though a fogbank had crept across the plain. The girl's clothing melted into shadow. Darkness poured from her like water and the birch tree, too, started to change. Its trunk grew wizened, its branches gnarled. The curved cage of bones propped on its limbs began to shake, as with a sound like ice shattering the skeleton reared into the air. Leaves leaped from the tree to cover it; strands of ivy shot up like spears to wrap around ribs, skull, fibula, sternum, until the entire form was clothed in greenery. Only the eyes remained free of leaves, such a deep black they seemed to glow. On the ground beneath the girl watched. Her stupor suddenly broke, and with a sharp cry she clapped her hands.

The leaf-cloaked mannequin lifted its arms. Ivy fell from them in a rain of green, and other vines sprouted as well, leaves larger and less variegated than the ivy, with pale yellow tendrils coiling like fingers about its shoulders and throat. Tiny globules erupted from these vines, burgeoned into darker globes that began to ripen, until a crawling mat of purple covered the green man. He thrust his head back, chest exposed to the rising sun. Bunches of grapes exploded from him, raining onto the ground and bursting, their juices soaking into the earth. I could smell them, a sweetness so intense my mouth watered.

"Not now," a voice said softly. "Turn quickly, Lit, don't look—"

Strong hands closed around mine. I ignored the warning, and strained to see what was happening as he pulled me after him.

The taiga was gone. In its stead was a softer landscape, hills climbing into mountains, slopes covered with trees, sunrise touching their limbs with gold. Of Ralph there was no sign. But the girl remained, unclothed, her breasts and pale skin and hair turned to copper by the dawn. At her feet poppies rippled in the wind—I could see their papery petals, white and red and pink, the green-furred stems and, on some of them, the swollen seed-calyx where the blossoms had already fallen. Once more she was embracing someone, not the man-woman but someone else, a tall man with hawkish features and dark hair that fell to his shoulders. He was naked, and in one hand held a staff topped with a carven pinecone. As he crushed the girl to his breast, wine streamed down her back, staining her hair reddish-violet.

"No more!"

I was yanked away roughly by the man-woman. In the

deepening sunlight his leather robe looked burnished. But as we ran the robe seemed to unfurl like a long ribbon, until I saw it was not a leather robe at all but a gown of dark-green cloth, embroidered with five-petaled flowers. His careful braid unraveled, long hair snaking in the wind. Ahead of us the sunrise grew blinding. I shaded my eyes, found that I could make out an eerie darkness within the brilliance, like spots on the sun's corona. I staggered after my rescuer, and with each step the darkness grew more palpable and took shape, until I was staring at a rectangular pillar in the air.

But it was not a pillar. It was a door, only a few inches taller than the man who led me and half as wide. A door made of shadow and light, the shadow the utter blackness of a starless night; the light more blinding than the sun, brilliance like a red-gold sea boiling up from the portal's center.

"Close your eyes!" the man shouted. "Stay beside me!"

His voice was familiar. But I had no time to question him, no time to do anything but race, gasping, until I was beside him.

Before us the portal opened like the world's molten core. A moment when I felt the ground beneath me drop away; a moment when air and wind and even the flesh upon my face were sucked away, devoured by a ravening heat. A column of flame ripped through me, erupting into pure white light as a voice shrieked deafeningly.

"Jump! *Now!*"

I jumped. There was silence and annihilating darkness, no sense of falling, of being; of anything at all. Then with a roar the world crashed all around me. I was thrown facedown onto a cold floor. The core of light exploded into pain, and for an instant I blacked out.

Then I heard a sound, a soft repetitive thumping, the murmur of voices that were not forming words. When I managed to open my eyes, I found myself lying on the floor of a darkened room, window casements thrown open so that a spatter of icy rain came down, and scattered oak leaves. I was back in Bolerium. On the floor beside me, holding her head and moaning, was Precious Bane.

PART THREE

The Eternal

Well the Cadillac
it pulled out of the
graveyard
pulled up to me
all they said Get in.
Then the Cadillac,
it puttered back into
that graveyard.
Me, I got out again.

—"MARQUEE MOON,"
TOM VERLAINE

13 &
White Light/
White Heat

It took me several minutes to catch my breath. I didn't just feel winded by falling, or whatever I'd done to return. My heart pounded dangerously fast and my skin burned; whenever I tried to focus on the room around me, streams of cobalt and violet light flared and faded at the borders of my vision. Even my teeth ached.

But gradually all these symptoms faded; gradually the phantom lightning disappeared, and I could see that the casement above me was tall and narrow, with two sets of windows opened outward into the rainy night. Watery blue light filled the room, a long raftered space tucked somewhere under the eaves. The outer walls were granite, the floor unpolished wood and very cold. There were no rugs or furniture; only an odd, propane-blue light whuttering in the distance. I blinked, trying to bring the light into focus; and that's when I realized there were other people in the room beside myself and Precious Bane. In fact, there were a lot of people, all gathered at the far end of the chamber. Before I could figure out what to do about *that*, Precious Bane sat up with a groan.

"God, I *told* you I hate this place." She brushed back a tuft of cotton-candy hair. "Every time I come here I tear something."

She stared ruefully at the band of shiny black polyester that was her miniskirt. It was slashed as though by a razor. "See? You think Axel will pay for this? He won't. Thank god they're too busy to notice—"

She inclined her head toward the people at the far end of the room, then got to her feet, long arms and legs unfolding like an accordion doll's. She reached down to grab my hand. "Upsy-daisy, Miss Charlotte. My, your new party clothes *are* a mess."

I stood groggily and looked down at myself. My dress was ragged and filthy, stuck with twigs and leaves; my Frye boots caked with mud. I touched my hair. It felt like the reindeer moss, brittle and damp. Precious Bane gave me a sympathetic look.

"Aw, don't worry, honey. A little Prell, you'll look super. Come here and let's see what we can do to shine you up—"

"Wait—hang on a second . . ."

I slipped from her and darted to the window. It was set halfway up the wall, so that the bottom sill was level with my chin. If I slitted my eyes, the out-of-focus image was the exact inverse of that I had seen with the portal, its perimeter etched with light and the center a seething darkness. Very carefully I extended my hands, until my fingertips brushed the edge of the sill.

"Charlotte!"

"No. Wait—"

It was like being too close to an incredibly powerful electrical appliance. The air felt warm, almost furry; the hair on my arms stood on end. When I moved my fingers, threads of blue-violet light streaked between them, like paramecia swimming through the darkness. Out of nowhere words echoed around me, faint but clear, as though broadcast from a radio in an adjoining room. There was the smell of upturned earth, and my mother's clear voice reciting—

> *"Down with the bodie and its woe,*
> *Down with the Mistletoe;*
> *Instead of Earth, now up-raise*
> *The green Ivy for show.*
> *The Earth hitherto did sway;*
> *Let Green now domineer*
> *Until the dancing Sonbuck's Day*
> *When black light do appeare."*

"That's what it is," I whispered. "Black light . . ."

I took a deep breath, opened my eyes and firmly grasped the sill. As though I'd rammed my hands against a stone wall, a shock raced through me, from fingers to elbow and on to my shoulder. The pain made me shout, but I kept my hold tight on the window. The violet threads thickened, became ropes of light that encircled my wrists and arms, twisting about my shoulders until I could feel their pressure at my throat. Then suddenly the luminous bonds fell away. There was the summer-charged smell of ozone, a sound like the sea. With a gasp I let go of the sill and staggered backward.

Above me the window glowed like stained glass at dawn. Only it was not a window anymore. It was a portal. Flame runneled along its edges, blue-white deepening to indigo, feathered off into a desultory darkness that

I knew was the room surrounding me.

But I could no longer *see* the room. My sense of it came only from knowing that it was not the incandescent threshold, a threshold that made everything else seem bleak and inconsequential. It was not a room there behind me, or even a world, but a prison. Ralph's despairing voice came back to me—

More than anything—more than I have ever wanted anything on this earth, love or money or children, I've wished to be one of them—

—and I thought of who they were and what they might become, those Chosen Ones who could pass through such a door.

"Charlotte."

I stiffened, refused to turn.

"Charlotte. Come back. Come back *now*."

I shook my head, then felt Precious Bane's strong hand on my shoulder, pulling me away.

"You just got back here, honey," she said softly. "Don't be in such a hurry to leave. Not yet, anyway."

The portal was gone. Rain slashed through the open window. From behind us came a faint echo of laughter. Precious Bane put a finger to her lips, indicating the far end of the room.

"Remember: we are not alone," she said sotto voce. "Com-pa-nee!"

"Right." I sighed, looked over and saw who the company was—eight or ten people thrashing naked on the floor, bathed in the leaden light spilling from a single glaring bulb on a pole. I gulped and looked away.

But there was Precious Bane staring at me, so I had no choice but to watch.

"Oh," I said.

"Why look, Charlotte," she said. "They're making a movie."

Above the heaving group Page Franchini stood impassively, filming it all with a Super 8 camera. The blue light gave everyone's skin a wet, glassy sheen. It was less like an orgy than a school of dolphins arcing up through the floorboards, with only an occasional flash of a mouth or eyes to betray anyone as human. I stared, fascinated, until Page Franchini lifted his head from the camera and saw me.

"Hey," he called. He set the camera on its tripod, still whirring, and waved at us. Behind him I glimpsed an open door, jeans and T-shirts flung over it. "You! C'mere, we could use some girl action—Precious, bring her over—"

"No way." I spun around, and Precious Bane draped her arm around me protectively.

"Not today, Page," she said, drawing a hand across her brow. "Our aura is very weak today—"

She tossed her head, cherry hair cascading down her back, and escorted me to the door. We had to step over several men, none of whom took the slightest notice. Page Franchini shrugged, lit a cigarette and tossed the match onto somebody's bare ass.

"Well," sniffed Precious Bane. "Now we know how many holes it takes to fill the Albert Hall."

I laughed and squeezed through the door beside her. She kicked at a heap of clothes, then glanced back at Page Franchini angling in for a close-up. "Well, Charlotte. *That's* what comes of wearing white shoes after Labor Day."

"Was that, like, an orgy?"

"Very, very like."

We were in the corridor, back on the main floor. There were people here, certainly more than I expected to be wandering the halls a few yards away from an orgy. An extremely pregnant woman in a dashiki dress, holding a wine glass and looking very drunk; a naked man in a wig. Music ricocheted from an upstairs room—

> *I hear you knockin'*
> *but you can't come in . . .*

Just a few doors down, the corridor opened onto the music room. It seemed almost incongruously bright in there, all the lamps turned on and the candelabra alight atop the piano. Someone was hunched over the keys and a few people were gathered around, their backs to us. It took me a minute to disentangle their singing from the stereo upstairs and the resonant thump of dancing in the main hall.

But when we entered the room I saw it was Duncan at the piano, shirtless, his back slick with sweat and dusted with silver glitter, lank hair hanging around his face. He was banging out a ragged barrel-house version of "Moondance" and singing in his rich baritone, accompanied by a blonde high school chorus—Christie Smith, Alysa Redmond, Leenie Wasserman, all warbling cheerfully out-of-tune—and two predatory-looking women in tuxedos and stiletto heels.

"It doesn't look good for Marsha and Jan and Cindi," said Precious Bane. "I think I'll leave you here with the cheerleading squad for a few minutes. Just don't get lost. The party's not over yet."

She blew me a kiss and strode off. I nodded but forgot to thank her—I was too relieved to finally see my friends again, and something that looked like normal life. I hurried over to the piano. With a flourish Duncan finished the song. His face was glistening, his makeup smudged. But he looked astonishingly happy, and for a moment I almost forgot who I was looking at, Precious Bane or Dunc or the statuesque creature who had pulled me through the portal. The girls applauded, the tuxedo-clad women moved to touch their shoulders. Duncan looked over his shoulder at me.

"I wish my brother George were here," he said.

Leenie and the other girls gave me stoned, slightly damaged smiles, brightening when one of the women dangled a small brown vial in front of them.

"Wanna come with us, Lit?" Leenie called as Christie and Alysa followed the older women across the room.

"No thanks."

"Sure? Well, see you later—"

I watched them disappear into a corner, cheeping like goslings, then turned back to Duncan. "Hi, Dunc—"

He ran a hand across his face, leaving a smear of blue eye shadow. "Lit. Christ, what happened? You in a car wreck or something?"

"Or something." I angled onto the piano bench and lay my head on his shoulder. "Oh, Dunc, am I glad to see you."

"Yeah? How come? Aren't you having a good time?"

"No."

"Really?" He looked shocked. "Well—why not? I mean, who've you been hanging out with? Your parents?"

"Where *are* my parents? Are they still around?"

"Uh-uh. Nobody is—I mean, nobody from town. They all split around the same time, about an hour ago. Everyone but us, I mean. You know"— He flapped his hand, indicating the corner where Leenie and her friends appeared to be exchanging articles of clothing while singing "American Pie" —"the usual suspects. All our Kamensic heroes," Dunc finished.

I stared bleakly at the piano.

"Well, jeez, Lit, it can't be *that* bad—"

He struck a pose, head held high and candlelight glinting from a sequin stuck to his nose, then let his hands fall to the keys and began tinking out a few notes.

> *"I've BEEN to the most MARVELOUS—PARTY—*
> *I COULDN'T have—LIKED it—MORE."*

I shook my head. "Duncan, I don't think Noel Coward would have liked this party very much."

"Boy, you really are Captain Bringdown, aren't you? Here—"

He reached beneath the piano bench and withdrew the bottle of Tanqueray. A scant two inches remained. He took a long swallow and handed it to me. I hesitated, finally took it and knocked back what was left.

"There! That's better. Drunk Dunc and lit Lit." He took the empty bottle and let it crash to the floor. "What should we sing now?"

I got woozily to my feet. "I think I'm gonna try to find Hillary. Have you seen him?"

"Not for a while. He and Jamie Casson were talking about going down to the city—"

"Tonight?"

"Yeah. There was some show at the Mercer Arts Center, the Dolls and someone else, I dunno. They blew that off, but I guess something's going on afterward down on the Bowery, Jamie says he knows the band and he wants to get some people together and head down for it."

"What about Ali?"

Duncan wrinkled his nose. "Man, she's out of it. I tell you, I think Jamie Casson is bad news. He's got her shooting smack or some such shit—" He shook his head. "I just don't get it. All this pot and booze and great acid floating around, what's she doing messing with her head like that?"

"*Chacun à son goût.*" As I started to walk away Duncan called after me plaintively.

"What the hell does that mean?"

"It's French for 'Mind your own beeswax.'"

I sauntered off. The Tanqueray made me feel indestructible once more, but when I caught a glimpse of myself in an ormulu mirror in the hall I decided I'd better clean up. I found a bathroom, a cedar-paneled cubicle occupying what had once been a linen closet. That night it had obviously seen a lot of traffic despite its size. There was a pair of woman's red silk underwear wrapped around the light and a pile of shoes alongside the toilet. A joint was still smoldering on the sink, the porcelain beneath it amber with resin. Across the mirror, someone had scrawled TERRY TAKES IT UP THE ASS in hot-pink lipstick. I found a sock and cleaned off the mirror, smoked the rest of the joint, and did my best to make myself more presentable.

It was tough. I kicked among the shoes on the floor, searching for a comb or hairbrush, but found only a baggie that held a fine sifting of cannabis seeds and stems along with a pair of manicure scissors. I decided to save this, then tried to do something about my hair. All I could manage was dragging my fingers through the tangled copper mass.

"Ouch—"

I gave up. My dress was a lost cause as well. I plucked off as many twigs as I could, and scraped clumps of mud from the hem. One sleeve was hanging loosely. I tore it off, but then I had to tear off the other one, too. My bare arms were covered with scratches and insect bites. I examined them carefully, thinking of Ali and wondering if Dunc was right, if she actually had mainlined heroin. If so, is this what trackmarks looked like? My finger touched a small gash in the crook of my elbow. I winced, and glanced into the mirror above the sink. A mad girl stared back at me, ragged hair flaming around her mud-stained face, orange peasant dress in tatters, lips bitten and bloody-looking, pupils huge and very, very obviously stoned.

"Well, it's a look," I said.

I began to wash up. A few minutes later my face and arms were relatively clean and the sink was clogged with dirt and floating leaves. I was trying to get the drain to work when the door behind me flew open.

"Oh, hey man, sorry, I didn't know anyone was—"

I turned too fast, and bumped into Jamie Casson.

"Jamie!"

"Huh? *Hey*—ow! what the—"

He drew up, staring at me. "Lit? Is that you?"

"Afraid so."

He took in my ruined dress and hair, the mess on the bathroom floor. "Huh. I guess I must've missed something."

"I guess you did."

I made room as he edged inside, closing the door behind him. He looked tired and unhappy, shirt untucked and trousers hanging loosely from his hips. "I gotta get out of this fucking monkey suit," he said. He held up a jumble of clothes. "You mind if I get changed?"

"Uh-uh."

Immediately he started to undress. I wasn't going to be so uncool as to leave, or deliberately look away. I busied myself again at the mirror, dabbing my face with water and doing my best not to spy on Jamie.

But it was impossible not to see him. In the mirror his thin pale form moved like a wraith, shrugging off the white shirt, trousers sliding from his legs so that I had a glimpse of his underwear and the silver-blonde hair on his thighs. Then he was pulling on black jeans and a T-shirt that said RAW POWER, and fumbling with the laces of his black high-tops.

"Hey, thanks." He straightened, shoving a wisp of hair from his eyes, and balled up the clothes he'd just removed. "Guess I can just dump these here, huh? Boy, you really look bad, Lit."

I flushed, glancing at the wadded clothes in his hand. "Hey"— I looked back at Jamie. —"are those your clothes? I mean, would you mind if I wore them?"

He shrugged. "Hell no. They're not mine anyway— Kern gave 'em to me to wear tonight. He has, like, a whole closet full of these things, extras that he keeps around for *the help*. He wanted me in a fucking uniform, man, can you believe it? Like a fucking waiter. Here—" He tossed them at me. I grinned, and he shot a tired grin back. "—you'll look better in 'em than I did, anyway."

I took off my Frye boots and pulled the trousers on under my dress, then tucked the pants into the boots; made a half-assed attempt at modesty by turning sideways and tugging the dress over my head, and finally put on the white dress shirt. Jamie was insultingly indifferent, yawning and lighting a cigarette and leaning against the wall with his eyes closed. The trousers fit perfectly, soft wool and smelling of mothballs. I grabbed the baggie with the pot seeds and manicure scissors and stuck it in a pocket, along with a pack of matches. The shirt was much too big. I tucked it in, catching a breath of Jamie's sweat and a smell like burnt sugar, the harsh odor of car exhaust.

"Ta da," I said. I started rolling up the sleeves.

"Looks good," said Jamie. "A *lot* better than it did on me."

I tossed the dress into a corner and inspected my reflection in the mirror. It was a definite improvement on the madwoman who'd stared out at me before, even with the patina of grime that clung to the shirt, not to mention several cigarette holes. I still couldn't do anything about my hair, though. I ran a hand through it, sighing, and turned back to Jamie.

"Well, thanks. Are Ali and Hillary still upstairs?"

"She passed out. And Hillary took off—"

"He left the party?"

"I don't know. No, I don't think so—I think he was going to find you first. I'm taking off—going down to the Pit. You want to come?"

"The Pit?"

"Yeah, man. These guys I know are playing, a fucking great guitarist, it'll blow your mind." He began swaying, eyes half-closed, cigarette weaving figure eights in the air. "This amazing scene . . ."

Abruptly he leaned forward. His turquoise eyes were huge, their expression so intense it was like rage. "You hate it here, too, don't you. I know you do, Lit. And I know why. I know what goes on . . ."

"Wh-what—"

"This place—" He waved his cigarette, let it fall to the floor. "This fucking madhouse—"

The little room was filling with smoke, but as Jamie moved his hand the smoke directly in front of him disappeared. Not as though dispersed by the motion, but forming in a pattern. The reddish wood of the bathroom walls suddenly seeming to glow through the haze. He spread his fingers, turning them in a deliberate way that was both odd and oddly familiar. As I watched him, my own hands clenched. In the air between us the pattern grew darker, more apparent. The smoke took on a harsh metallic color, like the singed blade of a steel knife. There was a soft crackling sound of leaves burning, the acrid smell of incense. Another moment and a face hung in the air before me.

I gasped. It was not a face, but the image of a mask, one of those gaping terra-cotta masks that adorned the houses of Kamensic in the autumn. Its eyes were oblique, the mouth wide, upturned in a malicious smile; the high cheekbones two slanted bars of steely light. It was a cruel visage; and unmistakably that of Axel Kern.

"No!" I jabbed at the air. It felt as though I'd plunged my hand into a freezer. But the image was already gone. There was only a roiling cloud of cigarette smoke, and someone banging on the bathroom door.

"Hey, man, give someone else a turn, whaddya say?"

Jamie stuck out his foot and nudged the door open. In the hall stood Page Franchini. He gave us both a disgusted look.

"Oh, Christ, what are we doin' now, sneaking a ciggie? Fucking kids. Let me in, I got to piss."

He shoved past me. "Good morning, little schoolgirl. Comb your hair and put on some lipstick, I'll make you a star."

"Fuck you."

I stomped out. I was shaking so hard I was afraid to stop moving, afraid that if I paused to take a breath I'd shatter like one of those masks. I could hardly see the corridor around me, hardly see anything but that lewdly grinning face staring out of the smoke.

"Lit—damn it, wait—"

I stopped but refused to look at him. Jamie hurried to catch up, taking my arm. "Where did you go before? Were you with my father? Tell me, Lit, you have to tell me—"

I lifted my head, fury scalding me like acid, and stared at him, his sullen mouth and great bruised eyes. Not a god dying to be reborn, not a transsexual Amazon; not a redhaired girl gazing back at me across a Eurasian steppe four thousand years ago. Not any of these but a boy my own age who I'd met the day before sitting on a jukebox, a boy who'd just given me his clothes.

A boy who could make masks in the air.

Jamie was looking at me the same way he had in Hillary's car, when I thought I could confide in him about Kamensic. After a minute he nodded. I took a deep breath, nodded back; and socked him in the mouth.

"*Awwwowww. . . !*"

"You," I said, my knuckles aching. Jamie reeled and crashed against the wall. "You *bastard*. You knew, what did you know, tell me *what the fuck is going on!*"

"Ow—don't, don't! I swear, I just—"

He panted, one hand cupping his jaw. His lip was dark and swollen, but not bleeding. He looked a hell of a lot more awake than he had a few minutes ago. "Christ, Hillary was right—"

"Hillary?" I shouted. "What the hell did *Hillary* say?"

"In the bar—Deer Park—he said not to mess with you or you'd clock me—"

"Yeah? Well, you better tell me what the fuck you're doing here or I'll clock you *again*—"

"I told you! We just moved here—my father was supposed to do sets for some asshole project that Axel Kern is working on—"

"Wait—start there. How do you know Axel?"

"I don't—stop! don't look at me like that, it's the truth! I never met him before two days ago—he wanted me to park cars for the party. Then I saw him tonight when he paid me and gave me—"

"How did you do that?"

Jamie shook his head. "What? The cars?"

"No, you idiot—that thing in the air. The thing that looked like a mask—*how did you do it?*"

He rubbed his lip, looked anxiously up and down the hall. The bathroom door creaked open and Page Franchini emerged, zipping his fly. He glanced at us and bared his teeth in a derisive smile.

"It's three A.M., children," he called as he sauntered off. "Do you know where your parents are?"

"Asshole," Jamie muttered. "Look, let's at least go somewhere a little more private, okay? C'mon—"

He grabbed my arm and pulled me after him. We found an empty room, a small study with a pair of oversized armchairs in front of a fireplace where graying embers gave off a fitful warmth. There was a row of candles on the mantelpiece, and a half-dozen votive candles on the floor. Jamie dragged the two armchairs together.

He settled in one. I slid into the other, still glaring.

"This better be good, Jamie. This better be fucking *great*."

"My father," he said. "That's how I learned. But you must've already figured that."

I had a flash of Ralph Casson drawing a pattern in the air, a circle of fire blazing up around us. "Your father—"

"He doesn't know that I know," Jamie added. "Not that he's ever been what you could call discreet. But I've watched him, at home when he'd go off by himself and practice . . .

"He's always done stuff like that. We were always moving, trying to find some place that would give him tenure, or even hire him for more than a year. But nobody ever did. He'd start pulling this crazy shit, talking about cults, the doors of perception swinging open so you walk right through them—I mean, he was *teaching* this crap, it wasn't like he was just talking to my mom and me. He'd go down to the rec room to eat mushrooms and stare at himself in a mirror for four hours. And he never made it a secret, what he was doing at the schools. Same thing later, when he got bounced from Berkeley and all he could do was build sets for all those shitty monster movies. Because eventually somebody would always complain, about the wacked-out witchcraft crap, or the drugs, or the girls—"

"Girls?"

"Sure. That crazy stuff he was talking about in the kitchen—you know, 'go only with teenage poontang, for thus lies the way of truth'—you think he made that up? No way! Every time I'd bring someone home, that's how it would end up—my fuckin' father shagging her. That's how come my mother left—"

I made a small sound. I couldn't help it. I thought of Ralph holding me, the way he'd stroked my arm and tried to kiss me; then thought of him doing it to innumerable others like myself. I crossed and uncrossed my legs, fighting an absurd stab of jealousy. "Oh. I—I thought your mom joined a commune?"

"She did. First she became a lesbian, then she became a Jesus freak, then she joined a commune. And you know what? I don't even blame her. I wish now I'd gone *with* her."

He stopped, his voice ragged, and I looked away. He was close to tears. He punched the arm of his chair, leaving a dent in the worn leather, then lifted his head defiantly. "I'm splitting. Tonight. Ali says there's a train at 4:35—if the trains still *run* out of this place. I'm taking off. This is it."

"But—" I hesitated. "Well, I know you hate it here—but why?"

"Because it gives me the creeps. Because it's *sick*. But how would *you* know," he went on bitterly. "You're part of it, you and your creepy little town, all these fucking actors and Kern up here playing lord of the manor—"

"Me?"

"Yes, you!" He leaned forward and poked me, hard, in the shoulder. "Taking notes about everybody, pretending you're gonna write a play about all of us—"

"Who told you that?" I demanded furiously, but I knew who'd told him.

"Hillary. And Ali. 'Oh, don't mess with Lit, she's Axel Kern's goddaughter, she can do—'"

"Shut up!"

"*No.*" Jamie had moved so he was practically sitting in my lap. "Did you fuck him? *Did you fuck him?*"

"Who? Axel?"

"No—my father."

I almost laughed; instead stared at him and said in a snide voice, "No, I didn't fuck your stupid *father*—"

"What about Axel? Did you sleep with him? With Axel Kern?"

"What goddam business of yours is it who I—"

"Did you?" He took me by the shoulders, his eyes desperate. "Lit, please, you don't understand—"

"No." I stared at him with all the hatred and disdain I could muster. "And you let go of me, or—"

Jamie let his breath out, gazed at his hands as though they didn't belong to him; then sank back onto his own chair. "You didn't," he said in a low voice. "You swear you didn't—"

"I didn't sleep with Axel Kern. I never have."

"Thank god."

His tone was so earnest that I laughed despite my anger. "What, are you a Moonie or something? You hate sex?"

"No. Of course not. It's just that—well, this is all a trap, Lit. All of it here at this party—"

He turned to peer over the top of his armchair, like a kid playing hide-and-seek; then curled around again. "It's all for you. Axel Kern—I'm not sure exactly what he is, but he's sure as shit not just a movie director. Somehow or other my father conned Kern into thinking that he could do some work for him, but my father's not here to work. At least not *that* kind of work."

His voice dropped. "Have you ever heard of a man named Balthazar Warnick?"

"Professor Warnick?"

"God, you *do* know him—"

"No! I never even heard of him until tonight!"

"Well, he's here because of my father—and because of you. I don't know why, exactly—"

He began scratching nervously at his arms. "But I do know this—I know my father wants to hurt both of them. Warnick and Axel Kern. I hear him talking some nights, my father—talking to himself, but what really creeps me out is that it makes *sense*. I mean it's like he hears a voice, or voices, telling him things. And I can tell by his tone of voice that whatever it is he's listening to, he's hearing it for the first time. And once he *does* hear about it, well, all this weird stuff turns out to be true. Like this party—I heard him talking one night, we were still in the city—and he just sort of listened to whatever it is he listens to, and finally he said 'Fine, Kamensic Village, we'll go there.'"

"But Jamie—people *do* move here. It's not like you need some magic voice telling you about it. Lots of people have heard of this place."

"He hadn't. Not before that night. I know, because he had to get a map to figure out where Kamensic Village is—he thought it was in Massachusetts, or Maine. He didn't know it was just upstate. He's here because of you, Lit—you and Kern and that guy Warnick . . ."

His voice grew softer, more despairing. "Look, I *know* it sounds crazy, but you have to admit this place isn't exactly Walton's fucking Mountain. And my father is definitely into some weird shit. I think he's in way over his head. My mother did, too—she thought he was in some kind of cult, she was even trying to collect stuff for a book about it, maps and things, but then of course my mother also thinks she's the seventeenth incarnation of Mary Magdalene. So"— he lay his hands on his knees beseechingly. —"can you *please* tell me what's going on?"

"But I don't *know*. You—you drew that face in the air back there, in the bathroom—how?"

"I told you—I watched my father, and memorized what he did. It doesn't always work—I have to focus on what I want to see, and"— he opened his palms, clapped them together. —"*pffft!* Like that. *If* it works."

"But Jamie, why did it look like Axel?" He looked puzzled and I wanted to shake him, I was that frustrated. "The face you made in the air—it looked *just like him*."

"Kern?"

"Yes! Didn't you know?"

He gestured helplessly, his arms red-streaked where he'd scratched them. "But I wasn't thinking of Kern. I was thinking of those things you see here on the doors, those creepy masks . . ."

His eyes went dead, and somehow that was more frightening than the thought that he could draw faces in the air. All the color drained from them, the way a blue jay's feather goes from blue to gray if you strip the quills, and he stared vacantly into the air between us.

"I don't want to see them," he finally said, his voice listless as his eyes. I knew he was seeing something else in the room's shadows; whatever it was, my skin prickled to watch it mirrored in his face. "But they're always there. That's why I get bent—so I won't see them . . ."

He turned and grabbed my hand. His was icy cold, the long fingers flaccid as rotting leaves. I recoiled but he drew me closer, until his breath was on my cheek, nicotine and a faint green scent, crushed petals, the bitter tang of resin. "Come with me, Lit. You hate this place, you want to leave—come with me to the city. We can live cheap, practically for free. We can get high, we can hang out. If we leave tonight we can be there by morning. I mean, trains *do* stop here, right?"

"Well, yeah," I said slowly. "Of course they do, the commuter trains come every day, but I don't know about four A.M. on a Saturday . . ."

"Then we'll hitch! There's a place we can crash, a bunch of people I know are squatting there, it'll be so cool—"

His hand tightened around mine and I nodded, not meaning Yes, not meaning anything; just trying to buy time to think.

"Why? I mean, why do you want me?" I said at last. I looked up, trying to will a spark back into those wounded eyes. "Why not Hillary, or Ali?"

"Because you'd know exactly what you were leaving. Hillary's afraid to really go away—he just wants to hide at Yale for four years, and pretend this place doesn't exist. But it *does*, and it's not going to disappear—"

"But why not Ali?"

He shook his head. "Ali's too much like me: she just wants to get high. Little rich white girls scoring nickel and dime bags . . . she'd never make it. She's not tough, like you are. And she can't sing."

"*Sing?*"

"I'm getting another band together. I know these guys, they've been playing down on the Bowery for a few months now. We can get a regular gig there, and if we're squatting we don't have to make rent—"

"But I can't *sing*! I'm horrible at all that stuff . . ."

I blinked back tears, my turn to feel desperate. Because suddenly it seemed as though there was a way out of Kamensic, and this was it. I shuddered, feeling the rush of chilly prescience that overcame me sometimes when I was drunk—the same dizzying sense of hopelessness and relief, the same sickening perception that *this* was the real world, teenage drunks and junkies nodding out in corners, midnight's promise given over to crushed pill capsules and empty bottles and the same record playing over and over again on a neglected stereo.

And none of it, none of us, would ever mean anything. We would never be famous; we would never be rich. None of us would become what we were meant to be, beautiful and brilliant and enchanted, destiny's tots taking bows onstage and receiving armfuls of roses, reading our reviews in the *New York Times* and *Rolling Stone*. Ali would go quietly mad like her mother, Hillary would teach *Cymbeline* to yawning high school students and one rainy night drive his car into the Muscanth Reservoir.

Yet in a terrible way it was a relief to know these things. To imagine that life could be ordinary and barren; to know that nothing I did would ever matter, that the visions of another world and another self were nothing more than bad dreams, the bitter aftertaste of bad acid and too much Ripple wine. Whatever secret that Kamensic and the Benandanti held was trumped by what Jamie was offering me—the chance to escape, to go to the city and lose myself. No one from Kamensic Village—or anyplace else, any*time* else—would be able to find me. Not in New York City.

Not if I didn't want to be found.

"Lit?"

I looked up to see Jamie staring at me. I opened my hands. "I can't sing, Jamie. I can't even act, and around here that's like saying you can't read, or drive. Actually," I admitted, "I can't drive, either. But Hillary can sing, and Duncan—"

"They'd never come with me—too chickenshit. Can you play guitar?"

"Hell no." I bit my thumb, finally offered, "I guess I can dance. Sort of . . ."

"Well, you wanna write, right? We'll just do covers at first but we'll need songs, new stuff—"

"Songs? I can't write songs—"

"Sure you can." For the first time Jamie grinned. "Fuckin' A, look at you"— he took in my filthy boots, the cast-off shirt rolled up around my elbows, my snarled hair and dirty fingernails. —"you're a fucking mess! You're *perfect*."

"But—"

"Look, you're *pissed off*, right? You're mad as shit at the whole goddam world! You got a chip on your shoulder, I've got a monkey on my back—it'll be fucking great! Come on, come on, come on," he urged, rubbing my arm. "New York City really has it all . . ."

"But—"

I shut my eyes, dredged up the image of a hornéd man clawing his way through the trees; of a boy bound with ivy and Axel Kern in a rainswept chapel. I opened my eyes. Jamie was still there, his gaze no longer imploring but insistent. I sighed.

"But Jamie—if something really *is* happening here . . . if something is going on, and I'm part of it—how can I leave? How can I just go?"

"I'll tell you how." Jamie took his hands from me and slid from the chair. "Like this—you just put your legs together, and *go*."

He crossed to the fireplace, squatted there and stared into the ashes. After a minute he turned back to me. "Look, I don't care if you come or not. Or, no, I *do* care,

I guess, but I'm going whether or not you come with me. Or anyone else. But if you stay here, it's just like Hillary going to Yale, and Ali going to Radcliffe or whatever fancy place you all get shoved away in. It's a cop-out; it's a way of making sure you just keep coming back home again and doing what your parents did—

"Just like they always do, Lit. It's their fight and they drag us into it. Always, *always* the same fucking thing. But you know what?"

He stood. He didn't look wasted anymore, or tired. "This time I'm not buying into it. Whatever my father is involved in, whatever it is he thinks he's breaking into, I'm breaking out. I'm breaking the cycle. And I think you should, too."

I groaned. "Oh, God, Jamie, I dunno . . ."

Jamie said nothing. He just stood there, then began to sing in a sweet boyish tenor. *"I remember how the darkness doubled . . ."*

I leaned forward and cradled my head in my hands. When I looked up a moment later, he was gone.

"Shit—Jamie, no, wait—"

I raced into the corridor. It was empty. Thin cyanic light filtered out from a few half-open doors, along with laughter, the tireless whir of a Super 8 camera. I turned and began walking toward the main hall. I felt wired, almost frantic, and my eyes burned. When I rubbed them I looked at my hands, to make sure they weren't black with ash. Instead my knuckles were red, not with blood but something powdery, the color of brick-dust.

Ochre.

I touched my cheek and drew away fingers stained vermilion, then rubbed my face with my sleeve. The white cotton was streaked with rust. When I saw the arched entrance to the main hall in front of me, I began to run.

Music thudded from the monolithic speakers. Heavy bass, slivers of guitar noise; buried vocals that sounded like weeping. Beneath my boots the floor was awash in the party's spoilage—spilled wine, auroras of glitter and sequins, roaches and cigarette butts.

But there was a more ominous residuum, too. Crushed acorns, their meat like grubs nosing amidst scattered piles of oak leaves; pinecones and opium pods, papery petals frail as moth's wings. When I kicked through the detritus daddy longlegs raced underfoot, and spiders as long as my finger crept over broken syringes.

"Damn . . ."

I stepped inside. I expected to be blinded by the same carnival glare that had greeted me hours earlier, and shaded my eyes.

There was no need. The columns of ultraviolet light still marked the perimeter of the room, but all their otherworldly fire had been extinguished. There was only a faint flicker inside the tubes, like trapped lightning. The bulbs made a threatening sound, buzzing as though locusts hid within them. I walked past warily, making a circuit of the room and looking for someone I knew.

I saw no one. The dancers had all gone home. The hall seemed to be full of white-shrouded figures, frozen in the dying light. Something warm grazed my wrist; I looked up to see the candelabrums still hanging from the ceiling. Long streams of wax had spilled from them to the floor, hardening into veils and cataracts and tusks. It was these that I had taken to be cloaked figures; it had been a droplet of hot wax that spattered my wrist.

"It's okay," I whispered. "It's okay . . ."

My breath was enough to send a shiver through the

waxen shrouds. I walked on, tiny stalagmites crunching beneath my feet, and as I crossed the room the music changed. The droning bass was chopped off by the crackle and fizz of dust on the needle. As though it were water leaking in, the great hall filled with the sound of a chiming guitar and a tambourine's funereal jangle. But I could still see no one, and I could no longer tell where the music was coming from.

I shivered. My eyes ached from trying to focus on anything within the colonnade of ruined candles and black light. The music thrummed and droned, the tambourine became a tocsin. As I walked things clung to me, cobwebs or dripping wax, I thought. But when I glanced at my arm I saw long tendrils of pale green sprouting from the cleft of my elbow.

"Ugh!"

I slashed at them and the tendrils fell away. Immediately three long red furrows rose along the inside of my arm, oozing dark liquid that spun in long droplets to the floor. I gazed down, stunned, but before I could move there was a rush of wind that swept away everything, music, light, dead leaves and cigarette ash. Something touched my cheek and I recoiled.

The room was alive with whirling petals, a vortex of red and pink and scarlet, as though the mansion itself were bleeding. They erupted from the casements like broken glass and drifted from the candelabrums, and where they touched my skin it grew numb. My feet were mired in blossoms; when I tried to shout my jaw didn't move. The sound of wind in the trees grew deafening. It no longer came from outside but somewhere within the room. There was a smoky reek like hashish, the fruity odor of new wine. And still the papery blossoms swirled around me, sticking to the gashes on my arm and covering my face like snow.

As though unseen hands had slammed the windows shut, the gale stopped. The petals froze in midair; then, like iron filings circling a magnet, they made a shape— the ragged outline of a tree, limbs bare save where petals settled in the crux of trunk and branches. Something moved within those branches, just visible behind the scrim of blossoms; a shadow like a crouching figure readying itself to spring.

No . . .

I tried to summon the strength to move; but abruptly as it had appeared the phantom tree was gone. So were the falling blossoms. The music rang out again, thin and shrill. I blinked and drew an unsteady hand across my face. There were no flowers there; but on the floor faded petals mingled with broken wineglasses and oak leaves. I turned and started to walk across the room.

The sickly glow from the dying UV lights had faded. I could just make out a series of closed doors along the far wall, each a lozenge of deepest black with no hint of a lock or knob or window set within. I remembered seeing them earlier, almost hidden by a throng of partygoers. Now they seemed ominous as the doors to Bluebeard's castle in a Hammer horror film or one of Ali's ghost stories.

"Oh, Christ. Ali." I whispered, anguished, and opened my hand. A single crimson petal lay pressed against the palm. "Ali . . ."

I knew then that it was as Jamie had said. Bolerium was a trap, a labyrinth; and I was ensnared. The only way I could truly escape would be to do as Jamie planned— leave right now, taking nothing, saying no farewells, with no money in my pocket and no idea of what I was really doing, except running away.

But that would mean leaving Ali nodded out in an empty room upstairs. That would mean leaving my parents, and Hillary; leaving Duncan and all the rest of them—Mrs. Langford and Moe and Flo and Ali's father with his crapped-out car. It would mean leaving Kamensic itself.

And suddenly I didn't know if I could do that. I wasn't even sure if it was *possible*.

Because Kamensic wasn't just a town. It was something that had seeped into my veins like a drug, something that had filled all the hollow places in my bones and heart and head, until even if I died the shadow of the town would be there, taking my shape, using my voice— and how would anyone even know I was dead?

How would *I* know?

I shuddered. The smell of spilled wine grew stronger as Axel Kern's voice crooned in my ears, and Ralph Casson's—

Nothing happens only once . . .

She is their pathfinder: She travels between this world and the realm of the dead . . .

I thought of Ali's stories of the drowned village, of suicidal children given as tithe to a dark man in the back of an unconsecrated church. I thought of Hillary smashing a terra-cotta mask in a drift of autumn leaves, and Ali dancing drunk across her room, crooning *gimme shelter* as she waved a burning joint at me. I thought of all these things; and of my parents, and a silver-framed photograph of Axel Kern with me beside him, my hair crowned with a wreath of red flowers.

No, I had said when Ralph Casson held out the small

swollen globe of a poppy husk to me, *No, I don't want it.*

With every ounce of fury and despair I had, I beat my fists at the air and shouted—shouted until I drowned out the droning music and the entire hall became an echo chamber with only my voice roaring inside. The streams of candle wax snapped and shattered. From the long outer wall came a muted thump, and then another, as one by one the tall tubes of UV light flared like Roman candles and went black. My voice died into a rasp. I let my hands fall to my side and listened for the music.

There was none. A flood of frozen wax covered the floor, shards of white glass and metal threads. The French doors banged open and closed as the wind sent a spume of dead leaves into the hall. I watched them, but only for a moment. Then I turned away, terrified but resolute, and walked through the wreckage until I reached the row of closed doors. Some were veined with ivy, others covered with thumbtacked messages, bits of paper and strips of sequined fabric clinging to the wood like vines.

But there was never any doubt which entrance was meant for me. Toward the end of the long wall was an arched door of unpolished oak, its panels flaked with black; no knob, no latch. Set within the center, like a sundial in a garden, was a terra-cotta mask. Its slanted eyes glittered as though ruby glass winked behind them, or flame. Its mouth was set in a half-smile as though it were asleep.

"Axel Kern," I said, and raising my fist I smashed it.

There was a satisfying *crack*, more like bone on bone than shattered clay. I drew back, to protect myself from flying debris, but there was no hail of broken terra-cotta. Instead bits of torn greenery rained down, stems and stamens stripped of their blossoms, ragged petals, crushed lilies and the fragile trumpets of narcissus. They covered me, tangling my hair and catching in my sleeves, their fragrance thick and choking as honey.

"God damn it, let me *in!*"

I kicked blindly at the door. The panels splintered beneath my boot and a lancing pain shot through my leg. Still it didn't budge.

"Open!" I pounded where the mask had been. A rusty hand-shaped stain bloomed beneath my touch, grains of powdered stone trickling to the floor among the falling blossoms. *"Open—!"*

A sound like the tolling of a vast bell, a smell of burning leaves. As though it were a slab of ice the doorway seemed to melt. Its edges blurred into daylight. The storm of flowers subsided. I stood, breathing hard and glaring at the portal. Then I lifted my head, fists drawn before me, and walked through.

There was a sickening rush of vertigo, a flare of violet-blue light. My skin burned and my hair crackled with static. Then there was only darkness: no floor, no walls, no sense of whether I was falling up or down but only that the world had been ripped apart, like a tree torn by a hurricane. I couldn't breathe but I felt neither fear nor panic; only numbness and exhaustion. The darkness spiraled away, sucked into a point of radiance that grew larger and larger until it enveloped me.

And suddenly I *was* falling, plunging down so fast that when I tried to scream the air felt like a stone thrust into my mouth. I saw a room racing toward me, walls and chairs and windows atop jeweled carpets. The sudden hiss of air mingled with my own voice, shrieking, as I crashed onto the floor.

"Giulietta!"

I moaned, turning slowly onto my side, opened my eyes and saw someone crouching beside me.

"Giulietta—what have you done! You should have waited, I would have—"

"Aw, shit," I moaned again, sitting up. My head spun viciously. For a horrible instant I thought the whole scene was going to run backward, and I'd end up crashing back into some other awful place. But then warm hands were on mine. Carefully they opened my fingers and placed something heavy in them. I looked down and saw a cut-glass tumbler full of amber liquid; looked up again into the incongruously boyish face of Balthazar Warnick.

"Giulietta—"

I nearly dropped the glass, but he touched my wrist to steady me. "It's all right, Giulietta, you're here with me. Drink, it will calm you—"

I shook my head. "No way—"

"It's only cognac. Very *expensive* cognac. So please—"

I sniffed at the tumbler, glanced back into his sea-blue eyes. With a shrug I drank.

"Ugh."

He laughed. "That's a bit *fast* for cognac—"

I shoved it back at him, my eyes watering. "Gross! Take it—"

"Here, Giulietta. Let me help you . . ."

He took my hand and got me to my feet. I stood woozily, unsure whether it was me or the cognac making the room look unnaturally brilliant—a gorgeous, Pre-Raphaelite vision of a scholar's study, with paneled walls and Oriental carpets on the floor, rows of bookshelves and a huge bay window overlooking mountains.

And, while it had been after midnight in Kamensic, here sunlight streamed through the sweeping windows.

Everything gleamed with a primal intensity: the crimson and indigo of the carpet so saturated they looked wet, the gold letters on the spines of books sparkling like flame. Decanters on a small round table glowed as if they held paint rather than liqueurs—emerald green, blood-red, sunflower yellow. A daybed was heaped with tapestried pillows, and there was a small cast-iron woodstove set into one wall, its isinglass window glowing beneath one of several beautifully carven plaques inscribed with Latin phrases—

CONSILIO ET ANIMIS

It was all like some Victorian fever-dream, or a movie set. I rubbed my eyes, heedless for the moment of Balthazar's hand on my arm.

"What—what is this place?" I finally said.

"My study. You are at the Orphic Lodge of the Benandanti, in the Blue Ridge mountains. People come here to work—students, visiting professors, classical scholars. But only the Benandanti see the inside of this room— Benandanti, or their guests," he added. "Giulietta—"

I stiffened and drew away from him. "I'm *not* Giulietta. Whoever the hell she was. I'm Lit—Charlotte Moylan—"

I walked to the window, peered out at the mountains, a river threading between autumn-gold trees, all beneath a sky so blue it made my eyes ache.

"And I'd like to know what the hell I'm doing here." I turned back to Balthazar. "Where's Axel Kern? I thought . . ."

My voice trailed off: I wasn't sure exactly what I *had* thought. "I thought I would find him—through that door, in Bolerium—"

"You would have." Balthazar leaned against a desk, its surface covered with stacks of books, curling parchments, a silver tray holding the remnants of a meal. He still wore his formal evening clothes, though his iron-gray hair was tousled, his face more worn than when I had seen him last. He stared at me, so frankly delighted that I blushed. "But you were diverted."

He walked over and eased himself on the window seat beside me, gazing out at the mountains with a proprietary air. "You're not an adept, Giulietta—*Lit*," he corrected himself. "You're something far more unusual—and dangerous."

"What's that?" I snapped. I continued to stare out the window, desperately hoping he couldn't tell how frightened I was. Whatever had happened to me—falling through a tear in the fabric of the world, stumbling through doors at Bolerium and ending up on the Eurasian steppe—I very much wanted to believe that those things were accidents.

But even if I hadn't known I would end up at the Orphic Lodge, I *had* chosen to walk through that portal at Bolerium. And that seemed to have upped the ante in whatever cosmic game I was part of. I recalled a moment in my childhood—the aftermath of that same Irish funeral, a whiskey-fueled wake where I'd watched my father argue strenuously with an Augustinian priest. Something about free will, and living with the consequences of one's decisions no matter how dire . . .

I started as a breath of chilly air nosed through an open window, smelling faintly of river-mud. Balthazar reached to shut the window, gently touched my wrist.

"You're a sort of prodigy, Lit." He picked up an odd-looking toy that rested on the velvet seat cushion, a model of the solar system made of wire and polished stone beads. "A savant . . ."

"Ralph Casson didn't think I was a savant. He said I was a Malandanti."

Balthazar's hand tightened around the shining array of wire. There was a small blister on his thumb. As I stared, the blister swelled, burst into a red star that bled down to stain the cuff of his dress shirt. "Malandante," he said. "Malandanti is the plural."

He let the wire toy drop back to the seat and looked at me, his eyes grim. "And I hope very much for your sake, Lit, that you are *not* a Malandante."

Faster than I would have thought possible, he grabbed me by the shoulders. "Listen to me—you have no idea what you have walked into. This is a battle that has been going on for longer than there have been words to describe it. You have no part in this fight, Lit. Do you understand? You know nothing of the Malandanti—they would use you and discard you as casually as you would throw away a piece of paper. You would be destroyed—"

"So?" I spat, knowing my voice sounded thin and frightened. "So everybody dies, it's not like—"

"It is not like anything you can imagine. Because you would *not* die, Lit, any more than I have died. Not now that you have become aware. For four hundred years I could bear this world and my place in it, the constant watchfulness and the eternal, *eternal* waiting—but only because I knew you were safe. Giulietta Masparutto, whom I saw burned to death, but who was then claimed by the Malandanti—I knew that she slept, and would be reborn, and die, and sleep only to be born again. All of this for centuries, thousands of years, perhaps. And as long as she was not aware of who or what she was, she was safe. Even in life, she would be sleeping.

"And so always I was sustained by the thought that she

could be there, somewhere. Even if I never saw her, even if I was never able to find her again—it was enough. I could serve out my duty to my masters, knowing that she might be alive but with no memory, no knowledge of what she had been, nor of what she might be. And the cycle would have gone on, endlessly—if not for Ralph Casson."

"Ralph Casson!" I tried to pull from him. "Ralph fucking Casson didn't create me! I wasn't waiting for him to make me come to life—"

"I did not say he created you," said Balthazar. "I said he made you *aware*. Do you know why Giulietta was executed, Lit?"

His fierce gaze made me look away. "Because she slept with you," I muttered. "And they thought she was a witch . . ."

"She *was* a witch. By their terms—she had the sight, she knew I was a Benandante the first time she laid eyes on me, covered with dust and carrying my scrolls in a rotting leather sack. She did not know precisely what a Benandante was, but she knew me for something more than what I seemed to be. She was sixteen when we met, she had been her own cousin's lover for two years already—she was no child, any more than you are. And she did not know what she was, any more than you do.

"I was the one who told her of our work; of our fight against the Malandanti. Because I loved her; because I wanted her to join me. I—I thought that if she knew, it might be possible—that my superiors might have permitted us to marry—that she might then have helped us, helped me to fulfill my part in all of it . . ."

He fell silent. His grasp upon my shoulders loosened, and I drew back.

"I think you're crazy," I said. "But even if it were all

true—and I know it's not—why should I listen to you? You betrayed that girl—you let them burn her at the goddam stake—"

"There was no betrayal. I was going to help her, I had no idea that the Conclave had condemned her to death—"

"You were afraid. You were afraid of them, and you were afraid of—whoever she was." I tilted my head back and regarded him coldly. "That was how the story went that Ali told us."

Balthazar sighed. He ran a hand across his brow and sat back down on the window seat, shoving aside the model of the planets and watching me with bleak eyes. "They were all afraid of her."

"Because she was so powerful?"

"No. Because she was so angry. Not bad-tempered—she was good-natured, too easily led into bed, too kind when it came to helping her father and her cousins. But she had a very great rage, sometimes it seemed that everything would make her angry—babies dying of the flux, her own mother dying as she struggled to give birth to her tenth child, her friends and cousins becoming pregnant before they were fourteen years old—all of it enraged her—"

"No shit."

"—but there was nothing she could do about it. For herself, she took herbs, and was very careful in her lovemaking so as not to get with child. But she would shout at the others when they got pregnant, she would shout at the parents whose children died—she shouted at the village priest, and when he tried to force her confession during the sacrament of penance, she kicked him."

I laughed. Balthazar smiled ruefully. "I *was* a bit afraid of her, as much as I was afraid *for* her. Not that she would hurt me—she loved me, and we argued very rarely—but because I knew her rage would draw attention to her."

"Because she kicked a priest?"

"No. Because her fury is what gave her power. It's what fueled her sight, it gave her the dreams she had, where she could see things she was not meant to see. Her anger is what drove her to learn about the plants that kept her sterile. It made her lash out at the other women, who refused to listen when she tried to help them—"

He stood and crossed to one of the massive book cabinets, shelves bowed beneath volumes bound in leather, untanned hide, rainbow silks, parchment. A library ladder leaned against the wall, and Balthazar nimbly climbed it, looking like an earnest schoolboy in the shadow of all those somber tomes. Dust puffed out around him as he withdrew a volume and blew on its spine.

"Kirsten better see to those," he said as a pair of moths flew past his head. "Here, take this please—"

I hesitated, then walked over. I was half-expecting something exotic, or at least undeniably ancient—crumbling vellum, cracked leather and Latin—but the book he gave me was merely old and musty-smelling, its cloth binding frayed, its spine cracked as from much use. Disappointed, I turned it to read the cover.

TERRORS UNSEEN

THE ERINYES

AND

THE ORIGIN OF THE MYSTERY CULT OF DIONYSOS

By June Harrington

"Do you know it?" asked Balthazar as he clambered back down the ladder.

"Oh, sure. Are you kidding?"

He walked over to a narrow table set along one wall. Papers covered it, and an old Royal upright typewriter. I followed him, opening the book to read its title page.

> An inquiry into the Vegetation Gods of Old Europe, and their connection with the Ancient Women's Cults of the Mediterranean and surrounding regions. Cambridge University Press, 1904.

"Well," I said as Balthazar took the book from my hand. "It's not exactly *The Catcher in the Rye*."

He smiled and with a flourish pointed to a velvet-padded chair, its arms carved with whorls and griffin's-heads. "Sit."

I sat. He pulled a matching chair alongside me and settled himself into it, smoothing the book's cover. "It's a very important work, that's all. In my day students younger than you are could recite long passages by heart."

In your day guys were reciting Beowulf *in mud huts*, I thought darkly, but said nothing. Balthazar opened to the table of contents, an impenetrable listing of bizarre names and Greek characters, with a few bits of Latin thrown in for leavening.

"Do you know who the Erinyes are?" he asked.

"No."

"Really? Well, the name means 'the angry ones.' They were commonly known as the Furies, but also they were called the Eumenides, 'the kindly ones.' They are three women—usually old women, but not always. I have found depictions of them on black-figure vases where they are beautiful, and young, although they do have eagle's talons and wings. They were associated with terrible, terrible things. Even their names are bloodthirsty: Megaera, the Jealous One; Electo, the Relentess; Tisiphone the Avenger. They are the Punishers—June called them the death-Sirens, who would drive guilty people to frenzy. In ancient Greece, the very word used to describe 'rage' was almost indistinguishable from their name. They are far older than any of the Olympic deities; they may be among the oldest supernatural creatures of which we have any written record."

"What did they do?"

"They restored order. Not necessarily human order, and not divine order—certainly not divine order as we think of it now. Whatever their code of ethics was, it was far more ancient than anything we can even begin to imagine, and more horrible. June Harrington speculated that it was the order of the Mothers—of an unimaginably ancient form of worship. It is an extremely interesting thing, really."

I looked up, surprised at how his tone had changed. It was softer, more thoughtful, and his expression as he gazed at a page of June Harrington's book was almost dreamy. "So many of the images of women that we have from ancient Greece are terrible ones. Medea slaughtering her children, Medusa turning people to stone, wicked Clytemnestra plotting against her husband—

"But she wasn't really *plotting*," I broke in. "He murdered their daughter—he sacrificed Iphigenia, and Clytemnestra was just—"

"Ah." Balthazar raised an eyebrow, his sea-blue gaze mocking. "And how came you by *that* bit of arcane knowledge?"

"We had to read it at school," I said defensively. "At least we were supposed to read it, for one of my drama classes. We did all that stuff. Ali played Iphigenia in a scene for our acting class."

"Did she?" Balthazar smiled. Suddenly he no longer seemed so old. The burnished light touched his cheeks and graying hair with gold, so that his face looked smooth and timeless. He tilted his back back, and in a soft voice began to recite.

"A greeting comes from one you think is dead.
She is not dead
But alive. You are looking at her now, for I am she—
But come and save me from a life
As priestess in a loathsome ritual—
Save me from dying in this lonely land
Lest memory of me shall always haunt you."

I frowned. "I don't remember that part."

"It's a different play," confessed Balthazar. "Euripides, *Iphigenia in Tauris*. There's a happier ending than in the *Oresteia*, at least for Iphigenia—her father sacrifices a deer instead of his daughter."

"That was big of him."

"Ah! You think he was wicked—but the truth is, it was Artemis who demanded the sacrifice of Iphigenia. With the possible exception of Aphrodite, who was a bit of a latecomer to Olympus, none of the ancient goddesses were particularly nice people." I glanced at Balthazar curiously: he was talking about these characters the same way my mother might discuss a neighbor who drank too much before Garden Club meetings. "They could be helpful, but there was nearly always a price, and usually it was blood. Nowadays we think of Artemis as the Huntress, and picture her like *that*—"

Balthazar waved a hand dismissively at an Edwardiań illustration in the book, a demure young woman in long skirts carrying a bow, rather as though it was a tennis racket. "In fact, Artemis was a dreadful goddess, who didn't hesitate to slaughter anyone who crossed her. Look at this—"

He turned the page. A gray-tinted photographic plate showed an alabaster statue of a woman, her face cast in bronze—but really, the statue scarcely looked like a woman at all. It was more like a thick column, topped by an androgynous face that wore a cylindrical crown; an austere, even cruel face. Beneath it the column was ornamented with animals with staring eyes and bared teeth, and by vaguely obscene shapes, swollen orbs that hung in distended rows from the goddess's breast almost to her feet.

"The Artemis of Epheseus," said Balthazar. He tapped the page officiously. "Sometimes called Cybele. This is a representation of the very goddess who so enraged Saint Paul when he visited the city. He referred to her as Diana, of course, in the Roman fashion—'Diana whom all Asia and the world worshippeth.' Not that one can blame him for being so disturbed by her rites. To this day, most people associate the Ephesian Artemis with fertility cults. They think *these*"— He indicated a bulbous ornament on the goddess's dress. —"are breasts."

"Well," I said, squinting at the picture. "Aren't they?"

"June Harrington thought they were the offerings of the *galli*—the men who castrated themselves to Artemis, and not always willingly."

I grimaced, but Balthazar only turned the page and

continued in the same solemn voice. "She was quite a remarkable woman, June Harrington. We disagreed on the most basic issue of—well, call it belief—but she was a tireless researcher, and fearless. She was obsessed with the ancient mystery cults, with how all of them so obviously had the same origin. She believed that the Erinyes were manifestations of the beings that were the companions of Dionysos. Have you read *The Bacchae*?"

"I have it."

"Ah, yes," murmured Balthazar. "The classic answer from first-year students from New York, no matter how obscure the text: 'I have it.' Well, *bacchante* is one of the terms for the women who followed Dionysos. There are many others. Bassarid, Maenad, Thyiad, Phoibad, Lyssad. *Maenad* means simply 'mad woman'; *lyssad* means 'the raging one.' And we also have *Potniades*, which is particularly interesting because of its possible derivation from the far more archaic Minoan and Mycenaen *Potnia*, or—"

I exhaled impatiently. Balthazar looked surprised, even disappointed, but with a sigh he flipped through the volume in front of us. "Dionysos. The god of revelry, the god of ecstasy; the god of illusions. His rituals involve madness induced by wine or hallucinogenic plants; the apotheosis of the god was achieved in a state of intoxication, and often involved *omophagia*—the eating of raw flesh, of animals certainly but at some earlier point of humans as well. Most likely he is an Asian import, by way of Phrygia—Anatolia, that is, Turkey, and there are indisputable links with Shiva—and so from the same land that gave birth to the ancient matristic cults. They may literally have given birth to him—his mother is supposed to have been Semele, a mortal, but Semele is also a name for the goddess of the earth, the field that is wounded when it is tilled;

and Semele is also linked with Cybele—who, *as you will recall*," he added, gazing at me sternly, "is yet another manifestation of the goddess in her maiden form."

I blinked, trying my best to look interested, and Balthazar's expression softened. "Forgive me, Lit. You must be hungry. Here . . ."

He stood and walked to the far wall, where a small round device like a doorbell was set within the wainscoting. He pressed it. I heard nothing, but within a minute the hallway echoed with the sound of brisk footsteps.

"My housekeeper," Balthazar explained. Seconds later there was an equally brisk knock upon the sturdy oak door.

"Yes, Kirsten. Come in please—"

The door creaked open. A dour woman in a dark blue paisley dress entered. "Professor?"

"Would you be so kind as to prepare some sort of tray for us?"

"Tray?" The woman gave me a reproving glance. She was tall, head and shoulders above Balthazar Warnick, thin-lipped and black-haired, with eyebrows so dark and straight they looked to have been drawn in black greasepaint. "I brought up your lunch only an—"

"My guest is hungry," Balthazar said. "Is there any of that salmon left?"

"*Inkokt lax,*" the housekeeper corrected him with a frown.

Balthazar ignored her. "Do you like salmon?" he asked, turning to me.

"Sure." What I really wanted was another drink, but it seemed unlikely that Kirsten would be that accommodating.

"Good. Kirsten, if you please—"

"I had intended to have the *inkokt lax* for my lunch," said the housekeeper. There was no doubt as to who she thought was more deserving of it. "But I will see what I can do."

She turned and left. Balthazar watched her go, then gave me a sheepish look. "Kirsten is a devout Lutheran," he explained. "Here, let's sit, I'm sure it will take her a few minutes to pry the *inkokt lax* from the refrigerator . . ."

He walked over to the woodstove and thrust two small logs into its belly. I sat back down at the table, feeling light-headed, almost disembodied by the atmosphere of this sorcerer's den, with its Latinate inscriptions and stained-glass windows, the faint scent of woodsmoke and pine needles and the promise of food brought up by a glowering factotum.

And yet there was also something that was weirdly familiar, almost comforting, about it. I began flipping through one of the books in front of me, a musty-smelling folio containing tinted photographs of Greek vases and statuary. It was not until there was a knock at the door and Kirsten entered with a large silver tray, that I realized what it all reminded me of—my childhood visits to Bolerium, with Axel Kern's housekeeper bringing in platters of inedible delicacies while my parents and Kern sipped their way through Bolerium's legendary wine cellar.

"Here is your *inkokt lax*," Kirsten announced coldly. She nudged aside a stack of papers and set down the tray, which held not only dilled salmon but several porcelain dishes holding capers, cucumbers and sour cream, a knot of cloverleaf rolls and jam, as well as a small silver pot surrounded by wisps of steam and the blessed scent of coffee.

"Thank you, Kirsten," said Balthazar. When I opened my mouth to say the same, the housekeeper fixed me with such an icy stare that I hastily turned my attention back to the book.

"I will be in the laundry room, Professor Warnick. Goodbye."

Only after the door closed did I dare look up. Balthazar regarded me, amused, then opened his hand to indicate the heaping tray between us.

"Kirsten will have starved in vain if you don't eat something," he said. "Please."

I ate. Not very much, but enough to satisfy Professor Warnick. He dabbed strawberry jam on a roll and nibbled at it, finally set it aside and poured coffee into two cups.

"Here," he said. He handed one to me and pushed the tray to the other side of the table. "Do you feel better?"

I nodded. For several minutes we sat without talking. Balthazar stared broodingly at the bay window. I drank my coffee gratefully, pouring myself a second cup. When Balthazar remained silent I turned my attention back to the folio. At first its sepia-toned images seemed to share the same detached, rather prim gravity that all old photographs possess, each picture carefully numbered and named, dated and referenced—

> Symposium scene, red-figure cup by the Nikosthenes Painter. Late 6th century B.C., Museum of Fine Arts

> Fragment from a bowl of Central Gaulish ware, figure-type of the god Dionysos, 2nd century A.D., British Museum

But as I perused the volume, photographic plates like moths pinned to the oversized pages, the images began to take on a stranger, even malevolent, cast.

> Maenads in pursuit of the god Dionysos, one holding an *olisbos*, black-figure cup by Epiktetos . . .

> Red-figure cup by the Brygos Painter, religious orgy scene featuring woman beaten with a slipper before reclining figure of the god . . .

Dionysos . . .

I moved the folio so that its contents were not visible to Balthazar, lowering my face until it was scant inches above the page. The first picture showed three young women carrying branches, hair hanging around angular faces as they followed a distinctively unperturbed-looking man whom I guessed must be Dionysos. The man had lean features and slanted, blank eyes, and carried a long staff topped with a pinecone.

I turned the page. The next one showed an orgy, the women slim, unclothed save for fillets of ivy pinning elaborately tressed hair. The single male figure was naked, too, and had the same lean features, the same oblique eyes and dark locks framing an unlined brow. In this picture, the god appeared to sit in midair, one hand grasping an immense and swollen penis. His expression was neither lascivious nor even sensual. He looked thoughtful, even sorrowful; and more than anything else that unnerved me. I turned the page again.

This time I could not help drawing in my breath sharply. Unlike the others, this plate was in color, tinted in rich, dark tones like the embellishments of a medieval text. It showed a painting of a room, its walls daubed a lurid red and crowned by the repeating pattern of a labyrinth, all crossed squares and intricately linked shapes like swastikas. There were figures in the chamber, but also figures painted on the wall, so that the whole thing was a skillful trompe l'oeil of a room within a room, and the figures on the wall appeared to be watching those in the chamber.

There was a lot to watch. A naked man, bound, was kneeling on the floor. His head was crowned with ivy and what looked like pinecones, or acorns; his expression, unlike that of the Greek god, was anguished. Three women were grouped around him, also naked, but these had none of the detached calm of the Greek figures. Their bodies were rounded, where the Greek maenads had been slender and boyish, and their faces looked sly and gleeful and aroused, by turns. One stood with arm raised above the kneeling man. In her hand she held a wooden stake with a leather thong attached to it, like a flail.

> Flagellation rites involving initiates and the God of the Vine, from a religious series, 1st century B.C., Villa of the Mysteries, Pompeii

"Ah," said Balthazar, his voice tinged with distaste. "I see you have discovered the heart of the labyrinth. *Villa dei Mysteri*, where the initiates take their first steps into the underworld. Their experiences set them apart to such a degree that they had their own cemetery, the *bebaccheumeoi*. A remarkable likeness, isn't it?"

I said nothing, just nodded as he continued. "What is

most amazing is not that the god himself should be so utterly recognizable to us, two thousand years later, but that these images survived at all."

Balthazar moved his chair beside mine. "Because it really *is* a miracle, isn't it?" I could feel the warmth of his body, the wispy touch of his hair where it grazed against my cheek as he leaned over the page. "More of a miracle, in its way, than the death and rebirth of a god . . ."

"How could *anything* be weirder than that?" I said, my voice cracking. I tried to keep my eyes from the picture of the kneeling suppliant who was not really a suppliant but a god, not a god but a man I had eaten with, spoken with that evening. The same finely drawn mouth, its faint cruelty made exquisite by suffering; the same beautifully muscled arms, filigreed with ivy as though tattooed.

But what was most terrible was the young woman who stood above him, her ice-pale eyes wide open and staring calmly, almost dreamily, from the page, her auburn hair threading to her bare shoulders. With a cry I shoved the book and sent it flying onto the floor.

"How could *anything* be weirder than *that*?" I shouted.

Balthazar reached to comfort me and I yanked away. "Don't touch me! *Don't you fucking touch me!*"

Despair flickered in his eyes. "We didn't paint those frescoes, Lit—"

"I know you didn't fucking paint it! Who did?" I leaned down to grab the book, stabbed at the first page from the *Villa dei Mysteri* and turned to the next one. It showed the same red-haired girl, now lying on a settee and embracing the god while men and women watched, all with the same eerily calm expressions. "Tell me—*who did*?"

Batlthazar stared at me, then down at the book. "A

Malandante, an artist commissioned by the man who owned the Villa two millennia ago. The work is very similar stylistically to that of the House of the Stags, at Herculaneum, and also to the images in the Villa of Ariadne at Pompeii. The girl—"

He inclined his head toward the page. "The redhaired girl is Ariadne, beloved of Dionysos. Or his victim, depending on which account you read. In the version that Plutarch gave us, Ariadne rescued Theseus when he came to Crete—Theseus and a number of Athenian boys and girls had been given as sacrificial tribute to Ariadne's father, King Minos. It was Minos, of course, who kept the Minotaur, the monster who was half-man and half-beast, imprisoned in the labyrinth; and it was to the Minotaur that the youths of Athens were given to be slain and devoured."

"But that's not true," I said, fighting to keep my voice steady. "That's just a myth."

"A myth? More likely a memory—we know that there was bull-worship at Crete and the Cycladic Islands, brought there from Anatolia, where all sorts of animals were worshipped. Be that as it may, Ariadne fell in love with Theseus, and helped him escape from the labyrinth. In so doing, of course, she betrayed not just her father but her people.

"And her god as well. It is fairly evident that the story of the Minotaur is a remnant of a far more ancient religion, one that reaches us only as fragments—myths, stories, vase paintings and bits of statuary, rituals like the Crane Dance, which is still performed on Crete.

"Whatever happened there, Ariadne ran away with Theseus, but no sooner had they escaped but he betrayed her. He abandoned her on the island of Dia, near—"

"No!" I broke in. "It had another name—I just heard it, *where* did I hear it—Naxos! It was the name of the opera that Axel was going to do . . ."

My voice trailed off. I looked at Balthazar in despair. "But—it all fits together. *Why?*"

"Naxos is one name," he said. Gently he closed the folio. "Homer said that she was abandoned on Dia, at the command of the god Dionysos, who killed her there. Others said that she killed herself, and still others say that it was Dionysos who saved her, coming to the island and taking her as his consort. That is the version that made it into Axel's opera. Very likely Plutarch's version is the true one, since Plutarch was himself a Dionysiac *mystes*— and so, of course, one of the Malandanti."

I couldn't even begin to argue with this craziness. Balthazar just gazed at the scattered books and papers on the table, as though they formed a map, an archipelago of scrolls and faded tomes. Finally I asked, "Why did Theseus abandon her? I mean, if she saved him—"

"The Athenians worshipped Apollo, and Theseus was the son of the Athenian king, Aegeus. Theseus himself was a follower of Apollo Delphinos, and as such, Ariadne would have been tainted to him. On Crete, she would have been involved in the rites of both the Goddess and the Master of Animals—the god who over tens of thousands of years was known as Dionysos, or Shiva, or Cernunnos, or Orpheus; the master of song and the theater, of chaos and intoxication and death. The oldest god, save only for the Goddess, who was his consort—

"—and mother, and daughter." Now it was Balthazar's voice that sounded unsteady. "The most ancient rift in the world is the one which looms between order and chaos; between those who serve Apollo and his agnates, and those who serve our enemies. Ariadne was abandoned because she would not forsake her god. Even if she had recanted, Theseus would not have given her refuge. The first thing he did after leaving her was to sail to Delos, where he made a great sacrifice to Apollo. And then went on to become the greatest hero of Athens."

"That's a horrible story," I said at last.

"It is the oldest story I know," replied Balthazar.

"But it *can't* be true. I mean, you talk about all this as though it really *happened*—"

"But it *did* happen, Lit. It still does. Again, and again! In a way, it is the only thing on earth that really *does* happen: gods living and dying, their avatars struggling to be born and reborn."

"You're lying."

"I'm not. And you know I'm not, Lit—you've seen too much, you *are* too much—you could never begin to explain all this, any more than you could begin to understand it."

I shot him a furious look, but Balthazar did not notice, only went on, his tone patient and somewhat weary, as though addressing a favored child who was behaving badly.

"What has happened is that we have lost the ability to see these things. We no longer perceive the sacred in our world—but it exists, Lit, oh, it does exist! It is as real as this room, as real as this—" He took a handful of papers and shook them at me, tossed them in the air so that they came down around us like so many birds settling for the night. "—*More* real. We just don't see it, that's all. Not because it's not there, but because we have lost the senses that would enable us to perceive what is all around us. You are familiar with the work of Claude Levi-Strauss?"

"No."

"A very great man. Not, as many people think, an anthropologist. More of a mapmaker," said Balthazar, giving me one of his maddeningly secretive smiles; "a cartographer, and a very great aid to us in our work. In his *Mythologiques*, he wrote of certain sailors, the Bororo of Central Brazil and the Caribs of Guiana, and how they were able to navigate using the stars, just as sailors have for centuries. But the Bororo could see the stars in *daylight*. When Levi-Strauss asked astronomers about this, they scoffed at him—but of course the stars are *there*, and the Bororo, among others, really did use them to steer by in daylight. It is we who have lost the acuity that would allow us to see them.

"Look," he said more gently, and took me by the hand. He led me across the room to the bay window. "Look there, above that mountain—"

He pointed to a distant peak, crowned by gold-leaved trees. "What do you see?"

"Nothing."

"Keep looking. No, not at the mountain—at the sky. Try to concentrate. There . . ."

I stared, frowning, tried to see anything but the pulse of blue sky, blurring as my eyes watered. "There's nothing th—"

I gasped. Something *was* there. A starburst of white, and then another, smaller flare, and another. A whole group of them, clustered close together in the northeast sky. Like cracks in blue glass, or the refraction of sun on a windshield. But these did not move, even when I did, or disappear when I blinked and shaded my eyes. They remained, burning faintly but steadily above the mountaintop.

"The brightest one is Aldebaran," said Balthazar. "The eye of Taurus. That is the entire constellation, there—"

I shook my head, and this time the stars did disappear. "They're gone!" I turned to him in amazement. "How did you do that?"

"I didn't. You saw them, Lit. You didn't make them appear, any more than I did. You *saw* them, that's all."

"But how? That's *incredible*." I gazed out at the greeny-gold sweep of mountains, the river like a silver highway, and wondered what other marvels were there, just beyond my sight. "I've never seen them before."

"You didn't know where to look. You didn't know *to* look. And no, not everyone can see them—not unless one is trained to, or has the nascent ability—"

"But how did *I* see them? I'm not trained, and I—"

I fell silent.

"No, you're not trained," said Balthazar. He remained standing, staring at the horizon with his arms crossed. "But you can see; you have talents. That is what the Benandanti are; that is what we do. We find those who are gifted, and train them. Sometimes children are born to our order. There are families that can trace their lineage back over three thousand years. Others want more than anything to be born into it, but are not. They can only serve us, as researchers or couriers, and in other ways. But those who choose to work with us . . ."

He turned, eyes blazing. "Join us, Lit. Join me. Centuries ago I failed Giulietta, but I won't fail you, I swear it! Stay with me now and I will help you—I can do great things for you, I can show you the world within the world you know—"

His voice was pleading, desperate. He took me by the shoulders and gazed at me. "I would marry you," he said in a low voice. "The Conclave could not deny me that; not this time—"

"What?" I gaped at him, then laughed. "Marry you? I can't marry you! I'm only seventeen—"

"Lit! Please—"

"Let go," I commanded; then more urgently, "let *go*—"

He did and I withdrew from him, shoving my hands into my pockets. "I'm not marrying *anyone*. Not to mention I don't even *know* you—"

"Then don't marry me," he begged. "Just stay—no, not here, not with me! But with us. You'll be starting college next year—I can arrange for you to be placed at the University of the Archangels and Saint John the Divine. We can arrange for a scholarship, you'll be able to—"

"What?" I snorted in disbelief. "Don't you get it? I can't do any of this—this Benandanti stuff. It's crazy! And I'm already going to school—to NYU. Maybe."

I fell silent, thinking of Jamie Casson; of how even though the sun was shining here, it had been after midnight in Bolerium, and there was a train at four-thirty-five . . .

"I have to go," I said curtly. "I—I'm sorry. I'm sorry I bothered you, I'm sorry I came but now I have to—"

I was halfway across the room before I stopped.

Exactly *how* was I to go? I looked around, dazed. Balthazar shook his head.

"You can't go back," he said. "Not to Bolerium. Please, Lit. You don't really comprehend any of this—how could you? He *wants* you to return—he needs you, without you there will be no apotheosis. Without you he cannot be reborn—"

I looked at him as though he were nuts. "Jamie?"

"No! Axel Kern—"

"But he *is* born—I mean, he's *there*, he's not—"

"Not Axel Kern. He is just the avatar; the vessel. It is Dionysos who seeks to be born, and Kern will be discarded as though he were a ruined statue. He needs you, Lit. You're a lightning rod for him—you and your rage, your energy—that is what gives him power. It has always been like this. The god and his initiates are intimately linked—without them, any sacrifice is merely another death.

"But with them—with the girl who serves as his consort, and slayer—with you, it all begins again."

I listened, then asked in a low voice, "Is that what happened to Kissy Hardwick?"

"Yes. And to Laura Stone, Kern's mistress, and to others. *Many* others. If you go to him, Lit, you will die, just as they did."

"I don't believe that." I didn't care that he could hear how my voice shook, or see how my entire body was trembling. "I don't believe any of it. Because if you're right, and I'm somehow connected to your Giulietta, then I'm different from all of them—"

My hand shot out to point at the books strewn across the table and floor. "Is Kissy Hardwick in there?" I demanded. "Is there a painting of Laura Stone in the Villa of the Mysteries? *Is there?*"

For one long moment I stood and waited. Waited for him to tell me, *Yes, they're all in those books, there's nothing so special about you at all,* waited for him to say, *Hush, Lit, wake up, wake up . . .*

Balthazar Warnick said nothing. Behind him clouds started to gather above the mountaintop. Far below, the river darkened from silver to lead. Finally I turned, looking for a way out; looking for the way back to Bolerium.

There was none. Or rather, there was only one, and I knew what *that* was.

I would have to leave the same way I had arrived. My heart began to pound, but I focused all my will on keeping my hands steady, raising them in front of me and staring at the wall. There was no window in it, no door. I had seen two doors in that room, the one Kirsten had entered by, and another, battered door of wood set into a recessed wall and topped by a lintel with Latin words painted in faded letters—

OMNIA BONA BONIS

As I stared at the door the words seemed to glow, and I heard Ralph Casson's disdainful voice—

They call themselves The Good Walkers—Those Who Do Well—

And just as suddenly the meaning of the Latin words came to me, spoken by another, kinder, voice—

All things are good with good men.

"Join us," whispered Balthazar. The battered door glowed brighter, the radiance of a thousand suns striving to reach me.

But I would not go that way. Instead I wrenched my gaze from the door and turned back to the far wall, the shelves bowed beneath the weight of all the secrets they held, an entire world captured between leather and vellum and cloth covers. I held my arms straight, making my entire body go rigid until my arms and shoulders ached. I stood there and stared at the wall, willing my escape from the Orphic Lodge; willing the portal to come.

And it came. Like flame stitching the edges of a parchment, its outlines appeared before me: a ragged doorway with a threshold that burned so fiercely I blinked, then cried out as I almost lost the image to the darker silhouettes of shelves and wainscoting—

"Lit! No!"

Tears streamed from my eyes as I struggled not to blink again. Like a shipwreck rising from dark water the shape of the passage burned through the wall. Its perimeter glowed dazzlingly, but at its center was a blackness at once terrible and terrifyingly beautiful, a glittering penumbra like the remnant of a shattered star. Even as I fought to remain standing I was drawn toward it, sucked down as though I were toppling into the abyss. There was a roaring in my ears, the thunder of a raging fire. Behind me I could hear Balthazar's voice, faint and ineffectual as a sigh—

"Lit! Don't! You don't know—"

I was falling forward. Howling wind raked me, sent my hair streaming outward into ashes and smoke as I plunged into the portal.

"—you don't—"

"Get back!" I screamed.

The flesh along my arms rippled and burned, the darkness seared my throat but somehow I found the will to laugh. Because *I had done it*—I had created it, the portal was there and even if it destroyed me, even if I never drew another breath to tell anyone what I had seen, the making of it was *mine*. Around me was nothing but flame and heat and the void, and I shrieked even as the abyss took me and Balthazar's warning voice came one last time—

"You don't know what you're doing—"

As I fell, laughing, and shouted back at him through the darkness—

"Then I'll learn the hard way."

14 ❧
Harvest

This time it was not like crashing, but waking. There was no pain. Darkness and flame alike receded into a muted gray expanse that held the promise of vast space, an unseen ocean beyond the fog. The mist grew brighter, feathered with electric blue and violet. I blinked, blinked again as the realization dawned that I *could* blink; that I was alive, and awake, and definitely no longer in the Orphic Lodge. There was something familiar about the surface under my back, something that was soft without actually being very comfortable; something cold.

"Hello?"

It took a second to register that this was my own voice, croaky and tentative.

"Hello?" I said again, louder. There was no answer. I rubbed my eyes, trying to dispel the sense that the air was somehow fuzzy, along with everything else. It took another moment, but then I knew. I was in the room where I'd last seen Hillary and Ali; the room with the black light and the stereo and the sun spider. I was in Bolerium.

"It worked," I breathed. Beside me the sheet was bunched up, weighted by a knot of blankets. Without looking I elbowed it aside, then rolled to the other end of the mattress, groaning, and stood. "God, I can't believe it *worked* . . ."

My legs trembled as though I'd been on a roller coaster. Underfoot was the same rough carpet of acorns and twigs and poppy pods, above me the same ultraviolet light buzzing ominously in its plaster medallion, like a wasp in a rose.

And there was another sound as well, the monotonous click and scratch of a needle stuck on vinyl. I crossed to where the stereo sat in the corner, surrounded by a desolation of album sleeves and loose records, marijuana seeds and a broken syringe. I picked up the stereo arm, replaced it and switched the OFF button; then slid the album from its spindle, tilting it so that I could read the label.

BERLIN

I grinned wryly: that would have been Ali's choice. I glanced around for the cover but didn't see it. I stuck the record atop a stack of albums, turned and tripped over something round and smooth.

"Oh, *fuck*!"

I'd stepped on the glass globe that held the sun scorpion. Swearing, I kicked aside shards of broken glass and stone and a small gritty heap of sand. Something gleamed as it skittered across the floor, glowing cobalt in the UV light; then disappeared, as though it were a flame that had been extinguished. I hopped over the shattered globe. The fact that I had on heavy leather boots with two-inch heels somehow didn't seem much of a comfort. I headed for the half-open door, but when I reached the mattress again I froze.

Sprawled across its center was the tangled mass of blankets I'd shoved aside minutes before. One side of the pallet was bare, and still showed the faint imprint of my body.

But there was someone on the other side of the mattress, the side that was closest to me. Her body curved to form a question mark, arms drawn in front of her with hands clasped. She still wore her dress with the heart-shaped cutouts; in the cold light the flesh that showed through looked slick and damp, the color of a mussel shell. Her eyes were slitted, her mouth open and teeth bared, tongue protruding like a kitten's. Along the bottom of her jaw a silvery filament of saliva glistened.

"Ali. Hey, Ali . . ." I knelt, paused before touching her arm. *"Shit."*

I jerked my hand back. Her skin felt hard, cool as plastic. I swallowed, tasting bile; forced myself to look at her again, my gaze traveling from face to breast to abdomen, searching for some sign that this wasn't real, that I'd made a mistake and she was just sleeping.

She wasn't. I steeled all my courage to lay one palm against her breast. It was like touching a hot water bottle that's been left overnight, cold and slightly flaccid.

"Oh, Christ, Ali, don't do this, don't do this, please *please* don't—"

I lowered my face until it grazed hers. Her cheeks were cold, her hair stiff. I ran my hand along her arm, stopped when I reached the crook of her elbow. There was a row of tiny bruises there, each with a bright dot in the center, as though she'd been playing with a red Magic Marker. I brushed a dank tuft of hair from her forehead, let my finger trace the outline of her cheek, trailing down the side of her nose until it reached her upper lip. There was something sticky there, sticky and granular. I pulled away, letting a wash of blue light cascade from the overhead bulb onto her face. Sparks of purple and black glittered on her lips and around her mouth, as though she'd been eating poisoned sugar. I hesitated, then touched her mouth and held my finger up to the light. The same purplish gleam was there, flecked with grains of glowing violet. I inhaled, breathing in a perfumed sweetness that was also rank, like wisteria or fetid water.

"They look so peaceful when they're asleep."

A figure loomed above me, her sharkskin jacket and miniskirt given a sinister, inky sheen by the light.

"She's—she's dead." I stumbled to my feet. "Have you—did you—"

Precious Bane stared at the corpse. "'*Lethaeo perfusa papavera somno,*'" she said in a throaty voice. "Poppies soaked with the sleep of Lethe." She stooped and gently touched Ali's lips with her finger. "Opium soaked in honey."

She held up her hand, the UV bulb making her nails glow like so many lit tapers. "She must have eaten an entire cake of it—yeah, look, there it is—"

She pointed at the floor near my feet, reached to pick up a filmy piece of paper, its surface shiny like aluminum foil. "See? There was enough here to kill someone twice her size. Little slip of a thing like that."

Precious Bane flicked the paper so that it floated into the shadows. She knelt beside the corpse, lifting one of the arms to study it. "And she was using."

"She said she wasn't. She said she was just chipping—"

"Uh-uh. Sorry, honey, but she lied. Lesson Number One: junkies *always* lie. She was trying to find a vein—see?"

A shining talon tapped at the cluster of star-shaped bruises on Ali's arm. "But she wasn't very good at it. Junkies are stupid, too," she said flatly, and with a soft *thud* she let the arm drop to the mattress.

Rage and horror bloomed inside of me. I tried to hit Precious Bane, but she was too quick.

"That's enough—" She grabbed my wrist and I started to cry. Gently she pulled me beside her, smoothing the hair from my forehead. "First time you ever saw one of your friends OD?"

I nodded.

"Yeah. Well, it's not a pretty sight, even if it doesn't kill you. Here"— she held out a big, white, man's handkerchief. —"that's it. Aw, don't cry, honey, you'll rust. God, I hate it when they cry," she sighed. "C'mon—"

She stood, took me by the shoulder and guided me to the door. "You start shooting that stuff, you'll be hanging with the Lee sisters—Homely and Ugly. And then you'll be dead. Ha ha."

After the ghastly light of that room, the corridor seemed black as a lake-bottom, and as cold. Broken glass was everywhere, along with twisted muntins and powdery chunks of plaster. Every window we passed had been shattered. We sidestepped twisted tree-limbs and branches thick with wet yellowing leaves, and acorns everywhere like marbles tossed across the floor. Precious Bane made little grimaces and grunts of distaste, her platform heels clunking on bare wood. Occasionally she would stop to kick at a twig or piece of bark, nearly losing her balance in the process.

"God, this place. I *hate* this place—"

I followed her, too exhausted and frightened to fight any more, too horrified by what had happened to Ali.

There was no light, save what seeped down from the windows. The few doors we passed were small and invariably shut, with rusted hasps dangling from broken latches. The floorboards were so worn it was like walking over crumpled carpeting, the windows so deeply recessed that looking into one was like gazing into a dark kaleidoscope. All the familiar landmarks looked shrunken and out of place, the lake where the night sky should be, gale-tossed trees moving slowly back and forth, as though they had sunk to the bottom of a river. The fitful rain of early evening had grown to a steady downpour. Now and then voices would abruptly ring out from the surrounding darkness, but they sounded hollow and metallic, fragments from a soundtrack or a television left chattering in an empty room.

"Man, it's freezing." I rubbed my arms, grateful for Jamie's clothes. But then I had a terrible thought.

Had he known Ali was dead?

"She passed out. Hillary took off . . ."

I stopped, my breath coming way too fast. How could Jamie have left her?

How could I?

"You couldn't have done anything, even if you'd been there."

Precious Bane's voice was gentle, as was the hand she laid on my shoulder; but to me it was the accusation I'd been waiting for.

"But I *did* leave her! I *knew* she had no fucking idea what she was doing, and I still left her—I left and she— she—"

"No." Precious Bane shook her head. In the darkness her face was more masklike than ever. The heavy pan-cake makeup was faded, her lipstick chalky-looking, so that the masculine lines of her face showed clearly: the strong chin and square cheekbones, wide mouth and bluish unshaven skin. But her eyes were still garishly mascaraed and flecked with glitter, and her cherry-colored hair still flamed around her Medusa-like. "You couldn't have done a thing. Believe me, honey—I've been here before. People get hurt, and it always ends badly—"

"Then why are you here now?" I asked, my voice quivering.

"Why am I here?" Precious Bane smiled, lipstick seaming the cracks in her mouth. "Honey, this is what I *do*. You think there's a lot of job opportunities for a girl like me? I make movies for Axel, help to entertain the troops. And I schlep people like you back and forth"— she waved her hand dismissively, but her expression was enigmatic, almost teasing. —"here and there, hither and yon. Look, it's a living. And when I say it ends badly, that doesn't mean it ends badly for *you*, personally. You got spunk," she said, her Jersey City accent suddenly bursting through. "Plus you can be a real little bitch if the situation demands—hey, don't look like that, I meant it as a *compliment*. But you know, honey," she added, lowering her voice conspiratorially, "let me give you some advice. Lose the hair—"

She flicked at my tangled curls. "It's all the wrong color for you. And it's too long. You want my advice?"

"No." I yanked away. "I want to get the hell out of here."

Precious Bane laughed. "Well. Just remember, nothing makes a girl feel so good as a *new do*. Now let's just look over here and see what Carol has for us behind Door Number Three—"

She took my hand and gestured to where a door was set into a deep alcove. In front of it stagnant water pooled, and blue-white flickers traced the outlines of the doorframe, as though a live electrical current flowed through it. When Precious Bane reached for the knob I stiffened.

"What's in there?"

"Wonderful things," she murmured, and opened it.

The flickering light flared, the door creaked inward and thudded against a wall. Before us was a room. Not a large room, but it seemed cavernous after that endless twisting hallway swept with rain and the sound of wind. Shadows flowed along the walls, blood-red, violet. When I followed Precious Bane inside I saw that they were not shadows at all but threadbare velvet drapes hanging from long metal rods. Strands of ivy had been braided around the rods, ivy and grapevines and evergreen boughs heavy with pinecones. The floor was covered with candles, stuck in mason jars and upended terra-cotta masks. The scent of wax mingled with incense, a sharp head-clearing scent of juniper. On one wall glowed the bright square of a film being projected without benefit of a screen, or even a sheet. The projector was on the floor, balanced shakily atop a pile of coffee-table books. The scene juttering on the wall was badly out of focus; it seemed to involve a number of women and a very large animal.

"This is where I leave you." Precious Bane's expression was grave but not unkind. "Don't!" she commanded, and pressed her finger to my lips. "*Don't* freak out. You want my advice, pretend you're in a movie—"

I stared at her, disbelieving, then tried to bolt for the door. But she pulled me back to the center of the room, where a large mattress was set on a low platform, covered with paisley scarves and an old Victorian crazy-quilt.

Bottles were arranged around the platform—dozens of them, burgundy and brandy and Southern Comfort, sloe gin and Boone's Farm Apple Wine—bottles and incense burners, brass trays and vials, decanters and long-stemmed pipes and even a hookah, its tubes spilling onto the floor like entrails.

"A movie? Christ, it looks like a fucking head shop exploded—"

"Name your poison," advised Precious Bane. "It'll make it easier for you."

"Gee, thanks."

"I mean it. Have a little drinkie." She hesitated, head tilted; then leaned forward and kissed me on the mouth. "Good luck," she said, and crossed to the door.

Despairing, I watched her go. She stopped to look back at me, her oversized frame filling the narrow space; drew one hand to her mouth and blew me a kiss.

"Remember, honey—don't get even. Get *mad*."

The door closed. I was alone.

"Great. This is fucking great."

I went to the platform and sat. A more comforting scent hung here, patchouli and the musty smell of mothballs. I ran my hand through my hair and sighed, fighting tears, stared down at the ludicrous assembly of liquor waiting for me. After a minute I picked up a bottle.

CHATEAU GRAND PONTET ST.-EMILION 1964

There was no cork. I sniffed it, then took a swig. A spark of heat on my tongue, sweetness and a tart aftertaste like unripe apples. I drank some more, finally set the bottle down, knocking it against a dark-green decanter that sloshed as it toppled over. I caught the decanter before it fell, but when I replaced it I saw a cloisonné tray alongside, patterned with ivy and honeybees. There were little squares like fudge on the tray, wrapped in foil. Not aluminum foil but some thinner material that you could see through, like cellophane. I frowned and picked up one.

It was heavier than it looked, with a thick, perfumey smell. I peeled back a corner of the wrapping. The square beneath was sticky and dark, the color of burnt toffee and with the same faint sickly scent I had caught on Ali's skin. As though it had hissed at me, I yelled and threw it as hard as I could across the room.

With a *thunk* it struck the projector, ricocheted off and landed somewhere in the shadows. The jerkily moving figures on the wall trembled, then continued their monotonous posturing.

"God damn it!" I picked up the tray and sent it skimming toward the projector. Silvery cakes flew everywhere. This time I made a direct hit. The projector thudded to the floor; a blue-white arc swept across the wall like a comet and disappeared. The projector lay on its side, reels grinding as its lens glowed like a small imprisoned moon. There was a flash, the stink of burning film. With a soft *pop* the projector's lamp went dead.

I stared at it, a little fallen monolith surrounded by glints of silver where the opium cakes were strewn. My skin was cold and my heart beating much too fast. The wall hangings moved slowly in and out. A candle sizzled and there was a scorched smell, like burning hair.

From behind me I heard something walking; something far too big for that room. Its stride was heavy and uneven, as though it limped or dragged a broken limb. Where its head scraped against the ceiling chips of plaster fell. I held my breath as its shadow fell in front of me: the shadow of an enormous tree, branches like black lightning. It stood behind me, unmoving, inexorable. Finally I turned to face it.

It was not a tree, but a stag, the same monstrous creature I had seen slain upon the mountaintop. Its antlers curved upward, so huge it seemed they must hold up the massive roof of Bolerium; its legs like columns, ending in scarred hooves splotched black and green with lichen.

The stag lowered its head. Droplets of rain fell from the ridge of stiff hair upon its humped back, and I saw that one hind leg was badly wounded. Blood oozed from three long downward slashes in the matted fur. There was a shimmer of white within, the glossy pink bulge of exposed muscle. Its breath came in short bursts—*huff huff huff*—that smelled of sun-warmed bracken, goldenrod and yellow coneflower, hawkweed and beechnut. As it staggered toward me I cringed, helpless: it was too huge, it would crush me as it fell . . .

But it did not fall. Its shadow swept across me, and for an instant I felt its warm breath upon my face. When I looked up again, the great stag was gone. In its place stood Axel Kern. The emerald-green kimono drooped from his frame. A wreath of entwined ivy and grape vines sat crookedly on his brow, leaves tugging at his hair. Like the deer, he swayed slightly. His breath and even his sweat reeked of wine.

Yet when he reached to lay one hand against my cheek, his touch was steady and reassuring, the brilliant green-flecked eyes nearly incandescent; but not the least bit drunk.

"Lit." He smiled. "You came."

I stared at him, then scrambled to my feet. "Right. And now I'm leaving—"

"No. Not yet."

His hand shot out to grab my sleeve. I kept going; he yanked me backward and the sleeve tore. I turned furiously.

"You can't make me stay!" I shouted. "You can't—"

"Yes I can, Lit."

"Yeah? How? By killing me, like you killed Ali?"

The maddeningly calm smile never left his face. "I didn't kill Ali. Girls overdose all the time—"

"Around you they sure do." I tried vainly to pull my hand free. "Kissy Hardwick, Laura Stone—"

"Laura would be very flattered that you called her a girl."

"Fuck you."

Axel Kern sighed. "You are mistaken if you think I have ever killed anyone, Lit."

"Right—you just gave them drugs—"

"No, Lit." He wiggled his eyebrows and twirled an invisible mustache. "I don't *give* people drugs. I *am* drugs."

"You're fucking crazy, is what you are! You're a fucking psycho!"

To my surprise he let go. I backed away from the mattress, but instead of following, Axel remained where he was. He was staring at the opium cakes, gleaming on the floor like so many little fish left mudbound at ebb tide. After a moment he stooped to pick one up. He turned it back and forth so it glittered in the candlelight, then looked at me and asked, "Do you know what this is?"

"Yes," I snapped. "It's opium."

"No."

He shook his head. His long hair had tangled inextricably with the vines upon his brow, so that green tendrils and darker grape leaves seemed to thrust from the skin beside his temples, and a spiral of ivy nestled in the hollow of his throat as though inside the bole of a tree.

"No," he repeated. He lifted his arms. In a shimmer of green the kimono fell to the floor. He was naked, but his lean body had none of the softness I would have expected in someone my father's age. His arms were smoothly muscled, covered with fine dark hair like an otter's, his legs beautifully formed, save where a glossy red scar ran along one thigh. Only his face held that mixture of cruelty and amusement that I had seen so often over the years, as he told of some producer's fall from grace or the death by misadventure of an old, beloved friend.

Now he looked scarcely older than one of my own friends, though more broad-shouldered, his hair like a winter sky, his face heavily lined. I stared at him, too tired to be embarrassed or aroused. But then it was as though my vision grew fuzzy, as though this were a film that had suddenly gone out of focus.

Because I was no longer seeing Axel Kern. It was like one of those optical illusions that would leave me fuming as I struggled to find the Young Girl in a blot of ink, when all I could see was The Crone. For a fraction of a second both figures would be there on paper, maiden and hag, and then I would have to try all over again to bring one or the other back in focus.

The same thing was happening now. In front of me Axel quivered and blurred like a flame, while behind him—or within him, or above him—something else tried to flicker into being.

But it never quite appeared. As abruptly as it had begun, the eerie haziness dispersed. Axel Kern stood gazing at the ceiling, arms raised, a circlet of leaves upon his brow. He lowered his head, until he was staring at me.

"No." He extended one hand, fingers curled into a fist, then opened it. "Not just opium."

In the center of his palm was a single poppy calyx, mahogany-colored, the points of its crown standing upright like so many serrated teeth. He tapped the pod, once; then ran his thumbnail down the small swollen globe. A split appeared in its flesh. Tiny droplets oozed forth, milky white, viscous. Axel gazed at the seed-head measuringly, then at me; and tossed it onto the bed. "Never just opium. Much, much more . . ."

He extended his hand. His gaze did not leave mine. A sea-colored line ran the length of his arm, a vein slightly raised above paper-white skin. With his other hand he traced the vein as a lover might, let one fingernail hover above the crook of the elbow. The vein throbbed like a seed about to burst. Smoothly as though it were a razor Axel slid the nail into his flesh. He drew it back, opening a seam from elbow to wrist, and stepped toward me.

"It is a kingdom," he whispered. "It is mine."

Along the inside of his arm white liquid welled, thick opalescent drops that grew until they spilled down to the floor in a slow steady rain. Axel stared at it, smiling, then turned and offered his arm to me.

"Drink."

"No." I tried to shake my head but could not move. As he drew closer I cried out. "No! Please—"

He stopped and shrugged. "As you will," he said, and drew his palm beneath the open wound. He let the white sap fill his cupped hand, brought it to his face and drank. Then he extended his other arm, with a finger caressed pale flesh before once more dipping his nail into it. As though he were skinning a hare's belly he slashed downward, leaving a bright tear, like a scarlet fern. I tried to cover my eyes but Axel took my wrist, pulling me to him as he murmured, "This you *will* drink—"

He pushed me to my knees and clamped his hand on the back of my neck. Red flowed from his arm, but as he pressed my face into the crook of his elbow I smelled not blood but wine and upturned earth.

"Drink," he said, softly but urgently. When I struggled his grasp grew tighter. His hand slid upward to hold my skull. "Drink."

I clamped my mouth shut but he jammed his arm up against it, hard enough that my teeth rattled. *"Drink—"*

He continued to press his arm against my mouth, at the same time began to stroke my head. "Come now, Lit, drink, drink . . ."

And finally I let my lips part, and drank. Liquid spurted onto my tongue, heat like blood and the unmistakable burn of alcohol: wine. But stronger than any wine I had ever tasted, stronger than anything I had ever drunk—dark and rich as broth, so that I lapped at it greedily, warmth streaming across my cheeks and staining my shirt, drops flying as I tossed my head back and laughed, gazing up into Axel's eyes.

"Do you remember now?" he asked.

I shook my head. It was hard to see clearly—everything looked at once too bright and misty, as though I was in a steam-filled room. With a flourish, he let go of me. I started to stand, lurched sideways, and almost fell.

"Whoa," I said. The man laughed.

"Strong wine," he said. I nodded, grinning. When I tried to take a step toward him I stumbled and sat down, hard, on the mattress.

"Sorry," I mumbled. Smiling he sank down beside me.

"Now," he whispered. He took my hand and drew it to him, brought it down until I could feel his cock. I had avoided looking at it before. Now I glanced down and quickly away again. I tried to turn but his hand tightened on mine, forcing my fingers to circle what I had glimpsed. He was bigger than any of the boys I had fucked, but not grotesquely so. Certainly he was neither ludicrous nor monstrous, like the owl-eyed creature I had seen carved upon Bolerium's arched gate, or the hornéd man I had seen at Jamie's house. Beneath my fingertips I felt his skin, smooth and velvety, the rough fringe of hair below. He withdrew his hand and I let my fingers move upward, until they reached his glans. There was a tiny bead of moisture at its tip, rose-pink. As I watched it grew larger, swelling like nectar on a honeysuckle bloom. When I bent to touch it with my tongue I tasted a bright spark of the wine I had drunk moments before. The man groaned but made no other move—no fumbling for my shirt, no tugging at my zipper; no hand sliding frantically down my stomach and beneath the waistband of my pants. I waited, my breath quickening. Still he did not move. He sat cross-legged on the mattress, a hand on each thigh, his head tipped back and eyes closed. Along the inside of each arm a bright red line was drawn. There was no trace of white sap, no supernatural wine, no blood.

I stared at him, surprised, even a little angry. Then I pulled my clothes off, thinking that might be the problem.

"Hey," I said thickly, dropping my shirt. He seemed not to hear. I frowned, reached for one of the bottles on the floor. It was three-quarters full, the cork protruding a good inch from the top. I took the cork between my teeth and pulled it out, hefted the bottle and drank.

I drank way too much. But I drank anyway, until my mouth burned and my head buzzed, until I felt the same familiar three A.M. twanging in my skull that presaged those wild bursts of clarity I lived for at Deer Park with my friends, mad jangling music and ragged black light just outside my range of vision. When I tried to set the bottle down, it slid from my hand and smashed onto the floor.

"Shit," I mumbled. "God damn it . . ."

I leaned over to survey the damage. I saw no broken glass, no spilled wine; just a drift of white poppies, wrinkled as tissue, and here and there one red petal like a bloody thumbprint. I blinked and turned back, feeling as though the whole room turned with me. The ivy-crowned man was still cross-legged on the bed. His eyes were open, verdant eyes shot with amber like the surface of a stream.

"Lit."

He smiled and took my hand, pulled me close to kiss him. This time he tasted not of wine but of blood, a taste that maddened me. I tried to pull away but he wouldn't let go. I pushed at him, pounded ineffectually with one fist, struggled and kicked and flailed: no good.

So I bit him. On the cheek—there was a metallic spate of blood in my mouth, as though my own cheek had been pierced by a needle. He moaned. I shoved him onto the mattress and he fell onto the heaped scarves, their folds rippling so that I saw the pattern that had been there all along: scarlet vines and purple leaves, glistening black figs and clusters of grapes that exploded where he touched them, so that threads of red and purple radiated like cracks around his body, a living mosaic.

"*Your* turn now," I said drunkenly. "Drink . . ."

I straddled him, placed my hands on either side of his head. I kissed him, my tongue lingering on his cheek, the taste of salt and wine; rubbed my face against his until it was raw and left a smear of blood across his chin. Then I moved away, raising myself until my cunt was above his face. I lowered myself carefully, resting against his solar plexus as I inched forward, until his mouth was under me. I felt his lips, and his tongue: barely touching me at first but then harder as I moaned, his tongue tracing the edges of my labia and then flicking at my clit as I rocked back and forth. I felt wet, not just my cunt but all of me, arms and legs and breasts. I glanced down, gasping, saw my body mottled red and white and the air around me filled with blossoms. When I came it was like watching that small throbbing vein in his arm, a rhythmic pulse that finally burst, a wash of red across my eyes and petals on his tongue. I cried out and pushed myself from him, sprawling on the mattress with my hand across my eyes. I could feel him alongside me, his chest and the little hairs around his nipples, his cock nudging against my stomach.

"Take me, Lit." I opened my eyes. He was staring at me, his expression yearning, almost desperate. "Now . . ."

I forced a smile. "In a minute." I was exhausted, too drunk to think about fucking right now; almost certainly too drunk to focus on anything else. "Can't we, uh, just rest for a—"

"No." He sat up, his eyes wide and staring. "Now. The harvest cannot wait, ever."

I started to giggle, clapped my hand over my mouth. "That's a new one—"

He gave me a thin smile, his green eyes feverishly bright. "Bound and scored, flailed and bled, burned and consumed," he whispered.

"Down with the bodie and its woe,
Down with the Mistletoe;
Instead of Earth, now up-raise
The green Ivy for show."

He raised his arms above his head, crossed them at the wrists. I watched, unsure whether to laugh or run.

"One buries children," he recited, "one gains new children, one dies oneself; and this the race of men take heavily, carrying earth to earth. But it is necessary to harvest life like the vine, and that the one may be, the other is not. I am the son of the earth, and the stag that treads upon it; son of the earth and the starry sky."

His voice rose, cracking like a young boy's.

"To a terrible end I will send this young girl,
And I shall prevail and be revealed the Raving One,
And that shall prove all else to be true.

"Bind me, Lit!" he cried. "*Now*—it has begun—"
From overhead came a rustling. I looked up.
The ceiling was alive, a thrashing sea of vines and leaves, tendrils like grasping green hands and the dark filigree of exposed roots. In a writhing curtain they fell around us. I yelled, kicking at a long strand of ivy that encircled my bare leg, in a frenzy grabbed it and tried to pull it off. With a hiss like burning grass the ivy lashed itself around my wrist. I held not a vine but a snake, its triangular head set with eyes like obsidian flakes, its yellow tongue tasting the air as it tightened around me.

"God, no—"

I staggered backward and fell. The snake slid from my hand as my head banged against the edge of the platform. I felt dizzy, no longer drunk but delirious. Around me swept a coruscating tide of green and gold and black and brown, serpents and field mice, oak leaves and gnarled husks of beech-nuts, withered poppy blooms and bunches of grapes like dusty pearls. I flailed and beat my hands against them, but still they came: a yellow-and-black mat of crawling honeybees, ermines in their fuscous autumn coat, boughs thick with figs and olives and a tumult of coppery acorns: all of October's woodland harvest, a golden flux burying me, drowning me, devouring me—

And then it was gone. I blinked and let out a shuddering breath, looked around at the room. All was as it had been, save for scattered leaves and seeds, the slithering echo of something taking refuge in a dark corner. On the bed reclined the man who had been Axel Kern. The crown of ivy still rested upon his brow, and at first I thought there were vines across his lap; but when I pulled myself up, I saw that he held several coils of rope. Coarse hempen rope, the same kind of rope used to hang terracotta masks when autumn came to Kamensic Village.

"Where—where did they go?" I asked hoarsely. "Where did they *come* from?"

"It is always here," he said, his eyes dull. "I told you: it is my kingdom. That is why they name me *Kissos*, lord of the ivy, and *Dendrites*, the one in the tree . . ."

His voice died, but I heard another voice then, Balthazar Warnick's—

. . . the god of ecstasy; the god of illusions . . .

I stared at the man on the bed. Hatefully, feeling a new

rage clawing at my chest; rage intense and raw as grief, less an emotion than another being struggling to escape from inside me.

"You did that," I said. There was a blackness in the middle of my eyes, a darkness in my head that told me I should stop now, I was too drunk, I should run away . . .

But I couldn't stop. I said, "You drugged me, like you drugged Ali—" He shook his head. I went on, my voice rising. "—you've made all these things happen, it's like a—a *sickness*, like some kind of delusion. I don't know how you do it but *you made it come—*"

I sprang at him, screaming. "You fucking bastard! You think you own this place, you think you own everything in Kamensic—but you don't own me! *I am not your fucking kingdom!*"

He raised one arm above his face but I smacked it aside. I could see his chest moving in and out as he breathed, fast and shallow, could see the blood rising to his face like sap. "I am not yours!" I shouted. The ropes slid from his lap and I grabbed them, grunting as I pushed him down. He did not fight. He moved feebly, as though too drunk or stoned to control his limbs. I wrapped the hempen cord around first one wrist and then the other, the rope like a brand against his white skin, his veins the same glaucous color as the ivy in his hair. When I had knotted the ropes and drawn his wrists together behind his back I did the same to his ankles, pushing him down roughly when he struggled.

In a few minutes it was done. He lay on his side, long hair disheveled, the crown of ivy falling over his eyes. His cock was erect, no longer red but a deep angry blue, almost violet. In the guttering candlelight his hair looked gray-green, the color of old lichen. I knelt beside him, my breath quickening. With one I finger circled his nipple, teasing it until it stiffened. I took my thumbnail, pressed it against the base of the nipple and drew it upward, hard. He groaned, and a stippled line of tiny red dots appeared. I touched one, drew my finger to my mouth and tasted.

Blood, not wine. When I squeezed the nipple another bright bead flowed out. I licked it as the bound man moaned. Then I turned away.

There was an unused length of rope on the bed, caught in a tangle of paisley cloth. I took the rope and made knots at one end—one, two, three of them—then stumbled to my feet again.

On the bed the man looked like one of the slain deer you saw during hunting season, neatly trussed and heaved upon the back of a pickup truck. His head was thrown back, his eyes squeezed shut, his mouth twisted. I wondered fleetingly if he felt anguish, or ecstasy, or both.

"I was never yours," I said. Then I raised the knout, and with all my strength brought it down upon him.

I struck him, without mercy, again and again and again, and after a while without even feeling the rope in my hands. It rose and fell, the man at my feet moaned and cried out and screamed, and still I did not stop. Once he gave a long wail, a cry that ended with a groan and his bound feet twitching spasmodically against the mattress. My arm went up and down. My wrist ached, and my shoulder. My legs itched where something spattered them.

After a long time the pain in my arm eased and I felt only numb. The shadows of the room around me seemed to fade, and there was a faint musky smell, like fox-grapes, like raw honey. I saw nothing but an umbrous shape before me, a stain on the wall. I was conscious of only two things, the rise and fall of the rope in my hand, the muted sound when it struck. I felt like one of the figures in Balthazar Warnick's folio, girls with hands eternally lifted to the heavens, flails in their slender fingers or the shorn leg of a fawn.

But after a long time weariness overcame me; not even weariness so much as a sense that something was finished. I stopped, panting, let the rope slide from my hand. It felt wet as a strand of seaweed. When I looked at my palm it was creased with red. There was red on my legs as well, and my feet. I shook my head groggily and stared at the man beneath me.

He was still as death, but not dead. His breath came in shallow gasps, and though his eyes were closed they twitched beneath their lids, the way a dog's eyes move when it dreams of pursuit. His skin was dappled dark green and blue-violet, with here and there a starburst of red where the flesh was broken. There were darker spots beneath his ribs, small crescents where the skin had been flayed into petals of pink and scarlet, and in places the veins showed through, vibrating ever so slightly as though something swam beneath them. A glistening rope ran from his groin up to his breast; his cock had shrunk, and was curled between his legs like another soft brown seed. Gazing at him I felt neither pity nor remorse nor even horror. It seemed natural to me, that he should lie there thus. If he had been cast upon the forest floor rather than this room, you would not have noticed him at all: he would have been nothing but dead leaves and pallid fungus, acorn mast and a slug coiled in the roots of a tree.

"There." My voice sounded ragged; I wondered if I had

been shouting. Only a few candles still burned. The incense had been reduced to ashes upon the floor. "No more illusions, now."

I walked unsteadily to the wall, where the faded velvet drapes hung. One by one I yanked them down, letting each fall and turning to the next without bothering to see what mundane things they had hidden, moldering plaster or cheap rec-room paneling, doors that led nowhere or windows staring out onto the village where all of Bolerium's other guests now slept, restlessly or peacefully as they deserved. "All gone, all gone."

I glanced at the bound man. He was motionless, his face drawn into a grimace. Silently I turned back to the wall.

There were faces there. Terra-cotta masks and gargoyles carved in stone, doors in the shape of mouths and eyes—the walls were covered with them. Yet it did not seem that they were walls anymore, but a pitted surface of stone alive with animals. Hundreds of animals; thousands. From one end of the room to the other they raced and capered and fought—bison and mastodons, birds like huge penguins or auks, ibex and antelope and bears with teeth like claws, hares and snakes and squirrels and bulls.

And everywhere, deer. Dappled fawns and red deer, reindeer with arching horns and does whose bodies were waves and hugest of all a stag like an oak tree, the great Irish elk *megaloceros*, its legs mountains and its horns a thundercloud, flanks pierced by a hundred spears so that its blood rained down into the open mouths of tiny figures scratched below. Men, or creatures like men—two-legged forms with human heads, though their legs were furred and their feet ended in hooves. They held sticks or axes or S-shaped twigs, and some were obviously women, heavy-hipped and with pendulous breasts, with snakes for hair and faces like birds. I walked slowly, tracing the figures, and where I touched the stone the impressions of my hands remained, as though someone trapped within the rock pressed against it with her palms.

When I reached the center of the wall I stopped. There was the same figure I had seen at the Nursery years before: the owl-eyed man with a tail and paws instead of hands. Surrounding it was a series of simple images.

The first was drawn in charcoal. It showed a figure almost like a seahorse, its two legs bound together so that they seemed like one, its body represented by sketchy lines evocative of fur. Its ears were long and pointed, as was its nose, and two horns projected from its head.

The second drawing was like the first, although its execution was more graceful. A line-drawing like those on Balthazar's vase paintings, showing a slender man, his body curved, his hooved feet close together and his hornéd head thrown back as he danced.

The third and final image was not a drawing at all, but a photograph: a black-and-white film still of a man lying bound and gagged on a four-poster bed. Another man stood above him, holding a whip; the man on the bed stared at him wild-eyed. In the background I could just make out a small white face like a spot on the negative, a girl with tousled hair and blank staring eyes.

"You have to do it right," a matter-of-fact voice said from behind me. I turned.

"Ralph," I said dully.

"That's right." He stepped toward me—still wearing his ridiculous shiny blue jacket, though it was now torn and stained, his shirt pleached with filth. He stopped near the platform and looked down, grimacing, then back at me. "Looks like you enjoyed yourself, Lit. Looks like you had a bit of fun."

"Shut up. Don't come near me—"

"You?" He laughed, a sharp sound like an injured dog. "You think I'd want to get anywhere near *you*? Christ, look at you!"

He pointed at me. "You look like a fucking animal! You look like you killed him with your *teeth*—"

"He's not dead," I said. There was a thunder in my ears. "He's—maybe we should call an ambulance."

"An ambulance?" Ralph shook his head. "No, sweetie pie. The only way out of this is through it. Here—"

He held out his hand. In it was a small bone knife with a broken blade. "Finish what you started."

"No—" I started to back away. "No, I won't, you're crazy—"

"You have to." He grabbed my wrist, shoved the knife into my palm. "You can't leave him like that."

"Then *you* kill him!"

"I can't, Lit. If anyone other than you kills him, it won't be the apotheosis of a god. It'll be the murder of Axel Kern." He forced my fingers around the handle. "He's almost free now—help him, Lit. It's what you were born for. It's why you're here. It's why we're all here . . ."

He pushed me toward the body, his hand clasped around mine so that the jagged blade was poised above the man's chest. "Kill him."

I pushed back but it was no good, he was too strong. Slowly the blade drew closer to the bruised body. I could hear his breathing, so rapid it must stop, suddenly, like a clock; and Ralph's breathing, too, a slower, measured panting. It sickened me, but I could not keep myself from twisting my head to look at him, as I tried one last time to pull the blade free.

"No—you—*don't*," he gasped. "You little bitch—"

His face was contorted, eyes bloodshot. He smiled, horribly, and said, "Poor little puppet . . ."

And at those words something broke inside me. If before my rage had felt like another living thing bashing against the inside of my chest, now it burst free. With a shout I kicked, my boot driving into Ralph's stomach. He gave a strangled cry and went flying backward. The bone knife spun from my hand as I straightened and watched Ralph crash into the wall beneath the cave painting of the hornèd god.

"YOU!" I shouted, and the entire room shook. "YOU!"

I pointed at him. My arm felt as though an iron bar were rammed inside it. Before me the room swam. The wall with its gallery of ancient figures began to blur and fade. "YOU—ARE—*NOTHING*!"

As though I truly *was* a lightning rod, a jolt of radiance streamed from me, leaped from shoulder to arm and from my fingers across the shadowy space that separated me from Ralph Casson. With a scream he flattened himself against the wall, one hand in front of his face. Then, as though an immense hand had struck him, he receded *into* the wall—into it and becoming part of it, his arms curving upward, his face growing hugely elongated: eyes exploding into chasms, mouth swelling and then splitting in two, so that his lower jaw formed a great jagged threshold and his upper jaw a lintel. In between yawned a dazzling black space, and from that space echoed a scream that went on and on and on, fading at last into a low, ominous buzz.

Panting, I stared at the portal—the prison—I had

made. Then I turned and crossed to where Axel Kern lay upon the bed. He was motionless save for his shallow breathing, a trickle of blood down his breast. On his brow the crown of ivy and grape-leaves trembled, as though stirred by the wind. Slowly I knelt beside him, lowered my head until my lips brushed his; then stretched so that my body covered him. For a long time I lay like that, listening to the faint *shushing* of his heart, the rustle of wind in the leaves. Finally I drew back, my hand lingering upon his cheek; stood and for one last time looked down upon him.

He did not look peaceful, or asleep. He did not look like anything I had ever seen, except perhaps for the body of my friend lying blue beneath black light in another upstairs room. I stared at the bound man, his arms bruised and chained with ivy, the pulpy shapes of crushed grapes and figs beneath his cheek, the smear of honey on his thigh.

And as I looked it was like before, when his figure had appeared to blur and burn before me. Once more I felt that shiver of apprehension, a prickling along my arms and neck and it seemed that something would break through. There was a mystery there, a secret bound like the man in vines and blood, fire and seed.

But it was not *my* mystery. Not now, anyhow; not yet. As Precious Bane had done to me, I blew a kiss at the bed. Then I gathered my clothes and dressed.

"Very nice," someone murmured. "Your portal. The irony will be lost on Ralph, of course, but not on me."

I turned, pulling on my boot, and saw Balthazar Warnick standing in front of the door. A real door, an ordinary door, that opened onto a hall where wind sent rainy gusts of brown leaves spiraling into the night.

"You—you saw—" I stammered.

He smiled, a small rueful small, and stepped toward me. Then he stopped, frowning, and bent to pick up something.

It was the bone knife. He turned it over in his hands, carefully slipped it into the inside pocket of his wool greatcoat. "I'll take this," he said. "For safekeeping." He looked at the man on the bed. "And I will take care of that as well."

He glanced at the bottles strewn everywhere, the scattered opium cakes and bloodstained ropes. After a minute he turned back to me. In a low voice he asked, "Lit—will you change your mind? Will you come with us? Now, or—well, soon?"

I shook my head. "No." Then, trying not to sound so harsh, "No, thank you."

"Then go," he commanded. "*Now*."

But as I hurried toward the door he stopped me. "Wait. Take this—"

He took my right hand and prised it open, slid something onto the middle finger. I blinked. It was a ring, shaped precisely like the grotesque image of Ralph Casson's face that now served as a portal.

"So you'll always have a way out," said Balthazar Warnick softly. "Or back."

For a long moment his sea-blue eyes held mine. Finally I pulled away.

"Thank you," I whispered. "G'bye—"

I walked like a seasick passenger into the hall. It was dark, but through the windows a chilly light gleamed. Behind the watchful shadow that was Muscanth Mountain, dawn was gathering. I staggered down the corridor, found a stairwell and nearly fell down it, my boots sliding on the runners. When I reached the bottom I lurched into another corridor, and another, until at last I made my way to the great hall. There were bottles and ashtrays everywhere, candle stubs and light bulbs, torn clothing and record albums, the detritus of a dozen parties; but no people. I walked through the room and went onto the patio.

"Oh, man . . ."

It was covered with terra-cotta masks. All broken, so that as I crossed to the lawn I stepped through a wasteland of crushed mouths and hollow cheeks, beatific smiles turned to death's-heads where they had been trodden into the flagstones. At the very edge of the patio one lay, more intact than the others, eyes slanted beneath a crown of grapes. It shattered beneath my boot as I left the patio and walked downhill. It was still raining, fine icy needles that made my skin feel numb, but that was okay. Numb was okay. Numb was good.

I reached the drive and started down. I shoved my hands into my pockets and something pricked my thumb. I swore, fumbled in the pocket until I found something sharp.

I pulled it out—the baggie full of pot seeds and manicure scissors I'd discovered in the bathroom, right before Jamie found me and gave me his clothes. I held the scissors up, wiping rain from my eyes; then tugged thoughtfully at my hair.

"Huh," I said. "Well, nothing makes a girl feel better than a new 'do."

I began cutting. It didn't take long, once I'd figured out how to position the scissors and pull my wet hair taut so I could shear it off right at the roots. When I was finished, the sky had turned from charcoal to the color of tarnished tin. Wet curls stuck to my boots; I kicked them away, reached down to wipe my boots clean with a leaf. When I ran my hand across my skull it felt bristly, the hair spiky and ragged.

"Fuckin' A," I said. For the first time in what felt like days, I laughed.

Precious Bane was right. I felt great.

From the black ridge of western mountains came a long low wail: the four-thirty-five train coming down from Beacon on its way south to the city. I brushed myself off quickly, shoved the scissors back into my pocket, and began to run. I passed parked cars along the way, the same Karmann Ghias and BMWs and fake woodie station wagons that I'd passed on my way up.

And, past the curve where the road forked to go to Jamie Casson's house, an old blue Dodge Dart, two figures perched ghostlike on its hood.

"Lit! Jesus freaking Christ, Lit, where the fuck have you *been*—"

Hillary jumped down and ran to me. For an instant Jamie remained where he was, and in that instant I had a flash of when I'd first seen him scarcely twenty-fours hours before, frozen in the jukebox's glow like a dragonfly in amber, all the promise and beauty of flight and none of the risk. Then he, too, was alongside me, rubbing his hand across my skull and whistling.

"Whoa! Nice job!"

"What the hell did you do to your hair?"

"Where's Ali?"

"Where's your clothes?"

"Where's—"

From the southernmost slope of the mountain came another wail—the firehouse siren—then another.

Hillary frowned. "That's the ambulance."

I took a deep breath. I pulled away from them, and nodded. "We gotta get out of here."

"But Ali—"

"Ali's dead." I pressed my hand against Hillary's mouth, squeezed my eyes shut. After a moment I opened them. "She OD'd on heroin. Or opium, or some kind of shit. But she's dead, and if we stick around here we're going to be fucked."

"But—" Hillary looked at me, dazed. "She can't be dead," he whispered.

"Hillary. We have to go. I'm sorry—I know it sounds horrible, you have to believe me because I *feel* horrible—but we can't stay. At least, I can't stay."

I started for the front of the car. Jamie stared at me. I couldn't tell if he was stunned or just stoned. When I reached the door I stopped and looked at him.

"You said you had friends in the city. You said we could crash there and we wouldn't need money. At least not right away—"

He nodded. "Right."

"Do you have money now? Enough for the train?"

He swallowed, then patted the front of his black jeans. "Yeah. About a hundred bucks. Kern paid me in cash for the parking job."

"Okay." I let my breath out, opened the door and slid across to open the other door for Hillary. "Hillary—can you drive us to the station?"

Hillary just stood there, staring at me through the wet windshield. At last he got into the car and shoved the key into the ignition. "Where are you going?" He sounded like my father when he was so angry he couldn't bear to look at me.

"To the city. Jamie has some friends, we're going to jam together—"

"You can't play shit. You can't even sing."

"I can write. I'm going to write songs."

"The fuck you are," snarled Hillary.

But he drove us. In silence, none of us speaking though I have no idea what the two of them thought, if they believed me or if they were just as fucked up as I was; if maybe each of them had found a different door that night and walked through, walked through the world and came right back out on the other side in Kamensic Village, just like always. It wasn't until we reached the bottom of the hill that I turned to look back at the mansion.

It was in flames, towers and turrets and ruined chimneys blazing as the darkness behind it swirled and thickened. I gasped, but then a sudden radiance spilled over Bolerium's facade and I saw that it was not on fire at all, but aglow with sunrise.

And yet it was not that, either. As quickly as it had blazed the light died away. There was a faint forlorn cry, the howl of an animal that has been torn from its master and sent to shiver, alone, in the darkness. Then Bolerium stood as it ever had, black and forbidding yet also protective; keeping watch over the town and its children.

The car bounced around the curve, the mansion disappeared. In front of us was Kamensic Village, its dreaming church spires and white clapboard buildings, ancient courthouse and trees stubbornly clinging to their last yellow leaves. There was my house, just as it had been that morning, save the terra-cotta mask was gone. There was Hillary's.

And there was the station, burnished by the glow of the town's only streetlight. Hillary drove right up to the curb, braking too hard so that I had to brace myself against the dashboard.

"Goodbye," he said. He sat rigidly in the driver's seat, staring at the tracks in front of us. "Good fucking riddance."

"Why don't you come?" asked Jamie.

Hillary shook his head. His face grew very red, and he made a strangled sound. "You sure?" said Jamie. Hillary squeezed his eyes shut, nodding.

Outside, the train hooted. A silver thread unfurled along the tracks, deepened to gold and then blinding white.

"I have to go," I whispered. I leaned over and kissed Hillary on the mouth. "I love you, Hillary—you know that, right?" He nodded again, eyes still shut. "And I'll find you—I'll see you, for sure, you can come hang with us in the city, it'll be great—"

"C'mon," said Jamie. He stood outside the car, looking nervously back in the direction of the mountain. "Be just my luck, my old man shows up and fucks this up for me—"

"That won't happen." I stepped out of the car onto the cracked concrete of the parking lot. "Not this time."

We stood side by side, waiting for the train. Behind us there was the roar of a car engine and the sound of raining gravel. The roar grew fainter, as Hillary's car drove back up the winding road to Bolerium. I waited until I knew it was out of sight, and turned.

I looked at the town, drowsing shopfronts and tattered playbills, Healy's Delicatessen and the Constance Charterbury Library, and beyond them all the mountains and the lake and the woods, trees bowing to the coming winter and deer seeking pasture in the farmland to the south. Then there was a deafening sound as the train arrived, and Jamie Casson was tugging me after him across the platform and toward one of the middle cars.

"Come on! Lit, this is it—"

I looked over my shoulder as I ran, the wind cold on my shorn head; and leaped after Jamie into the back of the car. As the train began to move I stood in the open doorway and stared back at it all. I knew this was it, farewell to Kamensic, Kamensic with its trees and its children and the sleeping god who fed on them. The floor beneath me swayed back and forth, the trees swept past black as deep water as we headed south to the city. It had been a while since I'd visited but I knew there would be other gods there, sleeping gods and people who were sleeping, too, even if they didn't know it, half-dead and just waiting for someone like me.

"Right," I whispered.

I ran my hand across my ragged scalp and laughed, thinking of Jamie Casson straddling a jukebox while I sat in a Bowery bar and wrote in my notebook; thinking of all those sleeping people. I laughed, because I knew that even if it took a year—even if it took ten years, or a thousand—I would be the one to wake them.

Author's Note

In the course of writing this novel, I referred to the research of many people, including the classic texts on Dionysos, *Dionysus: Myth and Cult* by Walter Otto and Carl Kerényi's *Dionysos: Archetypal Image of Indestructible Life*; as well as scholarly work in mythology and folklore by Alain Daniélou, A.G. Ward, Eleanor Hull, E.O. James, Walter Burkert, Catherine Johns, Donald A. Mackenzie, J.D.S. Pendlebury, Arthur Evans, Walter Torbrügge, Ivar Lissner, Claude Levi-Strauss, and the redoubtable Jane Harrison. Most of all, I am indebted to the work of the Italian historian Carlo Ginsburg, whose books *The Night Battles: Witchcraft and Agrarian Cults in the Sixteenth and Seventeenth Centuries* and *Ecstacies: Deciphering the Witches' Sabbath*, first introduced me to the Benandanti and Malandanti. Any factual errors are, of course, my own.

The trial of Giulietta is adapted from the late sixteenth-century trials of Paolo Gasparutto and Battista Moduco, as recorded in *The Night Battles* and translated by John and Anne Tedeschi.

Some of the history of Kamensic Village was based on *God's Country: A History of Pound Ridge, New York*, by Jay Harris, as well as material compiled and published by the Pound Ridge Historical Society and safely kept for lo! these many years, by my parents. Thanks, Mom and Dad. I drew as well on the memories of my friends Kathleen Hart, especially her poems about Whitlockville, the drowned village beneath the Mianus reservoir; and Anne Wittman, who twenty years ago worked with me at the Bedford Village Courthouse Museum (open weekends, Closed Today). However, anyone looking for the boundaries of Kamensic should keep in mind Melville's warning: "It is not down on any map; true places never are."

My heartfelt thanks to the usual suspects: Martha Millard, Caitlin Blasdell, Jim Rickard, Paul Witcover, Christopher Schelling, Richard Grant, and especially John Clute.